Praise for *I Been in Sorrow's Kitchen and Licked Out All the Pots*

"Straight's portrayal of a black woman's life is nearly miraculous in its astonishing richness of detail, its emotional honesty and its breadth of human thought and feeling."
—*USA Today*

"Elegant . . . As monumental as the tall, taciturn woman whose life it traces."
—*Publishers Weekly*

"How long has it been since I stayed up until four in the morning to finish reading a book? The self-contained, compelling world presented here, accessible though so very strange, belongs to its unforgettable heroine."
—APRIL BERNARD, *New York Newsday*

ALSO BY SUSAN STRAIGHT

MEMOIR

In the Country of Women

FICTION

Between Heaven and Here

Take One Candle Light a Room

A Million Nightingales

Highwire Moon

The Gettin' Place

Blacker Than a Thousand Midnights

Aquaboogie

CHILDREN'S

The Friskative Dog

i been in sorrow's kitchen and licked out all the pots

A NOVEL

susan straight

COUNTERPOINT
Berkeley, California

I Been in Sorrow's Kitchen and Licked Out All the Pots

First Counterpoint edition: 2019

ISBN: 978-1-64009-363-8

The Library of Congress Cataloging-in-Publication Data is available.

Cover design by Michael Schwab

COUNTERPOINT
2560 Ninth Street, Suite 318
Berkeley, CA 94710
www.counterpointpress.com

Printed in the United States of America
Distributed by Publishers Group West

10 9 8 7 6 5 4 3 2 1

For my Gaila girl:
Live as large as you want,
as large as you can—live big large.

i been in
sorrow's kitchen
and licked out
all the pots

south carolina

pine gardens

1959

day

She was supposed to sit quietly with her mother in the slatted shadows of the wooden stand, learning to make better baskets than the clumsy-started circle that could still fit into her palm. The long strands of sweetgrass shot out from the woven round, making it look even smaller in her hand, and she dropped it to the ground. She should have been bending the spray of grass, coiling the strands around, and listening to the hum and fade of passing cars on the highway and the echoing murmurs, rising and falling, of the women's voices.

The women walked back and forth in the morning, after they had gotten settled, edging into each other's stands to compare peaches and straighten baskets that looked slightly crooked to an eye coming from the front. Rosie, Pinkie, and Laha would come all the way to the end, the last of the six stands, to see her mother.

Marietta watched them. Her mother sat each morning, never looking at the baskets Marietta hung on the nails, or the peaches she lined in the box. Rosie would reach up to the shelf where the round-bottomed baskets sat, pushing one over a few inches, and then she'd turn to Marietta and say, "Get up there for pull that fanner basket right. You so tall and don never see it straight."

Marietta stood and tapped at the wide, circle-shaped flat; it wavered a moment before facing out to the highway. She went back to her corner and with her head lowered watched Pinkie. Laha would nudge Rosie's baskets, Pinkie would move Mary's, and only her mother sat motionless but for her hands.

Even her fingers were still this morning, the half-finished bowl of a basket on her stomach. She nodded at Rosie, and her eyes were too fixed for her to be listening, Marietta saw. Rosie said, "This heat make so hard for sleep, have me wake half a night. I too happy when this air break."

Her mother was quiet, and Rosie said, "How you rest, Josephine?"

She shook her head and answered, "No rest for me." Then she bent over the sweetgrass, and Rosie looked at Marietta.

"You still ain finish one, girl?" Rosie said, one side of her mouth lifting when her voice rose. "I swear, you ever was resist and hardhead." She dipped a finger onto the nearest peach and turned. "Your tree the oldest, Josephine. Got the best peach for everybody, so big and sweet." Marietta thought she was gone, but she paused again and said, "You let she put em up too high, maybe. Marietta reach up there for somebody want buy that, she don even need pole. But maybe nobody don see em good, so high for look. I ain sell a big one too long time. This summer for hard. But I keep mines easy for see." She went out, her feet crunching the dirt.

Marietta looked at her mother, but she had her finger and thumb on the skin between her eyes, pulling gently again and again like she did, like a foot tapping or a baby sucking a rag. Marietta took a step into the middle of the tiny stand, where the top baskets were close to her head. She hunched her shoulders, hearing Rosie and Laha and the others saying, "She cain get no taller. She what—fourteen? Something wrong she get bigger than that."

She had thought putting some of the baskets on a high shelf would give the peaches and new baskets more room. Her mother kept making them, all the women did, and none of the white people who stopped their cars seemed to buy more than one little oval to hold rolls, or maybe a small bottle holder. Baskets crowded all the slats of the stands, hanging from nails in the sagging boards, sitting on sand near the women's feet.

She pulled down the two biggest, the tall one with a flaring lip at the top and the big-bellied round that closed into a small mouth with a cap. Leaving the high shelf empty, she tried to put them on the ground near the front, but they looked squat and undignified sitting there. Her mother didn't look up. Marietta put them back on the top shelf and rearranged the peaches.

Rosie was still in Aint Sister's stand, next door, and Marietta heard them complaining about the wet heat, but then the first car slowed and their words faded. All up and down the line of stands, the women grew quiet. Marietta stood at the back of the stand, near the narrow rear opening between the two folding chairs, and saw the sun bars floating through the slats onto the dirt. Now the dust would come. The stands were at the edge of the woods, on the water side of the highway from Charleston, and when a car swerved toward them or pulled back onto the road, a layer of gold dust hung in the air for a long time. The women waited for car doors to open and feet to emerge, and Marietta pushed herself through the back, away from the fine roadside mist that came toward her. The cloudy air and hum of throats were what she hated.

Before the car doors even clicked, her mother put the cupped base of the basket down and looked at her hard. Marietta sat down, picking up the sweetgrass circle again, trying to work a new tail of strands into the shape. She saw the white people, two women in pointy sunglasses and scarves thin as spiderwebs over their hair, and a man with his belt cut deep under his egg-belly. She might scare someone if she stood, her head above theirs, her shoulders wide into the air around them, so she hunched over her hands.

Marietta wondered if her mother would fall asleep in her chair. Sometimes she did now, because at night she twisted in the bed beside Marietta, rolling back and forth, calling out. If she sagged in her chair, Marietta would slant herself out the back of the stand. She wouldn't stay to watch, to learn. She never had. Each beginning of a basket grew blurred under her fingers, the edges of grass loose and dirty from her handling until she threw the coil behind her chair and someone else picked it up, sucking her teeth and waving it at her mother. Marietta crept in among the orange butterfly weed every day, inside the bushes that grew thick at the fringe of trees behind the stands. Someone else would help her mother stay awake.

When she was younger, she used to lie in the soft, sandy shade behind the huts and play with her doll, or throw pebbles at Rosie's baby boy, Johnny, who was only a heap in the corner of her stand, where he slept all day. She was four then, or five? She remembered the stripes of light across her knees, the doll's creamy feet and cheeks that grew brown-smudged with dirt. Down the road, she used to hear Pinkie's two girls, Crystal and Cynthia, argue with their mother about boys and nighttime. She saw Crystal's and Cynthia's eyebrows grow thinner and wispy, then blue appear underneath the brows, and Pinkie shouted at them all day between slamming car doors. Now they were gone to New York, and Pinkie always talked about them when certain voices and license plates stopped during the summer. And Johnny went with the other boys to the landing and the boats, walking behind their fathers and uncles to the water, where they cast nets for fish and shrimp, pulled up crabs on baited lines, packed them on the landing to take in Big Johnny's old truck to the cannery in McClellanville. But Marietta was told to stroke the sweetgrass, around and around.

The feet had gone back to the car already, and Marietta lowered her head to peer through the slats; the hands carried nothing but purses and a cigarette and a small bag lumped with peaches. She watched dusty feet and listened to the roar of the engine, tires popping over the grit. Her mother stood suddenly. "I cain make it," she said, and Marietta got to her feet quickly to meet her mother's elbow with her hand.

In the humid end-of-July heat, when nothing swayed or blew during the day, only quivered under the pressing sun, her mother didn't last the whole morning by the road. But today was the earliest she had ever given up. She had to go back to the house to lie down now. Like all the other women, she refused to walk through the woods behind the stands, the forest that separated the houses from the highway, so Marietta gave her an arm for the long way.

It was hotter beside the asphalt than on Marietta's path through the trees, she thought for the hundredth time, and the voices she hated began with Aint Sister's leaning boards, her grumble through the back. "Go on get you rest now, Josephine. I take care. Drink you some a that tea I beena bring Sunday. Drink fe hot, now."

Rosie's stand, Laha's, Mary's, and then Pinkie's, each one saying, "Get you some sleep. Too hot for rest right. We keep a eye." Marietta kept her eyes on her mother's ankles, no bones showing, just plump-stretched skin that swelled like water-soaked wood. She didn't want to meet the eyes hard on her. "You herry back, Marietta," Rosie called.

They walked in silence on the sand. At the crossroad, they turned onto the scattering of gravel someone had left years ago, worn now into the sand, and then the dirt grew harder from so many shoes and wheels packing it down. They passed the bare lot beside Pearl's store, where no one sat outside to tell stories; only Laha's husband Jerry and his brother Dell squatted in the shade of the cinder-block wall, waiting for a ride if Mr. Briggs or one of the other white farmers should need some day labor. But they always brought their trucks down before the sun rose. Jerry and Dell nodded at her mother and looked away, but their knees stared at Marietta, hard, bony faces through the cloth.

A few houses lined the road, but after a mile the swampy land close to the creek was empty. The bridge's wooden planks had been washed out by the flooding creek and then rebuilt more times than she could remember. Sometimes the water rose with a flood tide or rainstorm and filled everyone's fields, even their garden plots and pig yards. A storm had hit only a few weeks earlier, but it was mostly wind that knocked down trees and branches, which still lay scattered everywhere. Marietta looked down at the clear brown water sliding sideways under her feet. Creeks cut across two sides of Pine Gardens, and the coastal waterway edged the back. The highway from Charleston to McClellanville was a blacker river.

Past Rosie and Big Johnny's house and the others after the bridge, she and her mother turned down the soft-powdered, narrow lane that led into the woods, where the oaks and pines towered over them to make the path cool and shaded. Her mother stopped twice, after Pinkie's house and then before the curve in the lane, but she never said a word; her breath was harsh and quick under Marietta's chin. Farther in the trees, Aint Sister's broom guarded her porch. Marietta's mother walked slower, to the small clearing and then their house, just before the brush and vines ended the lane.

Her mother didn't tell her to go on back, didn't say to get her a rag or bring water—nothing; just pushed down on Marietta's arm when it came time to climb the two steps to the porch. Then she went straight into the dark doorway. Marietta heard the soft pop of her own lips, the way they let go of each other when they'd been pressed together all morning, but then her mother was inside.

She looked into the doorway and saw her mother already lying on the bed. The bedroom was almost black, with the two window shutters closed and the sun on the other side of the house. In the other room, she checked the stove. The ashes still glowed pink from breakfast. The two rooms were already so hot she didn't think the embers would make a difference, and she made sure there was water in the bucket, in case her mother was thirsty. A clean Mason jar, too, and then she went back onto the porch and looked down the lane.

"Herry back," she whispered to herself. Starting into the woods, down her own path leading back to the highway, she walked slowly. Something—she was forgetting something. She kept on, frowning, but whatever it was, she wouldn't go back to the stand. Sit patiently, eyes down and fingers flickering, when white people came to tilt their faces at the baskets. They thought she was a woman. Grown. Their eyes swept right past her shoulders and hands, skimmed her dress—Rosie's dress, too old and small for Rosie's plumpness and too big for her mother, whose skin pulled tighter and tighter while the flesh underneath melted away.

The print hung loose on Marietta, but the hem barely covered her knees. "You beena get dress fe Rosie, you don care bout no print. You get pants this winter fe wear underneath," Aint Sister had said.

Her mother had said softly, "Girl have fe wear dress. And now you moontime come, every month. You keep you head cover, like Sister say. Keep you body clean and cover."

She hated how the dress felt when she hunched in the chair, the tight-soft creasing under her arms, the cloth smelling of smoke and bleach—she watched people enter the stand and their pale eyes flew past her, quick as moths. Their hands flapped at the flies hovering over the peaches. She stepped carefully around the swampy ground that covered her path, hugging close to a tree trunk to walk on the roots. If they knew she wasn't grown, their voices would be different, sweeter and direct, and they would buy something, feel sorry, give her money for soda or chips. But they wouldn't look at her. She heard the smiles and giving in their throats when Laha's kids hung around the stands. Could she say, "I ain't old," and take off the scarf tight over her hair? Would her forehead help? But if she stood up, none of that would matter.

She never said anything but: "Big one fifteen. That one seven."

The trail was only large enough for her; no one else ever went into the thick brush, and huge oaks hung with moss on this side. Laha's kids, all thirteen of em, Aint Sister always said, never crossed into the trees. They played only in their tromped-bare yard where Laha's mother kept an eye on them. The men chopped wood on the other side, too, past the church and the graveyard. If anyone came down this way to Aint Sister's or Mama's, they stayed in the middle of the lane, never venturing off to the sides. Beyond her mother's house were the old plantation gates.

When she had first started wandering in the woods, after the roadside dust began to fill her nose and mouth, she found twisting paths all overgrown—no thick trees to block her, but creeping vines and brush that only possums and raccoons slid through. She had knocked the brush aside with a heavy stick, like she saw the men do. Now she came to the huge fallen oak that walled off this path. People always said the tree had fallen years ago to cut off the road to the plantation, so that the spirits living there would stay where they belonged. She leaned against the gnarled trunk, so high she couldn't see over it. PINE GARDENS, the wrought-iron gates said, but Aint Sister just called it "the House." She told stories about the windows boarded like shut eyelids, and the plat-eyes and other spirits roaming there. Laha's father and the men said the old landing where the mail boat had come years ago to bring supplies to the House was a good place to fish, but more haints and rushes of darkness that could knock you down hovered there and in the gardens.

She trailed her palm down the oak's roughness and came to the hole she'd dug at the base. A piece of car fender, once thick-silver and now rusted, was wedged into the wood to keep her magazine safe from the wet.

Sitting against the tree, she opened the cover and looked at the ads first, at the same narrow, chiseled faces with noses as small as the knuckle on her baby finger. She had stared at the faces hundreds of times. The women's knees, in tight short pants, were sharp as knives.

A man had dropped the magazine by accident when he held out his hands for the two baskets his wife had bought—the shiny roll dropped from under his armpit. "Don't you put those in the trunk," the woman said to him when he turned. "They'll get oil on them somehow, I know it." They stood at the back of the car, arguing, while Marietta watched the magazine swell and plump itself, open its own pages against the sand. The car thrummed suddenly and swerved away, and she bent to touch the glossy cover.

"Motor tour on the historic South Carolina coast: Charleston and the Low Country." That patch of words on the cover was penmarked in spidery blue. She turned to those pages again, found the pictures of the waterway where Big Johnny's boat and the others left each morning and came back slowly in the dark. A sleek white boat she had seen on the water showed people standing to face the wind, wearing silvered sunglasses. Big Johnny and the others called them snowbirds.

She turned the page to the photo she always looked at longest. Under oaks and moss, a man and a woman sat in a small boat. He leaned into her shoulder, his mouth close to her ear, his brown hair ragged like bird feathers, and her smile was small, her hair yellow as corn. You could see half a boy who was Rosie's color, sitting behind them to push a long pole in the water. "Cypress Gardens—lush and romantic under dripping moss and stately oaks. The gardens are exquisite."

Lush—she read the word and studied the photo again and again. It meant the pinkness of the flowers beside the black water, the pink of the woman's lips. Dripping—that was exactly what the moss looked like.

"Charleston is the jewel of the coast, replete with old-world charm." She traced the wrought-iron gate; women with drinks in their hands leaned from the balcony to wave at someone below.

"Gullah speech, quaint and often unintelligible, is still spoken by Negroes in the Low Country." Quaint—she knew how they talked was how Mrs. Green, the teacher at school, didn't want them to talk. She beat you if you said the sentence wrong. "That Gullah chatter won't do in the real world!" she said. She beat you if you wouldn't say the sentence at all.

The heavy, ripping whine of a truck came through the woods, pulling up the highway and fading. Marietta stretched her neck to look into the branches, trying to see what time it was. Maybe eleven—she had to go back to the stand. More white people usually stopped just before or after lunch.

Pushing the thick curve of magazine back into the hole, she fit the metal over it. Her feet made no sound on the padding of oak leaves and pine needles, and when she brushed a branch or vine, the wetness and green of summer made them fall back without a crackle for Aint Sister to hear. For weeks, rain had hung in the air day after day, collecting on necks and foreheads, making fingers slide. "Either too much wet or not enough," they all complained. "Cain nobody breathe when it like this."

She heard the shaking and mumble of the road already—the heat making things vibrate, the road shimmering and women grumbling—and she pressed against the bushes to look into the backs of the stands, to wait for a car that would distract the eyes watching for her. She heard her name, she knew she would, in the tilting shade of Aint Sister's.

"Marietta no help out here. She mama need fe whup that girl, but she ain get the strent." Aint Sister's heavy voice was too deep to come from a face thin and hard as an apple someone had forgotten at the bottom of a box, Marietta always thought.

"Josephine no better, huh?" Rosie said, her voice trailing off to fly on the last word, the way she did.

"She ain make it through too many more summer, now," Aint Sister said, and Marietta felt new cold on the back of her ribs, pricking under the dress. She knew drops of sweat fell from her leaning forehead to nudge the sand. "She got that pressure, them headache. Pressure do that, go right fe she head."

A car roared past, sucking away the air for a moment, and Marietta didn't want to listen, didn't want to move.

Rosie said, "You want some more iced tea?" in a company voice, and Marietta remembered the cousin visiting from New York—Janey, the one with hair swirled high and stiff, not hidden under a scarf.

"Josephine no bigger now than the day I birth that baby," Aint Sister said. "She call out 'Marietta' and I beena think, Huh, this girl never fit no name like that. Name frilly and sweet, make me think fe lemon pie, and baby bigger than the mama, seem. See she now, tall and wild fe tree. Rip and run, no sense."

"Won't settle," Rosie said, her words wet.

"Look just like she daddy," Aint Sister said. "Tall and dark so like Freeman."

"Ain she like him?" Rosie trilled.

"Wasn't he a island people?" the woman named Janey said. "I never did see him, but I only come for visit a few time."

"You beena see Freeman," Rosie said. "He never taken no time for talk."

"Huh," Aint Sister said, and Marietta heard the shaking head in the word. Her father—no one ever talked about him in front of her.

"One a them blueblood mens, look like he directly from Africa." Aint Sister stopped, and the dry sweetgrass rustled from the bags at their feet. "Bullet head. Hair so tight it a scrape you hand you try fe comb it. I know. You see Marietta hair so short? Ain none a Josephine in she child."

Marietta pressed her cheek into the sand on her shoulder, rubbed the grains with her jaw. "Somebody tell me he get kill before the baby even come," Janey said.

It was quiet. Mary said, "I only little myself that time."

When no one spoke, Rosie said, "He catch he some a anything, Freeman. Johnny always tell me Freeman think he too good cause he from the island. Didn't want on the boat with nobody here. And every time, have more fish, more shrimp. Girl, I don care if all em come back with small-small bit on some bad day, Freeman go off lonesome and he boat too full. Like he and them fish have a consolation, and they say, 'Follow here. . .'"

"But how he die?" Janey pressed, and Marietta felt the water leave her skin like a spiderweb being lifted; she wanted to crack through the branches so they would see her, but she wanted to hear her father's name.

"Freeman never go long with nobody, just Josephine," Rosie whispered. Aint Sister's impatient puff of air came through her nose, but she didn't speak. Footsteps crushed the sand, and Marietta watched Pinkie peer into her mother's stand, then go back to Aint Sister's.

"That girl still gone?" Pinkie asked. "She stay with Josephine?"

"What you think? She run wild." Rosie's words flew again.

"Slow too much today. Where them lady?" Pinkie said. "I beena had one say she come back for get three."

"Huh. Almos kill bird don make no stew," Aint Sister said, and Marietta could hear that she was happy not to talk about her father. Freeman.

"You tire, Sister?" Rosie said. "You like for me take you back, you rest?"

"Ain nobody tire," she said. "Only my hair tire—all too many thought under there." Marietta saw Mary shift her feet, and she prayed for a car, one going so fast it would swerve in the dirt to stop, make the women gasp and stare. She didn't want to hear any she-she talk, and they would start on Mary's coming baby, their voices settled and comfortable.

But after the swirling rush of the next car, Aint Sister said harshly, "I don know what taken she fe marry that man."

"Whaaat?" Rosie sang.

"Josephine. She already thirty then, and he, I don know. Older. Josephine mama kept she in Charleston, bring she back here when they house burn down. I don know where she see Freeman. But she been on the island with he sometime—them peoples don took to she. Clannish."

"Mmm-hmm," Pinkie said.

"Josephine light as butter, so pretty," Janey said. "She mention her mama were cousin to you."

Aint Sister was silent again. Marietta held her breath, thinking of the butter glowing on the stove, shining pale in the rice she cooked. That was all her mother ever wanted for dinner. Her mother's skin glistening wet, just as gold, in the light from the fire. Aint Sister was oak-leaf pale, Rosie and Laha and Pearl red-brown as molasses. Big Johnny was dark, but only Marietta was blueblack. That was what they called her. She pressed her elbows to her sides.

"Josephine have too many weakness," Aint Sister said softly. "She have the sugar, have it too bad. That worse than she pressure."

"I know it," Rosie said.

"I see that baby taken too much out she, way back then. The sugar come with the baby sometime. Baby too big cause a the sugar, and mama ain never well since."

Rosie's voice went down into her chest, and Marietta saw her stretch. "She need for make that girl do some work, stead a lay up in the tree and run wild. Have she for do basket right."

"She just look too big for playin," Janey said. "She what—sixteen? Seventeen? Where her friend-boy? So tall, though."

"No, she just thirteen. Go on fourteen," Aint Sister said. "I know. I know all you day born, everyone on this place. Marietta eleven August."

Pinkie said, "A girl need for help. A boy different. She spend all too much time in the sun, blueblack as she daddy sure." She stopped abruptly to watch the two cars.

Rosie and Mary got up slowly and walked to their stands. The white people stayed in their cars for a minute, and then the big-armed man with his elbow facing them leaned out the window and said, "This is great, this is perfect." He turned off his engine. The woman stepped out and the car doors clapped.

and licked out all the pots

In her mother's stand, she swung her hand to lift the pepper of flies off the peaches, and she saw one of the men waiting impatiently like they sometimes did. He was a dark shape behind the wheel, keeping the engine running; the hood of the car glinted in the sun, shaking just a little like water in a bucket. She didn't sit; she heard them coming, but she stood with arms folded. One woman stepped inside the drooping tin cover and hesitated when Marietta raised her chin to watch with half-shut eyes. Then Aint Sister's fingers were digging into her arm to pull her down onto the chair. The woman smiled with her lips, no teeth, and her head turned from side to side like a turtle.

"These is some a the finest work on the highway," Aint Sister said, but the woman had already shifted to her leaving feet.

Aint Sister's fingernails were thick and yellow against Marietta's skin. "Sneak round," she hissed, and Marietta looked at the black-pink feet of her doll, the tiny toes and straight ankles poking out from a pile of sweetgrass beside her. Aint Sister went to meet the woman in her stand, and the smaller woman skittered past the doorway like a bird, going to the window to talk to the waiting man. He rumbled the engine in a burst of thunder and she ran back to the stand.

She was so small that her eyes were straight across from Marietta's and Marietta was on the chair; her hair so pale and wispy Marietta could see her ears through the strands. She moved around the stand, darted from basket to basket, then went to the doorway to look at the cars. Doors chunked now, and the other couple was already back inside. Marietta ran her finger around her forehead to catch the sweat at the edge of her headscarf.

"How much is this one here?" the woman said, voice skittering too, but she ran to look at the cars. Did she want an answer? Marietta swallowed to wet her throat. When she hadn't spoken all day, her voice came out deep and rusty. Now the woman fingered a roll basket, with a brown-and-cream pattern.

"You didn't say how much?" She held up the roll basket. "This one's the same price?" When Marietta's lips opened and she felt the cool on her teeth, the woman said, "No, it's not going to be big enough. It has to be a big, impressive present." She held her head back to look up at the fanner basket, flat and round. Aint Sister always said, "We use fe fan the rice this way and that, let them husk fly in the wind. Lady tell me peoples buy em fe keep magazine."

The horn blared out, so sharp and mean compared to the boat horns Marietta heard soft through the woods at night. And the man put his foot on the gas again; the woman never looked at Marietta, but she blinked and moved from basket to basket, twitching her hair off her shoulders, saying, "No matter what, it won't be right. Their mothers could never approve a gift—that would be against the rules, right? That would be approving me, and we couldn't let that happen." The horn sounded again, longer.

She threw her head back again, and her throat was white and curved as a gull's. "What the hell," she said, her voice trembling. "You didn't say how much this one was."

"Ma'am?" Marietta said, and her own voice was a dark growl after the high trickling words.

She stared at Marietta now. "Your big basket here. Is it expensive enough to satisfy a mother-in-law? Or do you have the same rules here? Is your mother-in-law ever satisfied?" She frowned at Marietta—at what, the voice, the face? "Could I see your big basket here?" She spoke slowly. "Is that yours?"

Marietta stood up, not looking at the face—the eyes would widen a little so white showed, and the mouth would close. She felt a puff on her shoulder because the woman let out breath when Marietta moved. The basket in her hand, she lowered it, smelling the sweet dry.

"It ain't mine," she said. "It's my mama's."

The hands were tiny on the curving sides, and the brown checks of pine needle wavered. "And how much is it?"

"Fifteen." Marietta could say the word, after so many times, without even moving her mouth.

"Fif-*teen?*" Her lips stretched straight in emphasis.

Marietta took a deep breath. "I said fif-tee. Fifty dollar." The words came out smoother now, not gravelly. She looked down into the woman's water-colored eyes, at the line through the middle of her hair. Then Aint Sister's voice shot past her elbow. "She just play, she only a chile. It fifteen, that one, and the other is ten and seven. They really the best one on the highway, got a lot a care in each one."

The woman's thin fingers landed again on the tiny dark squares. "That doesn't seem bad. They're made by hand, after all." She put the fanner basket down carefully, casually, and picked up a smaller one. She walked toward the car and Marietta saw the man throw his head sideways, impatient, like a bird tearing at a fish. But he gave her money, and after she'd left, the seven dollars in Aint Sister's dress pocket, Aint turned to Marietta. "I should beat you fe you mama," she hissed, the wrinkles in her neck hard as ropes, and Marietta turned to slide out the back of the stand. The car tires left the crunch of sand and were silent on the road when she ducked into the woods.

Even in the trees, the hanging mumble followed her. Flies and bees rested in the heat, but they lifted to buzz when she swept past their leaves, and in the close tunnel of her trail, sounds were louder until even the droplets of moisture in the hanging moss seemed to breathe. She began to run, elbows swinging wildly and knocking into vines and branches, until she heard quiet coming closer: the water.

Not the waterway, the salty coast where she watched speedboats skim past—the trees opened abruptly onto a still, wide creek. The creekwater was brown and deep-clear, like Aint Sister's eyes when the day was almost over, the sun going across the highway, and sometimes she turned to look; if Marietta was in the right place, she saw light way inside the eyes. "Don be in my face, nosy," Aint Sister would snap, and when she turned her eyes were flat again, closed. "You best fe check what peach done gone bad."

Marietta crossed her thumb over all four of her fingernails, held them down in a row, and said, "Don, don, don." She pushed out the fingers with a sharp flick, like Pearl did at the store when somebody said something she didn't want to hear. "I let them words go." Flick. Standing still at the edge of the water, she listened. Only water could sink all the sound and leave things clean. The creek trembled full with the tide coming in; the water could shimmer blue or black for a moment if the sun changed or a cloud shifted, but it was colored dark by the tree roots along the banks.

"Do, do, do," she whispered, excited, digging around in the wooden crate she kept behind a tree. A net, torn and mended many times, ragged with holes now, lay in a heap at the bottom. One of the men had lost it, and she had pulled it from a tangle of reeds only a few days ago. Picking up the heavy net, she smelled the dried water and fish in the cord, and a blooming rose in her chest. She would throw the net today; her mother might sleep for a few more hours, and Marietta could bring home enough shrimp and fish to sell to Pearl. Her shrimp would lie plump and curled for people to choose.

She brought home mullet all the time, fried them and felt the crunch of meal grit and the salty soft fish against her teeth, but her mother wouldn't touch them. Marietta caught the mullet on her line, and it was all they had to eat with the rice and grits besides the greens she picked behind the house, or cowpeas, maybe tomatoes. Unless Rosie brought a piece of ham or some crab and shrimp from Big Johnny—and then Marietta would have to hear the clucking and frowned instructions.

She'd throw the net farther down the creek, where the water swirled and began to meet the marsh. But she pulled her cane pole from beside the box first, pushing the end deep into the mud on the bank and propping it with the crate. Brushing her finger past the strange, furry insect she had tied onto the line, she felt the tickle and wondered if it would work today. Another man buying a basket had left this behind—it had fallen off the little ledge at the bottom of his car door. She had watched the bright thing in the sand, waiting for it to move, and then she remembered seeing pictures of white men standing in rivers, fishing with these bugs. She squatted on the small hummock near the edge and whipped the insect out over the water.

The quiet after the line dipped into the water was glassy blue, to the edge of the black mud and sharp green reeds. Flies were here, too, but they cut past and then were gone or landed, not hovering; no blurring dust and humming throats. The slurp of water was licking-sharp against the mud, the click of dragonflies fighting over her head, a bird screaming and then empty air. Only near the water the reeds and grass stood rigid, listening.

She couldn't see the traces of blue in her skin. She lay sideways on the hummock of drier earth, not caring about the dress, and looked closely at her arm. Her wrist, the skin inside her elbow, the smooth back of her hand were deep black with a sheen of sparkles like the shifting gold in the silt at the water's edge. Darker than the water sliding past her—black as the standing pools in the deep woods.

One picture of her daddy was hidden in her mother's box under the bed. Marietta had taken it many times when she was alone, going outside to see it in the lighter yard; the house was always gray-dark inside, with the shutters closed. Her father stood close to the camera, not smiling, so near she could see only his face and the thick, straight neck. No lines marked his skin, no hair stood out from the sharp curve of his face. He had eyebrows she couldn't see, maybe only a few hairs like she had over her eyes. No darker wells under his eyes like Rosie's, no freckles or paler patches on his cheeks—smooth black. She couldn't tell how tall he was; only wooden boards, nothing to measure him against, were behind him. His face filled the tiny photo.

She touched her eyebrows. She'd always wanted her mother's smooth, thin brows, arching over her eyes like markings on a bird's wing. Dark, perfect against the gold forehead. The only thing she'd wished for were those lines to stand out above her eyes and make her face looked more finished, somehow. Her lips were black, too, like her father's, everything blended into a sameness. The inside of Laha's lips were red as crab claws, a sliver of wet when she talked. She looked at the black of her arms and thought of the way Aint Sister's voice had sounded. Blueblood from Africa. Blueblack.

Something plopped in the water, but her pole was still. She lifted her toes dripping from the creek; her gleaming black foot, at the end of a dust-covered leg, was long as a man's. Her feet kept her from school. "I never see no feet that big on no girl," Aint Sister said. Pearl laughed. "Don nobody got shoes for fit them feets." She'd had a pair of sneakers until last year, but suddenly nothing fit, not her dresses, not the shoes, and her mother had said, "You cain go to school no more, not till we find you some shoe. You need for stay here and help me anyway."

Her father's feet. She had a pair of shoes, but when she wore them one day, the women all took in breath—everyone laughing except Aint Sister, who was angry. "Take them boot off," she shouted. "They not fe you."

The worn black boots were her father's, hidden, but she'd

found them years ago in the shed that had long since fallen down. She kept them under the porch, taking them out every now and then to play with when she was small; one day last year, she had put them on for fun, and they fit. She walked around the yard in the boots, felt her toes where they should be, felt the soft front-foot bend with her steps. But when she'd walked down to Rosie's house, where her mother and the other women were shelling cowpeas, and said, "I got shoes for fit me," her mother got up and went inside the open doorway. The hissing of all the mouths made Marietta lift her chin and say, "They good enough for go in the field when the man come around."

And she wore them when it was time to dig potatoes and pull beans and hoe rows of corn. She jabbed her long hoe blade as fast as Pinkie and Mary, kept her lips together so her throat was sealed and moist, and she didn't have to stop for water like the others, who were always talking and singing. Standing in the truckbed on the way home, she smiled at the other women's canvas shoes, the little white rings in a line where the laces were gone; she tipped the loose top circles of the boots against her shins.

Picking up the net, she tried to pull it into a shape, remembering how the men flung the circles out onto the water. A few times, she had hidden in the trees and seen them standing by the creek. Their voices and laughter carried through the woods, and she crept to the edge to watch their arms fly out and curve, fingers splayed against the sky while the net floated in a perfect bell. But most of the time, they were out on the boats far past the waterway, or they went in the creek at night, when the mullet were running.

If they saw her, if she showed herself and asked what she could do, Big Johnny and the other men said, "I ain have Rosie and Sister holler for me cause I keep you out here and you suppose to doing somethin else. Get on back where you missin from. Go on to the highway."

Girls could sell the fish in the evening when the men brought them back; sometimes Laha's girls stood near the highway with strings of fish while white people from the farms or towns down the road came to buy something for dinner. Pearl laid the fish and crab and shrimp out in big pans in her store, and before dark white men might go inside and come out with paper-wrapped packages.

The net was a heavy bundle in her arms; she had seen the holes in it when she stretched it out, but she didn't know how to mend them with sharpened palmetto slivers like Laha's father, Joe Pop, did; his hands would hold the net pattern out on the wall or porch before him. She threw it toward the water as hard as she could, and it fell in a knotted lump on the surface. Her face hot, she looked back into the trees before dragging the tangle back. The dragonflies smashed into each other, tapping sharp.

She arranged and flung the net again and again, and finally it floated into some kind of circle, settled on the water, and sank; she felt the sharp jerk on the wrist circle that attached it to her, and her heart jumped. Now what? She waited a few minutes and then pulled, hoping the net would be full of shrimp. How long should she let it sink? She had never gotten close enough to the men to hear about which tide, or where she should stand in the creek; sometimes they stood in the small rowboats, sometimes they stared at the creek, looking for the spot. The shrimp, scuttling along the bottom, the fish who were darting past now—the net cradled them all tighter and tighter as she pulled gently, and then the heavy-soaked mesh appeared on the bank, empty.

Flinging it out over the shivering water again and again, pacing up and down the bank, farther toward the marsh and the waterway, she made her hands finish stiff and bending backward in the air as if she were praying and shouting like the women did in church, welcoming spirits of love into their chests. She left her hands in the sky for long minutes, the sun hot on her throat and under her chin, and she dragged the net until cords of pain ran from her elbows up into the sides of her neck; then, angry, stalking back to the trees and slapping the net against a trunk, she lay on the damp ground near the water. The net slid to the base of the tree, sounding like a heap of just-washed clothes she had taken from the tub, and she felt furious water rise in her eyes and nose. The pole stood nearby; it hadn't even trembled. The man's furry bug didn't work on creek fish, and the net had so many holes that anything living in water swam through, twisting past her and going about its business. She pulled up the hook and lure to throw them onto the net. No one would show her how to mend the net; they'd just take it, saying it belonged to somebody and they'd see who. Even if that man didn't want it, they'd laugh and say, "Best be mend clothes. Take learnin for use the net. I give Rosie some fish and shrimp for you mama when I come back."

She thought of showing them the white man's insect and sucked her teeth. She'd have to come back tomorrow to her usual spot up the creek, and she'd have fish for breakfast, early, when the sun was only a line at the edge of the water, and her mother was already sitting on the porch. Tonight, only rice. As long as it was hot, when the breeze came maybe, and people were outside waiting for the moving air, she knew all her mother would eat was rice for dinner, grits for breakfast. Sweet yellow with butter and sugar heated into the grains.

Sugar—that was the something she'd been trying to remember all day. She crossed her arms and put a palm on each aching shoulder. Nothing had rustled in the can after breakfast this morning when she'd brought her mother's grits into the bedroom. Aint Sister had the seven dollars, and Marietta didn't want to face her so soon. Rosie would love to give her some sugar, if she could come inside and tell Marietta that the fire in the stove was too low or too hot, that the floor needed sweeping, and why hadn't she put up fresh newspaper on the walls? Lazy. Aint Sister would come with a tea, someone else with prayers, and they would all peer into the bedroom and stay to talk, poke a finger into the rice bag, stir the greens, and frown. And her mother would call softly from the bedroom to keep them there, words threading the air, her mother anxious for the sweet, low complaints and threats. "He do that again, girl, I swear. . ." "My washer ain work right for a week and them boy. . ." "You know she think she grown. . ."

Dreaming in the trees. . . that was how Aint Sister always finished up, when she came back through the doorway from the bedroom.

The sun was golder when she went toward the path. Her

mother would be awake now, maybe back in her chair at the highway, ready to give out a whupping because Marietta had stayed away too long. She was so much taller than her mother now that when she had beat her last, weeks ago, she had hit the backs of Marietta's knees, those tender grins of skin, with a peachtree switch, whipped so hard that even walking stung. She had swung like she knew these were the last whuppings, and Marietta was afraid at the silence, the lack of instructions and promises for future pain. Her mother breathed so hard and fast that she couldn't speak.

She went back to the marsh first and pulled a few bunches of rush, bending her elbow around the long, warm sheaf. To her mother and Aint Sister, she'd say she'd been gathering sweetgrass for them. The women never came to the marsh, where bugs and snakes waited. The men and boys pulled sweetgrass. Marietta started back through the trees, where the moss still hung motionless, always one strand curled off the end of each dangling fall, one strand alone.

Padding carefully around the edge of the clearing when she reached the house, she waited at the pump to listen. The pump sat on its own little table, a board held up by two thick pieces of wood, and she stroked the handle, which flew away in a dip like the ponytails she saw on those magazine women. The clothes she had hung out that morning on a line strung around the porch didn't dance; the air was still as a seen rabbit. At the base of the house, she crouched and went hunched below the windows. Her mother wasn't crying; her breath was high and light as a leaf rocking back and forth on the wind, zigzagging down to the ground.

Inside the house, where no light had been all day, the dark was much deeper than the daylight going behind the trees; the air was gray-blue as the inside of oyster shells, and still her mother didn't stir. Marietta hung her face in the sheet that separated the rooms, watching her mother's face glisten, the mouth a long sliver and only the cloth below her neck swelling slightly. No breath sounded going in, but rasping harsh it came out, and Marietta was frightened, imagining an angry possum in the night. She pulled back the sheet and picked up the bag of grits from their corner on the shelf. The Mason jar was still full of the reddish tea Aint Sister had told her mother to drink. Tea from the bloodroot, which seeped red blood when you cut it. Marietta swirled the tea—why hadn't her mother touched it?

Sugar—there wasn't any use to cook rice or grits without sugar and butter. She'd make both tonight, just in case, make them yellow as dandelions. No way to get out of having to go to the store, so she shifted the dress back on her shoulders and picked up the sweetgrass.

After she had left it on Aint Sister's porch and run down the lane, she slowed for the crossroad. They would be everywhere, looking and laughing and twisting around on chairs and haunches to see who was coming—oh, just Josephine girl, wild as she want for be. Laha's kids all up and down the road, playing with boxes and carrying buckets of crab. Joe and Ricky and Tina would see her and shout, "Here come Marietta! Ax her reach in a tree and get me a bird! I seen a lady had a bird in some cage, right on the seat. She have a bird in she car for sing to her."

She knew the backs of their heads better than their faces, because she always looked past them when she walked; in school, she had had to sit in the back and study their braids and barrettes and the beads of hair near the boys' necks.

They chased two dogs past her, the boys, and the girls held bags of potato chips and gleaming cans of soda. Marietta passed through them quickly, and only Jimmy said something to her. "Hey, Marietta, you so black till I scare a the dark when I see you."

Ricky said, "That one too old, boy. You not even funny."

The men around the store, sitting on crates and shadows in the creeping brown light, looked up. Big Johnny wasn't there. She tensed and passed them, but nobody said anything. A cluster of women's voices swirled through the door, but the men said nothing, not "See Helen's girl? Got them eye like she mama, seem like they almost green." Not "Naw, that ain Pearl grand-baby? Where she get them long leg? Her daddy shortest nigger I ever see." And they didn't wait until she passed and then say, "Big as a man. Probly whup a boy in the dirt he even look for her. Whup me any day."

Inside, the cloudy jar of pigs' feet and moss-green of pickles waited, and the tin of cookies, the plastic soda bottles that hung from the low ceiling to dangle near her head. Pearl smiled behind the counter, and Rosie, who was her cousin, sat on a chair. "How you mama?" Pearl said.

"She sleep," Marietta said. "Aint Sister get my money, and she gone, but I pay you tomorrow."

"Bring it day-clean, be fine," Pearl said, looking at Rosie.

"Just some sugar," Marietta said. Pearl measured out a pound of sugar into a paper sack and slid it over the black pocked counter.

"You don want nothin else?" Pearl said.

Marietta tasted the salty potato chips, like when she licked the inside of her arm if she cut herself, and she thought of how long the seven dollars might have to last, if the summer kept slow with business. "Just some butter," she said, and when she held the small mushy cube she said, "I be by day-clean."

"You don need no meat?" Rosie said. "Big Johnny ain back, but I bring some butts meat for you mama."

"I got shrimp," Marietta said. "More than she want." She bumped the door frame with her shoulder, making the bells tinkle.

Smoke drifted from each house now, wisping through the air, and she hurried back down the lane, cutting through the trees before Aint Sister's. She looked at the roof of her mother's house, at the pile of pine needles and moss gathered above the porch; the roof was steep, and sometimes she heard the sliding leaves and needles in the night. She went up the steps and set the bag on the wooden table by the stove.

Only Aint Sister's house and her mother's had the big fireplaces in the kitchen wall, and that was where Aint Sister cooked. She kept her fire banked all the time, had a pot at the edge of the glow, and sometimes something tucked into the ashes that flaked gray and cooked slow. But Marietta's mother was always hot this year, and when the weather had turned warm, Marietta had cleaned out the fireplace and put scrubbed pots there to keep them out of the way. The bricks were cool to her palm. She took a few pieces of lightwood from the porch and started the fire in the woodstove, thinking that the cooking smell might wake her mother. She put the big cast-iron pot on one burner for rice, and the white-enameled pot on another for grits. Sprinkling salt into each pot, she licked a few grains off her fingers. The washtub was still outside, and she brought it onto the porch before she pulled the clothes from the line. In winter, they would be stiff, but with the air so moist now, they were soft and limp in her hands.

She sat on the porch step to watch the last slivers of light cut through the trees. The moss moved for a moment, and air passed her neck. She heard the trembling of fire under the pots and closed her eyes, remembering the blue flame of winter in the fireplace, the hot roar they kept going when the wind blew outside and her mother and Aint Sister would sit close to the hearth and tell stories. Her fingers would move slowly, theirs quick as spiders through the blackeye peas, sifting and sorting the dried smooth peas and setting aside pebbles and bits of stem. Aint Sister and her mother cleaned all the peas before they put them in the sack for winter. They bought the barrelful of peas from Laha's brother, who farmed his land. Her mother couldn't farm the acre plot behind the house; trees and vines had taken over years ago, begun growing when her father was out fishing. "He hate fe clear and plow," Aint Sister always said. "Want fe sit out on that water till dark the light."

Her mother hadn't even been able to ride the truck and work

for the farmers, Mr. Briggs and Mr. Tally and them, last year. When they came around, Marietta went with the others and her mother stayed inside with Aint Sister, patching holes in clothes and cutting okra into crinkle-edged coins for canning. Marietta thought about Aint Sister's words today. Her mother shook in the winter, swelled and slowed in the summer, slept in the day and cried out at night.

Something rustled in the pile of lightwood on the porch, something small, making more noise than fit its little body. She used to jump at every crackle in the leaves, every brush in the branches, when she was small and first in the woods alone. She would freeze until she saw the beetle or moth, the turtle sliding into the water or the bird pushing past a twig. The pile of wood was low now, but she'd have to find heavy logs to chop for winter, when wind screamed across the ocean and sliced to waft through the cracks in the walls. Then her mother would sit near the glow all night, her face the same bright as the lightest of the flames, watching the deep blue heat that wavered at the bottom of the logs. It was bluer than water.

The rice bubbled white foam under the heavy pot lid. Marietta began to sweep absently, pushing the wood splinters and dust toward the door, thinking that when she asked Mr. Joe Pop to sharpen the ax she could stay and watch his claw-bent fingers knit and mend nets. She could ask him for some cord and say she was making a rope to hold baskets in the stand. She swept the dirt off the porch in a puff and heard Aint Sister's deep shout thud off the tree trunks, always her words coming before her small, slow form in the dark.

"You sweep at night!" The words never flew away in the clearing surrounded by woods or in the stand—they hit Marietta and dropped to the dirt; but this time she sounded angrier, even, than when she had taken the seven dollars. "Stop now! Don never sweep at night—you *know* that!" She grabbed the broom and held it straight through the doorway like a torch. "That so bad luck I don believe you fe do that to you mama."

Marietta's chest tightened. Aint Sister would wake her mother now with hot tea, and then tell her about the woman, about Marietta's mouth and the sweeping, too. She had forgotten about sweeping in the dark. So many bad-luck things to remember—following footsteps, salt and red pepper for hags, eggs and ashes and everything that could bring bad luck or make it leave.

Aint Sister poked at the fire and put the broom in the corner. She stared at the jar of tea, which hadn't been opened, and took the last, smallest pot off the shelf. "Go get the water, fresh," she said. "You beena know that, too. She need some tea. And don be linger out there, talk fe them tree."

Marietta took the pail outside to the pump. She could find it with her eyes closed, even smell the cool wet metal. The water began to slosh into the bucket and she heard a screech, a long e-e-e-e-e-e shooting through the air. Sharp and long as that car horn, but this was throat, shaky high pouring out of a mouth. She turned and grabbed the bucket—was it one of the wild pigs the boys talked about, with mean small eyes and shining-drooled snouts? Or a hag, riding someone way down the road?

She ran toward the house and the scream came again, from

inside. Aint Sister came out onto the porch then and howled again, her head thrown back, calling ye-e-e-e-e louder than church, louder than angry, longer than breath.

night

Rosie only came because she wanted to bring a packet of meat. No one had heard Aint Sister's call down the long, shadowed road; her voice echoed around the branches and moss over and over while Marietta stood, afraid to go past her to see her mother's face. Now Rosie hurried back down the road to tell the others, and Marietta stood beside the bed, where Aint Sister sat in the rocking chair and talked to her mother as if she were still alive.

Her mother's cheeks were dry now, the shine evaporated, and they looked soft and chalky-yellow as pounded sawdust. Marietta knew they would feel like velvet moss. She made her finger move over the sheet covering her mother's chest and arms, and the face was peach-skin smooth at her mother's forehead except for the two permanent frown lines that sliced up from her brows, thin as razor cuts. Aint Sister talked, talked, to her mother and the air outside the window, maybe even to Marietta.

"I beena forget how far they live now. I remember gone time, everybody house close. Hear everything—hear baby fe cry and when somebody have trouble. I de call and nobody hear now, all too far away. Everybody live by the road. But they fe come now, all fe come. Stay till day-clean, don worry."

Her voice grew gentle, smoother in her chest, and Marietta heard that it was for her mother. "We stay till day-clean, fe help you go when that time come. You soul go easy on the journey and we be here till then."

They would all sit with her mother until the sun rose, talking to keep her mother company until her spirit could leave her body with the first streaks of light. Marietta imagined how her mother's breath had looked when it left, how her soul would sound. The women would crowd the room, she knew, sitting wherever they could, getting up to clean the table again, cook something, talk and sing. Then, when the sun showed and the spirit had flown, they'd turn to her.

The woods would have liked to creep all the way to the pump and over it, to take back the outhouse and the porch and then the house, twining into the windows and pushing up the floorboards. Every year she had to swing the ax and clear the baby trees, the bushes and creeping trails of leaf that came closer. But she always left the baby palmetto and the crepe myrtle near the back window of the bedroom, because she liked to see the patterns they made at night. The palm fronds waved like her own fan in the moonglow, and then vines and moss grew over the trees like a cage, meeting the moss that dangled off the edges of the roof.

The shutters were open now, to catch the tiny breeze, and Marietta crouched in the mesh of branches and leaves, listening. She wanted to stay near her mother, too, look out the window and wait for gold morning, wait for that whisper Aint Sister said you could hear when the spirit flew. But she couldn't sit with the voices and clucking and hum, the eyes cutting her way now and then trying to decide.

"Josephine ain sell nothing but that little one yesterday," Mary said. "How it gon get better? People ain buy nothing this week, why they buy next week?"

"You don know what them people fe do. Why you gon expect the worse?" Rosie said.

"Well, all this rain been done wreck Tally crop this year. He field too much flood. He ain get nobody fe work this whole month, and all he gon need is clean the mess when it fe dry. That give we two day, lucky," Pinkie said.

"This baby just kick and fight me all night!" Mary said. Marietta imagined the baby's feet against the slippery insides, wet and covered with membranes like the pig's parts she'd seen slide out of the belly, and she pressed her palms against her own stomach, sickened. Crystal used to say that you could see the baby's foot push all the way out against the skin, pop out the mama's belly in a lump.

"He know you disturb," Aint Sister said absently. "He near time fe come."

"Definitely a boy, way you carry," Laha said.

Aint Sister blew air out her nose. "I ain fe worry that one yet. I worry bout the one out there in the tree. Beena just she and she mama all to now. Josephine mama been dead. All other people dead out."

Marietta lifted her chin from her hand and bit the piece of bark she held. All people dead out. Just Aint Sister.

"She mama name Christmas," Pinkie said. "Mmm-hmm. Too pretty girl."

Aint Sister said, "Long-long black hair, she braid all round she head. My cousin. She die when Marietta small-small, we beena take the baby fe funeral. Christmas been done buy her a plot in Charleston, say she never come back fe Pine Garden even when she dead."

"Josephine never belong to no bury society," Laha said. "Every penny for feed Marietta. Weren't nobody else in the family?"

Aint Sister was quiet while her pipe smoke floated out the window and wreathed the vines above Marietta's head. "Christmas have two boy. One die early. The other still live fe Charleston when we gone to she funeral. But he wild, Hurriah. Wouldn't be no good with a girl. Hurriah ain no good with grown woman, he so wild."

Rosie and Laha laughed, and Rosie said, "He not the only one."

Aint Sister said, "I don know Hurriah believe Marietta he sister child anyhow. He ain see she since she so small."

"If you seen she and been a stranger, you believe it?"

"Who gon believe? Nobody. She so much like she daddy. He blood powerful too much, crowd all Josephine out," Pearl said. She never spoke, just sat knitting the baby sweaters she hung from the wall in the store, little bulky coats Marietta saw on the new babies.

Babies. If she were still tiny, crying, her feet small as spoons and kicking in the air, they would all want her. But they would go around and around tonight, and they all knew who would take her. Aint Sister—and she'd never do anything right for Aint

Sister. If she scratched her head, Aint would snap, "You find that bug yet? The one you fe chase round you ear?" And her father—everyone would whisper in those scared-and-something-else voices, because now that her mother was gone she would look more like him every day. She closed her eyes and lips and made her face as hard as his in the photo, and as if they saw her, Aint Sister said, "Freeman never know how fe make people comfortable. He face never right around nobody."

"Wha-a-a?" Rosie said. "Why you say that, Sister?"

"She talk fe them peoples like Freeman," Pearl said. "Blueblood."

"Everybody act scare fe Freeman," Aint Sister said. "Except that buckra kill em." She stopped abruptly, and Marietta felt the watery tingle on her back again.

"What I gon do with she?" Aint's voice hurried along, trying to pass quickly over what she had said. "Don go long with nobody, scare peoples on the highway she know it or not."

"Sister, what you talk about man kill Freeman? He drown cause he out fe fish and snowbird get he. Just like Fix," Laha said.

"Them white folks never stop for neither of em," Rosie said. "Probably say they ain see nothing."

His face, Fix Green's, floated into Marietta's head even though she put her fingers on her eyebrows and pushed—his face bloated and water rushing out of his mouth and ears in streams when they pulled him up. She had been hanging around the waterway when she heard the men shouting that they'd found him. One of the big white yachts filled with people from the North who sped down the waterway in winter, getting away from the cold in New

York, Big Johnny said, that was who got him. Fix was rowing at the mouth of the creek, where it spilled into the waterway, and the snowbirds had swamped his small boat. But Aint Sister had never said that Marietta's father died that way; she just shook her head and said, "Fishing. He die fishing." And Marietta had never asked her mother anything since she showed her the photo from under the bed and her mother snatched it so quickly she left an ashy scratch on Marietta's wrist.

"I remember when they find Freeman, find he battoe. Everybody fe look," Rosie said. "Cause he go everywhere fe fish. Ki, yeah, Fix daddy Morris find he! Up in that creek past the House, yeah?"

Aint Sister said nothing. Marietta pushed harder at the bones over her eyes, trying not to see her father's hard face soft-blurred from days underwater, like Fix's.

"Nobody never know why he want fe go up there," Laha said.

"What you say bout some man kill he?" Rosie said. "Nobody never mess with that crazy nigger."

Marietta heard a chair scrape, and Aint Sister went out onto the porch, lipping her pipe hard in the quiet.

"Josephine never get over Freeman," Pinkie whispered. "She must been make up she mind fe die, miss that man so like she angry. She tell me once, say she never eat fish cause water take he fe dead."

Aint Sister came back into the room. "All my people gone now. Dead out."

"You forget Marietta, Sister," Laha said.

"No, I ain forget she one minute. How I forget and she be on me now, fe me raise? But she ain remind me fe Josephine, and I never see my cousin Christmas fe she face. Josephine hand and little finger like Christmas. I never see that again, cause Marietta blood all Freeman."

"She not so bad, Sister," Rosie said. "She take good care fe she mama all this time."

"She do," Mary said. "She can come fe help me with the baby."

"I never say she bad," Aint Sister said harshly. "I say what I gon do with she, look like she do, run wild? How I fe keep she on the highway? Never make no basket."

"She work too hard in the field," Pinkie said.

"But ain enough work in the field no more," Mary said.

"I never say she bad," Aint Sister said again, and Marietta's chest was so tight she couldn't push back her shoulders, couldn't let the air come in deep enough. "I say she in the wood right now, talk fe some tree."

"I give you shoe, Marietta, but you know we have fe special order when they that big—you know, fe that size." Pearl leaned over the counter.

Marietta stared past her to the baby coats. "How I gon go?"

Pearl crossed her arms and frowned. "Black," she said, "all I can do." She searched behind the counter until she found a pair of men's black oxfords, with a band across the tongue. Dull leather like a thirsty dog's nose, dusty under her fingers. Marietta slid her feet inside.

"You cain be walk round in them shoe after. They not pay

for. Don look right nohow—you bring em back and we order you some lady shoe."

Marietta felt the drops of sweat on her neck and forehead when she began the walk to Aint Sister's. The thick stockings she had taken from her mother's small chest-of-drawers were much too short. She put her hands in the hot pockets of her mother's black dress and stepped high to keep the shoes out of the dust.

They were silent until they reached the church, where her mother lay in the pine box Big Johnny and Jerry had nailed together last night while the women sat up. Outside the white wooden church, everyone stood in the packed-dirt yard, waiting for her and Aint Sister.

If any cars had stopped at the highway, no one had been there in the stands. All day, they had been cooking and waiting, because Aint Sister wanted Josephine buried the old way, when the sun began to set in the open grave.

Marietta wouldn't listen, when they cried and rocked and held their hands up. The voices circled like a net over her. Once a month, the preacher came from McClellanville to lead meeting instead of Joe Pop. Marietta would hide until her mother left for church; all the talk and shouting, hours and hours that filled her ears to bursting when she was small—she hated the praise house and the others' skin tight-pressed to hers. Aint Sister would make her come now. Marietta watched the fingers stiff and palms facing her mother, who lay paler than gold, her lips thin as the edges of shells, baby shells. Close up tight. They sang and cried, and she stared at her mother's hair, the fringe of broken strands waving around her forehead. Tiny jagged hairs around her ears, the ones she used to press down with petroleum jelly. The cries pounded against her back, and then people were walking slowly past her mother, some touching her face, some bending far over her. All black, their clothes and feet and hair, hats swaying near her mother, Laha and Rosie and Aint Sister's hands pulling her up.

Outside, the coins of light between the oak leaves turned silver, shining quarters above her, and the line of people walked toward the graveyard in the woods. She saw the splinters of pine wood slant away from the box. Water stood in the open grave, and Marietta panicked then, shouting to Big Johnny, "Don't put her in the water! Don't put her facc in no water!"

The men bailed out a few more buckets of water, and the sandy earth still glinted damp, shinier by the minute. "Fill up again!" Marietta screamed, and then, "Wait!" She couldn't stop her mouth, curled with sobs.

"Hush, now," Aint Sister said, holding her arms. "That only a little bit. You know you cain keep all water out. It always that way."

"She hate the water. She cain go in the water—wait, I get it out," she shouted, and Laha came to stand in front of her. "Marietta," she said. "Water sink back down in a minute, soon as they put the dirt in. Hush."

Big Johnny bumped the box, and her mother's face shook a little. Marietta pressed close, hearing Laha's children gasp ragged in fear, and she remembered all the times she'd been afraid of when they would pick up a child and pass him over the coffin. Once, twice, three times. Hand the baby or child over the granma or uncle, the family sending the child back and forth so the spirit wouldn't bother him, wouldn't hover over her unformed self. And she jerked back suddenly, thinking that this was her time, finally, that the hands would grip her now and push her into the air close by her mother's still mouth and hands. Her own face would be only inches away, swinging over the breathless nose, and she closed her eyes backing into Aint Sister's fingers, fighting.

The fingers let go. She looked down at Aint Sister's black straw hat dipping near her shoulder, at the other hats, the feathers and straw and ribbon of the women, the soft felt of the men. Only a few of the men's hats were higher than her own eyes, and no one came near her as the box slid onto the ropes over the grave.

Aint Sister's hand pulled heavy at the crook of Marietta's arm when they walked back up the road. A little wind moved the pine branches high up in the air, and Aint Sister said, "The Lord sigh cause she home now. She relief."

The flashlight wasn't as bright as the almost-full moon. The silver finger flashed only in the shadows where the moon couldn't reach, but Aint Sister moved it back and forth anyway, talking the whole way, and when the beam cut across the clearing to the porch, Marietta saw in the black window squares and closed door that she was already gone from her house, already sleeping beside Aint Sister, hearing old-woman snores, or lying on a pallet in the front room near the fireplace. She couldn't breathe, couldn't stop the ring of water tight around her eyes, blurring the front steps. She stumbled and the edge of wood slammed into her shin.

and licked out all the pots

"Watch you feet. You follow in somebody footstep." Aint Sister was so small her shoes barely whispered across the porch boards. "I need me some coffee fe finish up. We have two thing left, have fe do."

Marietta followed her to the fireplace, where she took out the clean pots and clanked them onto the hearth.

"Too hot for burn fire," Marietta said.

"Hot don matter. Only fire get rid fe death smell in the air. Not no stove fire. Go fe get some lightwood, one big chunk, too."

Marietta brought an armful of branches and one leg-thick log. She laid out the fire and Aint Sister told her, "You go get them match. I never fool with em. Gone time, we never have match. Never let no fire go out or we beena get whup. You see my fire bank right, don never die. Better fe cook in the fireplace. I ain never like fe cook on no stove."

The fire licked out at them for a minute, and Aint Sister nodded. "See? She blow a little down the chimbley, say, 'Clear out death. Now I relief.'" Aint Sister went into the bedroom and pulled the soft, tangled sheets from the bed. "I make some new one," she said, and began to rip the thin cloth and feed the pieces to the fire. "I tell you, we need coffee now. Go on fe get fresh water. Don be linger out there."

Marietta waited by the pump, listening to the drip of water after she stopped moving her arm, hearing the woods, the animals and rustling, the crack of flames inside the house. She could wait in the trees until Aint was finished, be patient until she gave up and went home. But with no light—she thought of the trees and the plat-eye spirits behind them. Fix—people said he walked by the waterway and moved boats. Aint Sister's voice rolled outside under the popping fire. Marietta picked up the bucket and smelled burning hair, the awful acrid smell of her mother's hair caught in the sheets and turning to ash.

Don't remember the box, please, please, Marietta prayed, sitting on the floor while Aint Sister pushed her stick into the fire. Rag by rag, it took so long to burn the sheets and clothes, and she didn't want Aint Sister to pick through the box under the bed, to hold up the photo of her father and shake her head. She didn't want to hear any more stories, see the curl of Aint's lip when she saw the flat stare into the camera. Please, please, forget, she tapped into the floorboards with her shoe.

"You take em back to Pearl day-clean," Aint Sister said abruptly. Marietta remembered, slipping the shoes off.

"I got shoe—I don't need these," she said. She knew Aint Sister would frown. "My boot is all I need."

"You cain go fe school in them boot."

So? She smiled, thinking Aint Sister was on the wrong track. "I ain go to school. I can read better than them anyhow."

"What you talk bout, you read better? You ain even go there half a last year. You go go this year. Oh, yes, you fe go every day."

"I got better thing for read than Mrs. Green. All she got is them old book."

"See that mouth on you? You need fe get respect fe you teacher. You ain too grown fe whup."

"But I too big fe whup," Marietta said, and stopped her smile.

Mrs. Green never came near her with the strap she used on Laha's boys and the others. She never said anything directly to Marietta, only talked about her to the other kids.

"She has to sit in the back, she's so big," Mrs. Green would say, shaking her head. "Sit back there refusing to talk, pretending she can read." Marietta would turn the pages of the encyclopedia slowly all day. The blood-red books sat on a shelf in the back, near her. "Do you see what a bad attitude does to a girl?"

"We gon get you some shoe," Aint Sister said, "so you don miss no more time. And you better wish people start fe buy basket rest of summer."

She think everything plan out, Marietta thought. I rather sit in the tree and read. She looked at the sharp-nosed girls staring down from the walls; their faces were yellowed, the newspaper was so old, but their eyes were still half-lidded and cool, their clothes belted tight.

She couldn't listen to the low, long voice anymore, not another story or another "don" for her. She pushed open the front door. I don't care she see me go. She grabbed the flashlight from the porch. Aint Sister said, "All them basket crowd. . ." and Marietta knew she thought she was headed for the outhouse. She walked through the cleared space and sat behind a pine tree to wait, light off and clutched tight in her hand. She would wait until she could get the box.

The fireglow in the windows turned red, and Aint Sister yelled, "Girl, you best fe get on back. I tire fe play with you. You near grown. Get on back here."

Between tree trunks, Marietta could see her tiny figure framed by the doorway; her shouts flew lower than her screams had the night before, circling the trees, and finally she went back inside. When Marietta came out into the clearing, all she could see was the swaying beam of the lantern and the tiny bobbing pink of the pipe.

After the two lights had been around the curve for a long time and it was completely black, Marietta stood up slowly. Too afraid of the woods to get her magazine, she realized she was leaving. She would take what she could carry. Where you fix for go? she thought.

At the steps, the smell of smoke hung under the roof, and she closed her eyes. She couldn't smell the sweat or sweet hair oil or coffee breath, nothing of her mother, and for the first time she lay where her mother's form had always pressed down on the mattress. Scraping her face against the mattress cover, she felt water rush out of her eyes and nose, so much that she thought of Fix's face and then her father's, and then she screamed into the buttons by her cheek, screaming from her chest like a mule. Hoarse and long—she couldn't stop until the breeze blew a branch across the window and she jumped, afraid it was a spirit, more afraid it was Aint Sister coming back for her.

Swinging herself sideways, drawing in long breaths that made her feel like a child, she reached under the bed for the box.

It was polished wood, reflecting dully in the flashlight beam. She hoped her father had made it. The dried flower petals inside, broken and almost dust now, slid into the corners. They were sweeter than dry straw or even sweetgrass. Her father's face looked at her. She put it in her dress—if she was running, she couldn't be wearing a dress. Running? Running wild. The wild man, too wild to take care of a girl—he was her family. His name was in her hand, on the browned scrap of paper kept in the box along with a key black from age, two smooth black stones, and a greenish penny. Hurriah Turner. Charleston.

If he was wild, he wouldn't care that she was too. She could take care of his cooking and cleaning, and he wouldn't care what else she did. She could buy magazines and read them, go fishing in the river she'd heard Big Johnny and them talk about. Two rivers on either side of Charleston. Head down the waterway and see the big bridge.

She picked up the black shoes and ran a rag around the toes and heels. They turned darker again. Leaving them on the table for Aint Sister to find, she thought they looked lonely there. She pulled on her father's boots and checked for the fishing knife in the long, thin pocket on the outside of the right one. Pacing back and forth, room to room, she found a pair of brown knit pants her mother wore under her dresses in the winter cold. She had to hurry. The pants, the dress, the boots—she was hot, but she rushed back to the stove and took the big cast-iron rice pot from the back. In the big cloth bag where they always packed the dried peas, she put the rice pot and a sack of rice. A spoon in the pocket on her left boot. Matches. Then she held the wooden box and knew it was supposed to be on her mother's grave.

They would bring things there soon: beautiful Milk of Magnesia bottles, her mother's favorite blue; shells to outline the grave; cracked flowered dishes her mother had admired. And Marietta should put the box there now, to stay close to her mother's spirit.

But how could she walk all that way, past Big Johnny and Rosie's, where everybody would be sitting under the Angel Oak, where pipe smoke and words lifted and shivered into the thick branches? She suddenly realized that she couldn't walk to Charleston, either. Not on the highway. She had always been afraid of the highway when it was enveloped in night. All the children had been warned over and over not to play near the asphalt, but this fear was of the drivers who saw black faces as sport, like slow possums. Marietta and the others had heard about Willie's father, who was so drunk coming home from a woman near McClellanville that he didn't see the car playing chicken with him. They found his body in the bushes days later. And Pinkie's left hand had a crooked little finger, the one she had thrown up to stop the bottle flying at her head. "That finger mind she how fool she been, walk lonesome at night," Aint Sister always said.

She could take a battoe, one of the small boats tied near the landing. Big Johnny hardly ever used his battoe since he had the outboard. She began through the woods, the flashlight swaying and the bag heavy on her back. People always said not to take a battoe on the waterway, like Fix, but they went out at night sometimes when the people on the big yachts slept somewhere and the waterway was quiet. She could row in the moonlight, maybe get close by morning so she could see where to go.

Laha's oldest brother had gone on a boat to Charleston, about ten years before. She had heard them talk about it over and over. He and his cousin were driving a truck on the highway and a horse ran wild into the road. Laha's brother couldn't stop the truck. When the horse was dying, a white man rode up on another horse, cussing the boys. He shot the horse, then shot the cousin. Laha's brother had run into the woods, found the house at night, and they gave him a small boat. "A goddamn nigger let the horse loose, and this goddamn nigger killed him. A horse worth more than both of em," the white man shouted. Big Johnny had told Laha's brother how to see his way to Charleston.

She stood by the landing and untied one of the battoes. The water lapped and shivered. She stepped into the battoe and settled her bag, and then she was floating, touching the water with the paddles. The banks were tall with dense trees, and the floating felt good—nothing under her. She had been in a boat many times when she was smaller, before she had to stay in the stand or go to the fields.

Watch for the creeks, she remembered them saying. She passed the spot where she had fished that day, where the marsh met the waterway, and then she slipped past the woods behind her mother's house. She dipped the paddle, but the water was taking her. Watching the woods, she saw a small cleared space, another landing, and she tried to remember. . . the landing for the House, behind the gates, the tunnel of oaks that led to the House. And Marietta froze—a small white man stood there, leaning against the pole on the landing. He stared at her, not moving, and the battoe slid past, so close she saw a cigar in his hand. Then the trees rose dark again, and she pushed harder with the water.

charleston

The bridge rose too high above the water, and cars knocked air against her where she walked near the edge. Marietta kept her eyes on the road, afraid to look backward to the bushes that hid the tiny battoe near the ramp, afraid to look ahead at the dazzling sky that stretched long and treeless. The fall of air below her and the blankness above made her dizzy when she breathed. It was morning now, and she prayed that none of the people flying past her would swerve or swing out a bottle to send her into the blue.

Staring at them and their cars might make it worse. She watched the concrete just in front of each boot toe, the sun hot on her scarf knot and neck, but the water was still there at the side of her eyes. Who would find her body when she floated in this huge river? The black, damp leather was heavy over her feet and shins, thumping soft, and she let the steps blur together, forgetting to listen for laughing in the car windows. Her father's feet, bobbing in the creek—in the boots? No—the boots had been dusty and forgotten in the leaning shed. Why wasn't he wearing them? She would sink to the bottom of the river in his boots, and the crabs would eat her, eyes first.

When she tried to focus her eyes again, swaying, the water was closer to her, and the mud of a small island glittered under the bridge after a few minutes. But the span lifted high again, and she had to look away until she felt the gradual slide toward land. When the cars slowed, Marietta smelled the stink of marsh and smoke, and she stepped off onto hard dirt.

Three men sat with feet dangling off a wall, like boys at home with strings looped around their fingers into the creek. But asphalt was under their feet, and they didn't even look up at her. One passed a long bottle to another, and she heard him laugh soft and mumbly as Laha's kids blowing through straws into their sodas.

Her arms were stiff-coated with mud and fish scales. She thought of the battoe; maybe Uncle Hurriah would have a truck to go and get it. She could hear men shouting in a wooden building nearby, and the sounds of machines humming. Uncle Hurriah. What would he say if she appeared this way, smelling of Pine Gardens? She looked until she found a water tap in the shade of another building, and she watched that no one came outside. Washing her arms and face, pulling her dress down over the pants, she felt her stomach small as a fist, her head empty as a bubble. Too hungry. The bag pounded against her back when she kept walking.

What should she do first? Maybe Uncle Hurriah was at work. She walked with her head down, but now that she was level with the water again, she was more afraid of the faces and buildings, and she turned toward the blue to follow along the river. Each time she looked up, she saw black faces or white faces, hats and thumbs and newspapers and eyes flickering onto her, darting up and down. Eyebrows jumping up to their foreheads or pulling together over their noses: Damn. . . Biggest. . . You see them. . . Boots. . . Spear. . . Where the hell she—

Street signs were everywhere, and she sang, "Sixty-one, sixty-one, sixty-one" to herself, the number she had memorized from the-small, cramped writing on the paper with her uncle's name. But the faces and the signs blurred, and all she could see was ships in the water, people's mouths, bells and laughter echoing in her head. Biggest damn—you see that? She walked faster and faster, the bells louder and louder, and she could smell rain in the sky, far away, maybe a few hours over the water. The people began to disappear, and she smelled food.

When it was quiet and she stopped, she finally saw something she recognized—the walls and black lace gates and piazzas where the women in the magazine leaned over and smiled. She looked up—the streets had gotten narrower, and the only sound was a mockingbird hidden somewhere in a tree; oleanders made black-green hedges, and then she heard another click-click-click, one too regular for a bird.

He was around the next corner, a small old man clipping the oleander that reached through a gate. White pearls of hair stood separate at the edge of his forehead. He watched her, his light brown skin wet with sweat, and she said, "Scuse me, sir, I look for this street."

When she had pulled out the paper from her dress, he puffed air just like Aint Sister. "What you doin way over here downtown?"

"I just come from up the way," she said. "I don't know where for look. I come off the bridge."

He looked at her boots. "Go back where you came," he said, and she took in a breath. He don't even know me, and he tell me go home. What Uncle Hurriah gon say?

"Back up that street," he went on, impatiently. "Up, up, maybe two miles, and you see colored folks. That street you lookin for go off to the left. It ain't hard to find."

"Thank you," she said, but he had already begun the clippers chirping again.

She saw his sliver-grin, his head thrown back to look up at her scarf, when she moved the bag over her shoulder. His eyes were half-closed.

A clot of noise rushed up to her head and stayed between her ears when she walked slow enough to see each street sign. She kept her chin level and looked straight at the teeth and eye whites of the black people she began to see, the people hanging in doorways and alleys, staring. The sky began to darken, and she breathed the clouds into her throat until she saw the sign above her, a small corner and then she turned, her wrist leading her around the sharp walls. A small grocery store with cans in the window, women's faces and curlers hanging in the next glass, but she didn't see any houses. A wafting rush of clothes washing, and then she saw the "61" over a doorway. She stood in the open space, and silvery eyes, tailfans and curled shrimp, looked back. The smell hung in the air, the smell she'd tried to wash off, the smell she'd left last night.

She went inside slowly, toward the hand wiping the counter, back, forth, never stopping. "Help you?" the man said, unsmiling.

"I look for my uncle," she said. "Hurriah Turner. He left piece a paper with my mama, say he live here." The man's face set harder when she said her uncle's name.

"Hurriah live down the street," he said, and then he turned away, dismissing her.

"He leave this number," she whispered, dizzy from hunger—the strong fish air didn't make her mouth fill with liquid, it went through her nose and into her head, dark and lapping water under the landing, under the battoe. She pushed her palm against the glass, covering a red crab claw. "Why he write this?" she said louder. She couldn't believe she raised her voice, but she said it again, hard, and he looked back at her. Then he lifted his shoulders.

"He live down the street, but he get his mail here. Go the other side a the alley, the green house. Green house."

The houses sat sideways on the street, their narrow sides and flat walls facing her; as she went past, she saw feet on some of the piazzas. The spindle-railed porches ran the length of each house, facing the back of the next building, and shoe soles looked over the railings. Big booted feet perched in V's on the wood, small black shoes crossed over each other.

The green house was pale, the piazza railings dark with dirt. Marietta stood at the edge of the yard and looked up at the soles. They receded, gray and speckled, gritting hard on wood. A man peered down at her. "What you want?"

"I look for Hurriah Turner."

"He ain't here. Ain't seen him in damn near a week. Why you want him?" The man's red-brown face was heavy in the cheeks. Another man laughed somewhere on the piazza.

"He my uncle. I come for give he message," she said.

The man said, "Shit, old Hurriah ain't told me he had some a them country folk. You can leave him a note. Come on up the stairs."

At the top of the creaking wooden steps, she saw him and the other man, sitting in the shadows at the far end. She breathed deep through her nose and said, "I blige for wait and tell he. Message bad news."

The man stared at her boots, at the bag. "So? I don't need no girl hang around, and ain't even convince you his family. What you want?"

"He my mama brother. She pass two days ago." She spoke as hard as she had to the man in the fish market, tilting her head up and making her eyes flat. "I need for wait and tell he, huh?"

"You one a them island niggers, huh. How old are you?"

"Eighteen." She thought quickly. "I have thing for give he, from my mama, just he to get it." She heard her words growing shorter and faster, like Aint Sister and Pinkie when they didn't like a stranger.

"Yeah. Lotta thing for Hurriah." He laughed. "You can wait a week. He be floating around. I don't give a shit who in the room long as I get my money, and the rent due in a week. Then you gon have to get on whether he come back or not." He went down a long hallway in the center of the piazza, slammed a door, and came back to give her a key. "Hurriah room on the end. Bathroom down this hall, second door." He went back to his chair.

She turned the last knob, and the dark, hot air inside didn't move. Eyes were on her back, on her bag—she closed the door quickly and leaned against it. Their voices came through the crack at the bottom: "Hurriah living in the bottle this month, he gon get one hell of a surprise one night when he come home."

"Shit, she surprise Jesus when she get to heaven."

"Look bout as much like Hurriah as I look like the Pope."

"Hurriah musta been drunk as a skunk to get in with that. Shit."

When she let the tears run, dripping off her face and into the front of her dress, she thought the water leaving her head would make it clear and free for thinking, but the faster she cried, screwing up her face to push out the heat, determined not to make a sound, the more her head filled with a rush and whirl. She stood there for a long time, her chest aching with the effort, her shoulders sore from rowing. The ache stayed even after the tears slowed and her face began to dry. She looked around the room now that the dimming wasn't so dark. One long and narrow room with two windows that faced onto the street—the windows she'd stared at. The light was brown as tea coming in through the ancient pulled-down shades, a mattress lay in one corner, and three wooden crates by the wall were filled with a tangle of clothes and newspaper.

The walls were gray, smudged with dirt that rose from the

floor like morning haze. She could tell that no one had been inside, no one had even opened the door for days, and she moved quickly to the windows. Pushing them open, she felt the wind that comes before rain. Her own breath could swirl through the room now. It was bad luck to live in a place where no one had drawn air for a long time, Aint Sister had told her again and again. She thought of her mother's breath wafting out through the cracks in the walls of their house, her own air still lingering near the fireplace. She blew hard. She would live here until her uncle came.

The windows turned pink and then the rain finally came, pouring heavy and blowing into the room. Marietta sat on her bag in a trance, watching the water drip down the windowsills and make clean lines on the dirty walls. The room still smelled like a man—smoky, musty, like feet. Around her, on the wooden floor, dirt was trodden into the cracks, not light everyday dust but hard-packed long-time dirt. It wasn't her dirt. And the mattress was brown with grease and sweat. She kept her knees pulled up, only her feet on the floor, and watched the rain until the sky turned black. She stood to pull on the light chain.

Inside one of the crates, she found two cans of pork and beans, a can opener, and a grimy spoon. Taking her own spoon from her boot, she rubbed it with the clean dress until it shone in the harsh light of the bare bulb. The beans were cold and congealed against her teeth, and she ate so fast she felt the half-chewed mass stop at her chest until she straightened and tried to calm herself.

No broom, no washtub, no stove. Uncle must don't eat here, she thought. Only sleep here. Where he eat, where he wash he clothes? She hugged her knees again. No one she knew went to sleep without taking a bath each night. She saw the five large washtubs set in back of Laha's house, heard the men at the store teasing Laha when she bought another one after she'd had more children. "I finish when I finish," she said. Her kids filled the tubs with water from the pump in the morning, and the tubs heated all day in the summer sun for warm baths in the evening.

Marietta's mother had kept her tub on the porch, and she liked the water hotter than sun-warm. Every night, Marietta dragged the tub into the kitchen and put all three pots on the stove to add to her mother's bath and her own.

She picked up the rice pot. The bathroom was down the black hallway—what was inside? Checking to make sure her knife was still in her boot, she went out to the piazza, empty now with water sheeting from the roof and pounding the yard. She smelled the bathroom when she entered the hallway. But inside, with the bulb on, she saw a toilet. Her mother, Laha, Pinkie, all of them talked about getting toilets someday. The damp floor smelled the same here as the outhouse. The sink was brown-tinged and black hairs curled in tiny circles around the faucet. But she turned the metal knob and water sputtered into the sink. She filled the rice pot in a few seconds, then sat carefully on the cold toilet seat. Her legs peeled away when she stood; she pushed the handle down, and water swirled around in the bowl, muddy brown. The smell was wetter, worse than the outhouse somehow, and she jumped when heavy, clomping shoes went past the door. When it was quiet again, only the toilet murmuring, she hurried back to the room.

Dipping her dirty dress in the potful of water, she sat on the bag again and dabbed at her bare arms and legs. She wore the clean dress, curled herself onto the burlap sack and a few of the cleaner-smelling shirts from the crates. The tangle of sheets and mattress seemed foul with something. What would she say to him when he came through the door? Was he covered with dirt, like those men who floated up and down the waterway with no home? She lay with her shoulder pushing the hard floor and listened to the rain.

Knocking woke her. She started up, but then she thought, My uncle don't knock. He live here, got key. She listened to the banging that came again, the footsteps stamping down the piazza. Someone shouted on the street below, and she sat up for a long time, hearing others laugh and shout and walk up the wooden steps.

On the third day, the other can of beans gone and her eyes dry in their sockets from thirst, she retied her scarf in the room filled with her air. Even pulling on her boots left her hot and sleepy. She had lain on the bag or sat on a crate, looking out the window, for hours, making sure no one could see her in the glass. People came to pound on the door during the day and night, but no one tried to open it. She wasn't even hungry anymore, and her muscles felt long and tight, but the heat of her eyes and her slow thoughts meant she had to buy food.

The sun hung on its way down, and a few men stood in the long, narrow yard. They looked up when she started down the steps, and she stopped. I ain't keep my eye down all day. They know I scare for who come in the room. She stared back at them until they curled their lips and turned; she would look back until everyone wavered, she wouldn't stay in the room and hide. When she started down the street, she fixed her eyes on those looking at her basket, her boots, her face, until they pulled in their cheeks and ducked.

The store was on the corner, she remembered. She had five dollars—what Aint Sister had left her to pay Pearl. She could buy a broom, and fill the rice pot with water to throw on the floor and sweep out the dirt. You clean, you plan for stay. That not you room for clean. But he don't come back, you have for go home. Aint Sister be worse, angry too much, and she fix for you every day. She never forgive.

The thoughts swam black in her head, filled her eyes, and she was inside the store before she could be nervous. She looked at the crowd of cans and plastic. In the far corner, she saw a broom. Her palm felt cool and dry on the handle, and she smiled to the straw. But what could she eat? No stove or fire—she hated the metal taste and thick jelly-sauce of canned food. A soda, which would have to last sip by sip, and two tins of sardines, fish for make me strong.

Her eyes slanting down at the man behind the counter, she showed him her basket. He said, "Take em out so I can see you ain't hiding nothing."

"How much?" she said, slamming the tins and bottle on the counter. Her heart beat fast.

He said nothing, just handed her the receipt and opened his palm for the money.

Pushing through the door, she gripped the broom, dizzy again: she saw Aint Sister, leaning against a pale blue truck. "Don sweep at night, bring bad luck," she said, her headwrap moving. "Wait till day-clean fe break new broom."

Marietta jumped, bumping the broom against the wall; it knocked the basket out of her hand and onto the street, where the sardines thudded into the gutter. She swayed for a moment.

"You de fall out, child?" the voice said, close to her now, and the fingers were sharp as always at her elbow. "What wrong?"

The white headwrap, the hard neck and small eyes, but the skin darker than Aint Sister's—Marietta stared at the woman's hand around a pipe. "You look same my aintie," she whispered.

The woman laughed then. "I look fe everybody aintie, everybody granma. That me," she said. She let Marietta sit on the curb and picked up the basket and the food. "You go fe sell basket at market? I never see you."

Marietta shook her head. "What market?"

"You not from here? Where you from?"

"I look for my uncle," Marietta said. "Hurriah Turner. I come from up the way. Pine Garden."

The woman took a deep pull on her pipe and turned the basket around slowly. "Pretty-pretty. You beena make nice work." Her voice was faster than Aint Sister's, but her smoke smelled the same, and Marietta answered without thinking.

"It ain't mine, it my mama's," she said, and her throat swelled shut. Three days, four days—when had she said that to the small woman whose money was in her boot right now? She pushed at her eyelids, ashamed that she couldn't stop her face from trembling. And if the woman hadn't moved to hold her, she would have been able to stop herself quickly. She hadn't cried in front of anyone for years—not since she was small and cut her foot on a piece of glass, kept on walking without pain until she smelled her mother's hairdress at her cheek, felt the softness of her elbow folds. Then the gash throbbed. She leaned into the woman, forcing her eyes open wide to dry the veil of water sliding over them.

When the tears went back inside, she took the basket and said, "That my mama work. I can't make no basket."

"You tell me, I beena forget, I so old. Who you fe look now?"

"Hurriah Turner."

"Oh, Lord," the woman said. "That you uncle? He always in there, eat every night when sun de red fe down." She pointed across the street. "Like so now, dark the light. You ax Sinbad fe you uncle?"

Marietta shook her head again. "Man tell me Hurriah Turner live for green house, but my mama have paper say number 61."

"Come we de ax Sinbad. Frank never crack he teeth fe nothin. But Sinbad a sweetmouth man. He love fe talk."

Marietta followed her across the street to the fish market. The same man stood at the cash register, three lines deep in his forehead, and she looked at him closely this time. He was all stripes. His hair had a gray streak down the middle and straight back from each temple; heavy black glasses made a line down the center of the temple-gray. And his mustache was a finger below his nose, his teeth wide and white under than when he lifted his lip and squinted at the older woman. "Your nephew didn't come back and get that truck running?" he said. "He went out the back with Sinbad, say he looking for a part."

"Lord God, Sinbad gone and I need some smile. Sinbad good fe smile. This Hurriah niece, you know that?"

The man had looked down again, counting money in the register. Marietta smelled fish frying in cornmeal, the hot oil swimming in the air. Two girls sat at one of the tables in the room, staring at Marietta and hiding their mouths with red-tipped fingers. Their straightened hair glistened in the light. Marietta wanted to sit, to hide her boots; the smell of the food made her stomach tighten.

"You been in here with that piece a paper, huh?" the man said, and she turned back.

"You think she a lie?" the old woman said. "Where you from?" she asked again.

"Pine Garden."

"See! Hurriah mention that place, I hear he tell, say he beena happy in hell but not Pine Garden." She smiled in triumph.

"Way he carry on, he be in hell soon enough," Frank said. He frowned at Marietta. "Hurriah use this number cause he like to travel, specially when something ain't going right. He go all over, sometime he come back here and tell me he been in Arizona, California. All kind of places. He travel and work in the fields. Like to be in a different place so new people can hear him play."

"He play that box so sweet till you fe cry," the woman said, softer, and she stroked her lip with her finger as if she heard guitar strings now.

"He always come back, and I keep his mail," Frank said, sharp again, looking down at his money. "But too many people be asking for him. I can't keep em straight, who he know and who he don't."

"Lord God, where that Michael go?" the older woman said. "Look, dark the light now and I have fe take my foot and go." Marietta stared at the shrimp, heard Aint Sister complaining about how fast the sun had set and how she didn't want to walk home in the dark. "I know where that boy gone with Sinbad. I gon find him now." She stopped at the door. "We de bring you corn Thursday. Day-clean, now."

Frank said, "In the morning, Miss Pat. I ain't island folks, huh? Have to stop and think about everything you say."

"I see you by and by," Miss Pat said to Marietta on the sidewalk, and then she walked around the corner.

When Marietta reached the yard, she saw three men in the corner, cigarettes glowing, and the hallway light was a yellow finger in the doorway shadows. In the room, she opened the sardines, eating slowly and crunching the tiny bones. She nudged the grains of rice in their bag, watching them turn and fall on each other. She took the rice pot to the faucet.

Pushing the mattress out onto the piazza, the crates after it, she poured potfuls of water onto the wood floor and swept out the flood of black water onto the piazza. "Watch, please," she called to warn the men, and then she flung the sheet out into the air, where it shattered into drops on the dusty yard. Sweep at night I want, she thought. Sweep out my uncle dirt. He ain't come back, I sweep when I want.

At home, night was pure black unless the moon shone into the open windows. But here headlights swept the walls at night, and the street lamp shone. She lay on her pallet. "The week be finish up. I need for find a job so I can stay, save money for move to better place." She couldn't sell baskets at the market—she only had one. Maybe she could find Miss Pat again and ask for work in her fields, wherever her island was. Maybe Miss Pat lived on the same island where her father was born. She slept, woke again, and heard water still dripping off the piazza. It wasn't raining.

Poking her head out the door, Marietta saw a woman shaking out a mop, dropping it into a bucket; then the woman sat on a chair in her doorway and lit a cigarette. The smoke joined the gray dawn and disappeared.

Marietta walked silently in her bare feet down the piazza, and the woman jumped when she saw her. "Shit, you scare me," she said. She was small and plump, with nut-brown cheeks round and full, but her mouth was small as a dime.

"Who you?" the woman said.

"Hurriah niece," Marietta said. "I stay in he room, wait for he to come back. I want to know can I borrow you mop and bucket sometime?"

"Shit, take em now, cause I won't be mopping for another week. Gotta mop somebody floor every day, and I ain't hardly interest in mine." She stared at the back of the next house. Her feet were small, too, propped in house slippers on the railing.

"You do day work?"

"Why else I be mopping?"

"You know any lady look for somebody?"

The woman looked hard at Marietta. "You do day work before?" Marietta shook her head. "Where you work?"

"Pick bean, tomato, corn."

"Huh. Nobody want to train you, not now. These ladies so particular till you can't please em. You best to find something else." She got up abruptly and closed the door, but she pushed her face out after a moment. "Bring me back the mop—don't be leaving it out. Somebody steal it in a minute."

Marietta decided to walk back to that leafy, gated street where the houses were so big. Morning haze hung over the streets. She smelled the saltwater, the pluff mud at the edges, the coffee floating from windows and doorways. People were eating grits, drinking coffee. She had finished her soda this morning.

She heard the clack-clacking in the yards, but it was faint and faraway. A woman stood outside one of the gates, though, polishing the brass plate on the side. Marietta stopped beside her and said, "Ma'am?"

The woman started, white showing all around her eyes. "Girl, you scare me half to death! What you want?"

"I look for day work, ma'am. You know somebody need girl?"

The woman drew her chin back toward her neck and said, "You ain't hardly dressed for looking to work."

"Yes, ma'am."

"No. I don't know nobody." She turned back to the gate.

Along each street, the servants she saw looked as if she embarrassed them. Blueblack—country—huh. And the white people, the men coming out the gates going to work, women going somewhere with scarves and black glasses, didn't see her at all. The shoe tips and glasses tips were all pointy and shined, and the eyes didn't swerve—not like the white people at home, Mr. Tally and Mr. Briggs, who always saw you no matter where you were, always smiled and said, "You doin a good job, gal?" or "Hot today, ain't it?" And you had to smile back and answer, "Yessuh."

After a few hours, she couldn't even feel her feet, just her hips moving her forward. Nothing in her hands—no grocery bag in the bend of her elbow, no purse on her wrist, no newspaper tucked in her armpit. She stared at the people walking past her, making their eyes widen only a little too round, and she remembered that night, sitting in the small battoe, rocking and floating through the dark. Looking into the black woods, streaks of silver from passing creeks with the moon flashing on their water. Afraid of the not-seeing, and her powerless voice all she could use if something flew out at her—a spirit, a man. The darkness that sent streaks of cold through people and paralyzed them where they stood on the road—only animals moved through blackened forest and could see the paths. Animals and spirits. Her face—

that was what people saw, so dark reminding them of night, the time of animals and plat-eyes. There were *her* eyes, moving, and if she smiled, her teeth would be white as the moon. She scared them, and they looked away first.

She knew she smelled fire. A knot of embers pulsed in the far corner of the yard, shadows passing in front of it now and then, and she leaned over the railing to smell cooking meat.

Grabbing her rice pot, she slid the bag of rice under her arm and filled the pot from the bathroom tap. But in the yard she realized that she had no wood, so she went upstairs for one of the wooden crates. In the yard, she smashed it with her boot.

"What the hell you doing?" the landlord called from the far corner. "You can't be breaking things."

She didn't answer him. The wood splintered, she arranged it, lit the match, blew. He came to stand over her. "Shit, girl, you heard me. Only one fire lowed in the yard. I can't have everybody building fires."

She said nothing, just squatted and blew softly, imagining she was in the woods, and he pushed at her shoulder. "You don't understand English, country gal?"

Marietta raised and whirled around, her face even with his. "You put it out," she said, her voice cracked and deep as always; she imagined her father, his lips square, his hands, "and I knock you blind."

"Crazy bitch," he said, turning so hard he brushed her. "Think she somebody. You be out on your ass tomorrow night, cause you ain't got no money," he called. "Be building fires back in them woods you come from."

She felt a chill—had he known what she thought? But she bent to put the rice pot on the fire, even though it was too high still. The flames licked the black iron, pitted and coarse, and the base of the pot seemed to pull them right inside.

Awake all night, she ate the whole pot of rice, handful by handful, and looked at her father's picture. I don need no mirror, she thought. They say that me right there. The box filled the air with dry-flower scent, and that was as good a picture of her mother, because when she smelled it Marietta saw the tiny, soft forehead hairs, flattened with oil in a veil along her ears, and the eyelashes moving all in one curve.

When the cars had stopped passing, and no more footsteps scraped below her window, she waited for day-clean. She would look for Miss Pat.

The last grains of rice between her teeth, she heard sliding quiet outside the door. This wasn't the people who tromped up the stairs and banged, calling out, "Hurriah? Hey, nigger, come on." The shoes stopped slowly and a hand tried the knob.

Marietta turned on her hands and knees and saw the feet in the crack of dim light under the door. A clicking scrape, a knife rasped beside the lock. She felt for her own knife, beside the box, and crawled silently to the door. At the side, she saw the dull knife tip and the shadow of the hand. She waited until the tip slid in and then she jabbed her own knife forward, into the shadow. It hit the web of palm and she heard a cry of pain. "Come on," she said. "Come on."

The feet ran toward the stairs and down. Marietta looked at the knife blade in the light from the window, but she saw no blood. Her heart beat so fast that she felt her shoulders, her cheeks, pounding, and she sat on a crate by the window until gray morning.

"Oh Lord, you so tall-tall. I beena forget. Ain see no gal tall-so since I child." Miss Pat and her nephew Michael stood in the doorway of the fish market. He picked up a crate of corn, and Marietta picked one up, too, following him into the store.

"In the back," Frank called, and the nephew told her, "I get it." He looked at Marietta until she put down the crate.

"Tall-tall, mmm-hmm," Miss Pat sang, and then she said, "Look, Sinbad, she see you face fe true, better than little girl you de sweetmouth. She look right in you eye."

Marietta turned and felt breath puffing above her eyebrows. "Sorry," he said, going around her to the swinging door beside the counter. A middle-aged woman stood in front of the counter and said, "That all you got today?" She frowned at the half-empty ice.

"Right now," he smiled. "Come back in a hour—we slow this morning."

"Humph, y'all *is* slow," she said, leaving.

"Hey, Miss Pat," he said. "You looking fine this morning." He tilted his head exaggeratedly and blinked at her.

Marietta watched his face. He had sharp angles, hollows under thin cheeks. Straight black eyebrows, and a faint line of mustache. He was carp-gold, and when he smiled, a thin gap showed between his front teeth.

"I know, I know, you want your money," he said to Miss Pat, counting.

"I too glad this girl see me today cause she de look fe job, Sinbad," Miss Pat said. "And I beena hear last week Frank look fe help."

"She from the island?" he said absently, not looking up from his hands.

Marietta felt Miss Pat's hand on her arm. "No, no, she Hurriah niece. You know, Hurriah always sing and carry on. She come fe look he, and need work." Miss Pat's small, slanted eyes smiled up into Marietta's.

"Where you from?" he said to the counter.

"Pine Garden."

"That don help me. Sinbad ain know nothing bout here." Miss Pat looked at Sinbad again. "She from by the water, she know how cook a fish." She put the money in her dress.

Sinbad closed the drawer and gave her his attention. "We don't need nobody cookin. We need a cat to do the nasty work, cuttin and cleanin."

"A cat?" Marietta looked at Miss Pat.

"He mean a man. He from De-troit, that how he talk. And sweetmouth—every woman put she foot inside this door. You safe long as he don out the light and whisper fe you ear."

A shout came from the double doors behind the counter. "Sinbad—get back here if nobody ain't buying," Frank yelled.

"Excuse me, ladies, I gotta clean some fish. And I hate to do that instead of talk to you." He pushed through the doors, letting out the strong, fresh-fish air.

Marietta watched Miss Pat, her red headscarf and eyes long and half-closed. Miss Pat took ten dollars from her dress and pressed it into Marietta's hand. She lifted her nostrils toward the swinging doors and raised her brows. "Go on. You de pay me back."

Marietta pushed into the dock smell from back home. Frank saw her and shouted, "Sinbad, what the hell going on? I been told you don't let your lady friends come in back."

"I don't know her—she just in off the street."

"No, I know who she is." He frowned at Marietta. "That don't mean you ain't already made friends with her."

"Naw, she want a job."

Marietta took her fish knife from the boot and grabbed the shrimp.

She stood at the sink, ran her sharp thumbnail up the curled back of a shrimp, pulled out his dark-gritted vein. Faster with her nail—so fast the heap of grayish curves rose next to her quick as Frank could take them away.

Their backs winged out when they were dipped in cornmeal and fried, pink inside, and Sinbad put them on plates with boiled corn, rice, coleslaw. She cooked the rice now, too, setting the pots on the back of the huge stove to steam perfect. From early morning, she wiped the red vinyl seat bottoms, the round table tops, and then she stayed in the back, boning, cutting, cleaning the fish that slid through her hands. All Frank had said was "Get some shoes." And when he paid her the second week, he gave her ten extra dollars. "Pay me back," he said. "But get some damn shoes."

She went to King Street, where Sinbad said colored people shopped, and faced the store windows. The women's shoes were narrow, pointed, like the ones she had always watched stepping out of car doors when she lay in the sand. Or their soles were thick and rubbery, black or white shoes like the maids and cooks wore when they came by the market on their way from work. She didn't touch any of those. She went to the men's store and tried on a pair of black leather slip-ons, ignoring the face of the light-skinned man with the knot of his tie kissing his Adam's apple who had handed her the shoes. They were like the ones she had worn at her mother's burying, but long enough so that her heel didn't crush the back. She asked the man for black socks.

In the men's section of the department store, she looked straight into the faces of the salesmen in the mirror behind her while she held to her hips a pair of black pants, slim and narrow at the ankles, like Johnny used to wear. A white shirt, long-sleeved. She wasn't going to look like an old woman this winter, like Aint Sister and the rest with four skirts piled on to keep warm. She would come back in a few months and buy a coat.

Happy birthday, she said to herself. She was fifteen that day.

In the mornings when she left the dim room, she held the muscles between her legs and walked quickly down the steps. She was afraid of the dark, pee-wet floor and tight walls of the hallway toilet, more afraid than she had ever been of the outhouse at home. Rosie and all of them talked about "indoor plumbing" and Laha always said, "I love fe flush that water at Miz Briggs;" and everyone told tales about snakes in the outhouse. Marietta had sprinkled lime and turpentine around the edges of the clearing, the way Aint Sister said would keep snakes away, and she kept a heavy stick inside the outhouse just in case.

But flushing—this gurgle of water wasn't worth the trembling she felt while she sat, vulnerable, in that dark closet while feet waited outside to burst in and corner her, and the instant gleam of water from the tap was a dribble compared to the strong rush from the faucet at Frank's.

She saw the light from the glass door when she hurried down the still-dark street. If the truck was running good, Miss Pat and her nephew would be unloading crates at the curb, and Marietta ran inside to the back room, hoping Frank and Sinbad were still in the alley or at the register so she could use the tiny bathroom near the supply closet. She took off her blouse, smelling the air near the sink, like Sinbad's cologne sometimes, and splashed water everywhere. Then she went back outside to help Miss Pat.

The day was long, and customers came in past dark, but she was glad not to spend time in the dim room, where she rarely slept, just listened. The landlord and his friends sat with their shoes up, and when they saw her enter the yard, dime drops of spit sailed onto the dirt. "Man clothes don't make nobody no man. A bitch is a bitch. Some bitches need to learn." But she dropped her eyelids and handed him money, silently, the first few times, and his palms were smooth pink, unscarred, when he took it. She wondered why he didn't take his key and go into the room, throw her things out over the railing, but nothing was ever touched. Sometimes she thought it had been a haint at her door that night—did haints and hags roam in the Charleston dark like they did in Pine Gardens? But she had sliced a real hand, and she knew he had told someone to try her.

At night, she read the magazines people left at Frank's, or the newspaper ads from the trash. It was noisy in the yard and the street, with sparkling showers of breaking glass against the walls and sidewalks. She lay on the mattress she had covered with a heavy cloth and pushed to the window, watching the silver moonlight or yellow street light, listening for footsteps. She imagined her Uncle Hurriah's guitar, his hands, his face, and after a few weeks had passed and the landlord took her money, cursed her back, but didn't touch her, she thought maybe Uncle Hurriah had something the man wanted, or something he didn't want.

Frank would know, but she couldn't talk to Frank yet. She didn't know how. She sharpened her knife in the back room after Miss Pat and her nephew were gone, after the fish had been picked up, and the shrimp slid through her fingers, the flesh of fish, but Frank and Sinbad stayed out front. Frank hollered and grumbled, paying for things and ordering others, looking in the back room at the boxes of napkins and salt, until midmorning, when the first rush of customers slowed and some of the older men came in to pass the time with him. They sat at the corner booth, arguing, sucking their teeth, laughing.

And people came in and out all day, stayed, hung at the counter, draped over chair backs, to talk to Sinbad.

She heard the boys and younger men joking with him about Detroit and basketball. He had played one year in college, and he always snorted at the boys his age, "Y'all niggers can't play no decent basketball. Shit, you can't even go to college in Charleston. Shit."

"Shut up, man, we got Claflin, we got South Carolina State," one of the college students would say.

"Uh, yeah, and ain't that way the hell up in the country? And ain't summer near bout over?" Sinbad would say. "Time for your ass to get on the bus, right? Unless you taking that black ass to the Citadel this year." He laughed.

"So?" another student said. Marietta wiped a table nearby, watching. How had she learned to tell the students from the others? she wondered. They had neat tags of sideburn hair over their ears, no mustaches, and their necks were straight inside their collars. They sat at the tables near the window and talked for hours. This boy said to Sinbad, "I don't see you in college."

"I done did that. Too boring," Sinbad said. "Don't know why I stay here, y'all so backward."

"Cause he probably got hisself in trouble with some woman in Detroit," a man called from near the counter, where Frank sold him coffee. "Or her mama." Everybody laughed, Sinbad, too.

Because the women came, too, all day. College girls Marietta could tell by their skirts and sweaters and the way they held their heads and hands. Sometimes they stacked books beside their chairs, laughing with the boys and leaning hair close to talk to Sinbad. And the two girls who were waitresses at a restaurant, who came in to paint each other's fingernails and smile at him. Girls came in to buy two pounds of shrimp, two pounds of spots, and they stood, shifting from foot to foot, for an hour near the doorway while Marietta tried to get close enough to hear what he said to them.

Night came and customers came to get plates filled. Sinbad whispered far in the corner, or in the street. She washed pots and dishes while Frank counted the money and straightened the counter his way; then she took her warm covered plate of dinner into the corner booth and ate, smelling the men's cigarette smoke and pants and coffee in the vinyl. Before she left, she ducked into the back room again to splash water on herself.

When she said, "Evening," to Frank and he nodded, she went slowly toward the glass front door, where she could see Sinbad's elbows at the edge. It was dark, and a girl was pressed against the brick at the corner of the building, Sinbad's hands on either side of her face. Marietta closed the door carefully, straining to hear. He said, "Why you wanna take the bus, baby? Leave them shrimp here, I'll put em in the freezer, and you can get em when you come off work tomorrow. You can take the Gray Line home, you get the best ride you ever had. I promise."

Sinbad Gray—he whispered to them, and sometimes his murmurs were the last voice she heard before she went back to the room, where all the night sounds were blended into the dark.

The sweater girls, she called them in her head, with their round shoulders and bangs in rolls over their eyebrows, had a whole table of people around them one day near the end of summer. Marietta and Sinbad were busy serving all afternoon, because it was Saturday and Frank was out, but Sinbad called over to the group frequently, "You better not let them girls leave before I get to say goodbye."

The students were all leaving for college, and the boy named Stan who often argued and laughed with Sinbad said, "I thought you wanted to kiss me goodbye, man."

"Shit, I'll be glad when your serious ass is gone," Sinbad said.

"But I'll be back sooner than you think, cause we got big plans for Christmas break. Plans that might even interest you, Sinbad."

"If they party plans, I'll be interested."

Stan, with his molasses skin and mouth wide and thin as a new moon, always curled up or down at the corners, said, "Kind of party we need. We gon party downtown, past Calhoun."

"What you talking about, Stan?" one of the girls said.

"We got a movement started, and I can't talk about it too much, but some guys at Fisk and North Carolina A and T are talking about what we have to do to get the message across."

"Stan love to talk in riddles," another girl said.

"I ain't saying nothing," Stan said then, ducking. "Y'all have to wait till Christmas break. But we have to get everybody involved, not just students. You too, Sinbad, and you," he turned to Marietta. "What's your name?"

She froze when they all stared at her, and one of the sweater girls said something low to her friend. They smiled and bit the red on their lips.

"You'll have to come down with us, too," Stan said, still looking at her. "Even old Frank needs to listen up."

Marietta was glad when Sinbad snorted and went around the counter. They all watched him push his tongue into the loose skin above his chin, making bumps ripple back and forth like Frank did when he was upset. "Naw, you ain't getting Frank mad for days, uh-uh," Sinbad laughed. "Me and her gotta be with the man long after you out the door." Stan glanced back at Marietta, and she stared at the counter so she wouldn't have to see the sweater girls.

The afternoons were quieter when they were all gone, but the evenings were just as busy with women getting off work, men in their boots muddy from the rain, and still the girls who ducked into Sinbad's whispers.

He had a car now, and everyone wanted to see it; she knew he lived in the apartment above the fish market because sometimes he told Frank, "I gotta run upstairs and get me another shirt." He parked the car, with its pointy fins, on the street, and all the men admired every inch. Most people walked in Charleston, but Sinbad said, "Man, I come from *Detroit,* I can't walk. It's against the law. Signed away that privilege on my birth certificate. I'm a Ford man."

But during the half hours when no one came in, and only the fan and slipping ice made sounds, he didn't say anything to Marietta. Frank was gruff and short with her, like he was with everyone, but Sinbad was just businesslike, quick. Maybe Frank had told him not to talk to her too much while they were working, but maybe her height and face were too much even for him, though he curved his lips and moved them close to ears of every color—pink and brown and black. If no one lingered for him at closing time, he would say, "See you in the morning," to her before he got into the car. He wasn't going home, though, because she rarely saw lights behind his shades. Most often it was dark, and she knew he slept in someone else's bed. She lay below the window, imagining what he was saying.

At the end of September, she woke one morning to feel the heat pressing down too hard; thc air was heavy and quiet, and she dressed, tied on a clean white headscarf. Only old women wore white ones at home, but she liked her two white shirts and white scarves; she soaked them in a pail, swirling bleach cloudy through the water.

She could smell the wind in the air, and remembered that they had heard hurricane warnings on the radio at Frank's the night before. When she went inside the store, Sinbad was waiting for her.

"Frank said hurricane's on the way," he said.

"Where Frank?" she asked. The tables were empty.

"I guess the hurricane already messed up his brother's farm down south or something. He called me this morning and said he was going down there, so we have to watch the store. He said if people come in, tell em ain't no deliveries today, so ain't no plates."

Marietta thought of Miss Pat. "Probably them island people wait for storm pass," she said.

"Gracie. Why they name hurricanes after women? Yeah, I wonder," he said, but he looked nervous. Nobody for stay and talk today, she thought. He ain't custom for that.

A few people came by for fish, but then the sky darkened and the wind picked up. Marietta and Sinbad wiped everything down, and he sat at a table drinking beer, watching her. She began to wash the windows, although they would have to be covered with plywood Frank kept in the back room. She liked the idea of washing them on the inside and protecting the outside from the wind and water. But when she looked at the color of the air between the buildings, she thought, I stay right here. I ain't gon sit in Uncle Hurriah room and water come for rush. She saw Aint Sister and the others, shutters nailed tight, around fires, telling stories, drinking coffee, listening, and she saw her mother's house, empty of breath and maybe full of floodwaters. Her palm circling the rag around the glass, she stared at the street, remembering the times the water had risen, and the bodies had floated from the bury ground.

Sinbad turned up the small radio and said, "You ain't even nervous, huh?" The wind outside pushed paper and leaves through the street, but with his voice and the radio's warnings, she couldn't hear the scattering for a second.

"We best put up the wood," she said. Outside, they didn't talk as they fit the plywood and boards to the glass. She saw a bird hovering over them, not going anywhere. Sinbad hunched his shoulders and went first into the darkened store.

First the radio was silent, and without the burble of music Sinbad stiffened. But he said, "Can't get no good stations here anyhow—not like Motown." When the lights went out, he didn't move from the table. Marietta heard only her own shoes scraping on the floor; she went into the back and found candles in the supply closet. As soon as she could see his face in the flame light, he said, "Shit, I can't stand the dark."

"You ain't use to dark?"

"Hey, my mama *paid* her light bill. It don't bother you?"

Marietta smiled to herself, thinking of the rooms at home, with her mother sleeping and the fire gone out. "This ain't dark." She listened. "This ain't no bad storm yet, neither. Already had one this year, name Cindy."

"Yeah, Frank said that, but I didn't see nothing that day," he said.

"Came bad where I live." Marietta corrected herself: "Where I live before. Knock down people tree—lotta fig tree, peach tree go. Left my mama peach tree."

He looked at her closely. She stood near the counter. "You had a house?"

"My mama house. She pass. Then I come here." She turned to check the windows; now that his eyes had focused on her, for the first time, she felt her scarf too tight, her lips dry.

"You all live in a small town?" he asked.

"Ain't no town. Some house, a store. Creek."

"Everybody live in a house?" he asked, getting up to take another beer from the refrigerator.

"Why you keep ax for house?" she said. "You don't like house?"

"Never lived in one. Always stayed in apartments. Sixth floor. Mrs. Gray's four rooms. Shit." He wasn't smiling, his eyes weren't wide, and she had never heard his voice like this.

"We only have two room. See?" she said.

"Forget it, I was just talking." He drank deeply and said, "Hurricanes. I don't even know why I stay here. You sure we shouldn't go someplace else?"

"Frank ax us for watch the store. Where you gon go in the wind?" she said.

Sinbad looked at the blank eyes of the stove, the cave of empty glass case. "Ain't nothing more pitiful than a empty restaurant," he said. "Look like sorrow's kitchen." He laughed.

"Where you talking about?" she said.

"Didn't your gramma use to say that? One a them old-timey things they always say, from the South. 'I been in sorrow's kitchen and licked out *all* the pots, boy.' Said that all the time."

Marietta shook her head. "I never listen. Where you gran from?"

"Mississippi. Backwoods, Missippi."

She sat at the table next to his and stretched her fingers. "Why you came here anyway?"

He was quiet, but then he smiled. "I got in some shit with the cops. Been a while. Been. . ." he stopped. . . "five years. Damn. Stole a car—me and my friend C.B. He got caught—short, bow-legged cat couldn't run for nothing. I went to my aunt's house in Cincinnati. Dead as dead, so I started checking places out. Went to Atlanta. Memphis."

"Why you came *here?*"

"That all you can say?" He smiled and put his feet up on the chair. "I heard when I was a kid somebody way back in my family use to work iron. Made wrought-iron gates and shit. I came down here, drove down them streets where all the tourists go, seen gates. Rich white folks behind em. So?" He smiled wide this time. "I wanted to see the ocean. I just didn't expect to see it up to my neck. I heard it floods like crazy when you get a hurricane."

"Sometime."

"You should know."

She didn't say anything. His lips popped around the neck of the bottle, and she stared into the dark store, away from his hand clutching the beer. Willie's father's hand—when the flood came, that was how they'd found his body, which had been hidden in the bushes beside the highway after the car hit him. His hand—that was what floated near Aint Sister's porch. Dogs must have chewed it off, torn it from the wrist. And the rest of him came later. He was a haint now, Willie's father, roaming the highway, Aint Sister said. Marietta closed her eyes, listened to the wind. She spoke without looking at Sinbad. "You think my Uncle Hurriah dead?"

He was surprised. "Huh?"

"He been gone two month, maybe more."

"I don't really know the cat, but he likes to sing. Doesn't like to talk, not no long conversation."

"Like you," Marietta said. She clicked her teeth nervously—say some word fast-fast. "How old you think my uncle?"

"I don't know, maybe forty, forty-five. He probably caught up somewhere, maybe doing some time. He ain't dead."

She kept seeing her uncle, his face an older, darker version of her mother's, lying beside a road, floating in the storm now, with her father and Willie's father, all of them riding the water face up, waiting for someone to find them. The wind knocked small branches scratchy against the boards, and she could hear rain. "If you scare of flood, you could go upstair. I stay here," she said, watching his mouth tighten.

"I ain't staying nowhere by myself. You the hurricane expert—you gon save me if something happen," he said, trying to show his teeth.

"Nothing for do but wait."

"You sound like a grandma. Like Miss Pat. How come y'all talk so funny sometimes and then sound damn near normal other times?"

She smiled back. "Depend."

"See? You sound eighty years old. How old are you?"

"Eighteen," she lied, without thinking. "And you?"

"I was eighteen when I left Motown."

"You twenty-three."

"I knew you could add—I seen you take money from people, and nobody ain't hit you yet." He was still trying to be funny, but his eyes were on the black windows. "Only thing I like to do when I'm scared is sleep. Slept on the bus all the way from Detroit."

"Go on sleep," she said. "I keep watch."

"Nuh-uh," he said. But he drank another beer, and when the candles were shorter, he lay on the long seat in the corner booth, his legs and feet flopping until he curled onto his side, and his mouth stayed open in sleep. She waited a long time before she stood near him to see his smooth jaw and the soft mustache up close. His arms were thick at the shoulder and wrist, but his ankle bones poked high through his socks. She sat there for several hours, listening to the wind subside and the water trickle from roofs and ledges, and she knew he'd be embarrassed when he woke up.

She ran to her room. The windows had blown in because they faced directly into the wind. She wrapped herself in several shirts and a blanket, rescued her two *Ebony* magazines from the floor where they lay with edges curly-wet. Would Sinbad be afraid when he woke up? Would he remember what he had said?

In the morning, the glass shards glinted blue on the floor, on the street. And Sinbad only smiled at her, briefly, eyes moving away quickly, never like he did to the girls with books and eyelashes and rolls of hair.

Her hair wouldn't grow. She tried to wrap it with string, heavy white string, like Aint Sister and Rosie and them did at home, like they had wrapped her hair when she was small, but the curls were too short to pull into her hand. The ball of string in her palm, she sat against the wall on her mattress. Aint Sister—her long hair in corded spirals hanging almost to her shoulders if you ever saw her without her headwrap. Her mother and Aint Sister had given up doing Marietta's hair long ago, because although the curls were soft they refused to grow as individuals; they nestled thick against each other and stayed close to her head.

Sometimes she wondered if Aint Sister and them thought she was dead, floating somewhere in water. The storm had dissipated by the time it hit Charleston, so she knew it hadn't hurt Pine Gardens badly, but she still saw bodies floating from the bury yard at night, maybe even her mother. For days, she had watched the landlord smile, listened to him say, "Bet it getting cold in some bitch room at night." She was afraid to ask him to fix the window, so she took plywood from Frank's and fitted it to the frames at night, taken it down in the morning so she could see. But she was afraid to ask Frank, either, and not Sinbad, who avoided her with his shoulders and face.

Miss Pat and Michael came twice a week now that winter was near, unloading potatoes and maybe cabbage, so she had finally asked Michael to help her with the window. He had stared at the crates, the new mattress on the floor. A customer had asked Frank to put up a note selling the mattress, and Marietta bought it. But even on the clean, slippery new material she didn't sleep at night; even after Michael had gone, silent, and the windows let in light again, she turned the pages of the *Ebonys* again and again.

Wherever she saw a man leaning close to a woman, or talking to her on the telephone, or resting his fingers on her arm, his mouth near her face, she read the advertising around the photos. "Life is a whirl for the girl with the clear, bright Nadinola-light complexion. Don't let dull, dark skin deprive you of popularity—give romance a chance!" "Skinny legs? Add shapely curves. . ." "Does he want to put orchids in your hair? Hair Strate—hair *can't* revert!" "Sex and your perspiration—the most offensive odor—Rub in Arrid. . ." "Let's talk frankly about internal cleanliness—Zonite is for 'the delicate zone.'"

At the store she stood before the pyramids and stacks of jars. "Lighter, brighter skin—a sure attraction! Black and White Bleaching Cream." The jars were all sizes—50 cents, 75 cents, 90 cents. But she looked again at the pages of the magazines and at the faces on the jars—the noses and eyebrows, the mouths, weren't hers. I need for save money if I'ma move, she thought. After I move, I have money for spend.

She decided to watch the college girls when they came back for the holiday break, watch the way they moved and smiled at Sinbad. She looked at herself in the store windows; the winter sky was clear and reflected in the glass, and she saw sideways her all-one-color cheeks and lips stark against the white collar and headscarf, the smooth fall of her untucked shirt, her narrow ankles.

The girls came, college and not, with red mouths, gold bracelets that jangled when they waved their hands. Hair sprang high from their foreheads. But their voices were nearly drowned out by the boys, Stan and Robert and Carey arguing about what to do with the white folks. Sinbad hovered, pulled a girl away to another table like choosing a grape, until Frank hollered at him, while Marietta listened.

"Yeah, you can buy on King Street, but you still can't go past Calhoun," Robert shouted. "Don't touch nothing in those shops."

"That stuff too expensive for niggers anyway," someone else said, and Robert got angrier. "That's not the point and you know it," he said, and a girl put her hand on his wrist.

"Don't get mad at him," she said.

"I need to get mad at anybody who won't help out when we need it," Robert said, and Stan motioned him to be quiet.

"What you need?" Sinbad said. "You *need* to tell me where the party at this weekend. I don't *need* to know any of this other shit."

Some of the crowd laughed when he did, and Stan said, "You don't know cause you don't have to know."

"What's that suppose to mean?" Sinbad said.

"You can pack up and go home. 'Motown,' you always saying. This is my home," Stan said evenly.

Sinbad rolled his eyes and sang, "Wa-a-a-y down upon the Swa-a-nee River," and Stan and Robert stalked out. Sinbad plopped down on the empty seat and said, "Let's talk about more important things. I don't need to shop with no white boys—I need to talk to some lovely ladies."

Frank told them all to be quiet more and more often before Christmas. He looked tired most of the time; the streaks of gray in his hair had widened, and his eyes were red-veined. Sometimes he let Marietta take over at the stove and counter, and she chopped the cabbage with the sharp cleaver, rocking it back and forth like she'd watched him do. She dropped the oysters and shrimp into the spattering oil while he rested in the corner booth, and she brought him a plate of mullet, his favorite.

On New Year's Eve, she asked him if she could use the stove to make Hoppin John—the rice brown with cowpeas and bits of ham and pepper. Hoppin John for luck, and greens for money—she simmered them on the back burner with the ham hock. She gave a plate to Frank and one to Sinbad, but they ate at different times, standing at the counter and taking bites now and then because the store was so busy. Marietta watched the people crowd in, the women thick in their coats like Rosie and Pearl, the men in hats. They were rushing to cook for family today, and no one hung around to tell jokes or argue at the tables. She knew Aint Sister and

Rosie spooned Hoppin John onto plates for everyone today, too. And greens. . . good luck for the New Year: 1960.

Frank turned the radio up one day in February and said to Marietta, "Listen. This must be what them boys was jawing about all last month." Four college students had sat down at a Woolworth's in Greensboro, ordered cups of coffee and cherry pie, and refused to leave.

Stan and Robert and Carey were back at the store in a few weeks, smiling at Marietta and Sinbad, saying, "Now you see what has to be done." More of their friends left Claflin and South Carolina State to come back to Charleston, they said, and organize. The store was filled with young people and the older men, shouting and disagreeing.

"We're gonna hit the five-and-dimes, the lunch counter, and the bus station," Stan said.

"Sit-ins ain't gonna make them white folks love you," Frank's friend Clarence said.

"I don't want em to love me," Robert said to him. "But I'll be right there, and they can't deny me."

"Why you want to sit with paddies anyway?" Sinbad said. "I done sat with plenty of em in Detroit. It ain't no treat to watch them eat."

"I'm not even gonna bother with you, man," Stan said. "But Marietta, she's listening. Come here, let me enlist you," he said to her. Frank and Sinbad watched her shake her head.

"I ain't need for buy nothing down there," she said to Stan.

He stood close to her. "I didn't ask you to buy anything. Come with me tomorrow, and I'll buy you a cup of coffee."

"Stan serious about this sit-in," the girl called Gina said, the one Sinbad whispered to the most.

Sinbad walked away, saying, "Let me know when you tired of sitting-in so we can stand up and dance."

"You coming?" Stan said to her. "I'll be by tomorrow, and you'll be a member of the Carolina Student Movement Association."

"She ain't a student," Carey said.

"She can learn tomorrow, man," Stan said. "That's why we left school, right, so we can spread it out." He went toward the door, telling Marietta, "Tomorrow morning."

She went into the back before anyone else could say something, her hands shaking when she scoured the utility sink. Why did Stan want her to come? He was asking everyone else. All those white people downtown, where she hadn't been since the day she walked for hours, looking for day work. What I say for white folks? Aint Sister always talk about "Buckra don't want talk, only want work. Why crack your teeth?" Why I sit next to white lady for eat? I cain say nothing to Stan and them, barely say nothing to Frank. But Stan kept repeating, "Everybody needs to go. Everybody's important."

Almost everyone was gone when she came back out; she had listened at the swinging door for a long time. Frank sat with the men, Clarence and Marshall and Anderson, in the corner booth, and she brought him a plate of mullet, crispy-hot. That was all he would eat now.

"You gon go tomorrow with that boy?" he said to the table.

"I don't know," she answered carefully, and he turned to Marshall.

"Don't you know what somebody told me?" he said. "Man told me to think about it—crab, lobster, shrimp, all them, they the roaches of the sea. Yeah, man. What they eat? Go long the bottom eating on trash, everything people be throwing down there. Dead bodies, all we know. You don't want roaches in your house, chase em away, and then come in here and order some ocean roaches!" He picked up a mullet, finger-long, and bit into the coating. "I eat me some swimming fish, that's all."

"Look at em," Marshall said, pointing to the case. "Maybe he right. But shrimp taste too good to me."

Clarence said, "I look at them fish and see white folks."

"What you talking about?"

"All this about they don't want to eat with colored, don't want to shop with them, sit with em. Got these men beating on them kids. I look at them gray shrimp—see em? That the color some of them white men face. Some red as crab claw—you know that. And them ladies with pink cheeks. Talking bout colored people—shit, what they think they is?"

"You crazy, Clarence."

"Naw, he right," Frank said. "I don't care to eat with em myself, but I can't deny these kids what they want. They ain't use to being told, and that ain't so bad."

Marshall said, "Easy for you to say, Frank. You ain't got no kids. I gotta raise three boy and they better get use to being told. I rather have em be told than be killed."

While she cleaned for the night, she tried to imagine the white faces that would shout at her if she went with Stan. She had only seen Mr. Tally, Mr. Briggs, their wives, close up, when she went to work the fields. The people who got out of the cars—she had hardly ever looked at their faces, just at the ground to see what they might drop, or at the baskets they might buy. The tiny woman with fluttering voice and hair, she had seen her face, but no one since. Marietta sat awake most of the night in her room, seeing the highway and the bridge and the flying bottles, the pale hands hanging out open windows.

Frank pushed her toward them, where they stood at the door—Stan, a girl with glasses like sideways teardrops, a crowd of students behind them. "Go on. Sinbad ain't going nowhere." She went forward and Stan pulled her arm.

"It's not a long walk," he shouted to the rest of them. "That's the point, right? It's not even that far, so we should be able to go there and do what we want."

They marched down the sidewalks of King Street, passing the stores where she had bought her shoes and clothes, and then kept on past Calhoun. Faces bobbed around Marietta, feet scuffed into the backs of her shoes, and she saw the lunch counter ahead of her quickly. Stan, the girl with glasses whom he called Loretta, and Robert sat down at the only three seats available, and the rest of the students stood behind them. Marietta edged toward the wall when she saw the white boys with short hair and thick jackets come in from the street.

The waitresses stood with arms folded, staring at Loretta, and she said, "I'll have coffee and a grilled cheese sandwich, please." They walked to the end of the counter where the coffee urns stood, and Loretta stared at the menu, her mouth turned up in a small smile.

Stan said, "Look, more vacant seats." The white people sitting at the counter had gotten up and backed away from the students. "Sit down, guys, maybe we can get some service now."

When more of the students sat down, pulling their overcoats around them on the seats, the white boys moved in behind them, and shouting began to echo off the mirrors and menu and linoleum crowded with moving feet. "I'll serve you, nigger! Here, have some a this!" Ketchup dribbled like blood onto Stan's head, and through the arms Marietta saw a lit cigarette slide into Loretta's straight, fine hair—the glow flickered for a moment inside the nest of hair before she brushed the back of her head and turned. Marietta felt the cool wall against her back and stopped breathing, thinking that the boys near her would stretch out hands for her throat, but she saw two of them look straight past her, their eyes not stopping at her face. She stayed still, and they reached for the girl with a black purse and red coat next to her. They ain't see me; I ain't no student. They see my headwrap, they see me, she thought, and slid against the wall toward the short swinging doors at the end of the counter. They ain't see me. Robert didn't hit the boy holding someone next to her; his hand stopped and he stood still. "Chicken nigger boy, ain't you gonna help your girlfriend?" the white boy said. "I'll help her out the door." The crowd shifted and turned, and Marietta pushed through the doors into the kitchen.

The two older men by the stove stood staring at her and at the noise that massed at the door. They were shiny brown with grease and sweat, white aprons clear at the chest with oil, and when she ran past them to the alley door, open and cold, they turned back to the shouting she had let in.

Marietta walked quickly back up to Frank's, stilling her face before she went inside, and when Frank and Sinbad looked up at her, she said, "They sitting in. I try to get back for lunchtime—they got plenty student for stay there." She went straight to the back and rearranged the boxes in the supply closet, but the paper napkins were the same as the ones she had seen on the counter beside Stan's arm, splattered with blood-red ketchup, and she closed the closet door, sat on an overturned bucket to breathe regular again.

Frank came to the swinging doors—she heard his feet—and she jumped up to wash her hands at the sink. He went into the closet for the large can of pepper and said, "So they okay? Downtown?"

"I don't know," she said. "Maybe police come."

"Why you come back by yourself?"

She looked at him. "I don't want for sit next to nobody. I ain't want for see no white people."

He nodded. "Maybe not now," he said. "Come on in the front and make some coffee, huh?"

They came again, after they got out of jail, Stan and the others, but this time when they tried to talk to Marietta Frank told them, "Naw, now, you all got out of school to do this, and you gon have to go back sometime. But Marietta gotta stay here and work. I can't let her go all the time." She stayed behind the counter as much as she could, letting Sinbad serve and smile.

"The courts got it now," the students said. "We have to persist." Stan and Robert sat at a table alone sometimes, hands moving across the salt grains and fingers bending. She couldn't hear what they said, but she watched them while she turned the fish and steamed the rice, and she watched Sinbad sit more and more often with the pretty, red-mouthed, girl named Gloria. She came in the afternoon, before she went to work at the airport, carrying a bag with a blue uniform edging out. But she never wore the uniform to the store—always narrow dresses with belts at the waist, and her collarbone making hollows below her shoulders.

And at night a girl named Pat came to buy shrimp. She carried books, but Marietta didn't know if she was a student—maybe high school, her face was so soft and her smile so small.

Loretta was polite to Sinbad, but she stayed close to Stan, and every weekend the students gathered and made more plans, but Stan didn't ask Marietta to come along with them. He and Sinbad rarely said more than "Hey," and Marietta gathered thrown-away newspapers to see what Stan and the others were doing.

The newspapers said that the Negro student revolt was dangerous and should be stopped by any means—"the knife, the gun. . ." Marietta watched Stan's face for wounds, but only his eyes were hard, and his lips thin and curved as fish-knife blades themselves.

The older men still argued about what the students were doing, and when Marietta served the women who came in the early evening, the maids and housekeepers and cooks who had already served one meal and were getting ready to cook another, they waited by the case, talking to Frank. Their purses hung from hands clasped over their stomachs; they rocked back and forth on their heels while she fixed their orders, saying to Frank, "Wash my hands down they throats three times a day. I chew up her baby's food on my plate. Hang up her draws inside so nobody can't see em drying. And she talking about, 'How can you let your girl sociate with them trouble-makers?' But she can't sociate with me at the restaurant. Chew up them babies' food every day and night."

"Ma'am," Marietta said, handing her the wrapped fish, and the woman said, "Thank you, honey. I fixing to cook this fish right."

His grins were wider than ever all spring, but never for her. He forget he ever say something for me, she thought. He ain't see nothing but my hand give him the plate or money. He juggle them two girl every day. Sinbad watched them like Big Johnny checked the tide—Gloria and Pat. She saw him in the alley one evening when she went to put the trash out, and he stood with Gloria near the doorway that led to his apartment. Gloria began to come by the store at odd times, though, and one summer night she came long after dark.

"See? Sinbad, you better tell this girl," Gloria said. He looked around quickly from the table, where he sat with Pat and her friend. Frank looked up from the register—it was near closing.

"I ain't playing, nigger," Gloria shouted. Her curlers were covered with a thin scarf, and her lips were still red, but her knuckles were pushed into her sides so hard that Marietta could see how soft her waist was. "You better tell her you was with me last night."

Sinbad stood up. He looked at Pat. "Yeah, I was," he said, and then he walked past Marietta and through the double doors to the back.

"Nigger, get back in here," Gloria yelled. "I swear to God, you better tell her something more than that!" Frank went over to her; Pat was smiling at the floor, and Marietta was starting for the back, too, when the curlered Gloria rushed past her. "No, not you, don't you go in there. I need to see him alone."

But she came back out after a few minutes, hollering still, and said, "He ain't there." She stood in the street, looking up at his windows, and after a long time she went away. Pat and her friend left then, and a few minutes later Sinbad came in through the front door, smiling at Frank. "I had to pick something up at the store, man," he said, and Frank frowned at him.

"Don't get business mixed up with foolishness," he said. "You ain't bringing in customers much as you bringing in trouble."

When July heat came and people slept behind shades in the afternoon before coming back out at night, the store was quiet for a few hours after lunch. Frank went out to buy supplies one afternoon, and Marietta pinched the heads off shrimp in the back, thinking that she'd been in Charleston almost a year. Stan and Robert had gone to Orangeburg, to protest there, and then to Columbia. Sinbad said, "Good—less competition," and he and his friends sat drinking Coke now. She dropped a shrimp, shook her head, and went to pick it up where it had slid across the floor near the swinging doors. Sinbad's voice rose above the rest.

"She got a nice ass. African ass."

"Only a yellow nigger care about a African ass," someone said. "Only a skinny nigger like you."

"I care! The behind the best part." The one named Gene laughed.

"Yeah, but who in hell gon touch that? She six damn feet tall. Sinbad only one tall enough."

"She exactly your height, then, Lijah. Fit you perfect."

Marietta's forehead was hot, but she stayed bent there, near the wide crack. Her fingers touched the shrimp shell.

"Uh-uh," Lijah said. "I don't want no woman looking me dead off in my eyes."

Sinbad said, "She got nice eyes, too. You notice that? Naw, you wouldn't. So black they almost purple. Plum purple."

"Sinbad, nigger, you talking about a woman could have purple teeth for all I know. She ain't smiled or spoke since she been here."

"Man, all women beautiful. Gloria got three little freckles on the side of her nose. You ever kiss a woman side of the nose? Naw, Lijah ain't that smart. All women got something beautiful on em somewhere. You gotta look."

"Look all you want—you ain't gon see no freckle on Marietta." Lijah laughed. "Nothing show up on her."

She slid herself back to the sink and threw the knife into it so that the metal clanked. She dropped the bucket hard, and when she came out with the shrimp, Lijah said, "Man, them crackers was talking some scary stuff to that kid on TV, the one at the movie theater. I ain't playing."

"My aintie sick," Michael said when he showed up alone to deliver corn. "My wife take care for she."

He wife? Marietta thought. He so young for marry. When the corn was inside and she had started shucking the ears, Michael said to Frank, "I bring more corn Thursday you want."

"Yeah, we boiling em up," Frank said. "What's wrong with Miss Pat?"

Michael frowned and took the money. "She just ail. She seventy year old."

All day she thought about Miss Pat, about the first day she had brought Marietta to look for work and said, "Look, Sinbad, she see you face fe true. She look right in you eye." Michael was married—he never talked to her anyway, but she missed Miss Pat's short laughter and pats on her arm. Why did she want Sinbad to talk to her? Last year, all her life before, she had run into the woods to leave she-she talk behind, those voices, but this wasn't the same. She wanted someone to laugh and tell her about going to Memphis and New York and everywhere else.

His breath puffing above her eyes. That warmth bathing her forehead for just the one second when she had turned around that first day—she remembered it, and when she lay awake listening to the voices in the street and the cars, she was angry with herself. That was a foolish thing to want; it was what all those other girls, curlered Gloria, the red-nailed waitresses, the college students, wanted. Aint Sister's voice grumbled in her ears: "Pinkie girl fast too much—follow she hip and not she head."

But she couldn't stop thinking about what his lips would feel like, not on her mouth but above her eyebrows, whispering. She traced the ridges and knew it didn't matter—she could never buy a dress, fit her long feet into a pair of shoes right for a woman, stroke paint onto the dark skin below the hairs she rubbed now above her eyes.

He had looked at her eyes, though. And nighttime—the dark. . . "Nighttime is the right time," Lijah always said. Sinbad couldn't see her face in the dark. She remembered the white man—the haint?—at the landing, and suddenly wondered if he had really seen her face clearly on the water. She traced her brows and the rims of her eyes.

Waiting and watching every day, she saw that it would never happen, and she wondered how he'd ever looked close enough into her face to even see her eyes. Whenever Frank was gone, she waited, but Sinbad counted money or stacked boxes in the back, or laughed at a table. Gloria was happy again, her hair stiff and perfect, her neck arched to the side when she came in after lunch. The fuzzy girl, Pat, with furred sweaters and hair cottony-soft at the edges, was happy, too, when she stopped by after dark.

But Sinbad kept his top lip down too far when he smiled now. Marietta saw. He was quiet when the men laughed and slammed hands on the tables; he rolled his eyes when Stan stopped by to say that the courts were going to order the municipal golf course to integrate. "That should make every nigger happy," Sinbad said. "We *all* play golf, right?" He want to go, Marietta thought. He restless.

"You look like hell," Frank told him one morning when he came in with his clothes rumpled, the same pants and shirt as he'd left wearing the night before. "Lijah?"

"Nigger had me at a party," Sinbad said sleepily. "They don't never give up." He went straight to the back and didn't hear Frank say, "We gon have a party today with this storm coming."

Marietta joined him at the sink when she had made the coffee, and their knives flicked elbow to elbow. Storm coming, she thought. He think I the hurricane expert. Maybe he scared.

When they were finished, Sinbad said, "Tell Frank I'm a go upstairs for a couple minutes, huh?"

"He gone to see the doctor," Marietta said. Sinbad rubbed his eyes. "You didn't hear bout you favorite thing?" she asked, keeping her voice steady.

"What?" He spoke into his palms.

"Storm off the coast. Maybe come today."

He laughed. "Just what I need. I don't even care today. Float my butt out to sea and rock me to sleep." He turned and went toward the alley door.

Frank was gone for hours, and Sinbad didn't come downstairs. Marietta made only a few leftover ears of corn, the pot of rice, and some mullet and shrimp. Even by lunchtime only a few customers had come, and they were distracted by the radio warnings. Long after lunch, Frank came back from the doctor's and said, "You feel that air? I seen a damn tornado in the sky, like they supposed to have in Kansas. Just like a finger reach down and run along the ground. Never seen anything like that in my life."

"Not like a wind?" Marietta asked.

"Like a tunnel, I guess, just picking up and wrecking. But it was gone real quick. They don't know what might come next, so people suppose to stay in. Where Sinbad?"

"He run upstairs for change clothes."

"Well, tell him don't drive tonight, just in case."

"What the doctor say?"

"My pressure up. He said to stop eating. Stop smoking. Stop everything. I'ma go home and take these pills he give me. You and Sinbad lock up, huh? You can go home, cause ain't nobody gon be in." He took the mullet and wrapped it in paper. "I eat whatever I want, not what nobody tell me. Goddamn tornado could hit me and I'll be chewing something good."

Marietta fixed two plates of food and waited. She washed her face at the little sink, went outside to the glass to look at her face, and pulled her headscarf straight. Last September, the rain and wind, and nothing for Sinbad to look at but her. She got the plywood out, just in case the radio said the hurricane was coming ashore.

When he came down, he had washed; she saw edges of wet near his ears, and he stroked his little mustache. "Where everybody go?"

"I tell you storm coming," she said. "Frank see a tornado hit over there where he been to the doctor. He gone home, and radio say stay inside."

"I'm tired a these damn hurricanes. What this one called?"

Marietta, she thought. "I don't know," she said. "Just stay inside, like last year." She said it right, looking into his face, and he brought his thumb and finger together again and again on his chin, smiling.

"That's right. You the hurricane expert."

She brought out the plates and set them in the corner booth. "You don't eat yet, huh? Here." She set a beer down by his plate.

"What's this? What I do?" he said.

"Nothing. You tire today," she said, and made herself sit across from him. She ate carefully, sweating down her back; she hadn't eaten in front of another person for so long.

"Thanks," he said, cutting his eyes at her, and she saw he knew.

"I gon clean up now, cause Frank tell me lock up and go."

"He did. Okay." He drank the beer, smiling, watching her empty the coffeepot and wipe down the counters. In the back, she looked out the alley door and decided not to put the trash out today. The alley was deserted, the bricks damp, and the sky lighter. This storm not nothing, she thought, but I ain't tell he that. Since I the expert.

Splashing water on her face again, she stopped to fill her chest with air. "Go on," she whispered to herself.

"I fixing go," she said, putting the key on the table. "You stay?" She waited till he stood up and then walked to the door, watching in the glass when he followed her. His shoulders were wider than hers, only their edges and the top of his head showing behind her. Her back was cold. He stood close at the door. "Ain't we got something to take care of?" he said.

"What?"

"Don't we have to put up the wood?" He laughed.

"Up to you." He play now, like he do, she thought.

"You sure you want to take the chance and walk home? You the Carolina girl, the storm professor." His voice had come closer, changed now to the dipping-softer one she'd heard him use so many times before.

"You see storm last year," she said. "Worse storm then."

"Yeah, but this looks real dangerous to me. The street could be hit at any time." His chest touched her shoulder blades. Her nose pressed the glass and she couldn't see their reflections.

The soft breath over her eyes, the tickle of his mustache there. He flicked off the light beside the door and his lips touched her eyebrows, the side of her cheekbones, her jaw. They pressed her neck soft as she had felt her own mouth on her arm. When his fingers slid up the back of her neck, cupping her head, something flew back and forth between her hip bones. Think with she hip. . . He pulled at the scarf, and the pads of fingers went through her hair.

The stairs in the alley were dark, and her head felt naked and cold. He held her scarf, kept a finger on either side of her neck, the palm at the back, and she went up the narrow stairway ahead of him. She couldn't see anything inside his apartment, but his hands went to her temples and he bent his head to hers. "I didn't know," he said. His lashes brushed her cheek.

I don't know, I don't know. He don't know. They lay on his bed and her hands felt rough at the sides of his back, where she touched ribs when he stretched to turn the sheet down. She pulled her fingers away quickly, but he caught them and put them behind his neck. I don't know. His tongue touched her teeth. He don't know. She opened her mouth.

When she woke, afraid to move at first, he was breathing harsh and slow in sleep. Even his shoulders moved, nudging her. She had only been asleep for a few minutes. What had hurt her was heavy against her leg, and she tried to touch it without waking him—the end was soft as new skin after a blister had peeled off. His hand came over hers, and gathering her up—was he still asleep?—he pushed her face into his neck and pulled at her hips again.

He was gone. "Where the hell he been?" Frank shouted. "He stuck in some girl's bed." He turned to Marietta. "Excuse my language, Marietta." Frank had to take money and wrap fish while she started the cooking, and he hated to reach into the case now. "I'm going upstairs and make sure some woman didn't kill him."

After lunch, he sat and ate with Marietta. "Sinbad like your Uncle Hurriah," he said suddenly.

"I never see my uncle," she said. "But I hear so much. I know."

"Here and gone people. Not just men like that, you know. You got women like that, too. My granma, after slavery time, she went around all by herself, couldn't settle."

On the third afternoon, he came in, shirt clean and pressed, gray moons under his eyes. "I gon let you go, you do this again," Frank yelled.

"You love me, Frank. I bring the ladies in and they buy lots of fish," Sinbad said, going around Marietta polite and slow to the counter. "Hey," he said, and then, to a customer, "What can I get for you, ma'am?"

Gloria came soon, her eyes pale-clear as honey, and purple shadow on her lids. Her fingernails rested pink on his shoulders, and Marietta felt that same twisting below her stomach, imagining his fingers, hers, raking through hair. Or did all women like that—the lines of rubbing through her hair that made her eyes close? They had to like it, because he knew how to do it, right away.

In the quiet morning, darker because fall had come, they stood at the counter pushing fish into the ice. "I thought you go see some tree in Boston," she said.

"What?" He didn't look up.

"You come here for gates, you read about thing all the time. You can see cherry tree in Washington, in spring. Disneyland in California anytime. Up there by Boston, tree change color in the fall."

"You been reading too, sound like. So where you gonna go?" He closed the case.

"I ain't here and gone."

He nodded.

She walked home that night, pulling her coat around her. Her room was cold, and she sat in her clothes on the bed, looking through the magazines, piling them in a stack. Outside the window, she saw the piazzas and the street, cigarettes flowing and bobbing, white clothes swaying on a line where someone had forgotten to bring them in.

He watched her the next day, but he said nothing until they were in the back. "Next question?" he asked, pulling at his chin.

Was it warm between you leg for two day? Do it be warm every time? Only first time? She bent her head to the knife. "Sinbad you basket name."

"What?"

"I said, Sinbad you basket name."

"Yeah, I heard you, but I don't understand. You talking that island talk."

"What you mama call you—Sinbad. What your outside name?"

"Nathaniel Calvin."

"Why you call Sinbad?"

"My mama didn't start it, she still won't even say it. I caught a stick in the eye and had to wear a patch for a while. Like a pirate."

But the next day, when he followed her through the doors, said, "Shoot," she was tired of the game. Do Miss Curler wear them thing at night when you sleep with her? How she hair look in the morning, and she eye with no purple and blue? Marietta saw them all, sweaters tight at their chests, hands small and delicate, feet clicking across the floor. I ain't have a basket name. Only Marietta. You never ax.

"Shoot," he said again. "Let's go."

"You make the coffee?" she asked, and went out to the front.

Something below her navel—like when a drop of water slid halfway down the crease between her cheek and nose, caught there and tickling, both her hands inside a fish, and she almost crying for the sweat-pearl to swell and fall off her skin.

She walked on the street until a night when she saw the shades lit gold, watching until she thought he was there without anyone, and she climbed the stairs to listen.

He opened the door after she knocked and said, "Marietta." When she stood in the room, with a tiny kitchen in the corner and magazines strewn everywhere, shoes covering the floor like sleeping dogs, he said, "More questions?"

She shook her head. In his bed, she kept her face to the side; in the light from his window, she could see only his fingers clenching the sheet beside her cheek. He was silent, no talking or whispering. His tongue was warm near her collarbone once, his wrists tight.

At work, she said softly, "You don't say nothing."

"I didn't think you came up there to talk."

She went again, two more times, and when he slept beside her, his breath slowing from what felt like angry to nothing, she dozed, woke, lay afraid to move closer to him and afraid to move away. She had stayed half-awake for so many years, listening to her mother's cries, waiting for her uncle's key scratch, guarding against blades in the door; now she was used to the hazy short rest, and she never let sleep sink deep enough for dream spirits to haunt her.

When the light shifted to three or four in the morning, she slid off the sheet and dressed, and then she waited near the door until she heard Michael's truck or Frank clattering downstairs. She ran around the block and came to the store.

But the last time she went, she slept, hot-sealed sleep near him, and then even in her room sleep began to fall over her at night like a sheet. She dreamed of Aint Sister and Miss Pat, the twin tails of their headwraps facing her when they sat rocking at a fireplace. And sleep fell on her one afternoon at work, like a net thrown onto her head, twirling down from the air. She told Frank, "I sit here for a minute," in the vacant booth. Her head dropped forward onto her arms, and she woke when voices said, "Hey, you all right?" Lijah and Gene leaned down to her and she blinked.

The warm heaviness enveloped her every day, and Frank said, "You ain't getting no rest at night?" He frowned. "Something wrong with your blood?"

"I never need no sleep," she said. "I just catch up now."

She scrubbed the floor, swept the back room, polished the metal trim on the display case. Sinbad was wherever she wasn't; he walked carefully around her. At night, she walked to the riverfront sometimes in the winter cold, touching her fingers to her neck, the knobs of her collarbone, and her throat swelled. The students gathered at Christmas, Stan and Robert still making plans, and she served them with her eyes elsewhere.

Every night now, after work, she walked where she could see the glint and movement of water; the cold air felt good against her cheeks, and she kept her hand closed around her knife, deep in a coat pocket, when she started back to her room. For weeks she walked, and when her stomach, always taut and hard, grew stiffer and rose under her chest, she still didn't believe there was a baby. All the sleeping, the mullet salty in her mouth, three or four laid aside on a paper towel while she was frying them. . .

She bought new pants, and under her apron no one could

see her belly higher. But in February, walking, walking, the first azaleas blooming in a yard, two men rushed at her, pushing her into a brick wall to get past. A police car swerved around the corner after them, and Marietta felt her heart thumping huge in her chest. When taps and an urgent sort of stroking began in her belly, she leaned harder against the wall. The baby was frightened. The bubbly circles she'd felt rising under her skin for days, like crayfish breathing below the water, turned to thumps, The baby was hers, and it knew her already.

Even the loose shirts and her apron grew tight by the next month, and Sinbad didn't look at her at all. They brushed past each other in the doorways, and if he touched her stomach, handing a plate or passing her, even his hand jumped away. Frank made holes in his cheeks, chewing on their insides, but he said nothing to Marietta. The older men in the corner booth creased their disapproval under their hat brims each time they came in.

But the men where she lived scared her the most. Whatever Hurriah had, whether he was her kin or not, the landlord and his friends looked at her now and smiled differently, saw her vulnerable as a turtle, she knew. They laughed: "How the hell *she* get bigged? Who in they natural mind gon touch *that?*" She sat up all night on the mattress, baby feet rippling and rolling like corn in the pot, fingering her knife and knowing how slow she had begun to move.

Frank took Sinbad down the street one day, to pick up more boxes, and she had to hand plates to a table of them: Lijah, Gene, Jameson. The baby turned, turned, rolled and twisted and banged against her skin like a fish trying to escape the bucket that crowded him. She went back for more napkins. They murmured when the doors swung, and she knew to listen hard.

"You know Sinbad done done that. Had to be him."

"The blacker the berry, man. . ."

"Not when the berry *that* big, knock you on yo ass in a minute."

"That ain't no berry. Ain't even no pie. That the whole damn *tree.* Too much for me, man."

The kicks lifted her elbows. She went close to the boxes and whispered, "All right! I ain't try for get shed of you. I tired. Now be good, let me get some rest."

The kicking stopped, to her wonder. Her voice calmed it, and she slid down to the boxes and sat, talking soft. When she heard the bell on the front door, she went back out to the front.

Straight to the table she went, and told them, "Who said anybody done done it?" Sinbad and Frank opened their mouths. She smiled wide, showing them all her teeth. But her lips felt stretched as her belly skin, so she let the smile fall and said, "*I* done done it." She went out the door and started down the street.

Would Frank take her? She wouldn't ask him and have to sit in his car, feel his disappointment fill the windows. She tried not to think of Sinbad, his eyes or hands, the polite half-circle he made of his mouth for her now. I didn't know, he say. He don't know. Don, don, don. Aint Sister and don. She wanted to ask Michael, but she didn't want Miss Pat to know, and he would tell his wife, who tended Miss Pat. She would have to pay a taxi.

He drove in silence over the bridge where she had floated in fear, and the water flashed by in minutes. The trees were thick along the highway; she nodded to the bushes that had hidden the small battoe, and that was what almost made her tell him to turn and go back. But the car sped past the trees and the sandy shoulder, and she saw how she and the others looked from a car, how the basket stands and the women were just blurs to the people driving so fast. The trip was so fast compared to the battoe, the walking, and she strained to recognize the stretch of highway where she never ventured, in the late-afternoon light. She saw the stands ahead, empty for spring, and told him hurriedly, "Stop here. I pay you now."

"Ain't no house here."

"House right there in the wood. No road," she told him, and when he had spun on the shoulder and gone back, she started through the stand. Where was her trail? It would be overgrown now, she thought, because no one had pushed through the forest for almost two years.

She stood in the brush for a moment, the baby turning, turning, and she thought, I have for go this way. Can't walk by Pearl store, can't walk down the road. No. She took the boots from her big bag, slid off her shoes, and pulled the heavy leather over her feet. The slight indentation of the path was still there, and two years wasn't long enough for real trees to have blocked her way. The vines and brush were thick, though, and she kicked her way through in places, boot first, then bag, then belly.

The shadows were long when she came onto the lane and crossed. Her mother's house—her house—stood gray and small, branches and leaves all the way up to the porch and shuttered windows. She pushed open the door and stood aside so any animals could rush out past her, or any spirits. Nothing flew through the doorway, and she looked carefully inside.

The room was exactly as she had seen it last, but for the blanket of dust trembling on the table when she closed the door. The burned-sheet ashes had been swept; the smell hung in the ceiling, where no one could reach it. Dropping the bag on the floor, she went through the doorway to the bare bed and lay on her back. The baby rested too hard on her heart, and she turned onto her side, talking. "This you mama house. Granma house. Great-granma." The feet traced across her skin, nudging her elbow, and she said, "Go on sleep. You walk soon enough."

pine gardens

Her mother, twisting and wet in the bed beside her until the sheet was soft and slick as an old headscarf—her mother, awake, palming the bones at the bottom of her back, saying, "You was behind here so long, kick me all night. . ."

Marietta put her thumbs on the round-shell bones there and arched her back. Her father would have been dead then, her mother alone in this room with the kicks, just like she was now. She sat up on the edge of the low wooden bed frame where she had been born, but the old mattress that she and her mother had stuffed and restuffed with moss was gone. She wasn't sure what to do first. Tired, she thought she could make a pallet and rest, but then it would be dark in a few hours, and the baby wanted fish. The bags of rice tucked into the pot wouldn't be enough for him, flipping and turning like a dolphin.

Him—why did she always think of the baby as a he? He—because he kicked so much. Laha and Rosie had always complained that boys were hard to carry.

The sun was April-pale through the trees. She circled the yard and found a heavy stick, knowing she couldn't go past Aint Sister's or near the dock. She headed down the old lane toward the House, hitting the brush; she thought she could find a way through the branches of the huge fallen oak and then head past the House yard. That old, rotted landing she'd seen when she floated down the waterway was a good place to fish, Big Johnny said, long as you left before dark.

She walked half a mile before the oak-lined road was stopped by the first gate. Pushing it open, she was thinking that she'd have to pull up a crab first to use his meat on her line; aged smelly crab was better. She suddenly remembered the strange white man who'd been leaning on the dock post at the landing when her battoe went past. A bum—or a haint? She pulled out her knife and held it flat against her wrist, whispering to herself, "So sharp don't even keep blood on the blade. So fast you never see it."

What had happened to the fallen oak that barred the road? She was way past it—she saw the second gate, the arched wrought iron greenish, with PINE GARDENS across the top. The wall was crumbled in many places, and she picked her way through an opening.

The House, up this road, was still shuttered. She saw the blank windows covered with weathered boards, faded the same color as her house. My house. Not mama house, not nobody but me. Yeah, and you, she said to the swirl of arm inside her. She looked at the three stories, each with a piazza; many of the spindles were broken or missing, making gap-toothed grins under the closed window-eyes.

A path led past the house and the old summer cookshed. Marietta made her way through the bushes and vines that had been the broad patch of lawn Aint Sister talked about, leading down to the landing. Woods edged the clearing; she said they had protected the House from the storms.

The smell of rotting wood floated to her before she reached the landing. At the bank of the waterway, the boards reached out only a few feet onto the water, and when she saw how splintered and leaning the posts were, she decided to just stand at the edge of the bank and drop her string. We catch a crab, baby. Should go back to the creek, but bad luck for turn round and start over. See? Why I think that? Only been here a minute and think like Aint Sister. Everything bad luck. She took off her headscarf and tied it around the hand that held the line, in case something pulled hard to burn her palm.

Cupped oak leaves on the ground still held moisture from the morning; the day had been cool, and shade always tried to keep water. She breathed in the smell her old days of walking through the woods and knocking against branches on her own trails, hiding on the pine needles. The baby kicked her side, and she said, "I get something for you. Patient, huh? I ain't forget you." She felt prickles on her back, thinking that the baby would follow her everywhere, into the woods, to the creek. She would never be alone again.

When she'd pulled up a crab, she took the meat out and baited her hook. Then she stood to throw the line as far as the weight would carry it, pulling it back toward her slowly. The pluck of the flesh into the water was the only sound, again and again. Nothing for bite. Nothing. She threw it and moved a little farther onto the first board, carefully pushing down with her boot, and after the next drop of the line, she heard someone coming down the path, heard feet crushing the sand.

Don't turn—wait and see do they speak. It just Willie—he like for wander. Spirit don't come in the day, don't make no sound. She stared at the rotted landing wood. He was spirit—cain no man stand on that wood. The feet stopped, shifting and mashing leaves, and she heard, "When we get this place, I'ma buy you a big nigger like that. Just for you, take you fishing and hunting. They know all the best spots."

A white man, his whisper hard and carrying like their words always did, even when they didn't try. She turned very slowly, watching his mouth open as her belly swung around. He wasn't a spirit. He had a little boy beside him, holding a BB gun to his chest. The man wore a plaid jacket and a cap; he stared at her stomach, at the white scarf around her hand, and she saw instantly that it would have been all right if she were a man. He would've said something joking—"Boy, you think the fish better here than down your way?" Like Mr. Tally and Mr. Briggs said to Big Johnny and them when they met.

But her belly, attached to her size—the man was silent for a long minute, and his son said, "Daddy? She got a baby in there?"

"You lost, gal?" he said, not moving.

"No, sir. Just catch some fish for my dinner." She said it carefully, clearly, lowering her head.

"You live round here? I ain't seen you."

"I live down the road, close by."

"Well, you better get home. It's gon be dark soon, and this private property." He cradled the shotgun in his elbow. "This is hunting land, you know, dangerous to be slipping around where people can't see you."

"Yes, sir," she said. "I going, sir."

He turned away and walked up the bank, his son looking back, head swiveling like a bird's. "She got a baby in there, huh?" he said, voice high as a bird's, too. "Like Aunt Doretta?"

Marietta walked quickly back up the path and toward the gate. She had left the crab at the edge of the water. The lane was deep in shadow, and she told the baby, "You gon eat rice. Plenty, don't fuss."

Stopping by the roadside when she had passed the second gate, she picked up small broken pine branches. Private property—was she off it? Her arms full of lightwood when she entered the clearing, she headed for the steps and the woodstove.

A few fat chunks, too—it would be cold tonight. She found the ax under the porch where she'd kept it and dragged one larger branch from the edge of the clearing into the yard. The smooth ax handle felt good in her hands, sliding up and back with each stroke, but her back ached and her head was light from hunger. She took the wood inside and closed the door.

Spooning up hot rice, she thought of the first nights she'd spent in her uncle's room, sitting on the floor and scooping huge mouthfuls of grain. This room was empty of breath, too, but it was still her air, and maybe the breath of the wind that had blown the squares of newspaper off the cracks they were supposed to cover. She didn't feel afraid, not of spirits or the quiet or anyone pounding at her door. She was only afraid that Aint Sister would come and find her. That was why she'd waited for night to start the fire, to hide the smoke from day.

The white man said the land around the House was private property; was it his, or was he just working on it? She listened for a car to maybe pass down the lane; maybe he'd moved the fallen oak. He must know Pearl and them, say he ain't seen me.

After she had arranged all her clothes in a pile on the floor near the stove, she listened again, but no car came. Where did he live? The House was still abandoned. Marietta felt the cool night creep up through the wooden boards; she put more wood in the stove, seeing with her eyes closed herself as a girl, huddling curled like a dog on this floor, telling her mother, "I don't want sleep with you. Stove warm, and don't push me. Leave me lone."

She was huge and forward-jutting as the lady she'd seen once on an old ship in the Charleston harbor, a lady painted and gowned, her golden hair cascading down to her outthrust bosom. Marietta stood by the pump, looking at the completely overgrown path to the creek, and knew she couldn't put her belly forward and cut through the brush and vines. Carrying the water, she felt her stomach ring in a tight circle. She would have to see Pearl.

On the porch, eating warmed rice, she put her hand on the

baby, who rode high and quiet now. She leaned back and closed her eyes again. What I say to Pearl and them in the store? Don't say nothing—just hand the money. No—tell em, say I been marry and the daddy dead. Say, he die just like my daddy—I don't want hear or say no more. They stop and don't ax. . . A hand traced her belly skin, a slow arc like the baby's fingers or toes did, seeming to test the covering, and then the hand pressed harder. From the outside—"Lord God, Marietta, I feel all-two of em!"

Aint Sister! A haint, long black coat that had floated without noise up to the porch—a spirit staring straight in her face, tiny hands on her baby! Marietta slid herself back against the wall, terrified.

"You great-gran were a twin. Lord God! I smell you, girl, smell ashes smoke and think somebody beena burn this place." Her hands were soft on either side of Marietta's stomach now, pressing, moving. "You ain got but a month. And try fe hide, but I smell you. Why you hole up? Ain you get sense yet?"

Marietta's heart didn't slow; it pushed harder at her chest bone. "I take care for myself," she said.

Aint Sister's voice was low, chiding soft like she was talking to her chickens. "Girl, I think fe you every day. Every day. You my kin, run and never come fe me help you. Look you eyelid, look you fingernail. Never eat good! What you need?"

Marietta closed her eyes again. Aint Sister's knuckles rubbed lightly across the top of her head, where her hair felt thicker than ever.

"Two?" Marietta said.

"Praise God, two of em. How you don know?"

"Just feel kick, kick everywhere. I think it hand and foot."

"What you need?"

Marietta looked at the smooth skin of Aint Sister's cheeks, the fan of tiny lines from each eye, the lips thin as dimes now, waiting. "They want fish," she said. "All the time."

She brought the mullet, as Marietta had asked her to, and wouldn't let anyone come to the house, as she'd begged her to. "You ain keep people away long," Aint Sister said, turning the fish in the pan.

"I don't want nobody see me big. See the baby later all right."

"See all-two baby." Aint Sister stirred grits. Marietta waited. "Where the daddy?"

"Die."

Aint Sister's lips disappeared and then came apart with a ffftt. "What you fe do all day till you time? How you plan fe eat?"

Marietta thought hard—she knew she had to give in on something; she couldn't ask Aint Sister to keep everyone away and not stay herself. "I make basket if you help," she said.

The circle expanding slowly in her hands, she listened. Aint's voice wasn't a growling hum now, on the porch or by the fireplace. She heard the stories rise and fall, heard people's words the way they said them, and though she kept her eyes on the basket's coils and not her aunt's face, she saw the Africa woman. "You great-great gran, from the boat," Aint Sister started. "She give you twin in you blood."

"The boat?"

"Yeah, twin—I know you have twin you ever find husband."

"Who come from boat?"

"Africa woman—from Guinea. Maussa get she from boat, just before wartime come. Guinea—that a people with straight nose, thin lip. He take she here, keep in he house. He wife dead out, child dead out. They get fever. He keep she close and she try fe run so many time till he put she in little box. He have a little box by the House, fe hold rice and corn on top, hold person below. Maussa make old woman sit outside box and talk to Africa woman, say, say, 'Maussa never hurt you, only want you work. He give food and house you work.' Africa woman stay in box."

"She my great-great gran? She you granma?" Marietta asked. "She live in box?"

"No, she come out. And he take she here, fe stay in my house. Build just for she."

"When my house build?"

"*You* house?" Aint Sister raised her brows. "Huh. You *mama* house. Build after, cause Africa woman have twin. Maussa give she twin girl. My mama and she sister. One come before midnight—name September. My mama. Other come ten minutes later—next day. Name October. You mama granma."

"What the Africa woman name?"

Aint Sister was quiet, her fingers flying to stitch pine needles into the design. "Name Bina. She Guinea people. Sit like this and tell me one time she name, how she come. Only one time. But Maussa call she Mary. Mary, from Bible. I call she Gran."

Marietta pushed the needle through, too. "What you real name, Aint?"

Aint Sister curved her lips, a smile small as a fingernail. "Eva. Call me Eva then."

"Why you Sister?"

"Cause I everybody sister. Nobody mama." She wheeled the basket around and tilted her head at it. "And learn how fe bring baby cause I never scare, never forget. My gran teach me. And I bring all baby, so they belong fe me. Now I gon bring twin."

"Good. You bring em and I come see when you done," Marietta said, smiling but keeping her head down, waiting to see if she was allowed to talk back—if she was grown enough to joke now. Aint Sister said nothing for several minutes, and Marietta closed her mouth.

"Laugh *now*, heh," she finally said to Marietta. "Promisin talk don cook rice."

They had gathered the hanging moss and cured it with hot water. When the spongy curls had dried in the sun, she and Aint Sister pushed them into the heavy mattress cover Aint had kept at her house all this time. "Fill too full, cause you heavy now," Aint Sister said. "I beena think you dead out, gone under water like Fix and you daddy. Then week pass, and I feel you not dead. I know you fe come back sometime." Marietta didn't want to tell her about Uncle Hurriah, didn't want to be scolded for seeking out the wild man. She didn't want anyone to know where she'd gone, so she said nothing.

She thought of the creek she hadn't seen since she came back. When she filled the bucket from the pump, she splashed water on her face and arms, wondering if her net was still hidden in the box. But she was too big to walk far now, and still the babies turned and turned. She lay on the soft mattress, her head supported by pillows Aint had filled, and they asked for fish. Every day. She crunched the hot mullet between her teeth, thinking of Frank. Sinbad had never liked the mullet—he would eat shrimp sometimes, but he always went out and got a hamburger to eat with his plate of rice and peas and corn.

"This my fish," Sinbad would say, laughing at the people who shook their heads. "Round, brown, of uncertain origin, and caught swimming through the ghetto streets—the patty fish."

He would come into her head now, his face and the thin gap between his teeth, his voice always laughing. She didn't ask him, didn't stop him. When she saw his gold cheeks, the paleness of his chest in the light from the window as he rose over her, she wondered what the babies would look like. What color—her blue blood and his gold?

The next day they fought her, bubbling angry and sliding, the round humps that had to be their behinds pushing out on either side. Thrashing all day, they made her tired, and when Aint Sister brought a large trout, Marietta leaned against the table over the dishpan to fillet the fish. The knife fell onto the meat of her palm. Blood grew straight as a toothpick, and when she sucked at it, stopped, sucked again, she suddenly craved the metallic saltiness, the satisfying weight of the blood in her throat. Turning away from the opaque flesh of the trout, she kept her mouth to the cut for a long time, sitting on the porch, sleepy and then full. The babies were quiet. They seemed to want the blood, to be lulled by it.

They clamored to come a week later, the night she sliced open her thumb on purpose with the sharpened fish knife, closing her eyes to feel the blood slide down her throat and into them.

"You best stop fool round and push!"

"I ain't wide enough!" She hated Rosie's eyes there, and Laha's, and those of Laha's mother Miss Belle, who never left her house. But Aint Sister said they couldn't be alone. Women needed to help, to wait and clean, and pray, especially with twins. They sat in the kitchen, but they looked through the doorway at her. She felt the pain lift her from the bed.

"Nobody sixteen and ain marry gon be wide enough," Aint Sister hissed. "But them two gon come out you like it or no. Push."

She held her breath and pushed, felt her eyes go even darker behind her lids, red blooms on black, and then Sister yelled, "Wait now!" Her hips bucked and Laha rushed in to hold her down. "Push now!" Her lungs met her hip bones, and she pushed.

The boys were big as ten-pound sugar sacks in Aint Sister's bony arms. They were reddish with blood, but even after she lifted them easily, washed each off, then brought them back to Marietta, their skins were so thin she thought she could see the blood right there underneath their chests.

Rosie spoke to her now, for the first time. "Two boy. Big and fine, all-two. You a mama now."

Laha stood near and said, smiling, "You done done it."

They brought the babies to her and laid each at a breast. For a month, she lay there and water, cloths, food, mouths came to her. The boys' skin grew thicker so that she wasn't afraid of touching them, and there they looked exactly like her: dark-dark, their legs soft and knees wide as clamshells. Their eyes were a blurred purple, their hands darting shaky as a drunk man's. But their eyebrows were Sinbad-thick already, straight and wide as windowsills over their eyes, and when they cried, she looked into their mouths and saw thin strings cut down the middle of their gums, where the two front teeth would have a gap.

"That one, come first, name Nathaniel. This one name Calvin," she said, and Aint Sister only nodded.

She was almost slim again when Aint Sister allowed her out of the yard after her month's confinement was over, and when the babies slept, she took the wooden box and walked down the lane. Past Aint Sister's house, with the broom leaning in front and chickens talking distractedly. Past Pinkie's white-board house, the patches of new tarpaper on her roof black as oil on the sand.

The crossroads next, and the huge oak near Rosie and Big Johnny's house overlooking a swept-hard yard, as always. Cigarette butts surrounded the big Angel Oak, where everyone sat in the evening to hear Big Johnny and Joe Pop tell stories. Marietta wondered if she would ever want to sit there with the others, listening to the voices in the dusk when they laughed and shouted and whispered about Buh Rabbit and Buh Buzzard, about Mr. Tally and Mrs. Briggs, about the spirits and haints roaming in the woods.

She kept on, all the way to the church and the cemetery far behind it, where the trees stood guard over the graves and gave the spirits a place to live. Pine needles and oak leaves covered the long, raised gravesites and floated down to join the plastic flowers standing on wire supports. Clocks were set at the time people had died—round-faced clocks set at four-seventeen and four-eighteen on two graves. Big Johnny's cousins, David and Julius, had been killed when their truck overturned on the highway. Eleven-forty—that was what the police had said the time was when Pinkie's Crystal was shot during a robbery in New York.

Marietta knelt beside her mother's grave. She knew Aint Sister had put the Mason jar and the dish, with a hole in the center, at the foot. She opened the box and took out a small shiny-red alarm clock she'd bought once at the corner store in Charleston. She set the time for eight, when the sun would have started down. Beside the clock, she laid on the dirt a tiny blue bottle she'd found at Frank's, and a silver spoon for her mother's grits. Then she walked back home to feed the babies.

They lay in the shaded sand, on a sheet, and the hum rose around her; dust fell like sparkles on their cheeks where they slept with lips crushed to the ground. She went behind the stand to nurse them, in case a car stopped, and then they lay in long cradle-baskets Aint Sister had made for them. If Mr. Tally or Mr. Briggs was getting people in the morning, she woke in the dark and fed them, tied Calvin in a sling on her back and carried Nate, who fussed. Sitting in the stand might mean fifteen dollars, but not very often, and she made three dollars for sure in the fields, hoeing beans and corn, tying tomato plants to stakes, then picking the ripe fruit. Her breasts wet the front of her dress and milk dripped onto her boots with each step when the babies woke on their sheet and cried. Pinkie or Mary kept up her row, and she sat on the ground to nurse them, looking at the tall stalks of corn or the dry-curled tomato leaves above her. She imagined snakes near the blanket, spiders in their ears, and ran back constantly to see, but the boys lay sleeping or waving their hands or squinting at the rustle of plants. They cried when the sun shifted onto their faces.

But when they began to wiggle and turn, when they could crawl? She didn't want to think that far ahead, carrying them in her lap in the far corner of the bouncing truck while Laha came from Mrs. Briggs's house, where she cleaned and cooked, and swung up into the truckbed.

Suddenly they wanted to nurse every two hours, greedy and pulling hard, and that week Mr. Briggs came every day to the store. She cut the hoe in around the rows without thinking, listening for their cries, and she felt heat ringing her eyes. When she walked back, Aint Sister called to her from the porch. "How them two?"

"They fine," Marietta answered, still walking, thinking of the diapers she had to boil. But when they fell asleep, she lay on the floor to stay cool, feeling the heat settle into her cheekbones. Blood pushed against her ears; she listened to them breathe. The air caught harshly in their throats when they began to wake, their hunger and excitement building, she could hear, as their eyes opened. That was how they spent their time awake now—thrashing arms and legs, rapid breathing, sucking on her knuckles or a rag to get rid of their energy.

They grew impatient and began to get louder, Nate growling first, then the howling going up in levels like the engines of passing cars, speeding fast and faster. But she couldn't move. Her legs throbbed with tiredness, her arms felt weak, as if they were asleep, and she told herself to get up—milk trickled down into her armpits, her breasts pulsing by themselves to let it go. Scared by her body—she couldn't move, and the babies' howling wasn't like dogs, steady ribbons, but it rose higher out the window, faster in their vibrating throats, pinning her down even harder to the floor, where milk found cracks and ran. All that noise catch in moss and leaf, she thought, and nobody ever hear. I cain move. We die—I cain do it.

She didn't know the door had opened, didn't even hear it through the piercing spirals of crying, but a hand came past her eyes, cutting through the square of muddy light from the window. Aint Sister shoved her hands under Calvin's back and then Nate's, flipping them over like pancakes to let each know that someone was there before she picked them up.

"You got fever in you breast," she said, feeling Marietta's forehead and hard-swelled chest. "Milk fever. Stop all that cry and moan—you ain kill em. You ain bad mama. You sick. Feed em. No, fever ain in the milk—in you. Let it out."

By the time she and the others were cutting the dry cornstalks down in the fields and turning over the earth, they needed her milk only in the morning and when she came back at night, because they stayed with Aint Sister, who gave them warm grits during the day. Her breasts still tried to feed them more. She kept pushing cloth into her shirt, standing in the corner of the truck-bed on the way home. Laha put her arm over Marietta's shoulder, and Marietta bit her lip at the aching points inside her shirt.

Nate would be screaming, outraged, when she neared Aint Sister's porch, but Calvin was always silent, in shock, it seemed, that she had gone away that morning. They attached their lips to her so hard she almost cried. Nate looked off to the room while he nursed; Calvin stared at her, and she worried that she had hurt him forever that day she let them scream. But he stayed quiet, and Nate stayed loud, and she saw that they were becoming themselves. Nate was all mouth, Calvin all eyes. And both hungry all the time. When the sky stayed silver in late fall, there was nothing to do in the fields and no tourists passing on the highway. The wind blew through the stands. Marietta sat with Aint Sister in front of the fireplace, watching the boys pull themselves along the floor.

"This October—last time Mr. Tally have snap bean," Aint Sister said. "Mary tell me. I know you don have money. What you fe do winter?"

Marietta looked at Aint Sister's neck, shadowy-thin under her chin in the darkened room. But she could see that Aint was testing her with the tilt of her head and mouth.

"They big and hungry as you was," Aint Sister said into the fire. "Look fe they get into thing so soon. What you think you feed me?"

"Go in the creek with Johnny and them, get oshter. I got net, too." She caught Nate by the armpits and turned him back on his belly.

"Them two need more than oshter. You owe Pearl for them diaper, too."

"She know I pay her back." Marietta waited. "What *you* think, Aint, what you axing me?"

"I give you few chicken, you get egg fe them two. And you need fe plant garden, in spring."

"Work in somebody else field, I ain't feel like work my own. Greens come up every year." Marietta caught Nate again, but Calvin bumped his head on the chair leg. She picked him up, wrapped her fingers around his head. "I rather fish stead a clear field."

When it rained and cold blew against the newspaper, rippling and cracking through the night, she stayed inside all day, and when the sky was clear and cold, she left the boys with Aint Sister and went to the creek, carrying buckets. Big Johnny, Little Johnny, Laha's Jerry and Willie, they skimmed past in their boats; sometimes she found them tonging oysters near the waterway. White people came in the afternoon to buy oysters from Pearl, sometimes all the way from McClellanville.

She pried the rough shells loose from rocks and roots near the channel after the tide had gone out, walking up and down the creeks throwing the net. She threw over and over, learned how to tuck it against her shoulder, take a piece in her mouth, and fling it with the same sweep Aint Sister used to scatter corn to the chickens.

There were rarely enough fish or oysters to sell, though. She got a piece of bacon, an onion cut in tiny pieces to simmer with oysters and make stew. Grits. Eggs from the chickens, who lived in the old shed Laha's Jerry came to straighten and hammer tight. He said, "Egg good for them two. And keep you from wander so much."

"I throw the net now," she said, smiling at him just like she had shown her teeth to Sinbad's friends.

"I know you do," he said, throwing back his head a little and laughing with her.

But they still wanted milk, after the soupy grits or soft-cooked egg. Nate clawed to be fed first, anxious and impatient, then pushing to get down and roll over and over on the floor. So when Calvin was in her arms, she held him longer, his hands kneading at her breast, touching her face, staring at her lips and eyes.

She sat in front of the fire for hours, sometimes hearing shots ring through the woods. Rosie said that the white man and his friends were hunting ducks, driving up from Charleston. "That man ain from here," Marietta said, buying sugar. "He voice different."

"He from Birmingham," Pearl said. "Got house in Birmingham, one in Charleston. Got three car." The shooting echoed in the silent trees, and the birds flapped like newspaper in the wind.

What had they done in winter before, she and her mother? She rocked in the heat of the fire, trying to remember, putting on more wood. The boys slept, woke, stared at her. When Aint Sister came that afternoon, Marietta got up as if in a dream, leaving the boys asleep on the bed, and went outside to chop more wood. The ax slid back and forth, and she remembered: Her mother and Aint Sister sewing and shivering, four layers of skirt above their feet, which stayed on the hearth. And Marietta had gone to school in the back of Big Johnny's truck, crowded coat to coat with Laha's kids and Little Johnny and the rest, their breaths floating below her nose. If the truck broke down, they stayed home, sitting by the fire. She remembered the woodstove at school, burning some legs and far from hers, and the dark blackboard like a huge window into the night. The teachers, different faces that made them read from books, correcting each word. Marietta reading silently in the back, all day, trying not to lift her head.

She built the fire outside in the shelter of a tree at the edge of the yard and dragged the old iron washpot Aint Sister had lent her when the boys were born. "Watch you put enough water in," Aint Sister called from the porch now, her sweater wrapped to her neck. "Don be lazy."

Marietta dumped bucket after bucket into the pot and fed the fire. She took the soaking diapers from the washtub on the porch and added the soap and bleach to the iron pot; when the water boiled, she stirred with a stick, poling down the cloth that bubbled to the surface.

After they hung on the line strung across the porch, she went back inside, where the boys banged spoons and pushed empty cornmeal bags across the floor. "Where they come from, them bag?" Marietta asked, frowning.

Aint Sister whirled around from where she bent at the fireplace. "I see you," she said suddenly. "Think this hard time. Think you so hungry, sadmouth too much. I make something fe you now. Sit."

"I beena sit, sit too much," Marietta said angrily, leaning against the table. "I can hear stand up."

The boys looked up at their voices, and their chins gleamed with spit when their mouths hung open.

"Way back, gone time hard fe die. Hoover time." Aint Sister shifted the ashes at the edge of the hearthstone. "No work, no food. Coffee? Take corn and burn in fire, cut off the burn and boil. Make black water you fe drink, keep you warm. Take grits and burn em in pan, add water and grits tea come. Brown water." The ashes breathed in heaps.

"Nothing fe eat. Nothing. Slavery time, make hoecake, my mama say. Put the corn and water cook on you hoe in the field. Hoover time make ash cake. Here." She thrust out a tin plate with grayish mounds inside. "Knock off ash and open. Then you taste hard time. And fill you stomach with hard time."

The cake was gritty and hot. The boys crawled toward her, eyes on the food because they always wanted what she ate now, and she broke off pieces of the mealy lump. "Here," she said, and Nate's lips closed around the bite. "And here," she said, pushing some into Calvin's, the bottom two teeth white in the darkness of his open mouth. "Aintie teach you bout hard time. I already learn."

"Heh! We eat with stick! Eat flour bake in some pan with nothing fe mix. Flat flour. So many hungry no possum left in the wood, no meat. Fish, only fish till I never want fe see a tail. You mama, too, hate fish after she grown."

"She hate fish cause my daddy love fish more than she, love water more than she," Marietta said, the boys pinching her legs. "Cause he die for fish."

"She hate fish long before she see Freeman," Aint Sister said, shaking her head. "But you keep hold fe you story. You keep hold. Go on."

Marietta went to the shelf for the bag of rice. The only sound was the popping fire and the boys' babbling—ya-ya-ya and ba-ba-ba. Aint Sister got up and paused beside them. Marietta knew she was touching their heads. "Look all that hair," she whispered to them, and Marietta spoke louder so she wouldn't have to turn around.

"Look, nappy till it burn you hand you try and comb it," she said, hard. "Nappy as they mama hair. Blueblack till they look African."

"Marietta, you don. . ."

"They not you family. You family dead out now, remember? This Freeman Cook family, he blood take over. Don't look like you, don't think like you. Blueblood. My family."

She stared at Aint's knobbed knuckles around the walking stick. "It dark outside. Best fe take you light," she said, and the old woman's lips were a thin line, straight as the scar on Marietta's palm, where she'd fed the boys her blood. She went and pulled them in to her with sweeping arms, held one on each hip, told Aint Sister, "Watch fe spirit on the road." She went into the bedroom and stood there in the dark until the steps creaked slightly and the swaying light was gone.

Wild azaleas came in March. Before any light worked its way through the pines and oaks, she heard the morning. Small stirrings, far away, maybe the chickens or a man calling someone far down the lane; maybe one of the boys hunching up in the bed beside her, trying to get away from the wetness at his belly. Sliding out of the damp sheet without waking them, she went outside in the darkness to feed a few grits to the chickens and carry their water. Then she opened their door, so they would be able to find what they could in the yard. She started the fire for the wash. All before light so she wouldn't have the boys underfoot and stumbling against her legs, trying to catch her ankles when her feet swung past. They hated her to stride back and forth out of their sight, even for a moment. Sometimes she stopped and said to them, "When I ever go and left you? When I ain't come back?" Their tongues trembled in their mouths they wailed so hard, angry pink tongues curled and shaking.

They heard her when she put wood in the stove, and then they growled. She tried to remember Rosie's baby Johnny—as he had stirred from his naps, when she was a girl in the stands, had he cooed and smiled, happy to be awake? Nate and Calvin called "rawwrr!" in their impatience to get up.

The grits began to bubble and the fire's glow faded in the

woodstove when the sun made the room light. She put chunks of yellow and white egg in front of the boys, on the oilcloth sheet where they sat, spooned cooled grits into their mouths, then moved them and the oilcloth outside to the swept-bare yard. While she started the diapers and the bedsheet, they were happy, not even looking at her but crawling to the base of the porch and standing to hold on to the board edges. Circling back and forth, moving the pecans and peach pits she kept there for toys, they put them carefully onto the ground, back onto the wood, dropped them into the empty soap boxes and back out. But let her take the ax, the bucket and pick, let her walk to the garden patch behind the house, and without even looking up—she watched them to see—they howled, pawing the earth like bulls, and set off after her.

They had to come. When she set them at the edge of the acre plot, overgrown for years, they crawled right off the oilcloth and into the leaves. Marietta bit her lips and chopped at the slim trees and brush. She carried the wood back to the yard when they fell asleep, and when they woke, resumed chopping and pushing. At the end of each day, their hands were numb with cold dirt and their pants held bowls of dried mud at the knees. They followed her into the field now, dragging right through to plow up the mud in ragged furrows. "You two mules now, huh? Think you help me? I can't throw no seed in there. But I have for wash you pants every day!" She scrubbed and rinsed in the dark, hung the clothes near the fireplace each night to dry for the next morning.

Turning the soil over with the pick, sliding the hoe edge

under the ground and scooping, then breaking the clods, she planned a small plot for peas, one for greens and tomatoes. She could can at the end of summer, like her mother used to. But she'd have to buy new Mason jars, because only one was left on the shelf, and she owed Pearl so much already. When she went to the store, she didn't linger to talk to Rosie or Pinkie. She let them exclaim over the boys while she bought the few things she could add to her credit. Then she wrapped Calvin in the long strip she'd sewed from a torn dress, tied him to her hip, and picked up Nate, who liked to try and hold the small package.

When the weather changed up, though, before she had put the seeds into the ground, the rain came in through the roof in two places, swirled around the wood blocks holding up the porch, came down the chimney and made the fire smoke. And it got into their lungs, so that one night they had fever. They didn't cry or babble, just whimpered, and she held one in her lap, the other in her arms, feeling the heat right through her clothes. They were like hot sweet potatoes against her fingers, their eyes swollen with pain, and she had nothing to give them. All night she rocked them in the chair, the fire low and gold, and she put water on their faces and necks.

They were still and heavy in the cloth wraps when she walked to Pearl's early in the morning. "I need lison molasses," she told Pearl, and Pearl said, "I can see that fever. But I ain got no lemon. You need fe boil it with lemon juice. You go fe see Aint Sister."

She whispered, "Don, don, don," against Calvin's cheek all the way there, her lips hot against his skin. "Heart don mean everything mouth say. Don hold you mad, let it kill any glad. Don get straight wood from crooked timber." She whispered up the lane: I crooked, I Cook. Hold mad cause it make me strong. Then she stood on the porch and knocked.

"Fever get em," she told Aint Sister, looking down at the bent headscarf.

"Go on and I come," Aint Sister said without looking up.

The bed felt hot, too, pulling in their heat and burning, so she lay on her back on the kitchen floor, her head on a pillow, and held them against her shoulders. Their breaths roared heavy in her ears, and when Aint Sister came in, their cheeks were sealed to her neck with sweat.

"Never see Rosie and nem floor like this no more. Ain like they don know how fe keep it clean." Aint Sister's voice was brisk. "You beena sweep it out with clear sand, like you should." The wide gray floorboards were smooth and slick under Marietta's back.

"You never say something bad bout Rosie to me," Marietta said slowly. "Never talk about nobody, only me. Always tell me what for do, tell me I wrong."

Aint Sister's forehead jumped. "You old enough fe hear talk now. You old enough fe talk about other people. You learn child can angry and pout, but woman say thing, hear thing, go on."

"I don't like she-she talk," Marietta said.

"Ff-ttt. No she-she talk, just people say thing fe pass some time." She stopped. "Listen how they breathe. Have whooping cough you don get up and do what I say."

Marietta laid the boys on the bed. "Watch for they crawl off," she said.

"Tell *me* watch? Go to the water, look fe little crab run in he hole. That one."

"Fiddler crab?"

"That one. Tide coming back in now, so you fe go quick-quick." She turned to the stove and took a root, wrapped in cloth, from her dress.

Marietta ran down her old path to the creek, the bucket banging against trees, and then she hurried along the creek-bank to the marsh. The pluff mud clicked in the sun, glistened with millions of tiny ripples and holes and scurryings. She was alone by the water now, a bucket and stick in hand like always, with the slapping quiet of something gliding into the creek. She hadn't been alone for months, breathing without watching someone, and she'd dreamed of sitting here to listen. Now she couldn't for fear she wouldn't find enough of the crabs; the water trickled into pools at the edge already. My boys, she thought. Sit with pole, throw out net with me. Listen with me. She started over the mud and bog carefully, looking for streaks of silver across the black-velvet mud that would show her the crabs.

The house was close and still. Aint Sister boiled the crabs in the big pot and Marietta heard Calvin draw in air and bark. "They start the cough," Aint Sister said. "But we almost ready."

She added the water from the boiled root and strained the liquid through white cloth into a cup. It smelled foul, but Marietta took it into the bedroom. "Bring some for Nate," she said. "He never wait for nothing."

When they woke in the night, she rocked Nate in the rocker

and Aint Sister rocked Calvin in the straight chair, her tiny back curled over him. They tested the fever with their lips until the hot faded and left cooled, sticky foreheads.

Nate and Calvin were identical twins. They looked exactly the same to everyone else, but she saw in their faces the ways they had inherited from her and Sinbad. They were completely different. Nate had tiny creases no deeper than thumbnail presses against skin beside his mouth from his smiling, boasting in syllables, moving his face. He loved to hear himself, like his father, and he raised his eyebrows in anticipation of anything.

But Calvin walked first, planting each foot as hard as if he could hammer nails into the ground. He ran away from Nate, who screamed and dragged his knees after him. Calvin's lips stayed pressed together in concentration, and he could carry a water-filled tomato can from the bucket to the peach tree. He wouldn't pour the water, but he would look at the tree while Marietta laughed.

They were one year old. At the stands, though, they were "them two." Everyone along the highway, in the store, at the dock where they pointed to the boats, said, "Them two in my way, now," and "Them two stubborn as they mama, heh?"

"What time them two sleep?" Rosie asked from the doorway of the stand. Marietta sat weaving coasters, and Nate and Calvin poured sand through the slats. Marietta shrugged. "Depend."

Rosie raised her hands to the roof to stretch. "Huh. Children need for sleep early. Have for put em in there six, seven o'clock."

and licked out all the pots

Now that they could walk and point and say "dog" and "duck-duck" and "Mama," she let them wander in the yard after dinner. They held peaches with both hands, and the juice ran down their chests, streaking trails of skin through the dust they had collected. Bits of collard green, fallen from their fingers, stuck to their stomachs like stamps. She waited to give them baths until their far-ranging loops turned to smaller and smaller circles, and they practically stumbled over each other. Then, each body dunked in the washtub and gleaming black in the lamplight on the porch, she let the still-hot air dry them, brushing sparkly beads of water from their tight hair. Calvin swayed against her, Nate in her lap, both dressed for bed, and yet she didn't carry them in.

When they finally lay snoring in the bedroom, she sat on the porch waiting for the moon, hearing branches move and maybe thunder over the water. Sometimes she heard nothing, and she thought of the music at Frank's, the constant chatter and singing. The only music here was the clapping and singing at the praise house, where she still wouldn't go. She listened to the faint rustles in the trees, waiting to see the moon red or yellow, full or slivered, chalky white above the dark trees. Just like the old people where she'd hated to follow her mother for visits. She had kicked the porch boards, sullen, while they talked about the size or color of the moon, the smell of rain, the way someone had heard an alligator roar a storm warning in the swamp last night. And now, her feet hot and pounding from the day and work, she sat here, too, watching for a veil on the moon or a ring of haze.

Aint Sister came, late. "Them two gone?" Marietta nodded. Aint Sister sat and lit her pipe. "Smoke keep skita way."

Marietta smiled. "Skita don't want me. I hear you say it when I small-small. 'Skita cluster round white folks, never light on somebody Marietta color.' I ain't get bit one time."

"You beena listen, huh?"

"Always talk about so black. But I see now."

"You beena hear with child ear. Folks talk everything, talk he black, she light, he skinny, she fat. Something fe pass time."

Now I pass time, too, Marietta thought. She breathed the sharp match smoke.

"Rosie hear owl call puntopa tree by she house. I too sorry that sign come."

"Nobody sick."

Aint Sister sucked her pipe. "Don matter." The breeze touched Marietta's neck, and smoke twisted above them. "You got bone fe cook tomorrow?"

"Mmm-hmm, thank you," Marietta said. "Got tomato. You want some?"

"I like only one. Seem my stomach only crave pea and bone from the pot."

They sat for a long time. Marietta heard only the pop of Aint's lips pulling in smoke from the pipestem.

"I eighteen today. Eleven August."

"I know. I know all day people born."

"Eighteen grown. Adult." Marietta watched the pipe glow pulse.

"Grown what? You birthday don mean nothing. Them day you son born what you recall now."

"Law say eighteen grown. Just thinking."

Aint Sister squinted at Marietta. "You been grown two hour

after you born them two. The first time you beena feed em, you grown. Adult mean you feed somebody cept yourself." Marietta thought she was finished, but Aint said, "Ki! White man come pass by Pearl today look fe you."

"Who look?"

"Man buy the land. He come by want people fe work at Pine Garden like old time, grow rice and thing fe tourist come look."

"He know I live here? Know me?" Marietta remembered the surprise at her belly, the little boy and his gun.

Aint Sister shook her head. "Look fe anybody. He come get we all day-clean, talk bout pay and work." She stood up, reached into her apron pocket. "You keep these. Belong fe my mama—you great-gran sister. October. I save them. Now belong to you." She put two gold hoops into Marietta's hand, circles the size of quarters. The two hoops Aint Sister wore had been in her ears so long that her lobes were pulled long and thin. "You have hole and thread when you been small-small, like Nate and Calvin. Thread fe keep hole open. If you poke, find them now." She turned on her flashlight and swept down the lane, singing to keep away the spirits.

Marietta poked the wires of the earrings again and again at her earlobes, and they tickled like Sinbad's lips were there. She stopped, went into the house for a needle, and put a sweet potato behind the lobe. The needle plunged through, numbing the soft skin.

The water sat on the dirt only a moment before it sparkled into the looseness, and Marietta poured one more bucketful around the beans. She knew if the earth glittered, like pluff mud did when a wash of ocean receded, the soil drank in the water straight to the roots of the beans. She ran back to the house to dress the boys. The white man, Mr. Ray, would be at the store soon.

They rode in the back of his truck, as if they were going to the fields, but she and Aint Sister held the boys. Mr. Ray, his hair combed back slick so grooves showed between the strands, hadn't recognized her at all, she could tell. He smiled widely at Nate and Calvin. Down the highway a little more than a mile, he turned into the forest.

"Where he go?" Mary said, and they saw the old moss-greened gate that said PINE GARDENS. Rough earth was piled near it, from the new road that had been cut into the forest, and the pines pressed in tight. The truck turned in to a parking area, where a tractor stood. The road led along the creek to the old rice fields, sunken green and swampy.

Mr. Ray got out and let down the gate, and they stepped into the cleared area—Laha's Jerry, Willie, Big and Little Johnny, Rosie and Pinkie and Mary. Nate and Calvin began to run toward the tractor, and Marietta grabbed their arms. They whined until she picked Nate up and held Calvin's neck in a half-circle of fingers.

"Well, I want to start out saying I hope y'all trust me," Mr. Ray said, facing them. "I know some of y'all were raised on this place and don't want to see it hurt. I plan to restore the whole plantation, having working rice fields and a barnyard, put the house in order and then watch the visitors come. Now I got a historian to make everything perfect—in fact, I got photos, got one of you, Eva, when you was just a lil gal." He smiled at Aint Sister. "But I think you'd get tuckered out too quick in the field nowadays. What I'd like is two able-body men and three of the younger women for the field, to plant, harvest, bag the rice. I'ma sell the rice at the house—call it Old Carolina Gold." He paused. "But the main thing is to let people see how a plantation works. Now I'ma stop right here and see what you all are thinkin."

Big Johnny put out his cigarette on the ground. No one looked at him, because they knew he would talk. "Well, sir, I got people look for my fish every day, so I too sorry say me and my boy can't help out. But what my wife probly like to know is the pay." Rosie ain't get in no field, Marietta thought. Big Johnny ax for we.

"I talked to Mr. Tally, Mr. Briggs, about the going rate and all. I pay fifteen dollars for a six-day week." Marietta knew that what flashed in her mind raced in the others', too—tie tomato four-dollar day, pick bean more. But he spoke again. "I know that's only two-fifty a day, but think six days every week. Winter, too, now, cause people come and hunt. They'll come down from New York and like so."

Laha's Jerry turned to look at the road leading to the rice fields. "You use tractor for rice, sir?"

"Naw, tractor sink in that mud. This one stuck here now. Need men to dig out them irrigation ditches, plow and do what the historian say to grow the crop right. Mr. William Thomas is the historian, drives up from Charleston every morning." He watched Nate slide his way down Marietta's front. "Look at him, rarin to go, huh? Well, like I said, I need two men and three gals. You, you, you," he said, pointing at Mary, Pinkie, and Marietta. "Y'all interested?"

"We like to discuss, sir," Laha's Jerry said.

Mr. Ray smiled again. "I'm a go make a fuss bout this tractor. And my generator giving me trouble, too." He walked up the long path toward the House.

Big Johnny said, "Rosie, you make more fe sell basket?"

"Rosie got you, get fish on slow day," Pinkie said.

"This six day a week, winter, too," Aint Sister said.

"Man smile too much, sweetmouth and crack he teeth," Big Johnny said. "He gon work people hard."

"But somebody go work fe that buckra, yeah, somebody," Aint Sister said harshly. "He ain hear no if people say that word. He custom fe hear yes every time."

"Who go in Mr. Tally and Briggs field?" Mary asked. "They come fe pick we up and get mad."

Laha's Jerry said, "Uh-uh. Laha say Mr. Ray already come fe talk, and Mr. Briggs want fe use them Florida people. They talk bout them people come for season, pick tomato and thing. Keep em in that shack by the field—they stay in a hole, you tell em."

"Winter," Aint Sister said. "Have money every week."

Marietta caught Calvin, but Nate ran to the tractor. Mr. Ray's face made her nervous, but she thought, tie tomato, pick potato, crate em: grits, milk, sugar, laundry soap. T-shirt. Shoe for all-two. She said, "I do it. But how you watch Nate and Calvin?"

"They sits in the stand I tell em. Bring toy. You go do it, heh?"

Mary said, "Laha mama keep my baby like same and I go, too."

"My mother-in-law ain go nowhere," Jerry said, laughing.

"My mama tell me bout rice field," Pinkie said. "Say that some hard work. Hard."

"Cain be no more hard fe winter," Aint Sister said. "Winter don starve now."

They walked up the old lane, and Marietta thought her trees hadn't seen so many people in years. A gaping hole was left by the moved gate. A man in a suit and tie, an older man with his face small under his hat, watched them come up to the House. He carried a notebook and didn't smile like Mr. Ray.

"Good morning," he said, and his voice was Charleston; Marietta remembered that voice from the gated streets. "My name is Mr. Thomas, and I'd like you to pay close attention to what I have to say from now on. This will be a complicated and exacting procedure, but it needn't be impossible if you listen carefully." When he turned for them to follow, Mary looked at Marietta and three lines appeared in her forehead. "You are Jerry, correct?" Mr. Thomas said over his shoulder, and Jerry caught up with him.

He looked at the notebook, got another book from the House, and as they walked around the grounds, he told them they would start on the gardens. "The rice fields cannot be planted until April, and work will begin on them in the winter. But first the azalea garden must be restored for the spring blooming season, when numerous visitors will come. February. And at that time, you'll be finished here and you will move to the fields to prepare them."

The rice fields were near the wide creek. The water was slow and brown here, and when they came around the bend and saw the fields stretched out for acres, squares hazily outlined by heavy brush and trees, Mr. Thomas seemed to watch their faces. "You haven't been here, all of you, correct?"

Jerry shook his head. "No, sir."

Marietta knew everyone was thinking of the haints that roamed the land. A band of forest protected the flatland from the salt and wind of the waterway, Mr. Thomas explained, and these fields were far too extensive for Mr. Ray's needs. "He would like only the first three rice fields cultivated, so that the visitors can look at the system. The rest of the fields are perfect for hunting, with numerous ducks and wild animals for our guests, but this means that during the ricebird season," he looked at his notebook again, "in August and early September, you will all be engaged in shooing away the birds that might ruin the crop."

His voice rolled along smooth as a marble on a floor, Marietta thought, and his words, long and gently peaked in places, wound around them as they walked. She didn't understand some of the words, but it didn't matter. He stayed close to them at each step, pointing and bending slightly, repeating himself and consulting his pages. His gray eyes flickered like dragonflies fighting, and to hear that voice sliding-even as the creek and see the eyes moving hurriedly over them made her dizzy.

"In former times," Mr. Thomas said, "the task system was used on a successful basis. I believe that is what you use for the farmers in this area, correct? You are allotted a specific task to complete, in a specific time? Well, you will not be asked to work as hard as people did under that system. We would rather you worked at a slightly more leisurely pace, because it will be necessary that you arrive at eight and stay until six, when late supper is served. Our guests would like to see you working, even eating and resting, but we ask then that you remain here for lunch."

Marietta and Mary and Pinkie dug holes and planted a hundred azaleas around the edges of the house and paths, and Marietta watched the newly glassed windows, the two white men in work clothes who came and went inside the house, hammering and painting. Mr. Ray shouted about the lack of electrical lines and the cost of the generator. Mr. Thomas hovered over Jerry and Willie, who were building a new landing and preparing lawns for seeding.

When Marietta walked back down the lane each night, she was silent and listening for the boys' cries and shouts when the others paused in their talking. Aint Sister had Marietta's doorway smelling of cowpeas and bone, and Calvin presented her with the peach pit he had carried for days, excavated from the yard and buried again. Nate touched her and ran toward the pump, chattering, "Wawa. Wawa."

On Sundays, she did heavy wash and cut down her own crops, leaving the field to the frost. She went to the store with the bills Mr. Ray put in her palm each Saturday evening, and after she had paid off most of her old credit with Pearl, she bought cans of beans and sardines for her lunch, crackers, and then bags of grits, flour, sugar, rice. Aint Sister said the boys ate all the time, and Marietta watched them with piles of greens, chunks of fish; they put shrimp in their mouths playfully, pretending they would chomp down on their fingers and smiling with lips closed tight around knuckles and food. Their shirts hung high on their bellies, and she bought jackets for winter.

Mr. Thomas asked the women to wear dresses; he even brought two dresses for each woman, long-skirted and full, which he said were "historically proper, yet of more lightweight material than that commonly used during the antebellum years." Marietta told him, "I wear a dress, but I keep my boot. Make me work better—I cain wear no shoe." He frowned, but didn't say anything else.

He was right. When the first group of people arrived at the plantation in March, the azalea banks were pink and red everywhere, and the women visitors wandered about in narrow dresses and matching shoes, talking and taking pictures. "Look at the piazzas!" Marietta heard them say. "And the workers—did you see those hoes? This is so unique." They looked at her boots, then smiled, smiled at her when she and the other workers walked past the house toward the rice fields, hoe handles on their shoulders. Marietta and the others made sure to smile back and nod.

Jerry and Willie had been redigging the ditches for weeks, with Mr. Thomas standing on the banks and talking about the system of trunks. The creek wound far from the waterway by the time it reached the rice fields, but the incoming tide still pushed fresh water in to flood the fields when the trunks were opened; when they were shut, the wooden gates kept the water on the ground. Opened again, they would drain the fields. Mr. Thomas stared out over the fields for hours, but Mr. Ray only came now and then. Mostly he drove around with the men visitors, Marietta saw, showing them the fields on his way somewhere else. Jerry said they went fishing and boating on the waterway. If it was still warm when Marietta and the others stopped for Laha, they saw the visitors sitting on the lower piazza with drinks.

Laha came to take care of the cooking and cleaning now. Mr. Ray had hired her away from Mrs. Briggs; Laha laughed and said he paid her three dollars more a week, but she felt sorry for Mrs. Briggs, and she took her daughter Willamae to Mrs. Briggs's house and taught her how to do most of the work. On the way home, Laha told them about the rooms upstairs, the wooden floors and rugs, the kitchen. She said, "Mr. Ray like me make them old-time dish, she-crab soup and that shrimp all the time. Mrs. Ray always want salad on the table. And drink—them men be drink till sun red fe down."

Mr. Thomas met them one day in the yard and said, "Mr. Ray has purchased a team of oxen, at my suggestion. It will not only be more efficient for the men to plow with them, as the fields are so boggy, but it will be historically accurate. Afterwards, they will be used with a cart we've found to drive guests for short distances around the property." He turned to the women. "Before I leave with the men, I will show you your duties for the next few days. You'll be cleaning out the dependencies."

He led them to the summer kitchen, the smokehouse, and

the granary. After he had gone, they reached up with brooms for the spiderwebs drifting over them in the dark smokehouse. "What Mr. Ray and them fe do with this?" Mary said.

"Just fe look, probly," Pinkie said.

Marietta kept the trash in a neat pile so they could pick it up later. Mr. Thomas had warned them several times about throwing weeds and garbage in the wrong places. They moved on to the granary, which was locked. He had given Pinkie a long metal skeleton key, black with age.

The heavy wood door pulled open, and inside was a tiny stairway hugging one wall and two small boxlike rooms separated by an iron mesh. The one room was behind the mesh; the other was open to the doorway where they stood. Mary said, "What kind food they kept in here? What don't beena fell through that gate?"

Marietta brushed her hand over the mesh, trying to remember where she had heard someone describe this. Keep she in box, somebody sit outside box and talk. Aint Sister had said it, told her about somebody who was in this room. She looked at the rough brick wall and the heavy iron, drawing in her breath. "Africa woman keep here," she whispered, her heart racing. "Keep she in box, make she stay here until she won't run."

"Sister, she granma," Pinkie said. "That right. You great-great gran. Sister tell me once."

Marietta wheeled around and ran outside, breathing hard to clear the too-fine dust of feet tramping on the earthen floor and walking in circles. She didn't see Mr. Ray or Mr. Thomas, no one, and she began to run again around the fading azaleas and down the lane.

and licked out all the pots

The boys carried tomato cans of water from Aint Sister's pump to the porch, where they watched the sheets of water slide off the wood. She felt their arms around her legs, the automatic comforting pats that made her smile; they had begun to copy the way she tapped them without thinking whenever she held them. When Aint Sister came outside, Marietta said, "I come home early, feel fever. I take em home for give you rest."

When she chopped with her hoe at the dirt clods left by the plow, the same way she did at home now in the first light, she imagined the Africa woman, silent as she was, listening to the others' voices as they moved up and down the rows. After the fields were leveled and perfect, Mr. Thomas instructed them to make sure that the trenches were deep enough, fifteen inches apart. He left and returned throughout the days, sometimes standing in the shade of the trees along the road to watch them.

"Please remove your shoes and listen carefully," he told them the next week. "This is traditionally done by women, who have more skill in the manipulation of the feet. I am not certain that this method will be successful, but I would like to try it because it is accurate and guests should always enjoy chancing upon the sight. It is meant to be very graceful."

They took the seed rice and dunked it in a barrel of thick mud. He hovered over them closely, and Marietta could see the tiny red bumps where he had shaved. "Now the rice is to be clayed, so that mud adheres to each grain. Then it will be spread in the sun to dry. This will prevent the rice from floating on the water when we flood the fields, which we will do *if* Jerry and Willie have proceeded correctly."

He stopped, distracted, and Marietta felt the wet earth near the barrel rise between her toes; she didn't understand why their feet had to be bare, and she felt ashamed of her long toes, which he stared at absently for a moment. They stood awkwardly there, with their dresses tied around their hips the way he had showed them, and pushed down at the bulges of cloth near their thighs.

He said in a soft voice, "There is a plantation called Cypress Gardens near Charleston, and several others in this general area. But this attention to historical detail will make your place of employment the most-visited in the state." He looked up abruptly. "Please follow my instructions."

He asked them to remove mud and rice from the barrel and tread on it with their feet, to dance carefully by pushing the wet rice and rolling it under their soles. They scraped their feet at first, and Marietta felt water behind her eyes for some reason; she could barely breathe when Pinkie's feet trod the mud delicately, and she kept her eyes down and open for a long time to lessen the pressure of the tears. Her feet blurred into four, moving below her.

"Take your time," Mr. Thomas said. "We will master this process gradually, as the guests should be able to observe you frequently. Tomorrow we will clay more rice in this manner, and I will schedule the guests' visit accordingly. When we're finally finished claying the seed rice, we shall plant it."

In the evening, she could watch the spring sky through the trees just after she came home. It lightened to white against the oaks, turning their edges to black lace like the gates she remembered, and she let the boys fall asleep on a blanket beside her, watching them root face first for a while and then grow still, their behinds high in the air.

If it was cold, they stayed inside. Calvin was fascinated with her fingernails, her earrings, and especially her boots. He picked mud from the leather. He tried to walk in them. He clicked his fingernails against hers, holding her hands firmly. He touched her teeth. Nate snapped splinters from the lightwood and tried to push them into the boot toes. He wouldn't sit in her lap, but Calvin would fall asleep pressed to her stomach in the rocker, his mouth blooming a wet flower on her shirt, his chest tight against her ribs. She could drowse, too, and then wake, feeling ashamed that she didn't want to put him down and wash the dishes. It seemed that she needed the touching more than they did; she rubbed her fingers across the backs of their necks without thinking until they ducked away in irritation.

When Aint Sister came to find her cuddling one that way, she would say, frowning, "You one a them kind—I never think *you* be a touchy mama. Way you so wild, I think you be push-away mama."

Marietta's face grew warm. "I like for hold em. My mama never hold me," she said without thinking, and she remembered when she was very small, trying to climb into her mother's lap and the heel of a hand blocking her way. "You too big—go on, I need fe rest," her mother would say. Then when she was older, leaving the heated skin of her mother for the cool wood floor.

Aint Sister said, "So? Some mama never do. Seem like it go

skip a family—the one what never beena hold when they baby want fe hold they own baby too much. Baby gon push away cause he cain breathe from he mama dress front," she frowned at the sleeping Calvin.

"He like it, he climb up here. Nate not so much."

"Be careful," Aint Sister said. "You spoil em, make em baby too long. They be two-year-old soon."

"Mama never touch my hair, nothing," Marietta whispered.

"You mama never meant fe have baby. She too sickly, too old. But she love you. She feed you. And you in the tree? She always hear talk from Rosie and them bout that, but all she say, 'Marietta like tree.'"

Every night she scolded Marietta for not teaching the boys to fall asleep in the bed, on their own, but Marietta needed to feel them pushing against her legs and tugging on the dirty dress. Then she sat on the porch like old people, watching the black.

Dropping the clay rice into a small hollow made with her bare heel, she dragged her toes across the soil to cover it the way he told them to. "I can't believe how rhythmic it is," one of the women visitors said from the road. Marietta followed Mary's white-flashing heel and Pinkie's bobbing head, not looking back at the small group, thinking about the peach-tree blossoms, the slurping creekwater, sliding pine needles. Stan's eyes peering up at her, questioning. Sinbad's hand at her neck, his fingers pushing through her hair. She jabbed her heel down and pressed the dirt over the rice as if in a dream, giving in to the whole night then, the lips under her ear and hands on her back, fingers deep in her muscles. They were all silent, Pinkie and Mary, too, and she thought they all dreamed of something as they floated and rocked across the long field.

Then she rocked Calvin in the dark when he woke from bad dreams; swaying in the chair on the porch, night and the woods quiet except for a falling branch or rustle of leaves, she stared out at the moonlit clearing. His short arms were thrown straight across her shoulders and his breath came fast and disturbed if she tried to stand. She liked it, almost, being so tired and dazed each morning, standing behind Mr. Thomas when the tide flood rose in the creek and water seeped over the trenches and her footprints. Her boots were heavy, rubbed comforting at her ankles when she and the others went back to the yard.

They sat in the shade and wove baskets during off times, though Mr. Thomas said he had already collected antique fanner baskets to be used much later when the rice was harvested. Marietta and the others piled their baskets at home, waiting for summer when Aint Sister would try to sell them. The tourists stopped to watch a few times, but there weren't so many people for Mr. Ray. Mr. Thomas wanted to stay in the rice fields each day, but now he went into the house all the time, and Mr. Ray was beside him, talking loudly.

"Drag hunting, fella told me about how they do it in Aiken," Marietta heard him say when they passed. "It's real English, people would love it. Hounds follow this fox-scented bag. We'd have to cut better trails through the woods and get some horses, but think of the money it could rake in!"

In the afternoon's hot quiet, Marietta's head nodded over her basket. "You sleep, heh?" Pinkie said.

"Calvin keep me up at night."

"He get new tooth?" Mary asked.

"Wake up cry from dream." She turned the basket around.

"Spirit hag he, heh?" Pinkie said. "Put broom cross you door, salt by where he sleep."

"Nate don't wake too, don't feel hag ride he?" Mary said.

"Nate sleep past thunder, wind, cry," Marietta said. "But Calvin sleep light like me."

He woke again and again, threading his cry into the night, and she had to pull him close in the bed; if she let him fall from her chest back to the sheet, he woke again. She finally listened to Aint Sister and Pinkie and sprinkled salt on the sheet, pepper at the bedroom doorway. She laid the broom at the front door. And he did sleep through the night, but probably because she lay awake now, making sure her arm pressed his, seeing her own spirits.

She could smell the dust of the granary when they sat and made baskets. The dust kept rising, forming shapes, when she had to pass that doorway, and the mud of the rice fields stamped into faces below her boots and her hoe blade. She asked Aint Sister about the Africa woman, if her spirit walked, if she was the hag who rode Calvin, but Aint Sister just shook her head now. "Only man spirit here," she said.

Marietta wondered how she had seen the man on the landing, smoking a cigar. Aint Sister had been born with a caul, she could see haints and spirit wanderers, but Marietta was afraid to ask her any more. She wanted to go into the House and look for the photo of Aint Sister; she was sure that her grandmother Christmas, maybe her mother October, and even the Africa woman were there, too.

But Laha left them each day in the yard, when she walked to the back entrance of the House. The kitchen was hers; no one else ever went inside. The wide piazzas had doors, and Marietta didn't know where she could approach the House safely. It was May now, the rice was shooting up, and they would have to hoe the baby weeds that had sprouted along with the rice before the second flooding of the fields.

She had seen only two guests this week, two men, and Mr. Ray was smiling too much again, saying to Mr. Thomas when they walked the grounds, "We better pack em in this summer, damnit. The advertising better pay off. My wife and boy are coming next month, and I damn sure don't want to be alone in the house with them and no paying guests. I got a lot of money in this, Thomas."

He and Mr. Thomas left in his car, and Marietta stood up quickly. "I'ma go round back and ax Laha for drink," she said, and Mary looked up.

"We suppose for bring drink, you know that," she said.

"Mr. Thomas say nobody in kitchen not train," Pinkie said. "Only Laha train."

"I know," Marietta said, and she hurried around the back, where the lawn led into paths and benches set where people could see faraway dips of blue water between the trees.

She slowed when she came to the back door, open and drifting smells of dinner. Was that Laha talking to herself, or was she talking to someone else? Mr. Ray say he wife and boy come next month. Marietta pressed against the wall. Laha began to sing softly. Laha sing, she lonesome. She only hear she voice.

Marietta slipped past the kitchen. The hallway was wood, with a long narrow rug down the center. She had no idea whether the photos would be on the second floor, but then she stopped, pressed herself against the wall and thought. When guest come, they want see some history first. They like for see photo soon. She tried to walk toward the front of the house without creaking the floor.

The living room—a chandelier with dangling pear-shaped drops, thick dark drapes framing the glass. She could see the small shapes of Pinkie and Mary down the sloping lawn. Laha always told everyone that she cleaned the house in the morning, just after breakfast, when the guests were usually out. But once she started dinner, the biggest meal, she never came out of the kitchen because she had so many pots going. Marietta breathed in the thick, slightly dusty drapes, but she didn't see the Africa woman rise before the wall. She stay in field, Aint Sister say. In field or in she house. Why she haint round here now? Why she come see me? Marietta went out of the living room and toward the front door. They want see history first.

She smelled pipe smoke in the next doorway, and there it was—the small room lined with pictures and a few wooden tables with open books. She stared back at the faces.

Most of them were ghostly white, women with furry-looking eyebrows and collars high to their chins. Their hair puffed mushroomlike from their heads, and the men's mustaches frowned at her, hiding their lips altogether. She circled the room too fast, looking out the window for Mr. Ray's car, listening for footsteps. Dark faces, dark hands—she whirled around and saw them on the far wall.

Framed in gold, the pictures were in a group, and a hand-lettered card below them said, "The Rice Harvest—1854 to 1894." Marietta leaned closer to see the faces in the largest photo. Ten or fifteen women, she couldn't stop to count, stood on a flat boat among piles and piles of rice sheaves. Even in the dark photo, the rice looked golden. The faces were stern, unsmiling, above folded arms.

Where Aint Sister? She scanned the line of faces, looking for a small girl, and found her thin cheeks nearly hidden in the rice. Two pale women, with tiny straight noses and hair braided close to their heads, frowned from opposite sides of the boat, and when she peered even more closely, her stomach pressing against the wooden table, she saw another small face in the rice, darker. The other women were all dark, so dark that their features could barely be seen. Their eyes, of course, but no teeth.

Squinting, she panicked. How I find she? Africa woman? That light girl Aint Sister. . . how I know who for look? Then she saw the line of white, shaky letters all along the base of the photo. At first, she thought they were string, floating in the water, but now she saw names running all along the bottom. Eva—yes, the pale girl, and Christmas, the other child. She was cold with fear, turning away to look out the window for the car, then trying to find the names again. September and October, standing far apart but exactly the same, yes, the thin cheeks that she saw in Aint Sister, the faces new moons floating against the stalks of rice. Her grandmother, Christmas, a baby girl with her mouth open. And Bina—she couldn't find the name and she started to shake, looked again and again.

Mary—Africa woman gave name Mary. She ain't Bina for he. Mary. She looked up from that name and saw a woman whose head appeared to have been cut off above her forehead. Her scarf was so white it disappeared into the sky, and the light shone harshly on the side of her face so that one half was silver and the other half completely night-black, no eyes or mouth, like a mask had been placed over one side. Marietta stared at the straight lip-corner in the sun, the clenched arms, and when she heard chunking car doors, she slipped on the rug, remembering to run.

The women on the boat—their heels pounding holes in the trenches; her heel slipped on the rug when she hurried down the hallway, sliding to stop before the kitchen. She couldn't see Laha, so she ran out the back door and brushed the azaleas. She wasn't even sure why she snatched a branch from the bush near her foot, not even sure why she pulled at the tough wood so hard it ripped into her palm, but when she came around the side, walking, the men were on their way past the tree where Pinkie and Mary sat, staring down at their work.

"You need something?" Mr. Ray asked, his face blank.

"Excuse me, sir," she said. "I see azalea leaf stay green even when it fall, and I try fe put some in my basket, make different. Azalea and pine needle for color."

"Fine," Mr. Ray said. "They need pruning anyway." He and Mr. Thomas went up the lawn and she sat, shaky, under the tree. Her stomach ached and she lifted her shoulders to let more air inside. "You gon get trouble," Pinkie said angrily. "Trouble by *youself.*"

"Trouble made for man," Marietta whispered, imitating Aint Sister. She looked at the deep green azalea leaves, pointy as knives. "Ain gon fall on ground, gon fall on somebody. See? She always say that, I listen. You tell Aint I listen." Her hands shook when she picked up her basket.

"Mama," Nate said. "Big dog." He pointed down the road. "Dog." He had been wanting a dog for weeks.

"We visit Pinkie dog tomorrow," she said.

"Mama," Calvin said, pulling at her bare feet. "Gran."

Aint Sister sat smoking beside Marietta. Marietta watched the boys' faces, their cheeks so wide she could see the edges rising even when the backs of their heads were to her, and she knew they were smiling. Their elbows were ghost-white with ash, their feet pale.

"Where they bury?" she whispered.

"Who?"

"You mama. My mama people. Africa woman."

Aint Sister kept her lips clenched around the pipe stem. Finally she said, "Why you ax?"

"I wonder."

"They suppose to bury at graveyard, far back from you mama. Old-time part." The boys screamed. "But Maussa take she body, Bina, and put she near the House somewhere. Nobody know. When they die, he take my mama and she sister somewhere there, too."

"Why he take em?"

"Cause they his. Want keep em."

Marietta watched the feet raise dust at the edge of the yard, where she swept everything into the trees. "What he name?"

"Who?"

"The man."

"Maussa."

"That all?"

"That all. Don ax no more. Time them two go bed."

"Where *you* think they bury?"

Aint Sister sucked her teeth. "I don think. You don think on that fe you work in them field—uh uh. No. Don ax no more."

The boys ran to touch her toes and then chased each other away, screaming again; their tiny voices sat in the branches like birds. "You tell them story for everybody else, all them year I sit by the road," Marietta said. "Why you don't want tell me?"

Aint Sister blew out smoke. "I see now how you listen. You listen about black, about skin and tree, and you ain let that go. Peoples listen about gone time, know it gone time. You listen and think hard too much. Make you face hard fee wood. You ain know story, just think. Hold you mad fe kill any glad." She stood up and called, "Come fe give Gran kiss. Give she sugar."

Marietta tried to look at her father's picture in the light from the stove, and then she went out onto the porch again to sit in the rocker and see his face by moonlight. But it was dark as the Africa woman's, Bina's. She knew the long cheeks, sharp by the eyes, well enough. Her face. Maybe Bina's arms were black as hers, but they were short, high on her apron. I take she frown, Marietta thought. She saw the half-face floating before her. The gate was down, the fallen oak gone—spirits roamed the lane now, rising from the ground where paths cut across and azalea roots reached deep.

She rocked faster and faster, every night as the air grew hotter, and she stopped speaking to all but the boys and Aint Sister. When Mr. Ray and the guests came near, she nodded and felt air on her teeth, but she sat under the tree in silence, hoed the trenches and raked the floating weeds and debris from the rice field with only her boots sucking at the mud. When she was close to the House, she saw women's bones white under the benches, the hedges, the grass; in the fields, faces floated on the stagnant water, burst in her eyes when she tried to close them at night. Dark faces, Nate and Calvin, half-faces and round heads, eyebrows like window ledges—they floated until the boys called, "Mama, Mama," anxiously in the morning.

"People can only take so much history, Thomas. Then they want some TV." Mr. Ray's voice carried across the field.

"You would think that if guests did all that you had planned, tramping through the woods and hunting and boating, they would sleep early and well," Mr. Thomas said, looking at Pinkie's hoe.

"These are New Yorkers, the ones we want. They never sleep early. They want some TV and then they want to read all night, dammit," Mr. Ray said. "I want you to get your connections in

Charleston to come up here and see about running electricity this way. The damn generator costs me an arm and a leg, and it breaks down half the time."

"Well, you're surrounded by water, with all the rivers and creeks, and you know you're fairly well off the highway, too. And don't forget that. . ."

Mr. Ray broke in, louder. "I know it ain't authentic, Thomas, but this place ain't got most of your money. If people want TV, they're gonna get it. Even my wife is saying she ain't coming to stay this summer if she can't watch TV. Talk to your city utilities friends and pull some strings, all right? Just get me a figure."

Pinkie told Big Johnny and Pearl the next night about Mr. Ray and the electricity. Big Johnny had been to McClellanville to ask about lines being run down to Pine Gardens, but he said people just laughed. "We too far from nowhere," he said. "But if they gon come for Mr. Ray, they come down the road for we."

Pearl had always smiled and shared stories with Mr. Ray when he first came to her store, and she went to speak to him, too. "Mr. Thomas one a them old-time Charleston mens, talk to anybody they do something for he. And Mr. Ray have money—that all he need," Pearl told Aint Sister. "I gon get me ice machine, refrigerator, I know it."

She did, a month later, when the lines were run into the House and then down the highway. Pearl got electricity, and the line ran down the crossroad, ending at Big Johnny's house. People on the crossroad accepted electricity when the man came around, and in a few weeks, when Marietta walked to Pearl's store, she heard television voices coming from the open doorway at Big Johnny's and Pearl's. The line above the road hummed in the night sky, and the complete quiet didn't return until she and the boys had turned onto the narrow lane in the trees.

But the television didn't make Mr. Ray happy, because only a few weeks later, she and Pinkie and Mary saw his face gripped like a fist when he talked to his wife, to Mr. Thomas, even to the little boy who had been only eyes on Marietta at the landing. He wore jeans now and rode his bicycle up and down the road beside the rice fields.

"Where are the damn history lovers?" Mr. Ray shouted at Mr. Thomas, who stood by the fields day after day, consulting his notebooks. "I'll tell you where they are—they're somewhere else cause of all the damn trouble down here."

On the way home, Pinkie and Mary said to Laha, "He talk bout trouble, trouble. I don see nothin."

Laha said, "They talk bout trouble in Charleston. I don't know."

On the piazza the next day, he shouted, "Goddamn city niggers, them goddamn bighead city niggers." Marietta heard his wife scrape her chair on the piazza. She had asked Marietta to plant zinnias, had told Mr. Thomas she always had zinnias in the summer. Marietta knelt near the side of the house, around the corner, tamping dirt around the baby plants.

"That's why I don't stay in Birmingham," he shouted. "Cause them damn niggers were crazy, stirring up trouble, and look at these Charleston niggers now. Thomas is always saying how happy they are, how they're different. They don't look any different to me." He threw his cigarette out onto the lawn; Marietta heard the tiny sizzle. "They're keeping the tourists away. Who wants to come all the way here to see niggers marching in the street, waving signs in your face? Trying to eat with white men."

"It's not violent like it was at home," the woman said. "It'll be over soon."

"Not with this fat-faced nigger King looking to stir it up. He's gonna spread it around." He was silent, and Marietta inched forward on her knees to finish the zinnias. She waited until she heard doors slam before she went around the edge of the lawn toward the rice fields, where Pinkie and Mary sat on the road. "Time fe go," Pinkie said. "Jerry and Willie late."

When they began to walk toward the House, because it was Saturday and pay time, Mr. Thomas stopped them at the beginning of the parking area. "Mr. Ray is very upset," he said. "He'd like to talk to you all for a moment before distributing your pay."

They stood before him on the lawn; he stared at them from the piazza. His wife was gone. "That all of em?" he said, and his words were blurred. His face was glazed with sweat, and he held a glass of ice and gold. The June evening beat down on their heads, and Marietta saw him catch his cheeks between his teeth before he started.

"Charleston niggers are marching and fighting and they're gonna make us broke. You, too, cause if I go broke, you ain't got jobs. They think they're better than you, and they're gonna wreck everything. You know that, huh?"

Marietta saw Stan's grin, the girls' pointy glasses, their hands steady on the counter edge. Pinkie spoke beside her. "City peoples too crowd, sir," Pinkie said, nodding. "That why they bad peoples. Not here—we fine. Plenty room here."

He focused his eyes on Pinkie, then on Marietta. "Yeah,

plenty room cause ain't no paying guests here." He looked past them to Jerry. "Well, Jerry, what you think about this marching and carrying on?"

"I don't know nothing bout that, sir," Jerry said. "Charleston too far."

"Yeah. Well, I want to tell y'all to treat people right when they come here, that's all I'm saying," Mr. Ray said, resting his drink on the railing. His voice was quieter. "Make em feel at home. Cause they might worry about foolishness they see on TV and in the paper, and I don't want no guests disturbed. You all understand?"

Marietta rushed to Pearl's to see the television. People crowded into the store, watching the Charleston people lining the sidewalks, carrying signs, singing. Every night she stared, looking for Stan and the girl, their friends, and once she was thrilled to see them, a glimpse of crescent mouth and then the girl's hair held back by a wide band, her mouth set. She couldn't help staring for Sinbad's face a few times, but she knew he was gone—in Texas, New York, maybe even California.

The fence of black people squared around buildings and snaked down the streets. Lips squared to shout at them from the sides of the streets, to spit and curse and throw things. But their eyes in the long lines were impassive. Pearl said, "These children crazy," and Marietta wanted to shout, "They not crazy. They carry book, they smile at me once." She wouldn't let herself smile, watching the marchers, listening to the voices on television ask, "What do these Negroes want?"

"They want to eat where they choose, to be served with dignity and respect," one of the older men who always spoke said.

"That them preacher mens," Rosie said. "They gon take em off to jail, heh?"

"Get all them chilren in trouble," Aint Sister grumbled. "Make peoples vex and get in trouble." She slapped at Nate's hand when he tried to reach for a packet of candy in the store.

The older men, in their suits, were shown in a court building soon after, and Willie said, "They gone now. They have fe give up."

But the marchers kept on, and though Marietta and the others tried to avoid Mr. Ray, no guests had come to keep him in his boat or driving in the morning to Charleston. He grew angrier each day about the smell of the water on the rice, telling Mr. Thomas he didn't know anything about money or land or business. "Nobody gives a damn about history!" he shouted. "In Birmingham, this would be over. The niggers would be taken care of right, but you Charleston aristocrats think you're too good to do anything right. You need to tell your friends to knock some heads in."

Mr. Thomas said nothing, and Mr. Ray slammed into the house, where his wife spent all her time. The boy followed Jerry and Willie to the barn, the landing, his voice asking and asking, and Marietta remembered his father telling him, "I'ma buy you a big nigger."

On July 12, the boys on television fought their way into a city pool, and then they twisted and arched in the arms of police. A policewoman was injured, and people in the crowd screamed.

"Mr. Ray gon be too vex day-clean," Pinkie said, and Pearl shook her head. Marietta clutched her box of soap, seeing a cigarette coal nestled in hair, seeing Mr. Ray's blunt reddish fingers on the piazza railing.

In the morning, she took the boys to Aint Sister and waited for Laha and the others on Sister's porch. "Bye," she called to Nate and Calvin, who waved without looking back at her. They never watched her walk down the road like they used to. She heard Nate say, "Gran sugar!" Calvin laughed. Was it a kiss, or the sugar they wanted poured into their palms?

They had to hoe this last time very lightly, catching the weeds that loved the long-flooding water just as much as the rice. The morning heat sucked up the moisture from the trenches and wrapped a veil around her legs. Mr. Thomas came again before lunch. "Tomorrow or the next day we will begin the lay-by flow. This water will hold up the rice heads until harvest. It is essential that your hoeing today be thorough, and equally so tomorrow, if you do not finish today. It appears that you won't."

It was too hot to eat, and Marietta slept with her back against the tree until Mary pushed her elbow. "Look, here come Rosie and Laha girl Janey."

They ran up the lawn, Rosie panting, her cheeks jouncing up and down with each step. Nate and Calvin! Marietta ran, too, and Rosie said, "They okay, Marietta! They not hurt!"

"What!?"

"White boys in a car done wreck all the stand," Janey said. "Yell bout nigger something, come off the road and drive all through stand. But Nate been play in the tree like always, and Aint Sister take Calvin fe get he. They at them bush when the car come. Piece a wood hit Sister in the back, she in the bed."

She ran all the way, boots knocking her legs, and found the boys screaming at Aint Sister's house, with Pearl's and Laha's kids and even Belle around Aint Sister in the bed. "Mama!" they screamed, and she pushed their faces into her legs. "Nate run in tree just like you, try fe sneak all too much," Aint Sister said softly. "We beena get he, or car take we, too."

The stands were a tangle of boards and palmetto fronds, and baskets had flown across the road or been flattened by cars. Marietta and Mary and the others stacked the wood in the butterfly weed. Rosie whispered, "I get headache and don't come today. So slow fe buy, no one come, nothing fe sell this week. Give me headache, and I stay home today."

They stayed in the kitchen corner at Aint Sister's, a sweet straw smell fighting the smoke, and Marietta weaved through the people who came to sit around the square table and watch Aint's bed.

"Marietta, make me pea and bone," Aint Sister called, and soon the others went home to cook, too.

It hadn't simmered all day on the back of the stove, so the broth was thin, but she brought a plate to the bed. The boys slept on a pallet beside her. "Look my back," Aint Sister said, and Marietta helped her roll onto her side. She unbuttoned the nightgown. A huge raised welt slashed diagonally across Aint's back. "Where the piece a wood hit, knock my rib and lung. Rub some a that white vinegar on there."

Marietta felt how thin the skin was covering the curved bones. She rubbed very gently, and Aint Sister whispered, "Bring my tea, heh?" The reddish bloodroot tea—Marietta swayed the liquid, tilted it in the Mason jar.

Aint Sister made her go to work the next morning. "I ain't want Mr. Ray vex. I tell them two bring me something now, they do it," she said, and Calvin watched her closely. "I need you tonight fe hot the water, get wood. Come by fe stay."

When Marietta got to the House, later than usual, Mr. Ray was waiting for her. She kept her eyes down, but he said, "Well, Laha has told me about the accident your granma had. I been telling people, ain't no good gon come from this trouble people stirring up in Charleston."

"Yes, sir."

"I went out on the highway and seen that y'all probly don't want to put nothing back out there till all this trouble settles down. And I want you to get your granma come over with you tomorrow. I have a proposition for her, to help her out. Ask somebody to bring her, huh?"

Big Johnny drove Marietta and Aint Sister in the truck the next day, inching down the tight road past the gate facing the highway; Marietta never went down this way. He let them off before the parking area, and they walked, each holding a boy's hand. Aint Sister shook her head at Nate. "Lord God, that smell!"

The stagnant water on the rice fields sent up a heavy stink that rose and hung in the woods. Marietta was used to it. "That long-water time, on them field," Aint Sister said. "I didn't never want smell it again."

They went slowly up to the piazza, where Mr. Ray and Mr. Thomas waited. "Good morning, Eva. I heard about your trouble, and Mr. Thomas here has seen your baskets," Mr. Ray said. "I think we might can work something out for you. Come on over this way."

They walked to the granary, near the deep shade of an oak tree, and that cool air held the dust smell, the wet mildew and iron smell. Marietta picked up Nate and folded her arms under his behind, breathing in the sourness of grass he'd rubbed into his hair.

"You can sit in this area here. The girls are gonna be doing something to the rice—what is it, Thomas?"

"They'll be flailing and winnowing and pounding," he said.

"They're gonna work on the rice in the yard there, and you can sit here and do your baskets," Mr. Ray said. "We'll keep a few on display inside the house, in the historical room, and you can show the rest here. You understand? I mean, I got too much overhead right now, and I'm not paying you, but I'm giving you a sure opportunity to make money. If you don't sell anything, I don't owe you anything. You understand?"

Aint Sister nodded, keeping her mouth curled and closed. He said, "But I'll let you use this space, and when you sell anything, you can give me a third." He picked up a basket. "How much you sell this one for?"

"That twelve, sir."

"So you sell this one, you give me four. For the use of the space." He looked at her again. "You understand?"

"Yes, sir."

"Scuse me, Mr. Ray, sir, my boy stay with her every day while I here," Marietta said.

"Yeah, that's great. They can play around here, nice and safe, as long as they don't bother guests. Maybe you can get em to help out. Look at how big those boys are! Just keep em in line."

Mr. Thomas said, "It looks fitting to have children around the yard, in the care of an older woman."

"Yeah, well, it better bring us some good luck," Mr. Ray said.

Aint Sister sat to the side, in the shade, but her baskets were arranged near the doorway of the granary. Marietta got her settled each morning with the boys, before she went to the rice fields, and she told Nate and Calvin, "Mind you gran. And don't go in there, else I whup you sorry. You stay out that place."

The water on the fields was changed often, but never drained because the flood still held up the heavy heads of rice. Jerry and Willie spent most of the days checking the ditches and trunks while Marietta and the others shoed lightly, jabbing the blade around the plants when the water was lowered and catching floating trash on the flat of the blade when the new water flooded in. At lunch, they sat on the grass by the House, and Aint Sister came to sit with them. She walked slowly, rubbing her back. Nate and Calvin begged food from everyone's fingers, and Marietta grabbed their arms to calm them when they ran in circles, whining and rubbing their eyes. They were sleepy as soon as they ate. Aint Sister and Marietta laid them on a blanket near the tree, where Aint could see them when they woke.

As Marietta carried Nate to the blanket one day, she smelled cold dust, dark and bricked-moist, in his hair, and she wheeled around to Aint Sister. "I smell it," she hissed. "They been in there."

"They beena play with Mr. Ray son. He try fe play hide-go-seek."

"I tell you I don't want em in there. Never," she said.

"You think I want em in there? I get em out, but they play. Mr. Ray son want play there, you have fe live with it." Aint Sister laid Calvin beside Nate. "I not go cross Mr. Ray son. Mr. Ray temper high right now. Look." She pointed to a broken window near the piazza. "Some guest call fe cancel, I hear he holler and then he go fe hit the winder. He wife run inside."

The hole in the glass was a starry flower from where they stood, and Marietta said, "I too glad no man round me for yell and stomp all the time."

"Huh. No man round you fe make money and chop wood, neither."

"Yeah. No man round me tell do this and give me that."

"Them two do that soon enough," Aint Sister said. "They stubborn."

"They go in that old jail again, they be sore, cause I whup em," Marietta said. "They ain't gon *tell* me nothing. I have fe go work."

Mr. Thomas sweated under his hat and coat. "Now will come a period of comparative rest," he told them all. "The ricebirds should begin their annual migration now; they usually arrive in August. This will confer twofold benefits, because while you will have fewer tasks during this time, we have booked two families from New York. The ricebird hunting will offer them some diversion."

Marietta and the women weeded in the garden and then sat weaving baskets with Aint Sister; they all moved to the shade of the huge oak down the lawn. Mr. Ray and the two men guests, with their teenage sons, went out near the fields in the early morning, and Jerry and Willie shooed the birds. Shots poked through the air for most of the day, and the two wives sat on the piazza with magazines. In the evening, they all went to Charleston, their car behind Mr. Thomas's, and it was quiet when Laha came out to join them.

Now Marietta could see how hard it was for Aint Sister to keep the boys near her. Since Mr. Ray was busy with the guests and didn't want his son tagging along, the little boy, Randy, was in the yard all day. He was six. He took Nate and Calvin to the edge of the grass again and again, leading them into the woods or near the barn; they loved him, screaming and chasing him, taking the twigs and rocks he gave them with adoring solemnity. Sometimes they all disappeared around the corner of the house and Marietta jumped up to see that they didn't go down the slope to the water, where Randy liked to play on the landing.

At home, they were content to stay in the swept-clean circle until she told them to come on and they followed her to the field or the peach tree. They carried a bucket each, and struggled to lift them half-full of peaches. On the porch, they held the huge peaches with two hands and bit; Marietta laughed, holding her breath, waiting for them to find the taste. When their tongues accidentally dipped to the sweat-salt left above their chins, when Calvin's tongue swept below his mouth and Nate copied him, she laughed at them licking that sour-sweet ring again and again. She remembered sitting on these steps near her mother, wearing a stinging spit-circle around her mouth.

But Randy called them—"Come here!" and "Hey, monkeys!"—and they scrambled to follow him. He had cookies in his pockets, play pistols and trucks. And Aint Sister was slower in the morning, all day, saying her back and her bones and her breathing ached where the piece of wood had hit her. "Take a long time old people fe heal," she said, trying to reach the spot between her shoulder blades where it hurt. "Hard fe take breath."

Sometimes Marietta came back from the fields where Mr. Thomas had them check the heads of ripening rice, and the boys were nowhere in sight. Their voices were hidden by the clinking of dinner plates and glasses on the piazza, or the hunting shots from the men. "There, your boys are in the woods, I think," one of the eating ladies said, pointing to the trees where the lane began, and she found them digging holes and moving army men Randy kept in boxes. "It's so hot, I told them to stay in the shade of the forest or the granary," Mrs. Ray said. "Little Randy is very fair, and I prefer him to keep out of the sun."

When she smelled the dust on them again, she knew Aint Sister was hiding it from her. Before she gave them their baths, instead of the crushed grass in their scalps and the peach-juice sweetness everywhere else, she breathed iron sticking to their lips and foreheads, drying in the peach and sweat. "You been in that place again," she said to them, and they shook their heads no, so hard their earlobes shivered. "I catch you in there, I gon get a switch."

But they didn't listen to her the way they used to. They concentrated on each other. Their mouths were always shiny and loose, tongues just behind their teeth, ready to laugh or spit. After lunch or dinner, their bellies huge under the tiny, delicate railing of ribs near their arms, they looked for each other or Randy, laughing; they were instantly angry if someone took something away, and their open mouths would shift from laughter to screams in a moment. She could hear them yell at Randy, at Aint Sister. Their favorite word was "Don! Don!" At night when she tried to hold them, they screamed "Don!" into her chest, and then in the morning, Aint Sister's "don" mixed with theirs until all Marietta heard was the poking threats.

Laha had to come and get her in the fields when it happened. Marietta thought it was Aint Sister taken sick when she saw Laha's blue headscarf on the road, and she walked along the bank of the field quickly. "Sister feel worse?" she called.

"Uh-uh," Laha said. "Nate and Calvin carry on something terrible with that boy. Miz Ray beena tell me get you fe take em home. They disturb the guest."

Someone had swung the heavy door shut; Mr. Thomas had the key, and he was in the woods with the men. Marietta stood outside the small building, listening to Nate and Calvin scream. Randy was in there, too, laughing and telling them to stop. Marietta's back grew cold, and she turned on Aint Sister. "How you let em in there?"

Aint Sister's face was blank and smooth. "I cain tell Mr. Ray boy nothing," she said, shaking her head. "He do what he want. Play in there what he want."

Marietta ran to the back of the granary, where the solid brick wall muffled their voices, and then she paced in front of the door, pushing Aint Sister's hands away from her. She slid the knife from her boot and heard the ladies standing on the piazza. "Oh, my God, look at what she had! In her shoe!" The knife blade slid into the crack above the door handle, just as it had in Charleston when the footsteps came to her room, but nothing happened. She yelled through the sliver of darkness around the door, "Nate! Calvin! Hush you scream, Mama here." They screamed louder, as if she should be able to get them out now, and the heat rose in her throat, choking her.

The women gathered at the end of the piazza, and Aint Sister said, "Calm youself, now, they want fe talk." But Marietta kept her back to the women, listening to the boys, and she stayed that way until Mr. Ray and the men walked into the yard.

"What the hell's going on that you have to send for me, get me all the way back up here?" he yelled at his wife, and she leaned over the railing.

"Those little niggers are naked, their mother has a knife, and who knows what's going on in there! They were running after Randy with no clothes on and he ran in there. One of em shut the door!"

Randy's voice rose when he heard his father. "Daddy! I closed the door and I can't get out! The niggers are hurting my ears!"

Mr. Ray looked hard at Marietta. She said, "I try open the door with my knife I use in the field, sir," and he brushed past her to insert the key.

Nate and Calvin rushed outside first and slammed into her. They shuddered when she tried to pry their faces from her thighs. Covered with dust and mud where they had cried, sweet sticky mud—she felt it on their arms. Leaning down, she could almost taste the peach juice all over them.

"They was licking theirselves like dogs!" Randy crowed. "Niggers lick theirself, like Bo does at home!"

Peaches lay strewn and smashed on the cool dirt inside the doorway—the peaches she had brought for lunch. She knew what he'd seen—Nate's and Calvin's tongues reaching for the running sweetness on their arms and chins.

"Even when they fall down, they laugh!" Randy told his father. "They take off their clothes—they do anything I tell em! I was putting juice on em so they would lick like dogs!"

Marietta felt the boys rub their faces against her thighs, imagined Randy running across the lawn and the ladies gasping at the naked boys behind him. She knew when Nate and Calvin realized they were in the granary again they might try to run: they listened to her threats sometimes. But he slammed the oak door, pulling it shut and smearing more peach juice on them. He came closer to look at the backs of their heads now.

"Just wash em off with the hose there," Mr. Ray said. "Stupidest thing I ever heard. What a mess—they're so black the mud's lighter than they are."

"But they hit me, Daddy," Randy said next, and his voice changed now that his father had turned away and stopped listening. "That one hit me cause I wouldn't let him out. See?"

He had angry red scratch marks on his arms, raising themselves already on the pale, smooth skin. "He scratched me like Bo," Randy said, lifting his arms to his father.

Mr. Ray turned to Marietta. "You better wash em off. They look like hell. And then you better teach em not to hit no white boy. Let's go—I want this shit over with now. I got things to do."

Marietta froze, with the boys' faces stuck wet to her legs through her dress. "Scuse me, sir?"

"Give em a whupping and then send em on home with Gramma here. She ain't gonna sell nothing today anyway. I want em away from my boy for today."

"They too scare for whup right now, sir," she said softly. "I whup em soon as I get home."

Mr. Thomas said, "We have weeds waiting for her in the fields, Ray. Maybe we should all just get back to work."

Marietta saw the women staring from the piazza, and one of the guests, the thin man with the beard and strange voice, said, "You really don't need to completely recreate the plantation ethic, Ray. Look, the colored boys are scared to death."

"Y'all got wax in your ears? They need to learn a lesson. Look how big they are—they're five, six years old, they need to know." He stared at Marietta. "She knows better, too. If she don't want to do it, Gramma there can go get a switch."

Marietta saw Aint Sister nod. She went to get the peach switch she kept beside her baskets, and when she handed it to Marietta, she whispered, "Beat em three time. Tell em so the hurt don come later, so buckra vex don kill em."

"I can't understand half of what they say," Mrs. Ray said loudly, and Marietta moved slowly. Tell em what? Tell em?

She pushed them away and whipped the bending branch at their bare legs. Pee rushed from Calvin's bladder and splashed the dust; Nate ran and she hit him once on the calf. "Don never hit nobody!" she screamed, chasing after him. "Never hit nobody!"

She ran so that no one would see her crying, and he made it to the woods. Then she caught him easily, held him close, her tears dripping onto his face, and she crouched for a moment to let them clean him off. Everyone would think they were his tears.

"I go next week after Saturday pay," Marietta said in the kitchen. "I ax Johnny take me in he truck."

"You ain go nowhere," Aint Sister said. She sat at the table, the food cold in front of her. The shudders that came after sobbing had stopped; the boys slept hard and silent.

"No, I gone," Marietta said. "You see he eyes when he look at em. 'They five.' They two-year-old."

"They so big almost to he son. They legs bigger than lil Randy legs."

"So? You beena help. You make my boy animal for whip," Marietta said. "You make em dog."

"I make them two survive. Cause you have you daddy blood, and them two have it, too. That blood kill boy, not woman. Get a boy or man kill."

"So I gone. I ain't have them scare and do what that white boy say. Mr. Ray and them smile at little nigger, like they puppy for play with. You see it!"

"Girl, you best be look fe how Mr. Ray see you. He see you

don do what he say. That man you maussa now. He pay you. What you gon feed them two, you run? Where you stay?"

"I survive before." She stared hard across the table at Aint Sister.

"Heh, you come back here and hide before. You gon go out and get more baby? Survive real good." Marietta felt as if she would upend the table, break the Mason jar of tea, but she stiffened when Aint Sister sucked her teeth. "You tell them two do what buckra say. So they don dead like they grandpa."

"Uh-uh."

"I'ma tell you. Tell you right now. You mama big with you and we sit here, this table. Here, Marietta. Knock come and you daddy say, 'Who that?' White man holler, 'Come on get you boat.' You daddy say, 'Stay here,' and he go out to the porch.

"That buckra want fish at night, like you daddy do sometime, and he tell you daddy, say, 'Get you boat we go fishing in that place.' Freeman tell he, say, say, 'I tire and go fe sleep now.' Buckra say, 'I tell you come, you come, nigger. I ax you three time last week and you say you busy.'

Marietta looked down at the wood, not at Aint Sister's lips stretching. "You daddy say, 'I tire and you ain nobody maussa.' Then we hear buckra laugh, say, I got you maussa right here. He say come get you boat, boy.' We hear Freeman foot down the step and we go fe look the door. He have a gun, that buckra—you can see by how he elbow bend."

Marietta imagined her father's face, set and still like hers.

"Nobody know you daddy place fe fish, in the swamp. They find him in the creek, swell up and think he drown. But I prepare he body—I find hole in he chest. Water don kill he. And buckra die, too, yeah, he die but they never find he body. He spirit rush me two, three time. Little white man in gray hat, smoke a fat cigar. He rush me in the lane, and I carry red pepper and salt fe throw on he head. I sing fe make he go."

A hat, a cigar—Marietta looked at Aint Sister, who stared into the fireplace. She had seen him—the man on the landing, the one she thought was a drifter watching her float down the waterway. The spirit standing on the rotted landing, the wood so soft Jerry and Willie had to beat it into the waterway and build a new dock.

"Only temper white men buy that land," Aint Sister whispered. "Only them kind. Get what they want, they temper make everybody scare fe jump. They happy when you jump."

"Mr. Ray ain't care if I go. He ain't come here with no gun," Marietta said. The spirit on the landing had never moved toward her, only watched. "I just he worker, he find anybody work in he field."

"You ain do nothing special today, Marietta. You ain do nothing bad, nor new. You feed them two, don matter. They been burn, now they learn."

"Learn what?" She stood in the doorway, listening to them. "Learn how for bark like a dog next time?"

"They learn what they do fe work. Play with white boy, that just they work now."

"White man burn in hell when he die." Marietta spat into the fireplace.

But Aint Sister laughed, and Marietta turned, surprised. "You think hell a hole and people do wrong fall in there and burn?" She laughed. "My mama tell me, say, 'Hell ain no hole. A hole be full by now!' You settle yourself, Marietta, quiet you head."

After she left, Marietta put her forehead on her wrists and breathed the table wood.

The boys sat, wary and subdued, near Aint Sister. Randy danced around them, offering soldiers, until he grew bored and went into the house. He came out one day and announced to Aint Sister that he was leaving, to go to a school where he would live. "I'm gonna be a soldier," he said, squatting near Nate at lunch. "My mama don't like it here. But I'll be back next summer. Maybe before then."

They all left for Birmingham, Mr. Ray telling Mr. Thomas he'd be back in a few weeks. Then Mr. Thomas was in the fields every day, because it was harvest time.

Marietta stood in the mud with Mary, Pinkie, even the men. The rice shook around her, near her waist and almost to the shoulders of Mary and Pinkie. They all swung curved rice hooks to cut down the plants, and the heavy heads of rice sounded like sparkles, she thought, when they rustled against each other. Sparkles like the shifting grains of black and white on Frank's old television, when he had first turned it on for the day. She imagined the sparkle of fish scales on her hands, the clinking coins in the register, Frank's gold tooth. Sinbad's forehead glistening over her. She swung the hooks Mr. Thomas had shown them how to use, trying not to hear Charleston every time he spoke.

"If Mr. Ray were cultivating the entire plantation acreage, we would be transporting the rice from the southernmost fields by flatboat, floating it down the creek to the yard. But as we are only harvesting these three fields, we will use the ox and cart."

The cutting was hard, and a hot spell came to make the harvest even faster, because Mr. Thomas said they needed to sheave the rice in the yard for it to dry. He was nervous, talking to them constantly, directing them to lay the rice on the stubble. The heat stayed in the house all day, and at night Aint Sister sat with Marietta while she lay on the floor, head to one side, her hands palm up, feeling the muscles in her back ache—the pads of meat at the bottom, the ones Aint loved to tear out of a chicken back, dense and chewy.

But Aint Sister was too quiet, and her back was twisted awkwardly when she rocked. She stayed home all the next week, when the threshing began, saying, "Cold get in my lung. I cain get it out less I sit by fire."

The boys straggled down the lane until Marietta and Laha picked them up. Mr. Thomas was frantic by the time they reached the yard, pacing and talking to himself. "A rain will ruin it, just one rain!" he said when he saw them. "Threshing is a long and tedious job, and we need to commence immediately before the rice is endangered."

The only good thing about threshing, she decided, was that they never left the yard, so the boys could stay in her sight, playing with rocks and sticks by the trees. She and the others beat the heads of the rice with flailing sticks for days, and Mr. Thomas brought parties of people on day trips to watch the work. They came in cars, then stood patiently while he talked to them, explaining everything from planting to harvest. When the shadows were under their feet, Marietta and the others moved to the tree and the city people went inside for dinner. The afternoons were quiet and laughing, with Jerry and Willie wrestling the boys on the lawn after Mr. Thomas drove back to Charleston.

The days slid by like dust riding on the creek surface. Mr. Thomas brought three fanner baskets from inside the house; they weren't new, but they weren't Aint Sister's. The designs were different. "He must beena buy em in Charleston," Mary said.

"Aint Sister basket historically accurate," Marietta said, "yeah?" But he think he got some better, she thought. He don want give she money.

"The fanning, or winnowing, and pounding are left," Mr. Thomas said. "Mr. Ray won't be back until shortly before Christmas, when I've booked a historic Low Country holiday tour. We'll need the rice harvest and processing done by November, so that you will have time to spruce up the grounds for Christmas." He paused. "Marietta, while the others prepare for the winnowing, may I speak to you now?"

He stood near the granary, where Aint Sister's baskets were piled inside because the weather had turned cold and no guests were around to look. "Your aunt is ill, I hear. Is she in grave condition?" he asked.

"She lung full of water, she think. She ain't heal fast since summer," Marietta said, looking down at his hat brim when he ducked his head.

"How old is she?"

"She born in 1880."

"She's eighty-three, then. And healing slowly. Well, I wanted you to tell her something for me. I feel as if I should give you this, and this message." He handed her twenty dollars. "Please convey to her my apologies for not using her fanner baskets in the winnowing process. I have chosen to use baskets that my elderly nurse made, years ago, even though they are in a different style, because they inspire so many memories." His voice grew distant, his gray eyes shifting to the yard behind her. "I think it was her many stories which began my consuming passion for history, and seeing her baskets used in the way she often described so nostalgically gives me great satisfaction." He let his words trail off, and Marietta wondered again at the rolling pebbles of his smooth voice, tumbling around her. She put the money in her boot and nodded.

"I tell she tonight," she said. "Thank you."

"I'd like the money to be kept confidential, if that's possible."

"Excuse me, sir?"

"Try not to tell the others about the money. Mr. Ray has discouraged lending among employees."

"Yes, sir."

"Let's begin the work, then."

The breeze came cool off the ocean, fall chilly, when they stood shifting the fanner baskets to throw the rice into the air for just a moment, then let it fall back onto the wide, flat rim of the fanner. The chaff blew away and the grains rustled against each other, back and forth. When Mr. Thomas was satisfied, he went inside, leaving them with the piles of rice and Nate and Calvin's shouts as they squatted near a crab Jerry had caught for them.

Pinkie said, "This how they beena get rice fe eat in slavery time. My mama and Aint Sister tell me."

"What?" Mary said.

"They tie up they skirt like Mr. Thomas tell we do when we go in the field, and when they beena fan rice, they let some fall in they dress. Shake it out when go home, and that be rice fe we. They whisper when they fan, Mama say, whisper, 'Some fe you, some fe we.' Sister tell them old-time story."

All day, Marietta heard Aint Sister's voice as she tossed the rice gently. "Don sweep at night!" Now she remembered the rest of it: Sweep at night, Maussa gon see rice you beena drop on floor when you let you dress down. Day-clean, he see rice by you door, beat you fe steal."

At night, Marietta and the boys stayed at Aint Sister's house, eating dinner there, building the fire high for Aint in her rocker. "Cold stay in there, my chest, don spread but don left," Aint Sister said when the boys had gone to sleep on the pallet near the fire. "I gone soon, before Christmas."

"Don nobody know when they gone," Marietta said. She didn't want to say that, but she didn't know how to comfort anyone but the boys. "You get better," she said.

"Some old woman get hag when they ready fe go. I not get hag, but I know. When you old, you know. I want you tell Big Johnny bury me by you mama."

"You ain't need fe tell me nothing," Marietta said, trying to get up and find more wood, but Aint's hand was sharp-fingered as when Marietta was small.

"Tell he where. Lord God, I want fe bury by my mama. But

she by the House. Put me by you mama and my cousin Christmas. We so close, me and Christmas, like them two when we small-small," she said, looking at the boys, feet nudging in sleep. "We talk so nobody hear we. We laugh like them two."

"I look fe grave," Marietta said into the fire. "I beena look since you tell me. But you ain't tell me no clue."

Aint Sister started. "Don search fe no gone time, I tell you. Make you soul hard, same fe you face. Look you face hard fe wood—that not the way fe raise them two."

"How you know they ain't bury by here?"

"This house build fe Africa woman. When she have twin, them two girl, he make somebody build you mama house, even then the girl only baby. When they fourteen, he make em marry somebody he choose."

"But slavery time over then," Marietta said. "That too late."

"Ki, over then, but Maussa got gate all round here, four, five gate, and nobody come this far back tell em that time gone. Not till them two girl have baby and catch fever. When they die, he take em fe bury. My house, you mama house far from all peoples, far from street. All them house gone—only we two stand now. Them other house burn."

"Where the street?"

"He have some house by crossroad, some house way deep near field. Only we house and Africa woman lonesome."

Marietta stared at the embers near her feet. The Africa woman, Bina, her face silvery to the sky, her white scarf and hoop earrings showing on the other side, silhouetted against the sheaves of rice. Never opening her mouth, like Marietta, only working and watching, but at night listening to the strange words of the white man who came to her house. Then hearing her children talk like him. "Marietta," Aint Sister said. "Don look fe gone time, look fe time now and them two. Stop you face like that. Get me that tea, heh?"

When Aint Sister had wrapped her fingers around the hot glass jar and finished the tea, Marietta helped her to bed. She emptied the slop jar into the outhouse, hurrying from the dark yard back to the reddish doorway, and then she made her pallet near the boys, watching the breathing embers for a long time.

"Pounding isn't really pounding, in the literal sense." Mr. Thomas frowned at them. "You cannot do it too vigorously, or you will crush the rice, but you must grind the grains hard enough to remove the outer husk and the inner cuticle."

They stared at him, then looked down, as usual, and waited for Pinkie to try what he said and hear him scold, "No, no. This way."

The fanned rice was poured, a bit at a time, into fat, hollow wooden stumps, and Pinkie ground the grains with a long wooden pestle. The smooth round ends rubbed the rice until the husks came off.

It took two days before they could do it right and he was satisfied enough to leave them, and two more until they did it without concentrating so that they could talk. At lunch, the boys mashed hands into her stomach and tumbled over her legs; their big cricket heads banged on the tree roots when they played rough with Jerry. She lined up her spine against the trunk and listened to the voices humming around her, the voices grumbling in her head. Trouble made for man—ain gon fall on the ground. Gon fall on somebody. You daddy blood—in you, in them two. Never hold you face right round nobody—that you job. Don live in gone time—that fe me remember. What you do fe them two?

She watched Nate try to hide from Jerry, behind an azalea bush, but even from the tree she could hear his giggles. The boys couldn't hide from anyone, with their laughter and screams bubbling like soap up from their chests. Nate ran all the way up the grass to hide by her back. Already now, at night and when they woke, they pushed away when she tried to hold them in her lap for a minute. She missed the arms at her neck and the warm bellies pressed to hers, but she thought about what everyone said, about coddling, and she wanted them to be tough. Nate sprang from her side and ran again when Jerry came after him, calling, "Plat-eye come fe get you!"

"You take care my grave when I gone," Aint Sister told her each night. "Don forget we grave, don forget fe pass them two. They my family."

"You stay by fire, you be fine," Marietta would say. "Here you tea." But soon Aint Sister was tired of sitting by the fire, and she walked slow and crabbed from the door to the porch to the bed, restless. She shook her head at the peas and bone, at rice, at grits. Marietta stared at the grains of rice on her plate, the husks on her arms, the cracked grains in her boots when she shook them out.

"I too full," Aint Sister said. "My heart get full—all them

gone peoples come fe visit, stay in there and full up my stomach, too. Give that plate fe them two. They still hungry. I too full."

Rosie and Laha and Pinkie came, Pearl came, for weeks while Marietta pounded the rice and listened they sat by Aint Sister all day; Laha had nothing to cook until the holiday tour, Rosie stayed inside during the cold winter and sewed, so when Marietta came at night, the two rooms were full of women and scraps of cloth and tangles of thread. Calvin collected the thread and made webs on his fingers.

"I gone soon," she kept saying, but she didn't go to her bed and lie down. Aint Sister began to go back out into the yard, just before dark, carrying her flashlight, to check on her roots. "My muscle and vein get lock up, I stay in bed," she said when Marietta scolded her. "I come back inside soon." One night Marietta sat by the fire watching the boys, growing sleepy over the mending she hated—the rips in their pants, tears at the elbows of their shirts. They had been spilling water from their Mason jars, hitting each other, bumping her all night. She checked Aint Sister, emptied the slop jar, and settled down in front of the fire.

The floor was warm now, but as the fire lowered to a sparkly rustle and the wind licked the windows, the room would get cold enough to wake someone, and she would put more wood on as if she were dreaming.

But when Nate cried and she stood up to feel her way in the total dark, she heard twigs breaking outside. Opening the door, she saw the tiny light bobbing in the trees. Then it fell. She rushed out to her aunt, who lay face down—the spirit Aint always told her about, had it rushed her, knocked her onto the ground? She said, "Aintie?" Nothing puffed against her cheek when she put her face by the quiet mouth; nothing beat against her arms when she picked up her aunt and carried her back into the house.

"Spirit steal she breath," Pinkie said, rocking back and forth by Aint Sister's bed. "Spirit stalk she, take she down."

"Them white boy take she when they wreck the stand," Big Johnny said, spitting off the porch.

"Old people hold a hurt," Pearl said. "She tell me that pain stay in she breath all the time."

"But spirit seek she since she gal," Pinkie said. "She born with that caul, see too much spirit. Sister see too much."

Nate and Calvin were silent, staring, not afraid but interested at Aint Sister's silence and lack of slapping, at her pipe cold on the table, at the people who stood in the two rooms all day and night, voices rising and falling. Marietta sat in the corner and watched Laha and Rosie do what they had done to her mother. She nodded when someone asked about the fireplace or the pots or Aint Sister's clothes hanging from pegs on the wall in her room. She had already told Big Johnny what she was supposed to, and he had looked at her as if she knew nothing. "Where else she bury?" he said. "I done mark the spot already."

The hearthstone where she cooked was clean. The clothes hanging on the wall were washed, arranged the way they always were. The pots were in the fireplace, lids tight. She sat in the church with the boys, hearing the songs and shouting with her own mouth closed and her eyes back in the house, where everything had to be perfect, she thought. Sister spirit happy? Aint tell me what for do. Nate's elbow rested on the bag beside her. The singing and voices rose and fell, and no one looked at her, at her eyes half shut and her still lips. They know me now. I grown now. I ain't change. She watched their faces, Rosie and Laha and Pearl and Jerry, when the procession to the bury ground started slow. They looked straight ahead and sang.

Calvin and Nate crossed the air over the wood coffin, still silent, their eyes locked onto hers as she nodded the whole time for them. They left Jerry's hands and came into Big Johnny's without a sound. Three times each, their palms stiff by their sides, only their heads moving to watch her. They stood beside her, at her legs, as the grave was filled in and covered with plastic flowers, the large round clock set at the time Marietta told them, and the dishes with holes punched through their centers. People began to leave slowly, and when only a few women were left, Marietta bent down and helped the boys cover the grave with shells and the shiny spoons Aint used to stir her root teas. A velvet bag she had kept by her bed, fingering sometimes.

Marietta walked to her mother's grave nearby and picked up the pieces of bright blue glass that had washed a few feet away with the last heavy rain. She found them all and put the shards back in the rectangle outlined by shells, straightened the shells, and pushed the clock's tiny feet firmly into the dirt. Calvin found more glass near a tree, and she didn't tell him to give it to her; she let him push it in carefully, just as she had.

She touched a few things on the grave that said CHRISTMAS

TURNER. Aint Sister cousin—Christmas. And she brother Hurriah Turner. Uncle Hurriah. He must dead now, too. All Turner dead out. Only me and mine left—we Cook. Cook family. The boys were back near Aint Sister's grave, with Rosie and Pinkie. Marietta pulled their arms gently to the road. Rosie and Pinkie were always the last to leave the bury ground, and she didn't want to change anything.

"I'm very sorry to hear that she's gone," Mr. Thomas said. He paused. "When an elder dies, a lot of history is buried, in addition to the actual person. I'm sorry."

The rice was finished. Mr. Thomas said they would have to bag it after Christmas, after this holiday tour. Old Carolina Gold—he said they would package it in bags bearing that name, he would instruct them on the process after New Year's. But right now, Mr. Ray and his family would be coming in a few days, and the women needed to help Laha do heavy cleaning in the house, while the men would store the rice and clean the grounds. "The season requires special touches, too," Mr. Thomas said. "We'll be adding holiday decor, such as trees and garlands. We have much to do."

Marietta and the others followed Laha through the back door. "This the first time you see inside, heh?" Laha said, leading them into the kitchen. She sounded proud, Marietta thought, when she showed them the stove and ovens, the sinks. "I take care here, but Mr. Thomas want all wood rub down with lemon oil, all them floor clean, all the drape dust. I show you."

"You never see this chanlier, heh?" she went on, heading down the hallway, and Marietta stayed last, biting her lip at the smell she remembered from that day she had looked for the pictures. The velvet that held dust, the rugs, the no-breath air inside the rooms. Laha showed them the living room, the study and historical room. "Pinkie, you gotta dust and wash that floor," Laha said, wheeling around. "We all work fast, we be done in two day. Wash, too, gotta wash them bedding."

Marietta stayed behind for a second, long enough to glance at the Africa woman and Aint Sister and the two women with pale faces—she had memorized their faces, and she only nodded at them before she caught up to the others near the stairs.

"You see them photo?" she asked Pinkie once they began on the floors.

"Where?" Pinkie said.

"In that little room, the study."

"I look at all them drape gotta be beat and dust," Pinkie said. "I ain see no photo."

"Look on wall when you in there," Marietta said. "See Aint Sister when she small-small, see all she mama and cousin and gran."

"I ain want stay in here long," Pinkie said. "This house have too many spirit in them drape, hide everywhere. My daddy always say haint fill this house. I want be done and gone quick-quick."

When loud voices floated upstairs as Marietta was on her hands and knees washing the base of the walls, she wasn't sure who had come until the high voice called, "Where are the monkeys?"

She went downstairs quickly. Randy was in the kitchen with his mother, while Mr. Ray stood on the piazza talking to Mr. Thomas. Laha was telling Randy, "Nate and Calvin stay at my house today, cause they mama work inside. They come fe play with you in few day."

Marietta said, "You turn soldier yet?" because Mrs. Ray and Randy looked at her expectantly.

"No. Just school," Randy said. "But I want to play with the monkeys now. Can you bring em?"

She nodded and went back upstairs, Mrs. Ray right behind her. The woman said nothing, just looked around, and then she went out onto the second-floor piazza. "Randall?" she said. "Big Randall. We have to go back to the hotel."

Mr. Ray came, with Mr. Thomas. "What?"

"We have to go back to Charleston, to the hotel, until this is all done. Look—the beds haven't even been washed, I can smell. And the women aren't done with the drapes. It's dirty in here."

"Miss High-and-Mighty can't sleep in a dirty room, huh?" Mr. Ray said. "I remember when you slept in a lot worse places than this, before I got you out of there."

"Remember all you want, honey," she said, sweeping out into the hallway. "I'll be at the hotel while you think back on the good old days."

Mr. Thomas told Marietta, "You'd better expedite the process. I think you and the others will need to be especially thorough, since you're not accustomed to working inside a house. I'll have Laha check your progress this afternoon."

She walked all the way to Laha's house in the evening, and the children's laughter and shouting flew across the road. During the day, only Laha's youngest boy, who was five, was home, along with Mary's boy, who was also five. Nate and Calvin played with them while Laha's mama watched. But the rest all came from school, and the house and yard were filled with tickling, singing, sticks and dogs. Nate and Calvin cried when she tried to pull them toward the road.

It was dark, and Jerry said, "You got too long fe walk in the night. Let we go ax Johnny take you back."

Nate and Calvin were thrilled to ride in the huge cab of Big Johnny's truck, swaying on the seat when he turned the corner into the lane. "Sister house dark don look right," he said when they had slowly driven that far, the moss and leaves brushing the top of the truck.

He waited, letting the boys touch the dashboard, while she ran inside and lit the fire already laid out in the fireplace. "I preciate it," she told him, leaning into the cab to smell the pipe smoke and fish.

They kept trying to tickle her, and when she asked if Laha's children had taught them that, Nate said, "Tickoo, tickoo baby." Calvin slapped his palm over his open mouth, the way Mary's boy loved to, making Indian sounds.

"You bring them boys in the morning," Mr. Ray had said before he left the house. "They can keep Randy out of his mother's hair."

She let them run down the lane ahead of the adults, their coats stiff-tight around their chests. Their shoe soles flashed quick, and they didn't turn around until the crumbled gate wall. "Hide-go-seek," Calvin said.

Randy was waiting in the kitchen. "Miz Ray say he too ceptible for cold to be outside today," Laha told Marietta.

But Randy said, "Monkeys! I got a jacket, I can go in the yard!" and he ran outside with them behind him.

Laha shook her head. "He do what he want."

"He so thin," Marietta said. "Why he never get fat?" His arms were straight as broom handles all the way to his elbows, no padding of strength or plumpness anywhere. His knees poked through his corduroys where he squatted with Calvin.

"Miz Ray tell me he born early, stay in hospital a month fore he even go home. He always been meager," Laha said, turning to her pots. "You better keep a eye. Miz Ray upstairs."

Mr. Thomas said, "The azaleas need fertilizing, the edges of the grass must be trimmed at the paths, and the granary must be arranged so that guests may view all the tools of the rice harvest. They will be here in one week."

"I take care for azaleas," Marietta said quickly, and the others looked surprised. "I plant em, so I know how take care." I look in the ground for grave, she thought.

She scratched the earth around the azaleas and scattered fertilizer, probing deep with her digging stick and hoe. What I look for? Wood? Wood be rot now. Iron? He bury, why he have iron marker? He know where they rest. She watched the boys and Randy, sitting on blankets near the piazza and playing with army men and plastic tanks. She could hear Randy's voice piping like a squeaky wheel, and the boys' tumbling chatter.

Cain be dig up no big hole here. And I dug hole fe these plant, me and Pinkie and them. Somebody see if grave here. She circled the fertilizer around each bush, looking back at the boys, at the trees, thinking about the woods and all the places the women could have been buried. But where he take em, where he want keep em? All land he got, land I ain even see—maybe they way at the other end, in secret place. She scratched the soil angrily, quickly, moving along the paths and around the edges of the lawn where the plants made a small hedge against the woods.

The boys played fine until after lunch, when Nate and Calvin wanted to wrestle with Jerry. "Uh-uh," he told them sharply. "Go on—I busy. Go play with that boy now. Stop." He pushed their tickling hands away and left, so they turned back to Randy.

"You can wrestle with me!" he shouted. "I wrestle at school. Come on, little monkeys."

Marietta caught Calvin's elbow. "You don be rough," she said. "He ain't like you friends. Don't hit, remember? Never hit nobody." She saw that they had forgotten the granary and peach juice, the switch.

Pinkie said, "They gon play like they want. They ain remember—they baby still. Don worry—we keep a eye."

"Mr. Thomas say for we go in the granary," Mary said, appearing from behind the house. "Say fix them tool first, so he can check."

They took all the things they had used out of the granary, and Marietta sniffed inside the cold bricks. The dust had settled, tramped down, by people coming in and out, and the granary smelled more of sweetgrass than anything else. She touched the iron mesh, feeling the rough rust on the strands of metal.

"They suppose to go in order how we use em," Mary said. "That what he want." Marietta laid the hoes, the rice hooks and the flailing sticks on the grass.

"Huh, use them damn hoe every day," she said. "Where that go?" Pinkie and Mary laughed, and Pinkie said, "You best hush. He come now."

Mr. Thomas moved things around with his foot, studied them, and took out a bag from his pocket. "I saved some of the clayed rice for display, too," he said. "Hmm—let me think about the proper order for a moment."

The women stood watching him. Pinkie said absently, looking at the hollow trunks for pounding rice, "Aint Sister palm trunk best fe pound. She use that when I small-small."

Mr. Thomas said, "Is that so?"

Pinkie looked startled. "I sorry, sir," she said quickly. Marietta thought, She best not say she know what work better. He suppose for know everything.

"I've never been able to find one like that," he said, and he went to his car quickly for his notebooks.

"What you done start?" Mary said to Pinkie.

"That man crazy," Pinkie said.

"Marietta?" Mr. Thomas said, walking back to them slowly. "You live near her cabin, correct? Are her things all sold or given away by now?"

"Nothing give or sell, sir," Marietta said. "They she thing."

"Come and show me the mortar," he said. "Pinkie and Mary may take a short break. We will drive my car."

"Sir?"

"I don't really like to walk in sand, as it hurts my calf muscles to no end. And to avoid damaging the lawn, we can go down the highway. I see that you approach the house through the woods, but we'll go around."

Nate and Calvin saw her leaving, and they scrambled up from the blankets, calling, "Mama! Let's go car!"

Randy said, "I'm coming, too!" Marietta looked at Mr. Thomas, but he didn't see anything except his book.

"You sit in front with Mr. Thomas," she told Randy. "They in back with me."

It was strange, passing the bare shoulder of the road where splinters of wood and scattered palm fronds were all that was left of the stands. The woods were so dark, the sandy side of the road so light, and the space where the women had all walked up and down was even lighter. Then Pearl's store, where Rosie had laid her baskets out along the wall. She stayed in the store with Pearl almost every day now. The houses along the wide dirt road, and then so quickly, the bridge clattered. In seconds, they were turning down the lane, and Mr. Thomas said, "My God, it's tight driving in here. I hope nothing scratches the car."

Aint Sister's house looked even smaller from the car. "There she house," Marietta said. When she got out of the car and stepped into the yard, then the door was in the right place again in her eyes. The window shutters had been nailed shut, like they were for a hurricane, but the door was unlocked. No one would bother Aint Sister's things.

He stared at the jars of tea, lined up on the shelf, the different colors murky and shadowed in the dim light from the doorway. In the firelight, they always glowed clear and jeweled. The bed was still made up, and the clean tin plate and spoon sat on the table. Mr. Thomas saw the palm-trunk mortar near the fireplace, and he rushed over to touch it.

The boys had all gone straight for her bed, because Nate and Calvin remembered lying in it, giggling while Aint Sister used to say, "Get out my bed! I come fe get you now!" Randy jumped onto the flat mattress and said, "It don't bounce right."

Mr. Thomas slid the mortar toward the door. The outside of the trunk was rough gray and wrinkled, like an elephant's feet and legs she had seen in a schoolbook long ago; the mortar was that thick and round. Inside, the pounding pestle had made the spongy wood slick as a baby's wet back. But now Mr. Thomas left the mortar and looked around the room. He poked inside the fireplace.

"How old is this cabin?" he asked.

"I don't know, sir." She shrugged, wanting to tell the boys to stop messing the bed. "Build for Aint Sister gran."

"Who?"

"Aint Sister—Eve—the house build for Eva mother mother. Come from Africa." She bit her lips and said, "Scuse me," going into the bedroom. "Hush," she told the boys, her throat closing. "Get up now."

Randy ran back into the other room, banging the spoon into the plate. "Who eats out of a pie plate?" he said. "It stinks in here."

"Let's put the mortar in the trunk," Mr. Thomas said, straightening up from where he'd been examining the fireplace. "I'm glad Pinkie told me about it."

Pinkie don tell you nothing. Pinkie just talk—talk fe pass time, Marietta thought, panicked. Aint Sister voice even come now. "People say don't take thing from dead," she said out loud, hesitant, when he moved toward the mortar.

"But why isn't the house locked then?" Mr. Thomas said.

"Cause she spirit might want fe use something," Marietta whispered, not looking at him.

"Don't you think she would have wanted people to see something she kept all these years? This is a piece of history, and it cries out to be seen in its proper context. History belongs to everyone," he said, brushing off his palms on the porch. The boys raced past him and he watched them with the same distant, curious glance he always gave them.

Jerry and Willie rolled the mortar out of the trunk and then frowned at Marietta. Pinkie and Mary widened their eyes when they saw it in front of the other mortars by the granary. After Mr. Thomas had gone inside to talk to Mr. Ray, Marietta said, "He don't listen. He too busy talk history. I cain say nothing for he listen."

"Next spring's gonna be so much better," Mr. Ray said loudly on the piazza, stretching his arms from his waist. "It's finally gonna come together."

Mrs. Ray blew on her coffee. "I bet." Marietta waited; Mr. Thomas had told her to go onto the piazza, because Mr. Ray wanted something.

"If I can't smell honeysuckle in the bedroom, I won't stay here all damn summer," Mrs. Ray said.

"I know, look, she's here right now. Tell her what you want. Where'd you have Thomas put the plant?" Mr. Ray said.

"You can tell her," Mrs. Ray said. "The plant's in back, I guess. Laha and I have to start the Christmas decorations." She went inside, and Marietta followed Mr. Ray around to the back.

"She wants honeysuckle in the bedroom, I mean, she likes the smell," he said. "I guess you can plant it here, and get Jerry to pick up a trellis for the side of the house here. That's the bedroom window, up there." He looked at the ground. "Look, don't worry about the trellis. The thing can start climbing up right there." He pointed to the lattice woodwork at the base of the house.

"Nate, Calvin," she called when she went to get the shovel and the fertilizer. "Stay round here." Then Mr. Ray came around the corner.

"I got all three of em," he said. They ran behind him. "I'm going down to check on things at the landing."

"You two stay here," she said to the boys, and they whined. "No—go get you trucks and sit," she said. "Now."

Randy said, "I want em to come, my daddy's gonna watch us. Come on," he called to them, and they ran after him.

"You two," she yelled, but they ran faster, trying to catch him. She ran after them to the landing, where they stood watching Mr. Ray walk out to the end and look down into the water. A fast boat skimmed past, and he waved—Nate and Calvin waved, too.

"Them two have for come back with me," she said. "I don't like em near the water, cause they cain swim."

"No, Daddy, I want them to stay here," Randy said, looking

straight at Marietta. "I want em to stay with me. You said they can't come over at Christmas."

"Mr. Ray," she started, but he interrupted her.

"I hope you ain't thinking that I don't know how to watch no kid," he said pleasantly. "Let em stay, and you get on back to the honeysuckle. We'll bring em back in a while. Look, they get a kick out of the water." He stared into her eyes until she looked away, at the blue. "They're big boys."

She stomped on the shovel, driving it deep into the ground near the base of the house. The honeysuckle plant was in a large pot, and she dumped it out onto the grass furiously. They ain't his boy. They my baby. They ain't big. They ain't his. I have fe whup em for he, teach em lesson for he. Monkey. They learn for be good little niggers. He buy two stead a one. Two little nigger for follow Randy.

She hit a rock and flung the shovel onto the grass. Now she would have to dig the rock out, or the honeysuckle roots might not be happy. Have for make honeysuckle happy, too. Grow big and strong to the window. She wanted to kick holes in the wooden latticework that skirted the base of the house; she picked up the shovel instead and plunged the point against the rock. Goddamn a rock. Probly big, too.

Scraping the dirt from around it, she saw that it was a flat, round rock, a little larger than the shovel blade. She rocked the point of the shovel around the stone, and finally it shifted enough so that she could reach in with both hands and lift it out. The dirt fell off the top and she saw MARY carved into the smooth face.

Mary. Africa woman. She name Bina but he call she Mary. Marietta stared at the blank white wood in front of her, with nothing special to mark this wall. She looked up at the window where the honeysuckle was supposed to reach. The bedroom. He bury she by bedroom, so he look out see her anytime. He keep she. Keep she close by. Marietta touched the carved letters. Who carve em? He make somebody carve she name, but don't bury she so nobody can see. Nobody never know where she rest.

Suddenly she remembered that the boys were still gone, somewhere near the water. Mr. Ray want keep em, like he keep she. Whatever he want, he get. Get my baby. She cut across the lawn to the trees, sliding through two azalea bushes, and ran through the thick brush and vines as quickly as she could toward the water. She heard them after a few minutes, heard the boys' voices. Mr. Ray was quiet. She walked slower, silent, and watched from the trees where they walked along the water. Mr. Ray kept looking out at the boats passing. Randy and Nate and Calvin followed him, throwing rocks and twigs into the water. "Big rock," Nate said. "Go boom."

Calvin said, "Go boom-boom-boom," and threw another.

They came to the landing, with her following their voices, and then they started up the lawn. She ran back to the spot where she had entered, scratching her arms with branches, pushing through the growth, and she emerged just when they came close to the freshly dug hole.

"You hiding in the woods?" Mr. Ray said, his face testing, tilted to one side. "You looking for something? Maybe you don't trust me?"

She shook her head. "No, sir. I find rocks in the hole, ain't good fe plant flower, so I throw em in the wood. One more." She walked over to the stone and picked it up with both hands again. "I get em out the way, like Mr. Thomas say. No trash in the yard. Excuse me." She walked back through the azaleas carefully, the stone cold in her fingers, and when the trees hid her, she knelt down on the leaves. Africa woman. Rest in the tree. I come get you later. Rest in my tree. Tree in we blood. It better here, better than window watch you. Tree watch you now.

Mr. Ray was standing near the hole when she came back, brushing her hands. "You digging it plenty deep?" he asked. "I hope the damn plant grows all the way inside the bedroom."

She looked at him and nodded. "Yes, sir. Plenty deep." After he went around the house, and Nate and Calvin began to crush the clods of dirt near her feet, Randy said, "I'm going to the barn where Jerry and Willie are. Come on, monkeys." They didn't look at him, and he said, "Stay then, stupid monkeys."

She dug a huge hole, fast as she could before Mr. Ray or Mr. Thomas came to look, wider and wider, looking for two more stones. September and October. But she felt only soft dirt against her shovel, through her sifting fingers, and she knew the daughters were somewhere else. He ain't need see them when he want. He put em away, cause they he blood, he think. But Africa woman spirit run. She took a last look at the trees after she had set the honeysuckle in its hole and filled in all the dirt. I come back. She took the boys' hands and led them around the front.

The next morning, while she looked out the door for Laha and them to walk past, she heard a car crushing the sand, growling closer. Nate and Calvin stopped chewing the pieces of bread she'd given them and stared at the trees. It was the big, black car—Mr. Ray's car, cutting slowly through the woods like a fish through tight reeds, floating and humming.

He and Mr. Thomas got out and looked at her house, at the clearing and yard. "Morning," Mr. Ray called to the boys, who had run out to the steps. "We need you to go get your mama. Come on with us to your granny's house. Go get her."

The car inched backward while she and the boys walked, facing the windshield and Mr. Thomas's eyes. Mr. Ray's head and elbow hung out the window and he said, "Goddamn! Like a tunnel in here! You're right—we'll have to move the damn thing."

They left the car in the lane past Aint Sister's house and waited for Marietta to come to the porch. "I want you to take all the jars and stuff out and keep them at your place," Mr. Ray said. "We're gonna move this cabin over to the main house, but we might want to put some of that stuff back inside for looks. Authentic stuff, but nothing anybody'd steal."

"You move a house, sir?" Marietta said, catching her breath.

"Yes," Mr. Thomas said. "This would be an original slave cabin, one of a very few extant slave dwellings in this area, and no one can even see it back here. Since your aunt is no longer living, it seems a shame to let this valuable piece of history go to waste, abandoned to roaming animals."

Animals? Aint Sister's spirit might come to eat, or to rest; that was why everything was left waiting for her. Marietta had been listening for a breath of something, but she wasn't afraid because the boys had been passed over the coffin. The spirit should be comfortable and pleased that all possessions were still hers or in her family. And no one came down the lane anymore, not to see Marietta, but they would still say, "Aint Sister place in the wood. Back there."

"Let's go," Mr. Ray said impatiently. "Find something to carry them in, or the boys can help."

"Excuse me, sir, but Aint Sister leave she house somebody," Marietta said. "House go from peoples to peoples in family. She my people."

He smiled. "And this is my land. All the way to the bend, where the third gate used to be. Yeah, your house is my property, too. I want this one on the big place, and in fact I hadn't even paid attention to this part of the title until Mr. Thomas here informed me of the buildings. But this'll be a great addition—it's gonna be a great spring, I can tell."

"Bad luck fe move house, sir," Marietta tried again, but he raised his chin slowly.

"In fact, I'ma have to start charging you rent for the house you and your boys there occupy. Of course, you can always get the rent deducted from your pay. Well, let's get on with this. Find a box or something. Thomas, what the hell is this?" He was staring at a chicken beak near his foot.

She didn't go back to the House after she had carried the things to her front room. The men didn't return. She walked back and forth in front of the fireplace, on the porch, Nate and Calvin playing with Aint Sister's plates and spoon and pots, with the ancient black iron spider she used to set in the fire, to cook something slow right over the coals. The graywood boards were slick against her soles, her head swollen with anger.

Bina house. Christmas house. Aint Sister house. Mama house. My house. All-two house gone—nobody land, nobody wood.

She watched the boys under the table. My boy—nobody boy. I whup em for make em weak, make em smile? Let em watch my face, they don't learn that. They see they grandaddy face. I make my face soft? They got he blood, no matter I do or no. Sister say I hard fe wood. Cain get straight wood from no crooked timber?

Dark crept into the clearing, then the house, and she built the fire higher and put the boys in the washtub near the hearth. They flicked drops into the ashes to hear them hiss. Their thick Sinbad eyebrows, her heart and bones and bodies—she was no threat, since a hard woman was only ugly and stubborn. But big boys—could she do anything to change their faces, or were their bones settling even now into square, even stares? Africa woman—she stone in the tree, wait for me.

Blueblack—blueblood. The deepest blue of the hottest flames; the sapphire blue of the glass on her mother's grave; the murky gray-blue of the oyster shells. The blueblack between the trees before night.

Her father's picture—her reflection in Sinbad's eyes—Nate and Calvin's still-soft faces, their baby skin plumped over his own, her own stark features. Hard bones of forehead and cheek and outlined lips.

Blueblack—cause trouble. Mr. Ray wanted them to learn from her, how to hold their faces right and hand things to him or Randy. How to show teeth. He wanted her eyes to open wider when he spoke, her face to somehow seem lower, closer to his, not inclined so that her lips and lids were flat and angled above him. The boys' mouths now, always moist and laughing, her own teeth always smooth and wet behind her shut lips, her eyes comfortable behind her lids.

She had counted the dollars in her mother's box under the bed a hundred times, but when they were asleep, she sat near the fire and counted again. How much for a room with a kitchen and bathroom in Charleston? She stared at the Mason jars on the table—the gleaming, clean jars full of gold and silver and ruby liquid. Opening one, she smelled the whiskey—snakeroot had to steep in whiskey. She sighed, running her palm around the rice pot. How much could she take this time? Then she remembered—she couldn't take the stone. She couldn't go back and get it. She couldn't leave the boys sleeping alone.

But the stone, Mary—Bina stone. She went into the bedroom and looked at the boys sleeping. Aint Sister, she prayed, come fe watch em now, just fe short minute. Watch no spirit come in here. Please.

She ran in the dark, flashlight slanting crazily in the trees, and because she wasn't sure what to sing to keep haints away from the road, sang what Sinbad had always murmured musically to women, the only thing she could remember right now. Please, please, don't go, she sang. No, I going, she thought. I gone.

At the gate, she turned off the light and didn't even let the song stay in her mind. It wasn't very late—lights were still on upstairs. In they bedroom. He bedroom. She inched around the edge of the yard, close to the azaleas, crouching when she heard noises. When she passed the path to the landing, she ran to the woods and went to the spot where she'd laid the stone. Mary—her fingers felt the letters. Bina—I cain change you, but I take you home. She lifted it up and started toward the azaleas, but she heard someone then, and she saw a glowing ember floating through the dark.

Maussa come get she! Spirit stand on the landing, see me. He smoke cigar, remember me from battoe. She crouched in the azaleas, smelling the dirt she had turned, and then the sharp smoke floating from the tiny fire, bobbing closer to her. Come on. I ain't run, I got stone fe knock you. This spirit stone, even knock spirit. She shivered against the leaves.

The pink ash flew toward her suddenly. She saw the silhouette of a man in the light from the bedroom window—Mr. Ray. He had flicked his cigarette at the azalea bush, and it smoldered near her foot. He went around the front and she heard the door close.

She ran then, around the edge again, but fast, before he could look out a window. The stone was heavy, clicking against the flashlight, and she clutched it to her chest, bumping her breastbone.

At the house, she left the stone on the porch and hurried inside to check the boys. They snored peacefully. One more small minute, she begged Aint Sister. Watch fe me, please. Watch fe Africa woman.

Down the lane, past Aint's dark house and Pinkie's smoking stovepipe, she passed the big Angel Oak, silent in the cold. No fire in the bricked circle in winter, no smoking and bubbling murmurs from people sitting around the coals. She kept on to the bury ground.

Spirit, Haint, please rest now, I bring someone fe join you. No harm now, please. She took a breath and entered the bury yard, the trees and moss ghostly, protecting the souls. Between Aint Sister's grave and her mother's, she placed the stone, resting her palm on it for a second. You blood here. My blood gone now.

She knew Little Johnny would be watching TV in the front room, but she listened to make sure he was alone. Big Johnny and Rosie must be out for visit, she thought. The TV light flashed silver and blue in the window. Marietta knocked on the door.

"Johnny," she whispered. "It Marietta."

"What you want?" he said when she was inside. He was surprised, his teeth silver, too, when he squinted in the television glow.

"You daddy truck here?"

"He and Mama gone to Laha's. They walk. Why?"

"I need you drive me somewhere. Hurry start the truck, I pay you three dollar."

Johnny looked at the TV. "You crazy. I ain't drive nowhere at night."

"You daddy take the truck day-clean," she said, moving to stand near the screen. "I pay you five dollar."

"Five dollar ain't enough to get kill for. Daddy be vex past reason."

"I have for get something by McClellanville," Marietta said, hard. "I go get my boy ready. You come in half hour, come on get we. You be back too fast. Please." She stepped forward and put her hand on his shoulder, and she saw that he was afraid of her. "One hour you come."

He nodded, said, "I come, okay?" When she let him go, his eyes fixed back on the silver-blue light.

charleston

"You ain't got no job, you don even know where you go," Johnny said, repeated like a verse, while she told him where to turn. The fish market was closed, plywood covering the windows, and she felt a stab in her chest—maybe Frank dead, no, maybe he just move he brother farm. Eat mullet every day.

The old house where she had stayed was dark, no one out on the piazza in the winter cold. Hurriah? He wander, he dead, he come back? No—he gone still. She told Johnny, "Turn right."

"You crazy. Plat-eye get you," he grumbled. "Talk bout go McClellanville and lie. Haint change you out."

She was tired of his voice, and she wanted to hear the boys' sleeping breath in the huge cab so she could think, remember the streets; she turned to him and said, "Plat-eye get me, change me fe hag! Spirit from the House change me, make me crazy. So close you mouth, I tire for you teeth. Just drive where I ax you!"

He clenched the steering wheel hard and folded his lips on each other. She looked back at the streets. Someone had come into Frank's one day looking for a room, and Frank had told him, "Go over there past King, up the way. That neighborhood cheap, but it ain't so wild like here. They got a bunch a rooms up there." She had walked this way a few times, and she tried to recall where she had seen the street with a long line of rooming houses and signs hung over piazzas.

The narrow streets ended in dead ends, in alleys, but finally she saw the slightly wider street she remembered, with tall apartment houses all the way down, and then the huge vacant lot that stretched to fences and factories. "Go slow," she told Johnny, and she looked at the piazzas and wrought-iron railings for signs.

"I ain't see nothing," he said. "You crazy. You ain't know nobody in Charleston—cain nobody find you in you house so far back in the tree."

"I spirit—my friend fly in the tree fe see me," she said. "We stay here till day-clean, when they put the sign out. Lean back and sleep—I keep a eye."

He snorted and grumbled, but after a long hour his head did nod crooked on the seat, and Marietta tightened the blankets over the boys, wedged into her legs. She smelled the truck cab, thinking of how angry Big Johnny would be in the morning. But I ain't go back again. Pine Garden gone. My house gone, my people gone. I stay here now. Lil Johnny tell em I crazy, I haint. Haint disappear day-clean, like I gone.

When the sky turned purple, she got out of the truck, arranging the boys close and warm for each other on the seat. She took out the pot filled with grits and rice and jars, took out the baskets filled with bedding and clothes, the boxes of tea and plates. Each thing she picked up off the truckbed clean and careful, like picking fruit, so Johnny wouldn't wake. She piled them in the dirt of the vacant lot where they were parked, and before the sun rose, she waited for the day-work ladies to open their doors.

Dim gold lights came on in windows, and a few men walked down the street in their heavy boots, heading toward the main street away from her. No one looked back to the lot. Soon the women came out in their coats, and then the older woman she had been waiting for hung the signs over her railing.

She ran down the street to the apartment house and knocked on the door. It was still gray-dark, and the cold air stung her ears. "Ma'am?" she said when the woman's face peered around the door edge. "I look for room, one with toilet and stove."

"Just you?" the woman said.

"No, me and my two boy. Small-small boy, not three yet."

"Huh. You sure early."

"Yes, ma'am."

"I got a room with kitchen and bath. One bedroom."

"Thank you, ma'am. Here?"

"No, down the way. Let me get dress and I be with you directly." She closed the door.

Marietta ran back to the truck and woke the boys. "Look, we take walk," she said when they snarled and squinted. "Look, we go see lady got candy."

"Candy?" they murmured, rubbing their eyes. "Candy?"

"Johnny, you go now," she said, shaking him. "I get my thing. Here five dollar. I ain't lie bout no money."

"Huh?" His head swayed for a second while he looked at the vacant lot. "What you say?"

"Say go home, hurry so you daddy don kill you. Here—take you money. Go!"

"You crazy—you stand in some street with all you thing and want me go?"

"I don need you. I take care weself now, so go." She glared at him with the look she had used all night, and he shook his head.

"Mama kill me I tell she how I left you," he said. "Stand in street."

"Tell she I fine. Tell she I gone," Marietta said harshly, pulling the boys away from the truck. She glared at him until he started the truck. "You go down to this street, turn left. When you see King Street, you go right. You see sign for bridge, or you ax someone for bridge to get on the highway. Go on now."

When the truck had turned the corner, she saw more people coming out to the street, carrying paper bags and purses and lunches. Women dressed for day work, men in dark uniforms and coats. Children came out onto the piazzas and ran back inside. Marietta took the boys' hands and led them down to the house where the sign hung.

"I got a two-room place, up closer to the main street," the woman said inside her apartment. "Bigger for all three y'all."

When Marietta found out how much it was, she shook her

head. "We look fe one room," she said. "My thing outside—we can go see the room?"

She led them back down toward the vacant lot, raising her eyebrows at Marietta's tiny pile of boxes and pots. "That all you bring?" she said. "This room ain't furnish. It only got a table they left behind. But I let you have a bed from my other place, if you interested."

Marietta counted her money again silently, pulling the boys up the stairs to the piazza of the old building at the end of the street, and said, "I think on it, ma'am."

The light through these dingy shades was the same honey-heavy beam and shadow she remembered from her uncle's room. The linoleum rug had worn through to the wood floor in spots, and the walls were filmed with smoke and grease. The whole apartment looked cloudy, like creek-water with sand stirred up from the bottom. After the woman had taken the money and closed the door, Marietta watched the boys. They ran from end to end, patting the walls.

The previous tenants had left a couch, too. The landlady was surprised to see it, but she said the people had left in a hurry. Marietta laid the oilcloth she had brought on the too-soft couch and tucked it into the crease at the back, and then she watched the boys run and poke and yawn until they grew sleepy enough from the long night to let her lay them end to end on the crackly cloth.

She touched her things in the middle of the floor and strewn about by the boys. Aint Sister's jars of tea nestled inside one peach crate. Marietta knew she would never drink them, and they were heavy, but she had wanted to keep the gleaming, gold-topped jars so nobody would peer at them and shake his head, so nobody would laugh and say, "Old nigger remedies, huh?"

Her pots—she put them on the sticky round table, white with flecks of color that didn't move under her fingers. Taking out the shells she had let Calvin put inside the rice pot, and then the small metal trucks Nate had chosen, she put their keepsakes on the windowsill, so they could reach them. She had an end apartment again, and the two windows looked out over the vacant lot.

She heard noises in the wall, gurgling and banging, and she went into the kitchen. She had forgotten about the water! The white enamel sink, dotted with black nudges where things had dented it, and the faucet that filled it with water in seconds. She listened to the whine of water coming from the pipe, and then ran to the bathroom.

Her mouth opened—a long white tub! Well, not white, it was brown-smoked around the edges, but when she bent and turned the taps, hot and cold water came out. She knelt and traced her fingers around the curves. And I feel too sorry I leave that wash pot for Laha, too sorry I tell Johnny give she all my thing. Nobody need no wash pot! Them boy gon swim in there, swim in warm water. She turned to the toilet, and then she closed the bathroom door. Nobody come bang on my door, nobody come fe get me. I sit here long as them two let me. The toilet seat was cold and damp under her, and a roll of thin, moist paper sat on the floor by her feet. She stood up and the rusty water swirled when she pushed the shiny handle down. Lord God. Water everywhere. The hissing toilet, the rushing water in the bathtub, the stream in the sink—she stopped and listened, eyes closed.

You got rent, too. You got one month for find a job. Then you rent due. Yeah, you was gon have rent you stay in Pine Garden. But you have food in Pine Garden. Have for buy everything here—no chicken, no field. She went back into the kitchen slowly after she had turned off all the water, and she turned the knobs on the small electric stove. Two burners coiled like snail shells; they turned fiery orange under her rice pot and the canned tomatoes she poured into the smaller pan. Playing with the knobs, she turned the rings to ashy red and let the food simmer. The boys' chests rustled evenly against the oilcloth.

She went outside to look at the street in the daylight, leaning over the railing. Below her was the sidewalk. Cain dump no water out there, when I clean. Have for sweep it down the piazza. She turned to go back inside. An older woman's shaky, birdlike voice said, "Yo two boy sleepin now?"

The woman was very small and thin, her face light brown with freckles near her eyes, and she sat on the top step of the stairs leading down to the street. Her gray-black braid was wrapped around her head in a crown, and she had loosened her coat in the morning sun.

Marietta nodded. How she see them two? She must look out she window all day.

"Them some big, fine boys," the woman said. "How old—five, six?"

"They near three soon."

"Hmm. They big. They favor you somethin hard. They good boys?"

Marietta nodded again and moved toward her door. She didn't want to hear questions about where she was from and why did she only have those few things in the street; she didn't want to wait until the woman got around to Where your husband? "I have fe go clean," she said.

The woman smiled. "That's nice—you fixing to clean. Was a young couple use to live there, no chilren, and they never kept no house. Runnin in and out, pile they thing on the piazza."

"Yes, ma'am. I have fe go now."

"You from one a them islands? You talk like them island peoples."

"No, ma'am. Pine Garden," Marietta said, standing against the door now.

"I never hear of no Pine Garden. Near Savannah?"

"Up the way," Marietta said. "Off the highway to McClellanville. My boy stir now, ma'am."

The woman nodded and turned back to the street.

Marietta set the rice aside. She took the middle pot and filled it with hot water from the sink, marveling at the gray rush and steam. In the small, empty bedroom, she began to pour the water carefully, keeping it in puddles on the floor and scrubbing until the rags and bubbles turned dark gray. Then she dumped the dirty water into the bathtub and did it again. Watching the water swirl around the drain, she thought, I ain't have for sweep it outside. Nothing like before now. I ain't have to go outside for nothing but find work. That old woman be like them at home, be watch and question every minute. She pushed with her knuckles, digging the rag into the floor. Never my dirt. Never my floor. Yeah, this my floor—long as I pay.

She knelt at the bathtub when they slid off the couch, and she jumped up, thinking they would cry at the unfamiliar surroundings, but before she could say anything, they were out the front door, Nate chattering away to Calvin. She heard them on the piazza and went outside, pulling her headscarf lower on her forehead, flattening her face. She heard a man's voice. My scarf down this far, no one see my hair. Could be gray, all they know. She thought of Mr. Thomas suddenly, his occasional stares at her face and hands.

A small man, his eyes only to her shoulder, was smiling at the boys. His red-brown face had curved sickle lines around the mouth, and his hair started far back on his head. "Juntlemon," he said, nodding at the boys. "I'm pleased to make your acquaintance." They froze like horses skidding backward, and they knew she was behind them, because they reached around for her legs.

"Or let me begin with your majestic mother," he said, smiling again. She let her head tilt forward and looked at him with her eyelids mostly down—this little man, talking like a hundred people lined the piazza, his long words skipping stones over the air. Sucking in her cheeks, she stared hard at him; she was in Charleston again. "Well, when you all are acclimated, I'd be happy to welcome you to the street," he said. "My wife and I live three doors down. My name is Larkin. But people call me Poppa." He turned and went back to the open door near the stairs.

"Get back in there," Marietta hissed at the boys. "Don't out the door less you ax. Never." She shoveled their behinds into the dark room.

The tiny kitchen was what fascinated her most. The small refrigerator—over and over she opened it to breathe the cold metal rack and rims cloudy with condensation. The stove and sink—she scrubbed off the syrup of aged grease until the enamel was thick white.

But the recklessness of what she had done fell slowly in the apartment with the second night's darkness. The boys ate their rice and tomatoes and then swam around the bedroom and the front room like mullet trapped in pools left by low tide; they darted into the dark caves of kitchen and bathroom as if they were little holes in the creekbank. Marietta turned off the lights, thinking about the electric bill. "We go out, Mama? Less go. We go now. Time for go, Mama?" they said into her knees where she sat on the couch.

She let herself wonder if Sinbad was still driving Charleston streets in his finned car. No. She knew he had found someplace else to disappoint him while he laughed and whispered and his eyebrows danced. She pulled softly at her gold hoops while the boys left her legs and ran. Taking off her headwrap, she made herself touch the back of her neck, the curve of her head above it, and then she tied the scarf tighter over her hair. The hoops felt heavy in her ears. Eighteen. Now I twenty. Wear black like them lady beena lose husband, keep my hair cover. People think I old.

Miss Pat used to say women from the islands went to the market to sell fruits and vegetables and baskets. But what would the boys do on the sidewalk—the street wouldn't be like the fields, where they could run. She went to find them in the bathroom, shooed them out while she fished clothespins from the toilet.

She had forgotten how the wind sounded different in the city. The heat clinked in the wall heater and the air brushed the window. Now that it was past dark, she let the boys stand on the couch underneath the front window and peer out the screen for a second. She listened to the air moving past the buildings with nothing to stop it—no branches or moss or bark to catch a sound. The cold wind rushed into the piazza, though, and moved the smells of cooking and cologne, and she could hear pots clanking, faraway voices, and right next door, through the walls, she heard radio music.

All night, after she had laid the boys on the pallet beside the couch, she lay there under the window and heard the sharp singing and guitars and underneath it all the quick little beats. It was a small radio, she could tell by the tiny music. And the voices were so different from Laha or Rosie singing in the fields or the truck, or the people singing at church. These voices sounded closest to the children, Laha's kids and the rest holding hands, chasing each other and chanting.

All the other sounds stopped eventually while she smelled the rusty screen air above her through the window crack—the cars, which seldom came down the dead-end street, the steps of boots and heels on the wooden piazza, the click of door locks and TVs—but the radio trickled drums and horns and voices through her wall until early morning. No chair legs scraped next door, no one coughed, but before the sun rose, the door next to hers trembled shut and soft feet padded down the stairs.

By the time she raised her head to the window, she saw nothing moving, just the dark shapes of the apartments that led in a shadowy tunnel like oaks down the lane. With her cheek on her arm, she watched until a few yellow squares blinked down the street and the outlines of houses showed. Then she poured grits like sand into the boiling water and stacked the baskets inside each other. Only two—the large round-bellied one Aint Sister had helped her make when the boys were almost six months old. It was the same shape as the one the tiny yellow-haired woman had fingered that day in the stand, the day Marietta's mother lay breathing silently in bed. Aint Sister's fingers had been all over this one, tightening the pine-needle contrast, smoothing the sweetgrass. Inside the large one was the tall jar-shaped basket, which she had filled with the forks and spoons and socks and shirts she grabbed while packing to leave.

How much did they ask for baskets here in Charleston? Only two left. She closed her eyes and saw the baskets lining the stand, swaying in the wind, breathing sweetgrass dry over her all day. She smelled the belly of the round one, and then she went to wake the boys.

It was just light when she pulled them down the street, their eyes sleep-slanted and mouths warm from grits. She pinched the oilcloth tightly under her arm and hurried. The sky was gray-cold, and people walked with their heads down until they disappeared into stores and buildings; all she could see was the men's hat circles. No women walked yet. Marietta found the old market building, and she slowed, set her face. The other women were settled behind vegetables and baskets, only a few women, and she didn't see Miss Pat. Who could she ask? The women were impassive, or weaving and murmuring, pulling sweetgrass from paper bags at their feet or rounding their hands over turnips and cabbage. They didn't look at Marietta.

Where I spread my thing? How much they ax for tall basket here? She kept the boys moving, their hands away from the colors, and walked around once more, still searching for Miss Pat's face. A few older black women holding the hands of white children, Nate and Calvin's size, came in now and touched the vegetables. Marietta watched them and thought, I sit and put my two basket out, I got no sweetgrass, nothing few do with my hand. I sit here with nothing don't look right. Like I steal these two basket.

She let Nate and Calvin pull her out the door. They had seen a store with Christmas tinsel in the window, toys and packages and even a tree. They ran ahead of her and tried to push open the glass-topped door before she remembered.

"Get back here! You cain go in there," she hissed at them, snatching their arms away from the brass knob. "Come here!" She dragged them down the sidewalk, and Nate's face cracked, outraged, into a howl.

Charleston—she had already forgotten that they couldn't go into the stores below certain streets, that the boys would have to learn not to run ahead of her and touch until they were in the right neighborhood. There was nowhere in Pine Gardens they couldn't go—Pearl's store was the only one they had ever seen. Pine Garden sound good, huh? Yeah, and they cain go in the House soon as they bigger. Can go in the granary anytime now. "Walk right!" she told them, angry, when they slumped and dragged on her hands, trying to pull her back. "Now!"

She waited until she saw black faces and smelled the right smells. Then she let them go into a corner store. Crackers and milk. She let them choose sardines. "Mama, look he get cookie!" Nate shouted, watching an older boy. "Less get cookie!" She thought of the few times she had let them take a big cookie from the Murray's tin at Pearl's, the sweet crumbs that stayed on their tongues only a moment and in their minds forever.

"Less get cookie, Mama?" Calvin whispered to her, his face thrown all the way back to look up into her eyes. She counted out the coins at the counter, numb, the cashier's face blurred in her unfocused eyes.

"Big truck!" Nate said outside, clutching the cookie with both hands. "Look big truck!" Calvin stared at everything, one pointed tooth coming down hard on the corner of his lip again and again. She walked back toward the apartment, and the cookies became only pale speckles around the boys' lips, hanging magically onto their cheeks until she brushed at them. Calvin squatted in the gutter when they got to their street, his head down to look for anything valuable pasted to the curbside. Marietta looked across at the muddy field and the smoke rising from the factories far across the lots. Them women in the market maybe don't sold nothing today, but they got chickens, they got the creek at home. They got greens. She touched her cold key in her pocket and told the boys, "Come on, we go upstairs. Eat some fish." The sardine can slid across the basketweave.

She missed the rocking chair. Her legs cramped up when she lay on the couch, like her muscles were spongy as the squashed-flat cushions already. She let the boys run wild, and they were crazy as chained dogs, stuffing clothes into the empty refrigerator, filling the bathtub with a pounding rush of water. The radio was soft and insistent toward night, like baby birds in a nest under the eaves. Behind the shade, the window was open a crack, and the screen let in night air and voices. After she put the boys to sleep, she listened to the older woman's trembling words and the deep answers of men. The small red man must be she husband. Marietta listened for the "don, don, don," in the older woman's throat, but though she kept still, intent, watching the boys tumble out onto the piazza in the morning as helplessly as if she were a child, she heard no scolding tongue against teeth.

Nate and Calvin came back to the door holding striped candy canes. "Mama! Candy! Christmas!" they shouted.

"Who give you candy?" she said, looking out the door. They whirled and pointed to the small woman coming down the piazza, smiling.

"Them boys ain't got nothin for Christmas?" she said, her voice high and rising. "Let em come on over my place and I make em some Christmas cake."

"Cake! Mama!" Nate said. But Marietta looked at the fan of lines wide around the woman's eyes, her teeth small and even, her two skirts. The "don" lingered there in the wrinkles and folds. Who was this woman? She no kin to me. She want something.

"Thank you, ma'am," she said, planting her fingers into the soft meat of the boys' shoulders and pulling them inside. "We have thing fe do today." She closed the door, seeing a wedge of skirt fade away.

Dressing in her black pants and white shirt, she cleaned the boys' faces of the candy-cane juice and waited until the piazza was quiet. They clattered down the stairs and down the street.

Heading toward Frank's, she stopped at each of the small cafés and lunch counters, holding the boys' hands and asking, "Excuse me, I look for work. I use to work at Frank's, fish market down the way. You need help?" She tried to look soft in the eyes of the women behind the counters. The young women, with red lips and fingers—were they some of the same ones who had come to Frank's and painted themselves, watched Sinbad? They shook their heads, staring at the boys, at Marietta's size and smile. She found herself looking at the tops of their shiny curls when they bent their heads to the counters.

"Christmastime, now," one man said. "We full up." "You need some experience in a restaurant, not a market," another man said. "This a lot different."

She held the boys' hands, walking them from store to store, from window to window with painted letters and dangling tinsel and Christmas music inside. After a few hours, they began to snatch at things in the stores, to cry for candy and cookies and rolls, and people smiled at their sullen lips and eyes. "Look them two," they said. "Twins—look how they get mad the same. Poke out they lips like they done practiced together."

She bought one candy cane for each and led them back to

the apartment. Her eyes felt as if hot, dry cloth lined the sockets. The rice in the bag was a small pillow. The grits bag was still full, and she put a stick of butter into the refrigerator, where it sat like a fat grub on the rack. She moved it to the side and closed the door.

Children shouted and warbled in the afternoon, and even though Calvin and Nate trod on her legs to stand on the couch and look out the window, she didn't let them out. They ran to the windows overlooking the field, hollered and pointed at the kids playing, and she shook her head. Until dark, they spun in anger, whirling at the door, and she sat, staring, listening and thinking of the smoke rising from the factories. They were past walking distance if she took the boys.

A smell floated inside, something sweet and black that she had never smelled before—smoking burnt sugar and butter? She counted her money, lay as if her legs had turned to fallen oak branches, and dozed. Sardines. Milk. Cookies—she could almost hear the crunch of cookies against the boys' teeth, loud as their shoes on the gritty sidewalks. I keep em inside, they cain see none a that in the store, cain ax for cookie.

What you think? You cain find no job here less you ax. This ain't winter in Pine Garden—this Charleston. Have for be work someplace. Ax them on the piazza. Aint Sister say you grown when you feed baby. Cain keep em inside with no rice and grits.

The next day, she took the sullen boys, who snatched their hands from hers and tried to run down the piazza, to the woman's door. She heard TVs and laughter and scolding from the other apartments, saw kids running on the sidewalks. After she had knocked, the woman's head peered around the door frame. "Scuse me," Marietta said.

"Darlin, I gon have to get back to you," the old woman said, looking back into her apartment. "I stop by your place in a while."

She closed the door abruptly. Marietta walked slowly back to her door, her mouth filling with water. That smoky sugar smell had coated the screen, made her hungry for sweets, too. She remembered when the boys were first born, how she had craved a chocolate bar, a cookie, something sugary, and she had no money; she'd had to stay in the house and mix sugar and flour into a sweetish powder to rub with her tongue into the roof of her mouth.

She paused before the silent, always-closed door next to hers. No radio burbled, no one laughed or spoke. Inside, she told the boys, "Wait. That lady come for tell Mama something. Go on play in the tub."

A lemon smell tickled her nose now, and she sat on the couch, her head buzzing. She would ask the woman about the factories, about anyone who knew where there was a job. But she couldn't concentrate on anything, with the lemon smell growing stronger even when she went to the kitchen and turned on the faucet to remember how exciting the water looked rushing in a straight stream. She stood there with her hand in the hot water until she realized that the smell was everywhere and someone was knocking.

"I don't never smell nothing from here," the woman said, her circle of heavy braid so far below Marietta's chin. "And nothing to hide it between your door and mine—next to you a old man never eat. Don't never eat." Her don'ts were sharper than Aint Sister's—fingers on a porch railing, impatient, clicks against her front teeth. But the lemon cake in her hands was shiny-glazed. "I make this to welcome you, but I couldn't invite you inside cause my husband sleep. He work at night, and need his sleep. Here, sweetheart, this for you." She had to bend only a little to place the plate inside Nate's hands.

Marietta saw their nostrils widen and knew she couldn't keep this tiny woman away from them. The boys turned their faces up to her so high that their mouths had to fall open, and she told them, "Go on, give it here for I cut we all a piece." She turned to the woman. "Thank you, ma'am. You like for sit down?"

"I likes to have chilren close by." The woman smiled. "I glad to see you and these boys. It bad luck if you don't bring some food to a new neighbor, but I never see y'all and always dark in here, nobody cooking."

They sat at the off-balance table, its spidery metal legs clacking against the floor whenever somebody moved an elbow. The cake was thick, dense, the yellow so buttery and the clear lemon glaze stinging sour-sweet on the tongue. "They can call me Momma like everybody else do," the woman said, watching the boys collect yellow crumbs on their cheeks.

"That you husband, say to call he Poppa?" Marietta asked.

"Mm-hmm. But they really calls him Baby Poppa. He so small, and peoples only remember my baby." She had eaten a few bites of cake, but now she sat with her hands curved up in her lap, straight as a schoolgirl. "When we come from Bamberg, we had a little girl, only tiny baby. One month old. And we come here cause Poppa cousin had him a job at a hotel, say the job waiting on him. But my baby pass on to the promise land, she got that fever when that fever were goin round. Take so many chilren, that fever."

"I too sorry hear that," Marietta said. "Lose a baby worse than all. People tell me that before, but I don't believe cause I beena lose my mama. But now I have these two, I know they right." She stopped, embarrassed by how much she had said, and brushed specks from the oilcloth.

"Baby teach you plenty, huh?" The woman smiled, her front teeth small and square as the checks on her dress. "But they been call him 'the baby poppa' all that time she were sick, and then they just kept on. Cause he taken it so hard, oh, harder than any man I ever seen. And we won't able to have no more, cause wait and wait, but weren't no more baby in me. Look these two—they want some more cake. Act like they never eaten no cake."

Marietta saw how she did it—not like Aint Sister, who came straight out and said what she didn't like—this woman didn't look at her, just said something light in a maybe voice, but she was handing them another piece of cake. She gon get she way, what she want, Marietta thought, staring at the cheeks, the spongy braid, the eyes much rounder and slower than Aint Sister's. Her hands were just as thin. Don, don, don—she watched the woman smile at the boys. Marietta made up her mind looking at the woman's cheeks, smooth and full in the center, too round for her tiny body.

"They ain't have too much cake before. We come from up

the way, like I tell you, Pine Garden. Hard time up there. My husband dead." She waited.

"You ain't had a job wait for you when you come?" the woman said. Marietta shook her head. "Where you fixing to look?"

I work in a fish market before. I try the store and restaurant, but nobody need help. I want ax you bout them factory across the way."

The woman shook her head now. "Girl, you better know somebody work in there to get you a job. And you gotta have experience. Them jobs hard to come by. You try the hospital? You ever work in a hospital?"

"No. Where you husband work?"

"He the night man at that big hotel, the one you seen with the pretty door and all the glass. You ain't seen it? Yeah, he been there twenty years. But ain't no openings there."

"You stay home?" Marietta asked.

"Shoot, no, I got a lady for day work. You been seeing me home cause she gone to visit her cousin for the holidays. She coming back after New Year's."

"You know any day work?" Marietta said.

"Well, these Charleston lady very particular. They likes references, all that. You done domestic work before?"

"I work in the field, but day work can't be no harder than that." Marietta remembered cleaning the House when Mrs. Ray came back. "I done a little domestic, too. But mostly work in the field."

"Huh. Yeah, well, you might see how hard." She looked at Marietta's hands. "Who watch them boys?" Marietta was silent, remembering them running in the yard with Randy. "You wasn't studyin bout take em with you, now? Huh. Well, I gon go now. I ax round, see maybe I get somebody help you. I got my dishes to wash still. You all keep that cake."

They avoided calling her anything. She kept instructing the boys to call her "Momma," but when they were out of earshot, Nate would say, "You the mama. She little."

Calvin squinted, concentrating hard, and said, "She tiny. Tiny like bird."

"She like granma." Nate said it as a challenge to Calvin.

Calvin shook his head. "Nuh-huh. Granma small. She tiny."

When the woman waited for them to come up from the field, where Marietta let them play while she watched out the window, they called her "you." "You make some cake? You want my mama?"

She called them to her door, and Marietta went. "Come in, let me see them two." Inside, her front room was covered with crocheted blankets and doilies, and Marietta smelled greens' steam heavy in the air.

"Come here, look what Momma got for you," she said, going to the table. She pulled two pairs of pants from a shopping bag. "Look what I find at my lady house. Nice and thick for rest of the winter. You know, yesterday was New Year's, so she back today. You all eat that Hoppin John I bring you? You ain't eat that, you ain't have no luck. Nineteen sixty-four. The New Year. Mmm-hmm."

Nate and Calvin took the pants and walked around the table, dragging the corduroy dutifully. They wanted cake. "Thank you, ma'am. You ain't have for do that," Marietta said.

"Didn't do nothin. Just found em in a closet," she said, looking at the boys, not at Marietta. "I try to think on somebody for you, but tell you the truth, I'm not so sure, cause it look like a hard time for you all get use to me. See, ain't nobody said 'Momma' once. Call me 'ma'am.'"

"You mean you see some day work, uh, ma'am?" Marietta said, not knowing how to answer the question of who was a mama.

"Well, I tell you. My lady so old, so feeblish I ain't got much to do over there except she have a party or a tour. Good thing, too, cause I ain't young, neither. I just got the three room, really, in that big house. I go in the kitchen, cook her dinner, the bathroom and wash her towels, and make up her bed in the bedroom. Do laundry. All them other room close up until spring, when them tourist come. They tour the house, you know. Historic house."

Marietta waited impatiently, then forced herself to relax, breathe. No hurry—listen. She like for talk, and she ain't talk like Aint Sister. She ain't tell me what for do yet, she just love for talk. She watched the woman's hands, listened to her voice twist with the crochet yarn, dipping with her wrist and needle.

"Go on and look that TV, sweetheart," she said to Calvin. "Pull that knob there. Yeah, that one. See? TV light up. Go head and look. Well, I come home bout two, after she eat her dinner. She eat earlier than most, you know. Most these folks eat they big dinner at two, but my lady want eat earlier. And Baby Poppa come home from the hotel round three in the mornin. You go down there see his hotel with that pretty door yet? No? Well, he sleep till I goes in at seven, and then he up awhile. Maybe he watch them two boys in the morning, and I get em when I come in, so he sleep some more."

Marietta blinked at the pause in the voice. The quiet settled like a fly after a long journey around the porch. Baby Poppa?

"See, now, that's what I was thinkin. You ain't happy with that, but you know, everybody round this street like for Baby Poppa watch they chilren. He take em walkin, play in the field maybe. He keep a close eye. See now, you just ain't comfortable."

"I never see no man watch no child," Marietta said and stopped. Her words weren't coming out right. "I only worry bout he keep up with em."

"Huh—Baby Poppa faster than you think."

"And I worry bout how much." Marietta looked at the boys' heads near the glowing screen.

"How much?"

"How much I pay you?"

The woman lowered her head disdainfully. "We here anyway."

"But I like for pay."

"Huh. You give me that big basket, round one, to hold my yarn. I teach these two how to help me ball it up. That's how we start, huh? And they call me Momma."

Nate and Calvin's faces were rapt in the TV light. "You ain't find no day work for me?" Marietta asked.

"Well, next Saturday you gon go with Loretta. She live downstairs. She got a rich lady on the Battery, and they havin a party so she need extra help. That how you gon get reference, get regular work." Before Marietta could count her remaining money in her head again, before she could calculate the days until the rent would be due, Momma continued, "And go look in the pot. I bring some extra chicken—my lady so feeblish she don't eat nothing but the breast now."

Calvin called her Tiny Momma. Nate hid his giggles behind his hand, waiting for Calvin's whipping, but Tiny Momma smiled. And Calvin said, "My mama big." Baby Poppa said, "'Big' isn't a very descriptive term for your mother."

Marietta sat on the piazza during the afternoon sun, hunched over in embarrassment at the eyes of the neighbors, and when she let Nate and Calvin play with the other children in the street, she soon heard them say, "Nuh-uh. That Tiny Momma. My mama big."

She circled the apartment's two rooms, thinking about how to buy a bed, waiting for Saturday. That morning, she woke before dawn with a shaking stomach. Putting on her best dress and the flat black shoes, she carried the boys to Tiny Momma's warm doorway and nodded to Baby Poppa. "Your eyes are fearful," he said. "I haven't had a complaint yet." He sat there in his robe and slippers, his red face with the two small grins curving sideways around the real one.

Tiny Momma handed her a biscuit and they went downstairs to walk with Loretta to the bus. It was filled with other domestics, and they murmured against the cloudy windows. "She ain't got no uniform," Loretta said to Tiny Momma.

"Your lady got some extra in a closet somewhere," Tiny Momma said.

Loretta raised her eyebrows and turned away, and Marietta stared out the dark glass, knowing what she thought. Not that big—ain't nobody got nothing to fit that big.

The other women began to get off, and Loretta didn't move. Tiny Momma left, and the bus was almost silent. "We on the Battery, the last stop almost" was all Loretta said.

These houses looked across their street to the ocean, which was gray and choppy in the dawn. The piazzas were shadowed the length of each house, three stories high; some of the roofs had circled towers, and rounded archways lined some piazzas. Marietta could hardly swallow, and still Loretta was silent until they went in through the garden of a gray-and-white house and neared the back door.

"I'm fixing to cook all day, so you suppose to do the heavy cleaning. Momma said you never clean before. You got no idea?"

"I clean couple time. Just show me."

Loretta smiled once they were in the kitchen. "Well, you gon have to learn quick. When Miz Simmons having a party, she subject to nerves all day."

The woman who came into the kitchen had hair in a smooth helmet and lips that were pale pink, silvery-frosted as a winter morning. She said to Loretta, "I can't believe how much we have to do." Then she saw Marietta and smiled. "Well, and you're here to help?" Marietta nodded. "Uh, you're a friend of Loretta's?"

"Yes, ma'am. She my neighbor. She good with cleaning."

"Let's get her started, and then we'll have to discuss serving, Loretta. You don't seem to have given that any consideration." Marietta saw Loretta's face grow hard when she turned to the stove.

Loretta told her to begin on the paneled woodwork in the living room and dining room. The squares and grooves had to be cleaned carefully, and Marietta pushed the toothbrush bristles gently into the corners and the carved sunburst on the mantel. The dents and notches and baseboards—she stretched and knelt to brush the dirt and then rubbed lemon oil into all the wood. She washed the floors and polished brass fittings. After lunch, she washed the windows, only the squeaking of her rag and the noise of the TV in the study close by to let her know anyone in the house was alive.

Loretta's kitchen was closed off, muffling the pots, and Mrs. Simmons stayed upstairs. Marietta heard the telephone's ringing, tiny as a dropped bottle on the street, but she heard no voices. She listened closely to the rushes of noise that burst from the study. Edging closer to the half-open door, she saw that Mr. Simmons was watching football. The cheering sounded like wind, pausing between gusts and roaring again.

She finished the windows in the early afternoon and went back to the dining room to polish the brass fireplace screen, with its curved flames at the base. For the first time since the kitchen that morning, she heard Mrs. Simmons's voice, imagined her smooth-flipped hair and her mouth.

"All you've done is watch that damn television. Football. I've asked you to check the liquor cabinet, to go get ice, I've asked you to lay out your clothes." She was nearly shouting, but her voice stayed deep in her chest.

"Well, I checked the liquor cabinet."

"You drank all the gin. I'm aware that *that* is low."

"It's your party. I just nod, pour drinks, and keep my mouth full. I'm practicing right now."

"That's right. Who cares? I only have one maid to serve, so maybe you can do that, too." Marietta moved the rag slowly, straining to hear.

"There's two of em here," the man said.

"See? You haven't heard anything I've said all day. You came up to the bedroom twice and didn't listen to a word. I can't have that other one serve. I don't know why Loretta even brought her, but of course Loretta doesn't care, either. Did you look at what she brought? That woman's so big and dark—she looks like a man, and sullen. She'd scare guests away from the front door if she answered it. Loretta knows better."

"She must be six foot. Not that hefty, though. Maybe one-sixty-five."

"That's extremely helpful to know, Carl."

"Defensive back size. Yeah, I'd say defensive back." He laughed.

Marietta heard his feet scrape on the floor like he was pushing out of his chair; she stood behind the open door of the dining room. Her heart hurt, with her shoulders caved around her chest, trying to make herself small behind the paneled door. The liquor cabinet—he wasn't leaving the room? She heard him go upstairs and the woman's heels click toward the kitchen.

Edging her way out of the dining room, she went back through the living room and around until she heard the heels click back again. In the kitchen, Loretta said, "She told me call somebody for serve. You can stay in here and help out with the dishes."

She stayed behind Loretta through the dinner, never leaving the kitchen, and she scoured the silverware and gingerly rinsed bubble-thin glasses. Mrs. Simmons gave Loretta the money to pay Marietta, and she never saw the shining helmet of hair again until all the voices had left. Mrs. Simmons looked at the plates and pots and her heels clicked across the floor, but she went back outside without saying a word. Loretta shrugged, handed Marietta five dollars, and they finished the stove and counters.

Sleeping on the couch that night, Marietta felt a racing tickle up her arm and onto her chest, the way only a spider's legs could hurry, she shook for a moment. But then she realized where she was, and she hoped the spider stayed, spun a web in the corner of the ceiling like the ones she had caught sticky on the broom all day at Mrs. Simmons's house. When the boys cut themselves, she would need the spiderwebs. She lay awake for a long time, seeing the silver-blond strands of hair spun together, hearing the rush of noise from the man's TV and his silence in front of it. Defensive back—she had no idea what it was she looked like.

And they did get cut, a few weeks after. She heard the screams from the vacant lot, where they were playing with the other kids just before dinner, and she rushed out onto the piazza. "Mama!" Nate yelled. "Calvin slip!"

"There Momma!" one of the other boys said, pointing to Tiny Momma, who was already on the sidewalk with Baby Poppa.

"No!" Calvin moaned, hobbling against Nate's shoulder. "My mama big."

"There Big Ma," the boy said when she passed Tiny Momma.

She sprinkled sugar into the cuts, pressed spiderwebs over the gashes. "Men be drink beer in them field," she told the boys. "Watch for glass. Baby Poppa cain see everything." Nate ran heedlessly, but Calvin bent to pick up the brown and green curves of glass; he brought them to the front yard and tucked them near the base of the house.

She had had only two other jobs, filling in for a woman down the street who was sick for a few days. The rent was paid, but they ate mostly what Tiny Momma brought. No one hired her for the domestic jobs she found in the newspaper or heard about from Tiny Momma. The women in the kitchens looked at her face, her shoulders, her feet, and they said, "I'd like someone with more experience. Well, you know, we prefer to hire older women. I require references. No, that position has been filled." Marietta walked home past the wrought iron, the pillars, the stores and windows, and when she saw Tiny Momma peering out from her lit doorway or waiting on the steps with the boys, Marietta shook her head.

Baby Poppa left for work at seven, and Tiny Momma always whispered her slippers down the piazza to Marietta's door soon after, when the boys had eaten. Sometimes Marietta would sit on the couch, watching them the way she had from her porch back in Pine Gardens, always thinking about their shoes, their wrists hanging too far from their sleeves, the cookies they craved. Sometimes she closed her eyes as Tiny Momma sat on a chair at the table and she heard Aint Sister, everyone, the voices it seemed would accompany each of her evenings for the rest of her life: the boys' singing and arguing and scraping things across the floor, Tiny Momma's chanted questions. "Them two ain't dress for bed yet?" They sleep when I decide, Marietta would think resentfully. "You feed em some a that ham I brought the other day? What they eat?" They eat better than winter; they ain't shrink yet, huh? "Look—Nate got a hole in his pants? Give em here, now." I fixing to sew that when he sleep.

Marietta was silent, watching their round faces bobbing in the dim light, hearing the refrigerator hum and click when Tiny Momma had finally gone and the boys were asleep, waiting for the haunting radio to waft its songs through the walls. Old women gon talk all round me, always. Ax this, tell that. I raise Nate and Calvin till they weigh much as elephants and I ain't do it right still. But that how they talk, old woman. When you turn a old woman, you hair turn light and you voice turn a question. She love them two, Tiny Momma—she want touch em, feed em. Long as I keep em—they mine.

Before spring, when the air began to warm and sweeten, women started to send word through Loretta and Tiny Momma and the neighbor women that they needed somebody to do heavy work, and they had heard Marietta was good. She became known as the one to get the day of the party or the tour, and the one for the mess of the day after.

She had three or four days' work each week all spring. Washing wood paneling, wielding her toothbrush; gleaming the floors; brushing the dust from the carvings in picture frames. She ironed the linens, scrubbed grainy cleanser into bathtubs and sinks and counters. She left the windows so that the guests would see themselves, and she stared at the glass when the dark fell, seeing her own face barely visible, imagining the pale reflections that would look out into the night.

Sometimes she left in the dark with Tiny Momma, and if she stayed for a tour and then a reception afterward, always in the kitchen, she wouldn't see the boys at all. They would be sleeping on the floor in front of Tiny Momma's television, and she carried them to the bedroom, where she had a double bed now. They hunched close to each other on the cold sheets for a few minutes, and she stayed, thinking of the three of them sleeping in her mother's old bed. Then she lay on the couch, listening under the window.

She scrubbed a white enamel sink one night, the double drainboard on either side with long ridges covered in gold flecks of chicken fat, peppery with dirt from scrubbed potatoes. She ran the cleanser-coated sponge down one ridge at a time, dipping hard into the scooped corner and sweeping down each row—like the even rows in the fields, hoeing in a straight line and beginning again, over and over.

Little Randy and his mother would be in Pine Gardens now, for the summer. She watched for them and for Mr. Thomas on the rare nights when she stayed during a party, but when she saw how nervous people were when they looked at her, how quickly adults glanced away, she realized that Mrs. Ray or Mr. Thomas would probably never see her. And children were always upstairs in these houses.

Pine Gardens—the fields of rice, corn, tomatoes, beans. Pinkie and Mary still moving up and down the rows—who worked with them? Laha's kids were getting old enough now. Aint Sister's house—how did it look, sitting near the granary? Or by the barn? The ancient fireplace must have crumbled when the house was moved. And her mother's house, her house—maybe the vines grew tight in the shutter cracks, or maybe Mr. Ray had taken it, too, to make his own tiny slave street.

After one party, Mrs. Despres, Tiny Momma's frail lady, ran to show Marietta water rings on two tables. "I can't believe someone would be this careless!" she cried. "Everyone knows about my furniture! This table was my great-great-grandfather's." She took a cloth from Marietta's hand and rubbed, her small hand whirling in circles, her face tilting up to Marietta's. "Do you understand what I mean? These tables have outlived people. They're a part of history. Two British generals sat and wrote letters on these tables!"

Marietta helped her rub out the faint circles until the wood shone clear as syrup again. Mrs. Despres touched her arm when she gave back the cloth, and Marietta was shocked at the coldness of the skin, at how Mrs. Despres trembled with fear that the tables were marred. "You want me help you up the stairs, ma'am?" Marietta said, afraid Mrs. Despres would fall. She supported her, both holding the polished banisters, all the way to the bedroom, with its tight spread and tiny lamp glowing.

Marietta walked slowly around the two rooms of her apartment that night when she got home. History. Mr. Thomas, Mrs. Despres live in history. Aint Sister thing gone but what I keep. She washpot with Laha, I hope. That washpot from gone time.

She remembered the pitted, coarse black iron of the washpot, and she went to the kitchen cupboard. The spider was there, the small three-legged circle of a cooking pot she had tucked in the bottom of one of the peach crates when she had packed that night, waiting for Lil Johnny. Why had she brought it? I think I might have fe cook outside, I cain find no place soon. Maybe cook in a field like cross the street. She ran her finger over the black roughness, trying to think of where she had seen that same metal. The wrought-iron gates—she had polished the brass nameplate on someone's house wall, and when she stood close to the gates, which had always seemed so smooth and lacy, she saw that they were pimpled with pocks and rust.

The palm-trunk mortar was in the granary, or in Aint Sister's moved house. History. She took down the Mason jars and wiped the tops clean. The colors hadn't dimmed: silver-clear, deep red, gold, palest green. Tiny Momma had seen them several times and asked, "What you keepin them jars for? We might could use em for some preserves this summer, you want."

Marietta had said, "I save this tea, I might need for drink sometime. Never know I get sick."

"You been had it forever, seem like. I seen you sick couple times, but all you do is polish them jars." She shrugged and cut more okra.

Who could she tell about Aint Sister? Only the boys had known her—and she was blurred-gone from their memories. My history. She walked around the apartment again, touched the tall vase-shaped basket, and ended up back in the kitchen, fingering the rice pot. Basket, pot, spider—all for work. No table, no old baby clothes press in boxes and lay out on little beds. No tiny boots somebody have when they small-small. No pictures. She opened the wooden box and sat at the table, staring at the picture of her father. One picture.

She spoke as little as she had to, even to Tiny Momma, who didn't seem to notice when she came each night. She sang a few words to the boys now and then, but they talked to each other, happy to keep her legs within touching distance on Tiny Momma's couch or her own while they played on the floor with the toys Baby Poppa picked up here and there. Baby Poppa watched her sometimes when he was home on the weekends, when they sat out on the piazza on chairs lined up to face the street and the field, where the kids played in the late fall heat. "I'm looking for the night spot to come free," he told her. "Quiet, easy, leave you to yourself. I see you prefer that. Night man keeps talking about wanting better hours. I'm waiting."

She was tired, more tired than she had ever been. She never knew if there would be enough money for the rent, and even though she worked enough days and nights to not hide from the landlady when she came knocking down the line of doors, each first day of the month frightened her. They ate the food Tiny Momma brought home sometimes. She thought about the job Baby Poppa described at his hotel, cleaning the lobby and the barroom in the early-morning hours when no one would have to see her, when no women would hover over and behind her to watch everything she did, or jump when she came around a corner and gasp when they surprised her in a room.

But when she tried to think to herself why she was so tired now—maybe it was because she only sat at the table or lay on the couch when she was finished with the cooking and washing, with no field or yard to work, maybe her veins and muscles were locking up, like Pinkie always said—when she thought about why the hours seemed longer as she went up and down the stairs at the big houses, she thought in surprise that it was the quiet. No, it wasn't her wrists aching from the wringing out of rags a hundred times, or her eyes stinging from ammonia, because she got used to that. The day of the party, cleaning, and the day after, the stains of wine and coffee in the tablecloths—she loosened the splashes of color with a paste, washed them out, ironed the heavy linens. She rubbed the tables, swept ashes from the floors she had waxed, blew the breath from the air. At home, she washed the mud from the boys' clothes, cleaned the brown ring from the tub, rinsed their shirts again. When she held them up to the light, the T-shirts white and dripping into the tub, she felt great satisfaction.

But she realized for certain one day, upstairs in a bathroom at one of the big houses, that it was the silence. She'd thought that couldn't be true. Only the cloth squeaking on the counters, the mirrors, her still face appearing everywhere against the pink curtains and walls. It was a shock—quiet? No one sang or talked. Lord God—she missed those humming voices? Rosie and Laha and Aint Sister? In the fields, laughing over the rows, Rosie singing, "Someday he'll come along, the man I love," and Pinkie shouting, "You been with Big Johnny since you fifteen! What you fe say!" Rosie laughing and saying, "Like I beena say, Someday he come along, the man I *love.*" Everyone calling out, "Hush!" Mary snickering to the others, "And Laha say Miz Briggs on a diet. Don eat nothing but fruit all day." "Lord God, I hate for be Laha and wash them draws this week!" "Hush, don be nasty!" "*I* ain nasty—I wash my own draws!"

The fish market—Sinbad's spinning lines of talk around girls, and his cartwheels of laughter with the men. The chatter of customers and ring of the register. She missed that? She scrubbed the bathroom sink now until it gleamed, pearly and shell-like, and then she began to wash the mirror above it. Sinbad—he was never quiet; even when there was a lull in customers, he read from the newspaper whether Frank wanted to hear something or not.

She reached to the side of the mirror and pulled the edge toward her to grasp it better and rub into the corners, and a hundred marbles fell out, clanking and cracking into the porcelain sink, bouncing onto the floor and even out into the hallway. The sound froze her, each marble seeming to land against her teeth, glass on her jaw, hard and gritted as tooth and bone. They bounced and rolled forever. Why had this white woman planned to trap her this way, she thought in panic. Was there money in the medicine chest that someone had stolen before? A few women always let quarters peep from rugs, or left dollar bills in chair-cushion creases. Had someone told this woman that Marietta stole? She couldn't move, afraid of the round glass that would pull her onto the floor and afraid of the woman whose running steps she could hear down the hallway now that the clacking had subsided.

Margaret, the regular maid, told her that night on the bus home. Mrs. James's mother-in-law was at the dinner. She always made excuses to use the upstairs bathroom, to straighten her stockings or check her hair, and then she snooped.

"How you know?" Marietta asked, incredulous.

"Miz James tell me. Complain all the time in the kitchen bout her mother-in-law, thinking she hide things all the time and don't tell her. Miz James in that kitchen complainin bout that woman so much I have to nod and uh-huh, cain't get nothin done."

"Why she don't tell she mother-in-law stop?" Marietta asked, and then she thought. No, I never tell Aint Sister or Tiny Momma stop nothing. But who got time for play with marble like that? How she get em in there? She didn't want to ask Margaret that.

Marietta heard the echoing rooms of all the houses when she walked up her street. She checked on the sleeping boys and sat at the table with Tiny Momma, who had cooked greens and ham hocks. Tiny Momma's voice wove around her as she ate, talking about Nate's new song—he loved to sing—and Calvin's hole—he'd dug for hours since someone had told him he could dig to China. They were getting grown—past four now, five in a few months. The radio next door was a trickle when Tiny Momma took a breath before the next story.

For the first time, she began to look carefully at their hair, from the back, when they were talking to the gardener or the other maids. The stiff curls and cloud sheen of the older women, the flat sheets of long hair framing the faces of the teenage girls. Bristled short fur standing straight up on the boys' heads. They were home from military school for the holidays.

The men had comb marks and stubble at the backs of their necks as they sat listening to cheering roars from the TV sets again, sometimes several of them in a den arguing about football during a weekend afternoon. She vacuumed in the other rooms with the same chopping motions she had used with her hoe, around the chair legs, in the corners, with the same familiarity that let her think while her arm swung: Defensive back? The noise of the vacuum gave way to her cloth, and then she could hear the sudden blare of shouts and cheers.

And the women who paid her, told her where to polish extra carefully—their hair sat in twists high atop their heads, or that smooth helmet with curls near their cheeks or shoulders. Their hair dryers were giant mushrooms that fit over their heads while they read; curlers in rows like sausage covered their scalps while they talked on the phone about which parties to attend for Christmas.

Once, the water wouldn't drain in the tub she rinsed, and finally she pulled the stopper; the long stem that reached into the drain was caught by a tangle of long hair, wet and matted, green and muddy as weeds in the marsh. Mud! Dirt washed off their bodies, too. She tried to look at the arms and legs of the woman who paid her that night, but the skin was covered with nylon and sleeves. The long brown hair was tight-circled at the back of her head.

Defensive back. When the boys had stopped whispering and shoving in their bed, and Tiny Momma went home, Marietta closed the bathroom door so the light wouldn't wake them. Then she took off her headwrap. Rubbing her scalp, washing her hair, lying in the tub water with her eyes closed, she imagined the warm water of the marsh, the long tangled grasses and reeds. Then she patted water from her ears and stood; in the cloudy mirror, her face was smooth and one-colored as always. Her hair was softer now than when she was a child, but not longer. She lifted the edge of hair near her temples with the comb, made the circle of close spirals even around her face. She looked too young like this, with the soft arch of her forehead free and exposed. She didn't even like Nate and Calvin to see her without her cloth and set mouth. She didn't like anyone to see her twenty-one.

She rarely had to whup them. She'd told each enough times that she would, but that wasn't it. They seemed to see that everyone else was respectful, even slightly fearful and distant, to her face; standing next to Tiny Momma and Baby Poppa, her size and face were even more intimidating, she knew. She had slowly become Big Ma, what the children called her to distinguish her from Tiny Momma and the mothers. "Big Ma mean," she heard the neighbor children whisper when she yanked Nate and Calvin into the apartment. "She don't never smile."

"Big Ma could whup anybody. Big Ma taller than yo daddy. So? She keep Nate and Calvin inside after dark. Big Ma mean."

People nodded to her when she walked home from work or took the boys with her to the store or went with Tiny Momma to pick up sheets. The neighbor men who sat on the piazza watching TV with Baby Poppa during the summer days when heat wouldn't be chased from the apartments, Joe and Victor and Richard, lifted their chins in greeting, or told her if the boys had been doing something they shouldn't. Two sisters who had moved in downstairs, Carmen and Jean, worked at a beauty salon, and they smiled but didn't speak.

She rarely had time to hug the boys, either, but time wasn't the whole of that. She kept remembering what Aint Sister said about spoiling them, making them soft, and it was easy with her arms full of clothes or still ashy-rough from scrubbing to keep that inside-the-elbow skin away from them. She hugged them only when they were hurt, whupped them only when they threw rocks in the field or ran into the street without looking.

But this Christmas, with the extra dollars she made working all the parties, she had bought them more than clothes and jackets. She had found bicycles with training wheels. Two. She didn't want them to have to share everything.

She asked Baby Poppa to come to the store with her, since she would have to put some money down and pay every month until the bill was gone. They walked to where the bikes hung shiny and small, and Baby Poppa shook his head and smiled.

"Your sons are so tall and husky that nobody seeing them on these bicycles will believe they're going to be five this summer," he said.

"They daddy was tall," Marietta said. "Higher than me."

"I'd guess so. Well, we'll have to get these gifts home somehow."

"Wheel em, huh? Keep em at you place till next week?"

Baby Poppa said, "I have a better idea. You know Jesse, just moved into the house next door. The gentleman with the wife and new baby?" Marietta remembered: Jesse was about her age, square-bodied and smiling. He and another man wearing dark green uniforms had unloaded a pickup truck full of furniture and boxes while a woman held a baby in the cab.

"That's his truck, the one he keeps parked there in the side yard," Baby Poppa said. "We can approach him and see if he'll pick up the bikes. I can keep them in the bedroom."

Walking home, he said, "Well, I'm glad you asked me to accompany you today, because there's an idea I'd like to discuss with you now." Marietta kept her pace slow beside him, swerving to avoid people on the narrow sidewalks. "I bought the boys books for Christmas. Children's books, at that same store we just left. The woman looked at me like I was crazed, of course, but I'm accustomed to that by now. When I open my mouth, I always have to decide how to talk to them."

Marietta hid her smile with her free hand. She loved to hear Baby Poppa's studied voice, the one he used most of the time. He slipped into an everyday voice now and then, especially when he watched sports with the men on the piazza.

"You will probably be as skeptical about this as you were about letting your sons stay with me when you first went to work," he said now. "They'll turn five at the end of May. But I'm betting you don't have a birth certificate for them."

"What?" Marietta said. "You lose me now."

"They were born at home, right? And no one recorded the birth?"

"My aunt. She pass now."

"That's what I thought," Baby Poppa nodded. "Well, they look older than they are. And they're advanced, Marietta. They love to look at the magazines I bring home from the hotel lobby. They pretend to read the newspaper when I do."

"What you talk about birth certificate?" she said, frowning. What he want—he cain have em. No.

"I think we should enroll them in school in the fall." He walked with his head down for a moment, so that she could see the dent at the back of his neck, under his grayed hair.

"School?" She saw eyes flashing past her, mixed up with the shine of the red-sparkled paint on the bicycles still gleaming in her mind. The dull, faraway blackboard. . . the stick across her palms. . . the voice of the teacher distant as an owl when Marietta stayed in the back row, refusing to look up or answer. . . the long walk, keeping herself apart from the others when they waited for Big Johnny's truck. . .

"Why I want em in school early?" she said.

"I know what you think of school. I know where you're from," Baby Poppa said. They turned onto the narrow street and she automatically listened for Nate's shouts and Calvin's laughter, but it was cold, and they were inside with Tiny Momma, probably eating. "Marietta," he went on, closer to her shoulder now. "I remember school, too. But this is different—this is a city, and if the teacher doesn't have a thousand Negro children in one classroom, your sons might learn something. They'll get a quicker start, and they learn fast. You've seen that more than I have. They are small versions of you."

She thought of them sitting on his floor right now, licking

cookie crumbs—What he want? "You ain't got time fe watch em, I find someone," she said harshly.

Baby Poppa said, "You're assuming something that isn't true. Listen—school keeps their energy harnessed, we hope. The field is full of kids who like trouble."

"You want em talk like you," she went on, walking faster. "You think I cain teach em nothing."

He laughed, breathing harder to keep up. "Every Negro speaks two languages! You're angry right now, and you're talking differently. I speak the same number of languages as you—maybe Nate and Calvin will speak three."

"They suppose fe be six go to school," she said, going ahead of him up the stairs.

"You have plenty of time to consider it," he said.

She heard them through the window. "Mama on the stair," Calvin said. "Mama comin."

Jesse and his friend Milton were groundskeepers at Charleston College, Tiny Momma told her. Baby Poppa asked if they would help with the bikes, and Jesse's round face almost hid his eyes. "Oh, no," he said, laughing. "Them two big old boys I seen playing gone have them some bikes? I plan to stay off the sidewalk for a long time."

His wife's name was Colleen; her tiny son was Jesse Jr. Marietta sat in their front room for a minute, waiting for Jesse's friend Milton, because they were expecting him. Jesse and Colleen's apartment was larger, the whole top floor of the house, and the baby had his own room with a crib and tiny pillows. Colleen laid him down gently, and he trembled his hands to his mouth. Marietta bent over the crib railing to smell his breath. Nate and Calvin were asleep in their room, and Tiny Momma was listening for them while Marietta went to get the bikes. When she took in the milky-clean air rising from the crib one last time, Colleen saw her. "I thought I was the only one like to breathe that," Colleen said.

"I forget how that smell," Marietta said, embarrassed. "Been long time." When she and Colleen went back to the front room, the man named Milton was there talking to Baby Poppa. "Let's go," Jesse said. "Santa Baby and his helpers got things to do."

"Wait, now," Milton said. "You didn't introduce me."

"Yeah, yeah," Jesse said. "This Marietta, she live next door. We on the way to get bikes she done bought for her boys. This Baby Poppa, you met him when we moved."

Milton nodded at Marietta. "Nice to meet you," he said. She nodded back, turning away from his stare. So? She so big. . . she so tall. . . she so black. . . I know. You ain't see nothing surprise me.

She rode in the cab with Jesse, uncomfortable, while Baby Poppa and Milton perched in the bed. "How old are your boys?" Jesse asked.

"Four. They five end of May."

"Little linebackers, huh? I see em out in the field. Wait till my boy gets out there, too. He's gonna give em a run for they money."

"That a long time from now." She smiled, getting used to his loud voice and wide forehead creasing. "He crawl for they money first, huh?" Jesse threw back his head and laughed.

"Well, he gon do that good, too," he said. "I want a tough one."

The two men put the bicycles in the back while Baby Poppa nodded. In the cab again, Jesse said, "I know they daddy proud of em, huh?"

Marietta said, "They daddy dead, back where we come from. Dead before they come."

Jesse nodded. "Sorry. Well, he can still see em from up there, and he probably keepin a eye on em." Marietta stared straight ahead at the dashboard, smelling the cigarettes and leather, clean and rich, no fish odor like Big Johnny's truck. Sinbad, watching the boys? She imagined Sinbad driving, saw his face twist above her, a drop of sweat fall from his forehead onto her chest, his chin drop to her ear—the bouncing cab made the twist in her belly even sharper.

"We takin the bikes to Baby Poppa's?" Jesse said. She nodded. When they pulled up in front of the house, she saw that Tiny Momma had kept the shades down, in case the boys woke up. Milton and Jesse carried the bikes up the stairs and into Baby Poppa's. When Milton came back out, he said, "Santa bring these bikes?"

"I bring em," Marietta said.

He smiled. "Nice. My mama always gave us pajamas and socks."

"Mmm-hmm," she said.

"Maybe I'll have to come by and see how they ride sometime." He turned when Jesse came onto the piazza. "Hey, man, you ready?"

"Yeah, we better hurry before Colleen gets mad."

Milton reached out his hand and said, "I'm glad Jesse got nice neighbors. I'ma have to see these boys sometime." Marietta touched his palm with hers and nodded, going to her door.

On Christmas morning, after the books and clothes, Marietta sent them down the piazza, saying, "Go get me some sugar from Tiny Momma. Hurry." She followed behind them and leaned as they opened the door.

"Bikes! Bikes! Look, Poppa! Wheels!" they screamed, and after they had danced around the spokes and tires, Marietta carried the bicycles down the stairs. Baby Poppa kept his hands on Nate's handlebars; she held Calvin upright. Tiny Momma shook her head and said, "I think she crazy—got cars on this street and don't look where they going. Gon knock they heads silly and we have to take em to the hospital. They just babies." Marietta tried not to let herself grin, but she couldn't help it when their hands shook on the rubber grips and Nate's mouth fell open in rare silence. Then he tipped toward the sidewalk and screamed before everyone's hands snatched him back.

When she didn't have a job, she and Baby Poppa spent the days with cold wind on their cheeks, shuffling next to the bikes until they were out of breath. Marietta could see Nate's behind shifting on the seat, his frown as he tried to position his weight, and she felt Calvin's hands pull on the handlebars to right himself when he swayed. They breathed so hard in their determination it was as if they didn't hear anything she or Baby Poppa said; they would find out how to balance themselves. She sat on the bottom stair to rest, and Nate howled when Baby Poppa took Calvin up and down the street a few times while he had to wait. "Come on," he said, trying to drag her up, and she shook her head. He got back on himself, but she jerked herself back onto the step. The old-woman voices in her head said, "He gon fall and crack his head! He be brain-damage—what kind mama you?" But she watched him fall slowly sideways onto the dirt of the yard, bouncing on his shoulder. He didn't cry. He got back up and dragged the handlebars as he had her hands.

They were exactly like her, in some ways—their faces when they concentrated, their impatience with instruction, the straight fall of their calves from their knees, their hair never growing away from their head but staying nestled and close.

But Calvin loved the water more than Nate. When spring came, he would abandon his bike sometimes to squat in the filling gutter, building dams and watching the rainwater rush past him when he sliced an opening in the mud-trash barrier. He stalked the huge puddles in the field, ruining his shoes—he even lost several pairs when he waded into the mud, and Marietta couldn't find the cheap canvas sneakers until the sun was persistent enough to dry the pools and leave the shoes bare and mud-crusted.

She hardly ever had work on Wednesdays or Thursdays, and sometimes she would sit on the curb in the sun with Calvin, looking into the trickle of gutter water where he dammed it. He dropped stones and pebbles inside, and she saw how the water was clear and brown-bottomed like her creek. This he creek, she thought, touching the surface to make it shiver in the sun. She followed him to the field, where a ditch held greenish water, and insects hummed at the edges. "Bugs live here when the water come, and they go when everything dry up," he told her. "Baby Poppa got a book show all the bug names—grasshopper, beetle, and all them kinda ants."

"Baby Poppa got a lot of books," she said.

"He always read," Calvin said. "Tiny Momma watch TV."

Marietta nodded. She and Calvin walked back to the yard, where Nate lay on his stomach in the dirt, shooting plastic guns at Robert, Carmen's son, who was ten. Two other boys from down the street hid behind the stairs, and Robert sneaked up on them, spitting bullet sounds from his mouth. "Y'all too easy," he said in disgust. "You babies."

Nate said, "You ain't hit me! Your head bald as Jesse Jr. *You* look like a baby!" Marietta laughed. Robert had his summer haircut, from his mother.

Nate was as quick-mouthed as Sinbad, always able to look quickly and say the right thing, even to adults sometimes; Marietta had to tell him over and over, "You teeth need catch some breeze every minute? Stop you mouth now." He and Calvin were darker, taller than any of the boys near their age. Nate walked with his shoulders back, telling smaller kids what to do and lecturing older ones if he could get away with it. Calvin circled him, watching, listening, always ready to back Nate when he was challenged. But it was Calvin who got pushed down one afternoon while Marietta happened to be hanging clothes on the piazza; Nate flew at the older boy's chest, not head down but smacking breastbones, and they rolled until Marietta wedged her hands into the tangle.

Her first thought of school had been of boys like Randy, and his shrill call "Monkeys!" But as Baby Poppa said, "Integration can't make children go to school together. All that fighting over drinking fountains—you won't see Charleston's white kids drinking after ours in school hallways, I know that." And he was right, she realized; all the women she cleaned for sent their children to private school now.

She asked Carmen's Robert where his school was, and followed him the three blocks and down the little side street. She walked past the building after that, when she went to the store alone or came off the bus by herself. But who could tell what was inside? On the playground, the kids screamed and ran in aimless and planned patterns during recess—so many faces, peach yellow and brown and darker brown. A few tiny faces black as hers, as Nate and Calvin. She saw Robert, and Eric and Shirley and Angie from down the street. But then bells clattered and the children disappeared inside, and she couldn't imagine what the teachers looked like, or the rooms. They were warm, she thought, no woodstove and gold light coming through cracked walls, but they still had blackboards, and the backs of rooms, where too-big children had to sit, were still dim.

She knew Baby Poppa was biding his time, letting her think, and she realized that of all of them, Aint Sister and her mother and Rosie, Tiny Momma now, only Baby Poppa had ever figured out who she watched and considered without saying, "Sneak and listen all the time? Just ain't right how she do." Tiny Momma still crocheted her talk, and Marietta listened right, but she knew sometimes Tiny Momma wanted more words to mesh in the air with her own, like different strands of yarn making a pattern.

On a Sunday in late summer, Jesse brought crates of peaches for everyone who gave him a few dollars. She and Tiny Momma made preserves, boiling the new Mason jars and drying them, stirring the bubbled fruit in pots until the steam dripped from the kitchen walls and their foreheads. Then they let the filled-bright jars cool on dishtowels. "You gon put em up there next to that tea?" Tiny Momma said, sitting at the table.

"Yeah." Marietta smiled at her. "But we gon eat em. Don't worry."

She went down to the lower porch, where there was a tiny locked room that had been empty for years. Jesse and Baby Poppa had found a used washing machine somewhere, and Marietta, Colleen, Tiny Momma, and Carmen had all given a few dollars to buy it together. She washed the boys' clothes and hung them on a line strung around her corner of the piazza. Tiny Momma napped on the couch with the door and windows open to let out the peach-sweet steam, and Marietta sat on the ancient couch at the end of the railing.

Baby Poppa had trailed a long extension cord to the other corner, where he set the TV on a straight-backed chair. The gloom of the piazza was enough in the afternoon for the square of the screen to flash. Bats rang when they hit balls, and Baby Poppa said derisively to Victor and Jesse, "That's it—only action in the whole game. How can you even care about these slow-moving fools and this simple sport, Jesse?"

Jesse said, "Look, it got strategy, too. Where he place the hit, or maybe he fixing to bunt. Football ain't everything."

But Baby Poppa said, "It's everything to me. It takes thought and muscle at the same time. I'm just passing the weeks here with you, waiting for the real season."

The kids had borrowed shovels and rakes and hoes from Jesse's truck, and in the field they dug and heaped wet dirt to make walls and trenches. Marietta listened to the boys' jeans drip water onto the wood and even way down onto the grass and dirt yard. She remembered that first summer here, when she had taken a heap of clothes out to the white-corded clothesline in the tiny backyard. A cluster of gray, faded pins hung at one end. She stood in the dust, pinning, and she saw streaks of mud along her palm, lines of mud on the white T-shirts. Puzzled, she leaned closer and saw a mountain of dust on each white plastic cord. No one had used the line for months.

She rubbed at the dirt marks on the wet clothes. Then Baby Poppa came around the corner of the house with a jar full of bacon grease swaying dully inside the glass. "Good morning," he said to her. "I can never keep up with this excess." He looked at her clothes and said, frowning, "You're not trying to hang those up, are you? I see the dirt. No one hangs clothes back here because someone will come in through the fence off that alley and relieve you of your garments, or your sons' garments. Sometimes they can sell clothes."

"Steal clothes?" she repeated. He went to the back fence, which leaned crazily in toward the yard, and poured the grease carefully into a hole near the base of the wood. He brushed dirt over the hole with his shoe and came back to her.

"People steal whatever they think they need," he said. "You'd better hang those on the piazza where you can watch them."

She pushed the wet clothes now with her finger. In the heat, they stiffened quickly. Baby Poppa still teach me, and I grown. Tiny Momma still teach me. Loretta have for teach me that first day in the house, how for clean right. Nate and Calvin know more than me cause they little and live here, they learn bout the city and swim pools and cars. They gon go to school next month.

Nate's face was sometimes hard as hers now, and Calvin rarely smiled. What did she want for them? They gon go school, get smart, know a lot more than me. They gon be so tall, so big, so black—like me. Like they granfather. What they fe do? They talk back to anybody—they never see no white people. Maybe they have big mouth, big shoulder, big head, and they get in trouble. Maybe they go work like Jesse and Baby Poppa, they have for see white men all the time tell em what fe do; they don't crack they teeth, they lose some job. She listened to the men shout at the TV again; the boys were receiving long and detailed orders from the older kids about where the trenches should be directed.

Milton pulled up in his old battered car, and she saw him look up at her and smile.

"He sweet on you," Tiny Momma said, right behind her, and Marietta started. "He ain't a bad man. Work over there to the college, on the grounds, that steady work. He seem real nice."

"You scare me," Marietta said, and Tiny Momma smiled.

"I scare you? Or he scare you?" She went into her doorway to get more ice tea, and Milton came up the stairs.

"Nigger, you ain't invited!" Jesse yelled. "This a private party—unless you got some beer!" They all laughed, and Milton held up the paper bag like a prize.

"I ain't no stranger," he said, looking at Marietta. "Right?"

She leaned against the railing, shrugged, and watched him settle down on one of the folding chairs. "But does your ticket have the right name on it?" Jesse said.

"Nigger, I brought your Pabst—don't fall out," Milton said,

pulling bottles out and setting them on the wood. "But they ain't gon stay cold for long."

"They won't *stay* long with Jesse here," Baby Poppa said, and everyone laughed.

"Marietta, you want a beer?" Milton said, his eyes still on her. She shook her head as one of the kids ran up to the yard.

"Big Ma, Nate say he can keep a knife. He find a knife in the field," the boy sang. "Calvin say he can't."

"Calvin right," she said, looking down at the dirty upturned face and bared teeth. "Tell he bring me that knife."

"He said Nate had the knife," Jesse said.

"But Calvin only one can get something away from Nate," Marietta said. "He know how to move him, where he ticklish." She got up and started down the stairs.

"Big Ma?" Milton said to Jesse. "They call her Big Ma?" She walked quickly to the field, where Nate and Calvin were still shouting at each other, and she didn't hear what Baby Poppa and Jesse said, but everyone laughed again. She waited for her face to burn with anger—but instead she felt only the sun on her shoulders. They say what they want—maybe they laugh at Jesse, maybe somebody drop the baseball. I don't care no more. She stepped into the dirt and said, "You better use you head, Nathaniel, before I slap it."

The dirt-crusted butter knife in her pocket, she turned to see the men all turned back toward the TV, Tiny Momma's face peering out of her doorway, and her boys' shirts like stamps against the dark piazza, the big face of the apartment house.

All afternoon, Milton smiled at her, asked her questions, and Baby Poppa, Jesse, Victor, and the others argued about baseball. When he asked, "When's your birthday?" she said, "Eleven August," without thinking because she was watching a pitch. "That was last week!" he said. "Why you didn't tell nobody?"

Baby Poppa looked at her. "She doesn't like birthdays, maybe."

Marietta kept her eyes on the TV. "I got the boys' birthdays for worry about—I too old for birthday."

"I doubt that—how old are you?" Milton teased, moving his knee to hitch his chair closer. "Too old for presents?"

She looked at Baby Poppa's light brown eyes, Milton's slightly red, Jesse's small slits in his smiled-high cheeks. "Old enough," she said.

"You too old to eat without your boys?" Milton said then. "Too old to eat out with me?"

She didn't realize what he was asking at first, until Jesse and the others looked away carefully, thumbnail smiles on their lips, and she remembered that stiff, formal way the men in the fish market had held themselves whenever one asked a girl out. He wanted to take her to a restaurant. Milton smiled, his mustache thick as a paintbrush over his lips, his teeth square and small for his wide face and body. "I old enough for that," she said, and the men all relaxed and let their shoulders go, their hands moving for more beer.

She lay on the couch listening to the radio next door. Friday—she and Milton would go out on Friday, and Tiny Momma would watch the boys, of course. The songs tinkled and beat, and the announcer's voice was deeper, fuzzy in the plaster. She never heard anything but the music—no rattling dishes, no voices not filtered through the radio's tiny mesh, not even footsteps. No one ever changed the station. But she had stayed awake many nights to watch the man go—only a bent back and dark hat over the door lock when she put her head out her own door. He pulled the knob shut silently and turned toward the stairs, so she never saw anything but his back floating down the dark street.

For a long time, when she first came back to Charleston, she had imagined that the silent old man was her Uncle Hurriah, that his music was now the radio she heard all night, until he left at midnight, even after he was gone. She had finally asked Tiny Momma who he was, and Tiny Momma said, "He a hermit—he ain't never spoke to no one, not even the landlady, since he been came here years ago. He leave her rent money in a envelope under her door."

"He leave the radio on even after he go to work," Marietta had said. "Who there for listen?"

Tiny Momma shook her head. "Nobody else there. He must leave it on for the roaches."

She purposely avoided asking anyone else about the man, calling him Uncle in her head. She knew he wasn't, but sometimes she thought about all the old men in Charleston, floating on the streets, drunk or nodding or walking to work, smiling at the boys. She turned over on the couch, away from the window that let in the street light, and thought of her old room, her uncle's room. Sinbad. When she looked in the travel section of *Ebony* at Baby Poppa's, or asked him for old travel magazines from his hotel, she put Sinbad's face in the photos, but she knew he would find a street like those she never saw in the pictures—one with a fish market or hamburger joint or café, with dark faces bobbing and weaving in the streets, long feet flat on porches and in doorways. He might have ridden the cable cars in San Francisco, licked fog from his lips; he might have gambled in Las Vegas, where neon lights wrapped around the streets like snakes and fireflies; he might walk underneath tall shadows of skyscrapers in Chicago or New York, but she knew he slept in places on streets she couldn't find in the magazines.

He been you excuse. He been some lips you think on so you ain't have for bother with nobody. You never see him again—nobody ax you bout he no more, cause he dead. You always say he dead. Let he dead then.

He one more spirit, she thought when she sat in Milton's car. He one more haint—Aint Sister, Mama, all watch me go out for eat. Milton turned on the car radio and bent his elbow out the open window. "What you want to eat?" he said. "You name it."

But in the restaurant, which she had picked because it wasn't far away and she remembered coming to ask the manager for a job, she sat across from him in the booth, uncomfortable. Milton's face was always across from hers, when they stood, now when they sat, his eyes always directly on her face. She wasn't used to such close looking, to someone watching her lips when she chewed, her mouth when she spoke, her eyes wherever they moved. The boys, Baby Poppa, and Tiny Momma were all far below her; the people in the big houses always avoided her face, turned their ears to her as soon as they could. Milton—what he want? He laugh? He stare cause I so dark, so, so. . . he go to work tell Jesse what I fe do?

He talked about what he and Jesse did at the college. "Man, you should see them wild cats hiding in the bushes—them animals get *big* off what they scrounge from the students. And they be wailing at night, when they gettin ready to fight. Jesse says that's how little Jesse be wailin when he mad—like some wild tomcat."

She smiled. "I hear he holler sometime at night. Colleen have she hand full." Why you talk like that? Talk like Baby Poppa—you hear how. Why you talk like Pine Garden? You always make hard fe people.

Milton said, "Your two boys never hollered like that? Big old lungs they got, they must sound like bulls when they get goin."

She said, "I don't remember." But she saw them plowing along in the mud behind her in the field, growling when she left the room, roaring when they first woke from sleep. "Maybe lion," she whispered.

"What?" he said.

She shook her head and took a small bite of her meat. In his car again, driving along the waterfront streets, where the moon made the river and harbor pearly-silver, she was quiet, smelling the dashboard. Car insides, truck cabs would always make her think of men—the metal even breathed their smoke and liquor and cologne and hands. He seemed not to care that she didn't talk; he drove around for a while longer, listening to the radio, and when they came back down her street, he said, "You want to do it again?"

Jesse and Colleen encouraged it, and Marietta could tell they liked the idea of her with Milton, of the two of them settling down. Jesse would knock on her door and say, "Milt fixing to come by—you want to play some cards? You like to play tonk?" Colleen would smile at the two of them, ask Marietta, when they had gone out for more beer, if Milt had bought her anything or kissed her.

Tiny Momma loved it even more. "What you think he like to eat?" she said. "I have it ready when you get home from work, cause you at Mrs. King's tonight and she keep you late. I get off early and buy some ham hock if he want peas."

One or two nights a week he sat on the couch, a plate of cake or cobbler on his lap, their plates cleared off the small table. Marietta said to Tiny Momma, "You ain't have for leave yet. I need you help me iron them two clothes for school. Baby Poppa say school start Monday."

Milton sat politely while Tiny Momma sprinkled and rolled the stiff clothes and Marietta pressed with the heavy iron. He and Tiny Momma talked about the college; she always asked him about the beautiful buildings and the students. Marietta listened to them and to the boys' whispers in the other room, to the radio's tiny taps against the wall, to the kids still playing in the street and the people talking on the piazza.

She didn't work that day—she told Mrs. Hendricks she couldn't come to do all the heavy laundry and windows until Wednesday. She and Baby Poppa moved with the mass of children and knots of mothers down the several blocks to the school, with the women hollering about no playing in the field with school clothes and school shoes, and where your money, boy? You ain't gon eat nothing for lunch *or* dinner.

Women sat at a long desk to fill out papers, and Baby Poppa stayed by Marietta's elbow when one older woman with high-teased hair asked the boys' names, age, address, birth date, place of birth. "You are their mother?" she said, looking up imperiously, and Marietta nodded while the woman's pen scratched over the papers.

They brought home papers with their names written in large, round letters, and the alphabet, numbers, in different colors. Baby Poppa left those books Marietta remembered—the house and the yellow-haired children, the thick pages and pointy roofs and brown dogs. She tried to read to them every night, their thighs pressed to hers, and she cupped their hands around pencils to practice letters.

But the week after, she noticed Calvin getting hurt almost every day, coming in from the field where the summer light still hung on. He stood close, nudging her like a calf when she stood at the sink or stove, and she didn't listen at first when he moaned about his cuts, trying to think of how she could wash the clothes that had piled up so quickly, and dry them at night.

Calvin wound in around her thighs until she sat on the couch and put her arms around him to examine the tiny scratch on his wrist, thin as a thread. "How this happen?" she would ask, and he said, "A-o-know." He pushed his head into her stomach and she touched the hard knots of hair by his neck, the ones she would soften and pull out with her fingers and the shampoo. Every day, it seemed, Calvin had one of those identical straight slashes on his thumb or arm, and he wanted to sit in her lap in the evening. Milt would stop by, and he and Tiny Momma had to sit at the table because Calvin didn't want to leave her legs. Nate would say, "You a baby, Calvin. Rock-a-bye baby." Marietta told him, "Hush and take you bath."

"He ain't gotta take bath?"

"He come." She asked Calvin, "Who scratch you up? You play with a cat?"

"A-o-know. They hurt, Mama. They was bleeding." She washed out the cuts and rubbed his back in the tub, frowning.

The teacher in their class sent a note home, asking Marietta to come in, and she expected it to be about Calvin. Was he fighting, getting cut by fingernails or even a knife? She left Mrs. Despres's house early with Tiny Momma, and she asked Tiny Momma to wait with the boys by the school fence.

The teacher was young, about thirty, Marietta guessed, and she sat behind her desk in a cement-block room filled with small wooden desks and posters and cutouts of letters. She was light-skinned, plump-faced, and her arms shook like Rosie's used to. She said, "Mrs. Cook, the boys are obviously twins, and obviously big." Marietta nodded. "Well, they're so much larger than the other children I think they're actually intimidated by the kids. I mean, Nate does fairly well, but when they're all in here and we begin a lesson, Calvin just refuses to talk, and Nate gets very defensive about his brother. Calvin seems to be disturbed about something."

"I think he fight with somebody," Marietta said. She breathed, calm, and smelled glue and wood. She imagined Calvin at the back, looking at the many heads stretched out below him, and thought maybe he was angry about the other kids. But she looked at the desks and saw names on them: Aaron, Aubert, Burns, Carvin, Cook, Cook. The front row.

"Have you seen them fighting?" the teacher said. "I haven't yet. Do you think Calvin has a problem with his schoolwork? Is it too easy or too hard for him? One of the other teachers tried to tell me that the boys had to be eight or nine, and they must have flunked out at another school, especially because you couldn't provide a birth certificate. I think they act as though they're six. I told her they were really six, because I had seen *you* bring them." She smiled, and Marietta tightened her chest. But she went on, "I have a daughter, and she's as round as me, unfortunately. I watched it happen."

Marietta let herself smile. She listened as Mrs. Williams said that Calvin had to talk in class or she'd have to consult with the principal about separating the boys. Marietta walked back through the dark hallway to the playground fence, but she didn't say anything until they got home and the front door was closed.

"Why you won't talk to the teacher?" she asked Calvin. He shrugged.

Nate said, "Cause he a baby, Mama."

"Nobody ax you," she said.

"Well, he don't know his ownself." Nate curled his lip in scorn, and Calvin said nothing, just stared impassively at the refrigerator.

"Close *you* mouth for a change and maybe he answer," she told Nate. But she watched them push and wrestle every night; in the morning before school, if she was still home, she saw Nate talking, gesturing, and Calvin studying the others. In the evenings, dressing the cuts that still appeared almost every day, she held Calvin alone, telling him stories about the fish that swam up the river and under the bridge, how they chased each other under the boats.

Tiny Momma said, "He playin with a cat, cause that the only thing make scratches like that." Marietta pushed the reddish meat from the ham hock into the greens and said nothing.

She stayed home for three days, telling the women who had hired her she was sick, telling Milt she had the flu, and after school she watched out the window. Calvin wasn't in the field on the second day; she saw Nate, trying to hit a rock with a stick, and she saw another boy and girl. She opened the door quietly and went down the stairs.

He was behind the house, where a tangle of rusted mattress coils and a pile of boxes hid him from the street. She padded as quietly as she had near the basket stands, peering over the orange-crusted metal, and saw him sitting on a peach crate, holding a razor blade between his fingers. He was examining his forearms. She drew away from the junk and placed her feet carefully in the dust, going back to the apartment to wait.

On the stairs outside, she held him while the dirt yards up and down the street grew cool and moist with the night. Tiny Momma called them inside to watch TV, and while Nate lay on the floor in front of the screen, she kept Calvin half in her lap, half listening to Tiny Momma say how Mrs. Despres had coughed all day, but she was thinking of the slice in her palm and the blood she had swallowed for the pounding, twisting babies. She traced her fingertips near his ear, remembering the sweetness of her mother's neck when she was hurt, remembering how she'd turned tall and no one would touch her gently.

She went to Baby Poppa in the morning. "I see one or two cut every other day," she said, after she'd told him about the razor blade.

Baby Poppa put his finger and thumb into those half-circles around his mouth and ran them down again and again. "Boys come to the street to fight them," he said finally. "I've seen them come all the way to the vacant lot to look for Nate and Calvin. They stand out at school, I imagine; they're different, they're big, and they always have each other. They're targets."

"I don't see em with bruise or cut like that," she said.

"No, you don't. Nate talks a lot, trying to scare the boys, but it seems like they want to fight Calvin. Everyone wants to hit the quiet boy, make him talk or cry. And they both get teased a lot about the way they talk. I don't know. I think they'll have to fight for years. I was too small to have to prove myself."

"Why boys always want fight? Girl tease and yell, but boy. . ."

"Too much energy," Baby Poppa said. "See, they watch everybody fight and they want to do it. But that's not the only reason Calvin's doing that to himself."

"I know," she said. As the blade sliced his skin, did he think that no one could hurt him if he hurt himself? She knew he still wanted her eyes and hands, but she was careful not to touch him so much that Nate and the others would tease. She watched closely for when he wanted fingers and attention, and she pressed grains of sugar and fine spiderwebs into the cuts.

When Milton came by in the evening, the boys were asleep. He said, "Come outside for a minute. I know, they sleepin, but just for a minute."

He leaned against the railing with her; the fog was rising over the field. "You want to go to a movie again tomorrow?" he said.

"I have for work a party, all afternoon and night. Halloween party," she said.

"When I'ma see you? Seem like you always busy now," he said, moving behind her and putting his hands on her shoulders. "I thought you have more time since the boys in school now."

"Fall usually busy, and then the holidays," Marietta said. "Boys busy every season." He turned her around and pulled her to the corner.

"When's Milton season?" he murmured, and his lips, hidden under the mustache, weren't soft like Sinbad's, but tighter against hers, and the hairs prickled. His head wasn't bent; his mouth was straight and hard on her. "Can't you be Marietta and not Big Ma a couple nights a week?" he said when he pulled away.

She didn't answer. He pulled the backs of her shoulders toward him again, and she didn't mind his mustache as much this time. He fanned out his fingers across her back and kissed her harder, until her lip burned from the sharp hairs and pressing. "I have for be up early," she said. "I have long day at work tomorrow."

"I'll stop by on the weekend," he said. "I'm sure you can find a few hours for me then, huh?"

The house where she worked the next day was huge, with a circular staircase that had a banister to be polished, with marble floors in one large room, with a chandelier collecting dust on the pear-shaped droplets of glass. And the windows, as always—she washed them last, when the afternoon wind tossed the tree branches outside in the walled garden. It was strange not to hear the wind, the rubbing leaves. She wiped the glass, tasting her lips with her tongue and biting them with her front teeth. Milt just pressed, moved, on her mouth; Sinbad had somehow softly twisted her lips open, tasted the undersides, even his teeth gentle. She shook her head. Sinbad lips dead. They spirit, kiss women all over the world. I still here. She moved to another window, watched the silent wind, remembering her mother's house and the wind that lived inside with them—lifting her collar in summer as she stirred rice by the open door, pushing through the cracks to raise her mother's hair when they sat in bed winter nights.

The wind had scared Nate and Calvin when they were tiny, and they would hold her in bed while it screamed through the trees, coming hard off the water. It always reminded her of the hurricane, the first night with Sinbad, and she had to work hard to forget him then. Months would pass and she'd be fine until summer when she knelt to pick tomatoes in the row behind the house and she felt hands smoothing across her back, between her shoulder blades, the same place where Milton rested his fingers last night.

Nate and Calvin would explore her blouse, press palms lightly on her to feel the texture, and then one or the other would lay his cheek and whole chest across her back where she bent, while palms patted her gently. It seemed that they were marveling at her, draping themselves on her all that summer when they were past one and just walking. Then a caressing hand would rub dust into her neck to see how much could cling there, while they both laughed.

But after they were asleep, she imagined other palms traveling her back, the callused fingers exploring her rib cage and the slope at the base of her spine. Testing, smoothing, pulling—it was weeks again before she could forget those few nights with Sinbad.

Milton's hands covering her shoulder blades—they fit? Calvin's breath, puffing against her neck when he nestled against her on the couch, hadn't made her think of anything for a long time. But she wasn't sure about Milt—maybe he was part of the reason Calvin cut himself. She saw the razor blade, imagined it rusty and the cuts swelling despite the sugar, despite the ointment Tiny Momma added.

That weekend, after Milt had come over in the afternoon and watched football with Jesse and Baby Poppa, she told the boys, "I'ma go to a movie with Milton. You two think he okay?"

Calvin shrugged and said, "He ain't funny like Jesse."

"What you mean?" she asked.

"He don't never say nothing funny," Nate said. "Jesse make you laugh. Milton just sit and look. Stare at you."

Calvin laughed. "He Jesse best friend, huh, Mama? Best friends ain't zactly the same—they different."

"Not like you and Nate," she said. "Sometime friend opposite, cause they get along that way. Milt get along with me okay."

"He boring," Nate said, and she frowned at him.

"You ax fe opinion, not fe get smart-mouth," she said. "He grown, and you ain't, so I don't want to hear nothing disrespect."

She watched Calvin's face when Milton came to get her and Tiny Momma walked with the boys down to her apartment, but he smiled and waved. When she had hugged him goodnight, she felt the last week's shallow cut, only a beaded line of scab on his arm, dry and raised on his skin.

Thanksgiving brought several jobs, and she worked at Mrs. Despres's house for three days, moving the furniture carefully and lemon-oiling the legs of chairs and the tabletops. Mrs. Despres said, "I trust you with my heritage, Marietta, because you're understanding about its importance. Mozelle has told me many times about how you appreciate working here."

Marietta kept her cloth moving, but she frowned when Mrs. Despres left. Mozelle? Oh—Tiny Momma's name. She remembered when Mr. Ray had called Aint Sister "Eva." She whirled the oil around on the long dining-room table, where Mrs. Despres would have twenty people for dinner, where she would have vigilant eyes on the glasses and drops of water scattered by the guests who would leave her to flutter around the empty rooms and touch the shiny surfaces and delicate lace.

Marietta needed more money. Baby Poppa kept mentioning that the night man might leave soon, that he was unhappy with the hours. But nothing was certain, and the boys were eating platefuls of food, outgrowing jeans and shirts monthly, needing pencils and paper and balls and shoes. The rent would go up on the first of the year, Tiny Momma had heard.

And Milton paid for dinners, for movies, even asked her a

few times if she wanted to stop at the store to buy food or soap. "I can help you out a little," he said, but Marietta didn't want to owe him too much. She had grown to like the smell of his car, and she liked kissing him and feeling the bend of his elbow around her neck when they sat on a street in the leathery air. She didn't like sitting on the couch with him, where he pressed her onto the cushions; the vinyl seat of the car wasn't as frightening as her own front room with the refrigerator hum and occasional cries of Nate or Calvin.

She didn't want Milt to own her. Jesse and Colleen and Tiny Momma said: "You two so serious, now? I see that car pull up late. When y'all get settle? He just a lonely bachelor till he see you." She just shook her head.

"Not enough room for nobody else in this place," she said.

"So you two can move somewhere else," Jesse said, but then Tiny Momma would cut in.

"No, she ain't taking my boys far, now. Don't even think that."

"Everybody got a plan but me," she said sharply, and they all dipped their chins at her. "I can plan my own."

She wasn't sure if she liked expecting him, waiting for him, wondering what he did during the day and at night. He lived with his grandparents, Jesse said; he'd never mentioned taking her to meet them, or told her where his parents were. They probly light like he, probly fall out he take me over there. And fall out again when they see Nate and Calvin.

She didn't think he only came to her for fooling around, because she didn't even let him do much, afraid she would get pregnant again. He had to have patience or another girlfriend, she thought, but Jesse said he only talked about her. Still, she didn't like the familiarity she felt, and she wasn't certain why it made her so nervous. Sometimes she let him kiss her and start to work at the buttons on her shirt only because she didn't want to talk.

One day before Christmas, when the boys had gone around the corner to the store with Robert, Carmen's son, Marietta sat outside because the sun had come out unexpectedly to warm the wood all day. She laid newspaper by her feet to catch the walnut shells. Tiny Momma had asked her for a pound of walnut meat so she could make a cake. It was Tuesday, and she knew Milton would come around, but she had just settled herself with the bowl when his car came down the street.

"Hey," he called up to her. "Jesse home yet?"

"He don't live here," she said, but then she relented. "He up there. I see him few minute ago."

He would come over in half an hour or so. She watched him go into Jesse's, and she thought, I make some coffee, give he one a them tea cake Tiny Momma bring for the boys. Too early for eat a meal. You plan for he come round regular now, huh? She dropped the shells and picked at the walnut meat, just wondering where the boys were, when a police car cruised to stop next to Milton's car. She started, wondering what trouble Milton was in, and then Robert and Calvin got out of the back seat. She dropped the bowl and heard the nuts clack on the wood.

"Mama! Nate hurt!" Calvin cried, running up the stairs. She turned him back to the yard and the policeman said, "Mrs. Cook? This your boy?"

She said, "Where Nate, Nate Cook?"

"He ran out into the street and bounced off a car, so we took him to the hospital," the policeman said. "This little boy here's been crazy trying to fight us, wanting to come here first, but anyway, the other one's not hurt real bad. Kids bounce like rubber."

Marietta grabbed Robert's arm. "Why you ain't watch em?"

"I did!" he said, snatching his arm away. "Nate seen a dime in the street and he didn't look. He too quick for me."

The static voices over the radio barked out the car's windows, and Jesse, Milton, and Colleen came down the stairs. Baby Poppa looked out the door, awakened from his nap. Marietta ignored them and pushed Calvin to the car. "Take me to the hospital, please," she said to the policeman.

Milton and Jesse yelled, "Where you going? You need a ride, Marietta?" She slammed the heavy door and Calvin started to cry again.

Nate was still waiting in the emergency room, the other policeman with him, and his nose was swollen, his arm stiff. He sobbed into her shirt until the policemen left; he finally went to a room to see a doctor. "He got knocked on the pavement, mostly," the doctor said. "Burns and scrapes—here's ointment. I think his arm's okay—bruised pretty bad, but he fell on it right, on the good side."

She didn't understand half of what he said, but Nate had recovered enough to defend himself. She called a taxi, and while he said, "Mama, I look, but that car come round the corner. I seen money, Mama, in the street," she sat silent, looking at the red lights of the ambulances. She didn't want to think about what could have happened, what had happened, how the car had thrown him onto the sidewalk. She didn't want to think of the bill.

His arm had started to ache as the taxi drove home, and he began to cry again. Calvin cried, too, and they both fell asleep for a few minutes in her lap, in the back seat. She felt them start upward when the car stopped, and they walked like zombies toward the stairs.

Doors opened and light spilled out everywhere; Tiny Momma and Jesse and the others all ran to see Nate. Milton came to hold her, though, and she pushed him away gently. "They need for rest," she told him. "We see you all tomorrow." Tiny Momma followed her in the door, as part of the "we," and Marietta was glad she'd come to make coffee and hold one boy.

It wasn't until the front room was silent and empty, and she sat on the couch, that she began to shake. Nate's skin, pink-raw under all the scraped skin, now glistening under ointment—his eyes swollen from crying and nose with rims of blood she had rinsed, pink, too—everything pink and frighteningly exposed. She had seen his eyes closed, his mouth empty of air, in that moment when the policeman stepped from the car, she had seen water streaming from his ears or blood from his mouth, and everything inside her shook hard—her heart against bone, her hands on the cup of coffee.

Milton's voice came through the door. "Marietta? You need some company?" he called. She opened the door and he said, "You okay?"

"I ain't hurt, Nate hurt," she said shortly, and he didn't move past her.

"Can I help you with something, maybe just talk?" he said. "Take your mind off everything?"

She stared at his mouth, his eyes, the way he didn't ever smile now, just watched her as if waiting, and she thought, I don't want nobody more worry bout. Worry bout them two hard enough—and Tiny Momma, Baby Poppa old—they gon die. I see too many buryings already. No—ain't nobody bury now.

The whole idea of dying made her angry, made her see Nate's face again the way she'd been afraid it looked, and she couldn't stop her voice from cracking, like it had when anyone talked to her at Frank's. "I don't need no help—I need for you stop coming round every minute. I have too much thing fe do with you always here. I talk to you later."

After she had closed the door, she didn't hear his car start for a long time, and she thought, So go see Jesse and them—they need company every second. They cain live without talk. She kept seeing the police car behind Milton's, remembering that at first she'd been afraid for him.

It rained for several days after that, and she was glad to keep the boys inside, talking only to Baby Poppa or Tiny Momma, running back and forth from the bus. No money for Christmas, not with the hospital bill and the way the boys ate; only enough for clothes and maybe a few toys. She hoped Baby Poppa would get more books, that Tiny Momma would make plenty of cake. She avoided Milton for weeks, telling him she had a cold, that the boys were sick now, that she had night jobs. And then Baby Poppa came one morning to tell her that she did have a night job.

"If Mr. Powell approves you, that is. He's the manager, and

he wasn't confident about hiring a woman," Baby Poppa said, leaning forward on the couch. "I've been waiting since I started watching the boys for you, telling Mr. Powell that if Lee quit I had the perfect person to replace him. I knew Lee would quit—he's your age, and he likes to be out drinking and dancing during those hours."

Marietta said, "Mr. Powell ax me question? He want reference?"

"I told him you had a reputation for excellence, and that you'd been working in the Charleston area for some time. If you don't mind, and you probably do, Mr. Powell will probably just look at your physique, since he's nervous about hiring a woman. That shouldn't be a problem."

For once, she didn't tighten—she thought about herself, about this Mr. Powell's eyes, and she shrugged. "Ain't no problem for me," she said, smiling.

"We'll go down tomorrow, on the 28th, and if he approves, you can start work on January 1, 1967. An auspicious beginning," Baby Poppa said.

That afternoon her house was clean and smelling of coffee; she drank a hot cup, watching Jesse out in the street with Jesse Jr. and the boys, rolling a football to his son and getting Nate and Calvin to chase after it. The field was muddy with rain. She had cleaned huge houses around the smell of cedar and pine, watching women hang red ribbons and taste eggnog and wrap gifts. This hotel a regular job—regular pay. Next Christmas I buy Nate and Calvin something good. Maybe even for they birthday.

"I walk," Baby Poppa said.

"I know," she said, heading down the street with him. The boys were with Tiny Momma. They passed the stores on King Street, kept on toward the historic area.

"Why are you avoiding Milton?" Baby Poppa said. "Did he do something wrong?"

She told herself, He got the right. He can ax—don't vex cause he ax. "He ain't do nothing wrong. I just busy." Poppa waited. "I don't need nobody else for care about right now. Too hard with Nate and Calvin, too hard with you and you wife. Four all I can worry bout."

"But with a man to help worry, some of the burden would be lifted from you," Baby Poppa said seriously, looking straight ahead.

"Maybe," she said. She thought for a moment. "But I don't think Milton that kind. He want me—I don't know he want worry, too." She tried to change the subject. "How you talk at the hotel?"

She thought he hadn't understood, but of course he did. "Well, you have to look at the faces to judge which Negro they want," he said. "My schoolteacher voice—some of them don't mind. Oh, I wanted to go to college, when I kept growing in mind but not in body. I wanted to be a teacher like my great-aunt Helen, who sent me letters and books. My grandmother's sister. But they only hired women teachers then, and colored could only teach at colored schools, of which there were few. Everyone made fun of me on the farm, but here, well, you have to look closely at their faces, but of course you can't let them *see* you look that closely. You know all this."

"Maybe I don't know these hotel people, these guest," she said, but she remembered Mrs. Ray talking about going back to the hotel because the House wasn't clean and ready for her. This hotel? Another hotel? "In Pine Garden," she said, "we talk what they call 'old-time talk.' Nobody understand if you don't want em hear."

"You still do that now," Baby Poppa said. "I've heard you speak your other language. Even Nate and Calvin do it. But I don't think you'll have to talk to anyone but me at the hotel. And that's the way you like it, right?"

"Me and Calvin," she said. "But Nate favor his daddy. Love to talk, love hearing them word fly out."

"It took me some time at first to tell them apart, and I don't just mean Nate's mouth always open," Baby Poppa said. "But anybody who knows them can see."

"Calvin eyes bigger. Nate mouth bigger." Marietta smiled.

The lobby of the hotel was lit by a huge chandelier, which cast shifting sparkles onto one wall. The marble floor gleamed near the door, and the wood floor was thick with wax. The deep-cushioned couches were wine red, and heavy draperies touched the floor. Before they crossed the floor to the office, Marietta touched Baby Poppa's arm. "In summer, I be home with em all day. And after school now. Thank you, Poppa. I need something for count on, and I gon make you wife so much chicken for pay her back she tired of my chicken."

Baby Poppa was Larkin here. He was the doorman, bellhop, elevator operator, and general handyman during the night hours. They were early tonight, to see Mr. Powell, and Marietta watched nervously while Baby Poppa went to a door behind the huge lobby desk. The white man at the desk, thin and pale, put things into the mail and key slots behind him and then registered two men who didn't even see Marietta where she stood in the hallway.

He used his schoolteacher voice. "Mr. Powell, this is Marietta Cook, who I've told you is perfect to replace Lee. She's stable, reliable, and extremely trustworthy."

Mr. Powell had reddish cheeks—that was all she saw, as she was afraid to look directly at his face. She didn't want to see Mr. Ray's kind of face. But Mr. Powell was already putting on his heavy coat after he glanced at her. "She's your responsibility anyway, Larkin," he said. "Bring her in Friday during the day to sign the papers. And tell her to do a good job in the bar—Lee was sloppy." He stopped to talk to the desk clerk for a minute, and then he went out the huge front door, letting in a gust of cold air.

Baby Poppa raised his eyebrows at her. "I told you the place was mine at night," he said. "You're not supposed to start till Friday. I'll show you tonight what you'll have to do, and we'll add these hours in there somewhere. New Year's Eve is going to be crazy as usual, and I want you to have a quiet night to learn everything."

In the early evening, from seven to midnight, guests still came in to register, and Baby Poppa took care of their luggage, showed them to their rooms, and operated the elevator. Marietta was supposed to clean Mr. Powell's office, and toward midnight, when the lobby was mostly empty of the people who had sat there earlier, she vacuumed the carpet, cleaned the furniture, and washed the big windows in front. She cleaned the marble and wood floors with a mop, and Baby Poppa showed her the large closet where all the supplies were kept. He had an old easy chair inside, where he sat to rest now and then with the door closed. But mostly he was everywhere in the hotel, going up in the elevator with drinks late at night after someone rang the desk, disappearing into the bar, where laughter rang out sometimes. She wouldn't clean the bar until after it closed, at 1 A.M.

Tiny Momma had said, "I gon pack you all lunch for the first day she go," and at eleven-thirty they sat in the closet, where Baby Poppa had put a folding chair for her. They ate fried chicken and biscuits, cold sweet-potato pie. The smell of the cleaners and damp mops was strong, and Baby Poppa watched her sniff. "I'll tell you what we do," he said. "I eat this meal quickly, because we have a break coming at one-fifteen, when the bar is closed. I think you'll like that free time better. Save some of your pie."

After the last customers had been turned away and the big, square-faced bartender named Paul had left, Marietta and Baby Poppa went into the bar and closed the doors. "I'll have to stay watchful in the lobby," he said, "but this won't compromise our time too much. After all these years, it seems that I have a sixth sense for when someone wants something. Here—have a seat."

They sat at one of the tables near the long, gleaming wood bar littered with napkins, ashtrays, and crumbs of food. The floor was sticky under her feet. Baby Poppa was smiling, and he went behind the bar to get her a glass of ice water and a napkin. "This is the break I look forward to," he said. "Lee only had eyes for the liquor. I brought something else for us." He went back out and came in with two buckets. One steamed. He put the soapy-hot-water-filled bucket near the bar and brought her the other pail. Inside were rolled-up magazines, newspapers, even a paperback book.

They spread out the magazines on the table. "This a lot of new one," she said. "Where you get em all?"

"*Time, Newsweek, Sports Illustrated, Harper's, Ladies' Home Journal,* and the Charleston newspaper," he said. "People read when they travel, and they discard these when they leave. I find them everywhere, and one of the day ladies saves me the reading material from the rooms she cleans. Take your pick."

She thumbed through the *Ladies' Home Journal,* but all the ads for cleaning supplies only reminded her that the bar area was waiting, and she grew nervous. "Ain't we have for start?" she said.

"First day," he said, shaking his head. "You can't wait. Well, we have about forty-five minutes to relax on our usual schedule. Trust me—you can clean this place leisurely and be done by two-forty-five. We leave at three. But let's get started now, and you'll see how quickly it goes."

New Year's Day. Everyone crowded into Tiny Momma's as usual: Jesse, Colleen, Milton, Carmen, all the kids—everyone held plates of Hoppin John and Greens, chitlins and pigs' feet. The chitlins made the air heavy and ripe, their steam rising from the huge pot on the stove.

Milton sat next to Marietta for a moment, but she got up after she had smiled and went to make sure Nate and Calvin didn't have too much food on their plates. The covered dishes were on the table, and she adjusted the towels over the warm food. People stopped in and out all day. She stayed standing, tasting the peppery greens, giving Calvin more Hoppin John. Victor came in the door, with a friend named Joe and Joe's teenage son Christian. Baby Poppa said, "No, now, I don't want to hear that the Green Bay Packers gon win it all. Don't even begin that litany today—the Super Bowl isn't for two more weeks. And I want Kansas City—I'll take the Chiefs. The Packers are a football machine without style or soul."

"They got points." Victor laughed. "They ain't gotta have no soul."

"Milt!" Joe said, slapping Milton on the back. "I ain't seen you since we went down there to Mount Pleasant."

"How you doin?" Milton said. Marietta watched him talk to Jesse and Joe, and she moved to the kitchen to rinse plates and check the pots. Tiny Momma left her seat next to Carmen and came into the kitchen, too.

"You better go on and sit next to him," she hissed at Marietta. "Everybody see you ain't spoke but a word. What you doing?"

Marietta swirled water into the sink. "I'm cleaning dish," she said.

"That a good man," Tiny Momma said, pulling at her arm. "Go on sit down now."

Marietta kept her elbow stiff until Tiny Momma let go. "You actin like a child," Tiny Momma said. "Ain't got no reason to let that man go."

Milton stayed for another half hour, and she eluded him carefully, picking up Jesse Jr. and taking him to the bedroom to change his diaper, staying in the kitchen, keeping bodies between Milton and her. He said, "Thanks, Momma," to Tiny Momma, and then he leaned down to say something to Baby Poppa, who sat with the other men near the front door. After he had gone, and Joe and Victor and Christian had eaten and left, Jesse said, "Why you breakin my man's heart?"

Marietta sat on the couch near Colleen. "He heart ain't broke."

Jesse was angry. "He ain't did nothing wrong and you treat him like a stepchild. He ain't gon come lookin for you forever."

"Good," she said. "He need for look somewhere else."

Even Colleen said, "What you got against Milton?"

Marietta said, "I ain't got nothing for him." Tiny Momma sucked at her teeth and Marietta's face grew hot.

Jesse snorted.

"You got a problem," he said, and Baby Poppa told him, "You are all making her very defensive. Let it go."

She sat, blood rising to her neck and face, thinking, Don't none a you know me. Don't know my problem. What I need? I don't need worry. All I need is money. I need Nate and Calvin black—no pink show on they skin, no blood. That all I need. You all need for shut up. De-fen-sive. She stood up, saying to Baby Poppa, "I see you tonight."

All night, cleaning the floors and polishing Mr. Powell's big desk with its papers stacked in piles at the edges, the word skipped in her ears—defensive. Defensive. She heard it in the roars of laughter from the bar, tried to remember.

A defensive back stuttered his feet backward and threw out his arms to hit the receiver, or he ran, feet flying in step with the receiver, to knock away the football. She looked out the window of Baby Poppa's and heard shouts coming from Jesse's apartment. Tiny Momma was napping in her bedroom, while the boys were at Jesse's with Baby Poppa, watching the Super Bowl. Marietta studied the tangled patterns on Baby Poppa's TV, the waves made of players as they ran and hit each other, remembered the men saying all fall, "Look how slow he is! Shit, I coulda caught that. And they gave that quarterback, what-his-name, all the time in the world."

A defensive back was her height, not as padded with bulk as the men who crouched at the line facing each other; the defensive backs were dark, poised on their toes, their arms hanging loose, waiting for the ball to move.

In the mornings, the boys ate biscuits and grits, and then when they were gone to school, she napped, cooked for dinner, sat with Tiny Momma and sewed up holes in their clothes or read while Tiny Momma crocheted, winding words around her. "You been let that Milton go, I don't see how you gon get nobody else with you crazy hours and always close-mouthed. I don't know what you thinking about. Don't have no man around for help." The don't clicked like the crochet needle against a fingernail, and they were so small that Marietta only nodded and smiled.

With Jesse and Colleen, though, she kept her face wood. "Lotta people work nights and still speak," Jesse said. "But now my man Milton don't even want to come to *my* house, so he ain't gotta take a chance on seeing somebody who can't speak." Marietta kept silent, imagining her cheeks oak and her forehead pine.

She packed her lunch at six, kissed the boys where they lay by the TV, and walked with Baby Poppa. They passed each other in the lobby until break, ate quickly in the closet-room, and then she met him in the bar.

"I use to keep magazine in a car fender," she told him, and he laughed. They spread out the pages and read silently, or she asked him questions. Her favorite was *Sports Illustrated.* He let her pore over the football articles and ask him about the offense and defense, the pictures that were an unintelligible knot of arms and legs, and he helped her sort out the players, the positions and movements of the ball. The season was over, but he kept this stack of magazines in his room, and she agreed with him. Basketball was fast and exciting, baseball was subtle and boring, and football was the one she loved.

He teased her. "Now you're just saying that to please me."

"No." She stopped. Why did she like it? "I tell you sometime" she said, because she wanted to think about it. He went back to the lobby and she washed the tabletops and mopped the gritty floors.

Mrs. Despres sent her a message through Tiny Momma. "She say you the only one she trust round her furniture, sides me, and I too old to do all that she want. She havin a spring tour and she need you," Tiny Momma said. "I told her you need you rest."

But Marietta couldn't sleep more than a few hours during the day. She finished all her work and then didn't like to sit and think, to worry about the boys and remember Pine

Gardens, to pace around the small rooms. More money—she could save for birthdays, for shoes. The boys grew taller and wider still, and they ate three pieces of chicken, platefuls of greens, slabs of cornbread for dinner. A pie lasted less than a day now. She told Tiny Momma she would still work for Mrs. Despres, and she sent word to her other ladies that she would do party preparation but she wouldn't stay after three. They had never wanted her to serve unless it was an emergency anyway, and now she only cleaned in silence, all morning and then through the night.

She liked to keep moving, and each day was a swirl of walking, riding the bus, turning from sink to stove in the kitchen, circling the boys' bed to pick up their things. She saw Colleen in Tiny Momma's living room a few times, and Colleen's belly swelled. "My girl comin now," Jesse said, and he seemed to forgive Marietta. She knew why one day when he said, "Milton got a girl over there in Mount Pleasant, Tiny Momma. Say they might even get married next year." He looked at Marietta pointedly, and she grinned and shrugged.

"We finally gon have a baby girl round here," Tiny Momma said.

"How you know?" Colleen said, her hand always on her stomach. "Kick same like Jesse Jr."

"Feet don't make a boy or girl," Tiny Momma said. "Look how you carry, look you ain't so sick. That a girl."

"We got enough boys around here," Jesse said. "Even for me."

Marietta was glad that the heat of summer came and the tourists left, so that no one scheduled tours or parties, because she liked to stay home during the days with the boys. Even though they didn't want to walk with her or go to the store the way they did when they were younger, she could sit on the piazza and watch them.

She saw it when Nate chipped his tooth. The kids were stalking him in the yard, and his eyes were closed. Blindman's buff. Calvin sneaked right behind him, and Nate was so busy smiling and talking that he didn't hear anything. His hands were stiff in front of him, then waving around, but when he whirled suddenly he thrust his face forward, and his open mouth met Calvin's smile.

"Owww, Mama," he cried, running toward the piazza.

A corner of his left front tooth was gone, from the force of meeting mouths. Calvin was frightened, staring at the hole in the white line of teeth, and Nate cried, trying to hit him. The other children watched her nervously. "Big Ma mad," one whispered. "She gon whup em silly." But Marietta laughed, to their surprise.

"That what you get for have you mouth crack wide every minute," she said to Nate. "And now nobody think you Calvin, think he you." Nate ran inside to look at the mirror, and by the next morning, *he* was smiling broadly and showing a pink bud of tongue through the hole.

He went to school, running behind Calvin, and Marietta curled up on the couch as best she could. She thought of the gap in Sinbad's teeth, his sweet mouth. She realized with surprise that she could think about him now and feel only warmth between the hipbones, that she could think of Milton and feel a warm arm around her neck or waist; she didn't miss them, didn't feel angry or pushed, didn't feel anything but a pleasant taste like barbecue sauce tingling around her lips long after she'd finished eating the ribs. Not hungry anymore, just remembering. She slept all morning.

The radio never stopped, but the listener had died, and Marietta and the others found out only because someone from the hospital where he was the night janitor came to find out why he'd missed work for days. The name on his identification was Hosea Williams. Marietta saw the white stubble on his cheeks, a forest of gray hairs against the brown skin, whiskers that had kept growing even after he stopped breathing.

Nate and Calvin were eight now, and they watched with fascination as Hosea Williams's body was covered and taken away by the coroner. That afternoon, when they came home from school, Nate said, "How old Baby Poppa?"

Marietta didn't know. She knew Tiny Momma was sixty, because they'd had a birthday party for her that year. Nineteen sixty-nine—Tiny Momma had been born in September, 1909, she liked to tell everyone: 9-19-09. But Baby Poppa never mentioned his birthday. Tiny Momma said, "He hate that foolishness, so I celebrate for him, too. Give me his presents!"

Marietta couldn't tell that night, looking at his face, whether he would be angry if she asked his age. They met in the bar, and she studied the reddish skin, the deep half-circles around his mouth and crescents under his eyes. A face of curves—she remembered Frank's face of stripes. Baby Poppa held a magazine away from himself to squint at the page, and he said, "Look here at this—they had demonstrations at trade unions and construction sites in several big cities."

"Who?" Marietta said absently.

"Up-North Negroes." He shook his head. "Everybody thinks up North is better, they always try to tell me that, but the truth is, certain jobs we can't get anywhere. They won't hire a Negro carpenter over a white one up there, either. You can clean, though—just like this—all over the country."

His hands were so small next to hers when she took the magazine. While she read the article, he had gone on to the sports section of the newspaper, and when she looked up, he said, "Now here's the only place a Negro can hit a white man and not get killed. He'll get paid, even get cheered. Football. No marching to integrate sports—they couldn't keep the best out."

She kept hearing his words all week, because she saw Nate and Calvin as tall as Baby Poppa, towering over the other boys. Suddenly they were fighting again. Coming home from school, every boy in the neighborhood wanted to challenge them. Calvin tried to dissuade them, but Nate jumped ready, and one Thursday he came home with a bloody lip, breathing hard, and went to their room to change clothes without stopping to talk to her. She let him go, thinking she'd catch his arm when he came to the kitchen, but an older boy yelled in the yard: "Nate Cook, I come up here to whup yo ass! Come on!"

When she went outside to scowl at the shouter, she opened her mouth in horror. A boy slightly smaller than Nate stood behind the bigger boy, and his face was swollen and thick with blood. "Nate do that?" she said.

"He whup my little brother Timmy. You can hide him if you want, but I'ma kill him," the older boy said.

Marietta stood there, as breathless and shocked as she had been when she saw her boys covered with ancient dust and peach juice. Calvin came around the side yard, from the back, and the boy ran for him. "I ain't Nate," Calvin shouted.

"So? You was there," the smaller boy cried, and Marietta ran downstairs, where Calvin was rolling in the dirt with the big brother. She and Baby Poppa pulled them apart, and the older boy screamed, "I waitin for you, Cook." He ran down the street, and Marietta called Nate outside.

"He start it, Mama," Nate said. "Everybody start, not me. They always want to fight us."

The other boy's face had been terrible, grounds for a parent or principal to come see her. His eye was only a slit. She dragged Nate by his arm to the tiny backyard: "You come too, Calvin."

"I got an advantage," she hissed when they stood, facing her, and then her hand shot out into Nate's face. She hit him with her hard palm curved outward, on the back, the behind, the shoulders, while he ducked and cried. "I don't have no switch—just my hand. But you don't want fe hit me, huh? I got advantage—I bigger than you, stronger. That's what you got with all these boys, you too big and strong, and I don't care they come at you or no, you hit em once and tell em quit, you and Calvin hold em stop the fight. You stop em so they quit, not so they fixin to die. I never want see something like that again."

Nate's lips hung open with saliva and tears, and Calvin

sobbed, too. She let them run upstairs to the apartment, and she went to Baby Poppa's.

"How I gon tell em not to fight?" she said, burying her head in her arms at Tiny Momma's table. How could she explain to Baby Poppa, to the boys, about their faces? Her boys' faces would never be right for most of the teachers, for white people, for other kids. How could they win before the blows by carrying themselves right? She didn't know how to talk to them like that—they were supposed to learn from watching a man, doing what he did. And Baby Poppa, across from her, was a small red man with a beautiful voice—not a Cook with blueblood and her eyes.

For once, Baby Poppa said nothing. All the way to work, she wasn't sure if he was angry at her for beating Nate, or disappointed that she hadn't let the older boy fight Nate to settle things.

On Saturday, Baby Poppa gathered all the boys in the neighborhood at the vacant field. She watched them hunch over suddenly, combing through the high spring grass, and they collected sticks, bottles, rocks, cans. Pieces of broken glass were held aloft like prizes, and their pile on the street grew. Then Mr. Sims, who lived a few houses down, pushed his lawnmower down the street and began to cut the grass. It took him an hour to show them how, and then the boys pushed the mower up and down the big field until the green was short and thick. Not level, but they assembled and Baby Poppa shouted, "You need gloves and balls and bases for baseball. You need a court for basketball. But you all are big enough and smart enough to play the real sport—football. Let's go."

She sat on the stairs and watched; from that height, she could see them running all summer in lazy circles and confused bumping. Then they learned a few patterns, and they began to fight over who should play quarterback. Baby Poppa let them all try, and Jesse got out there, too, with Jesse Jr. trailing along. Nate argued that because he was so tall he could throw the ball over anybody trying to defend him, and Baby Poppa only smiled. "We'll see," he said.

Walking to work one late summer night, not a holiday, she and Baby Poppa smelled barbecue smoke hanging heavy in the streets. They came upon crowds of people milling about, women by smoke-wafting barbecue drums, even kids running in the dark. "The hospital strike," Baby Poppa said. "Those women think they'll get a dollar thirty-five an hour starting pay."

Marietta stopped by a lamp post to watch the people laughing, talking quietly, resting near buildings. She looked nervously for white people to career past in cars and wreck something, but only dark faces looked back.

In the bar, Baby Poppa shook his head. "Those hospital administrators aren't going to give them a dollar thirty-five," he said. "They don't have to. Marching, singing—oh, that was almost ten years ago, and white people are just as hard."

Marietta closed her eyes for a moment, saw Stan and Loretta, the white men's thin lips pulled back so tight they disappeared. Baby Poppa said, "All that struggling we did to eat and drink and swim. . ."

She interrupted him. "You were there?"

He lined up magazine covers in a perfect stack. "Huh. I

wanted to be, but my wife was afraid. She didn't want to go, and wouldn't let me. She said that was for young people, because they hadn't seen enough to scare them off. Like we had." He was silent, and she thought, I hope he don't ax me. I young and still scare too much. Scare for everything.

While she cleaned, she thought of Hosea Williams, the man that had lived next door all those years, the shadowy ghost who walked to the hospital each night. She imagined him demanding more money from a man with a face like Mr. Ray's, but then, wiping down the windows and looking into the dark streets, she realized that Baby Poppa had called the strikers "those women." She read the articles about them in the newspaper, saw that their faces were as impassive and faintly smiling as Loretta's.

She told Baby Poppa in the morning, "Come with us to see someone. You read about she, come today." She took his shoulder, glad Tiny Momma was gone at work, and they brought the boys near the singing and pacing women to see the face of Coretta Scott King, Dr. King's widow, who led the march. Her sculptured features, her set mouth, her hair waved away from her forehead—she reminded Marietta of her mother. Baby Poppa shook his head. "Impressive," he said. "But white men aren't worried."

The boys liked the carnival atmosphere, the food and kids everywhere, but toward evening the crowds grew angrier and rocks sailed through the air. Marietta and Baby Poppa hurried the boys home, and they went far around the strike when they left for work, because sirens wailed through the streets. "Boys carry rocks," Baby Poppa said.

But the women won. Marietta slapped the rolled newspaper next to his hand where it rested on the shiny bar table. "I'll be damned," Baby Poppa said. "They got the raise. A bunch of women."

Marietta smiled. "Women more patient than men any day. Stronger than you think." She sat down. "And get they way without scream and yell, if they smart. I hear you yell at them boys in the field, want em learn everything in a second. I like em for see them women in the street, march patient."

Baby Poppa grumbled, "Your boys and the rest of them just want an excuse to try and kill each other. No finesse at all out there."

The boys weren't a team, not even close—by early fall they were still a bunch of kids who ran around the field hollering. Baby Poppa and Jesse sent them down the grass to catch passes. Marietta heard Baby Poppa say, "Let's be patient, now." He rolled his eyes at her. "Marching women. Marching boys. Let's run some drills again." When he taught them how to block, the only one who could stand Nate's blows was Calvin, and the two of them danced, hit, hugged each other all day. Nate tried to go around Calvin, and Calvin took the shove and turned, still facing his brother, covering him everywhere he twisted. Even after school began, Baby Poppa had them out on the lot whenever it wasn't raining, and sometimes it was just the two of them, sliding past each other and leaping to catch the ball Poppa threw.

She walked next door to Jesse's with Baby Poppa and Tiny Momma, but when Tiny Momma and Colleen played with Letricia, who crawled and smiled, Marietta sat with Jesse, Joe, Victor, and the men to watch football. Nate and Calvin burst in from outside, smelling of autumn dirt and leaves, and Nate said, "See! I'ma be quarterback and tell everybody what they gotta do. I'ma call the plays like he do."

"What you want to play, Calvin?" Jesse said. "You want to be Nate's wide receiver, since he throw like everybody ten foot tall? You the only one can catch what he throw anyway."

Calvin said, "Maybe." Marietta smiled at him when he lay flat in front of the TV to watch.

"You ain't gon be no quarterback," Victor grumbled. "Gotta change color for that. They don't like no black quarterbacks."

"They got that boy over there at USC, in California," Jesse said. "He's tough enough."

Marietta liked the quarterbacks, the wide receivers, and runners, but the longer she saw the game the more she thought the heart of football wasn't the throwing or running, but the players bumping in the middle, over and over. Watching the games each weekend with the men, she had found her eyes traveling to the ball, of course, but now she thought about the bigger men hitting each other and the gaps they filled or closed. Joe liked the defensive lines, and he argued with Victor about whose line was best.

"Naw, L.A. got the Fearsome Foursome," he said.

"But Minnesota got the Purple People Eaters," Victor said.

"They got a stupid name," Baby Poppa said.

"Four brothers and a Swede—you seen em? Marshall, Eller, Page, and Larsen. Check em out—they the toughest."

She studied the defensive line, the way they got past blockers. When Marshall and Page smothered a quarterback, a finger of fear traced her spine at these huge black men crumpling a white man like that, throwing him to the dirt like he was a pile of cornstalks and then walking away without even looking back.

"Oh, man, I love to see Marshall do that shit," Joe said. "Bart Starr ain't no good. Johnny Unitas ain't no Jesus. Marshall and Eller givin em a big nigger hug. Lemme see a brother throw that ball."

Mrs. Simmons hired her after Christmas, for a January Super Bowl party, she said. Loretta was still Mrs. Simmons's regular housekeeper and cook, and Marietta told her in the kitchen what the boys and Tiny Momma and Baby Poppa were doing. Loretta had moved to St. Philip Street, where she and her sister had bought a house.

"You watch football?" Marietta asked her.

Loretta shook her head. "Don't have time to fool around with that mess. Don't nobody in my house like sports. All women by us!"

"I ain't seen Mrs. Simmons' interest in football," Marietta said. "This Mr. Simmons' party?"

Loretta raised her eyebrows and stopped arranging cheeses on a tray.

"Huh," she said. "You know better." They both laughed.

Everyone at home was watching the game over at Jesse's, of course. Marietta put trays of crackers, cheese, olives on the long table; warming dishes of tiny sausages and meatballs and a fondue. Mrs. Simmons's sister-in-law arrived early with her husband, and Marietta heard them arguing in the kitchen. Then Mrs. Simmons went past Marietta to talk to her husband, who was in the den, as usual. He shouted, "We're having a dozen guys over here to watch a football game—why do we have a cleaning woman and a cook again, why do we have to get upset about which goddamn kind of napkins to put out and whether your brother remembered to bring a decanter?"

"Because those dozen men are bringing their wives!" she shouted.

"Well, shit, all we really need is two TVs and enough liquor for a Super Bowl Sunday. We don't need wives—why don't you ladies all go somewhere for a permanent tea, or an eternity of shopping?"

Marietta smiled at Loretta in the kitchen. "Gotta have her hand in," Loretta murmured.

"Twelve couple is a party," Marietta said. "Mr. Simmons ain't learn that yet? I learn, and I ain't even live here."

The women all sat in the parlor and the dining room; the men sat in the living room, where one TV played, and in the den, where the opposing team's supporters watched another TV. Marietta caught glimpses of the game when she passed doorways to collect plates. She heard one man say, "Look at that throw—what an arm!"

"And that little nigger can catch."

"The throw was on the money. Anybody can catch when the throw's perfect as that one was. Hell, I could catch it."

"Norm, you better stick to catching shoplifters," someone said, and they all laughed.

Marietta smiled to herself in the kitchen, bending over the sink. All that undivided attention to quarterbacks and running backs—the real game on that line, she thought. Defensive line stop the runner, blitz that quarterback arm and whole body. Offensive line force the hole, give that white boy time for look who he pass. That the work, up and down the field, on the line.

They couldn't play in the hard winter rains. They squirmed in the small rooms, growing and growing, downing platefuls of food and entire cakes and pitcherfuls of lemonade when the weather warmed. She took all the parties and tours she could for spring, coming home from the hotel to eat Tiny Momma's biscuits with the boys and Baby Poppa, walking with the boys partway to school and then taking the bus to the big houses. Like Tiny Momma and Baby Poppa, she never really slept, and so time passed too quickly while she napped on the couch or shelled peas and peeled peaches. Even now, she remembered Pinkie complaining, "I have fe go. I sit, I get all stove up, my vein stop. Have fe work."

She understood why Laha and Rosie used to complain about months slipping past when you had children, because in the hours of cooking and cleaning and washing, in the nights at the table with Baby Poppa and the afternoons at another table with Tiny Momma, time passed without her knowing. The boys were already ten, and nearly to her shoulders now. She measured the seasons by grass and football games in the field, then the games on TV with the men, and by the holidays. The February azaleas blooming and tourists filling the streets downtown. The heat of summer again, and school over to let the boys live in the field.

Tiny Momma checked on them during the night, a spirit in

her nightgown on the piazza, and if Calvin had a bad dream or Nate woke hungry, they went to her door.

Marietta sat, tired after a long Saturday at a house on the Battery. She had washed out their pots and stove burners, dusted picture frames and glass china cabinets and moved all the furniture to vacuum behind it. Her feet were circles of bone on the linoleum now—round aches under the heel and ball and each toe when she stood up to go check on the washing clothes.

When she sat back down, Tiny Momma had lain down on the couch. Marietta scratched her head. Even her fingernails hurt, throbbed all under the nail, through the pads, like the nails were pulling themselves loose from the bed underneath them. She stopped, pushed her fingertips under her scarf again, heard Aint Sister say, "Lord God, I so tired my fingernail hurt."

She'd always thought Aint Sister was just exaggerating—how could hard, horny shells hurt? What did they do to hurt? Wiping, plucking, wringing out—Aint's nails had been thick and spooned as duck bills, squared and swollen. Her mother's nails were so hard she'd trimmed them with a fish knife.

Marietta sat entranced. The first thing she ever remembered about her mother, the first memory in her mind, was the warm mouth around her fingers, biting off her nails. They must have been thin as paper then, like Nate and Calvin's had been when they were tiny. Putting her fingertips in her mouth one by one, she felt even the pressure and warmth of her tongue hurting them, the nails angry and pulsing. She took them out and blew on them gently, cool air against the wet.

But she had saved enough extra money for the boys' football uniforms.

She went to Baby Poppa that night in the bar, in the gloom of dark wood and smell of beer and cigarette ends and perfume. "You remember you ax me why I like it?" she said.

It took him a minute. "Football," he finally said.

"Mm-hmm." She took out one of the *Sports Illustrateds* and showed him a picture. "Mean Joe Greene. Look—he ain't smile. Look his face. I see those football player, black as me and bigger than anybody, like some people you know. They running over people, beat em to the ground, and white people love it, everybody love it. Scream and holler. Look my face. My daddy look just like me, my boy look like him."

Baby Poppa said nothing, just looked at the pictures, leafing through the worn, limp pages she had turned so many times at home. "You mean the intricacy of the game doesn't matter?" he finally said, smiling at her.

"Leave me lone," she said. "You tell me they learn all they can in the field. They ready for that junior league you want em in." She waited for a minute. "And maybe you ain't need to be in that field so much then. You getting tired, huh?"

He frowned. "Do I look tired?"

She saw his chin up. "I never ax you how old you are. I worry bout you throw and run all day with them two."

Baby Poppa went back to the bar for a glass. He poured a tiny bit of something gold into the bottom of the glass and said, "You're making me take to drink." She waited. "How old do you think I am?" he asked when he came back to the table.

"I don't know," she said. She didn't want to guess.

"I was born in 1900," he said softly. "My child died in the same week I would have turned thirty. You're not even that old, and you have boys playing football. How old are you?" he said, looking up sharply.

"Old enough," she tried to joke, but then she said, "I turn twenty-six this year."

Baby Poppa nodded. "Well, for all I know, you could have had gray hairs underneath those headscarves you always wear. Please don't judge my abilities as a coach by my appearance." He smiled and put his small, hard hand on hers.

It wasn't anything like the frozen tangle of bodies in the magazine photos, or even the faraway views from the television. All the players were easily scanned on TV, and she could track the play, watch the movements of the line and the receivers all in a glance.

Here, on a Saturday when she had refused a cleaning job, she stood beside Baby Poppa on a field and looked at the helmets, trying to watch Calvin as he crouched. On the sidelines at the junior league games, she could hear the cleats scrape the grass, hear the helmets clack like those marbles on the tile at first, and then when the heads banged inside, the plastic sounded heavy and hurting. The bodies fell hard on the ground. "Calvin get his man?" she had to ask Baby Poppa. She couldn't watch right from down here; she wanted to be higher up, like she was on the stairs or the piazza when she watched them in the field.

"He did," Baby Poppa said, distracted. "I don't know what

they think they're doing with Nate. I have a feeling they *are* going to use him as a wide receiver."

Calvin's smile showed under his face mask and above his chin-strap. This time she concentrated on the line, saw him taller and wider than the defensive man, and he lowered his shoulder to glance the boy off so that he could chase the quarterback. "That how you show him all these time!" she said, and Baby Poppa nodded.

Nate came in on the next play, and Baby Poppa said, "I thought so. He wants to be where he can get his hands on the ball, and he's been trying to talk the coach into wide receiver. Look at him—he's tall enough, but I don't think he'll remember the pattern."

Nate stood only slightly bent, and when the ball was snapped, he ran a pattern, but the ball went to the other receiver. Nate jerked his shoulders impatiently and she saw his pads move; he walked back to the huddle slowly. "He so impatient," she whispered. It was three plays before the quarterback threw to Nate, and then the ball slid past his palms and hit him in the chest.

At home, green-kneed and ashy-elbowed, Nate was still angry, even though the Cougars had won, 14–0. "I could play quarterback better. Baby Poppa always talk bout the coach right, I should play defense. I could throw, Mama."

Calvin said, "Huh-uh. You too nervous, always jump like a puppet when you looking to throw."

"Shut up."

"Mama," Calvin said sharply. "Baby Poppa say he our daddy when he sign us up."

She looked at him. "That okay."

"He ain't."

"No. He you poppa, *been* you poppa. Not you daddy. You daddy die. You know that."

"Where he bury?" Nate stared at her too, the way they fell in together sometimes like spoons in the drawer.

"I don't know. Don't know how he go either," she said, uncomfortable. "It don't matter. Baby Poppa like you gran."

"Well, he don't listen when I say tell the coach let me play offense," Nate grumbled. "Don't even want me play wide receiver. Want me play defense."

"Let me tell you something," she said. "You pay more attention to them game on TV, like I do. You gon see who in the action every play. And Nate, you crazy. You got a talent for see a shift and know how to get around somebody. I seen you all them time in the field and when coach try you on defense. Everybody think defense boring, but it the best part of the game."

"Mamas ain't suppose to know bout no football," he mumbled under his breath, turning to the refrigerator.

She let that pass. "You be fine on defense you give it a chance. Watch, sweetheart, like I tell you."

"Mama, what you know?" Calvin said. "You never play."

"If I did, I could whup you both," she said, laughing, picking up the light jerseys. After they were clean, Calvin came back out to the living room, saying, "But our daddy was big, huh? Bigger than you?"

She was surprised. "Yeah, taller, but he ain't fat."

"I thought he die," Nate said, behind Calvin, and she corrected herself.

"He wasn't fat before he gone," she said, carefully.

"We gon be taller than you," Calvin said.

"We gon be bigger, too, cause we men and you ain't fat." Nate nodded triumphantly and got a glass of milk. His feet were long and slanted on the floor in front of the refrigerator when he studied the leftovers.

"Our daddy skinny?" Calvin asked, staying in the doorway.

"No. Ain't been fat or skinny. Just regular." She folded her arms.

"What he like for eat?" Calvin kept on.

"Hamburgers," she said without thinking.

"Where he get hamburgers at home? I don't remember," Nate said. "I thought you said we have fish all the time."

She breathed in hard. "He don't get hamburger very much. We all eat fish at home, in Pine Garden. This you home—that my home long time ago."

"Our daddy catch fish?" Nate said.

"He work with fish," she said, remembering one of the ladies whose kitchen she cleaned, saying on the phone to someone, "Dan works with phosphates." She looked at the clock. "Go on, get to bed. Time."

She had not thought of taking them to visit Pine Gardens for many years, since she had decided she was a haint. But they had never asked about their father—if they went and saw the bury yard, they wouldn't find Sinbad. She thought of the stone with MARY carved into the face, wondered if someone had moved it, or put pieces of shell and glass around it. Haint move it there, that what they think. I just a haint for Pine Garden.

Nate and Calvin didn't ask her anything else, but she heard them say the word "Daddy" sometimes when they talked, and she knew they were comparing their arms and feet to hers, to other people's; she knew they looked in the mirror over the bathroom sink now and studied their faces.

The junior league season was short, and Nate stayed unhappy, but he tried to battle Calvin in the street and on the field. They were in junior high before Calvin talked him into trying defense, and Nate resigned himself to listening to Baby Poppa and the junior high coach. Then she watched from the sidelines when he played against another school in the city, in the still-hot fall air and the gray haze of afternoon.

Nate began to tackle like an alligator rising out of the water, clamping onto runners, slanting up from the line to crash through the offense like the other boys were reeds. He scissored his arms around the quarterback and fell on top of him. When he got up, Calvin slapped his hand on the sidelines, and Marietta knew he liked the feel of hitting and moving.

And Calvin stayed opposite Nate, as he had in the field. He was a pushing, nudging tree, a hundred trees in the forest when you were running and wanted to get through, he stopped the boys like Nate who came at him again and again, immovable in front of his quarterback or falling on top of a tackle just as the running back flashed past.

They were so much bigger than the other players that she saw boys cry when they left the field after playing against Nate and Calvin. Their mouths wouldn't open, but she and Baby Poppa saw their eyes red and cheeks wet.

"My wife deserves some of the credit," Baby Poppa said proudly. "She feeds them, too."

Marietta said, "I scared of em, myself." The school weighed and measured them when they began the eighth grade—they were both six feet two, 190 pounds.

Suddenly she smelled Sinbad when they came in at night, and she circled close to them where they put their plates in the sink. Before she went to work, she sniffed. Where was the sour, leaf-and-grass sweat that had risen from their scalps all these years? Was it floating above her now that they were taller than she was? They sat on the couch—no, she stood over them and smelled man sweat, a film of hard work and salt, dried and sharpened by the day until now it was Sinbad when he reached for something above her. She looked at Calvin's huge knees, wide as plates, and thought of those tiny knees that had dragged through the mud when they began to crawl. She had made rings around their bellies with her arms and carried them back to where she wanted them, while they spit and blinked and swam in the air.

She dipped her head into the washer and smelled the bleach in the tangles of long, white socks. She looked into the tub, where there was no haze of dirt, and she sat in the water, watching her knees dry, imagining them. They had played in the tub together, then grown so big they had to take baths one at a time. She imagined their knees high and always cold. Now they showered at the high school every day after practice.

"Did you notice that they're growing differently?" Baby Poppa asked one night when they all sat at the kitchen table before work.

"What you talking bout?" Tiny Momma said. "They eat the same thing—ten times much as anybody else."

Marietta said, "I see Calvin getting bigger, *when* I see him. They go to school early, got practice, till I only see em on the weekend." She finished her coffee. "But Calvin say Nate don't have the patience to sit at the weight bench like the coach want him to. Don't want to lay under that bar for the military press."

"Military?" Tiny Momma said.

"Calvin say Nate don't even want to interrupt the running of his mouth long enough to breathe," Marietta said. "He talking bout, 'I don't need as much bulk like Calvin do, Mama. I got the speed and I *know* where they going.'" Baby Poppa laughed at her imitation.

"As if he never thought of playing anything but defense," Baby Poppa said.

"I don't know why y'all always laughing bout football," Tiny Momma said grumpily. "Wait till one a them boys gets hurt and then you see what I been warning you bout all these year. That too dangerous no matter how big they get."

She wouldn't go to the games with Marietta and Baby Poppa. "I ain't gon watch em get hit. I stay home," she said.

When Nate and Calvin were sophomores, they both started on the varsity team, and Marietta and Baby Poppa went to the first game—September, 1976. Nate and Calvin's high school was playing a crosstown school, and all the arms and legs sticking out from the uniforms were dark. The Charleston schools were almost completely black, since after integration most of the white parents had sent their kids to private school or moved away. She always thought of the boys she saw during Christmas holidays, the ones in military school or boarding school.

If they get to some playoffs, they gon play outside the city, she thought. What gon happen when they hit a white boy? They hit somebody like Mr. Ray boy? Well, I done done it. Tell em it okay to pound somebody, encourage them for hit hard as they can. She watched the quarterback turn his head left and right like a turtle, Calvin bent over. No. I done done it.

The running back was slightly off center, poised, and the tight end was wide. Both receivers wide, but they bluffing. Marietta couldn't say how she knew, how she could usually feel the play, but this time, something about the way the tight end and receiver held their heads on their necks, the set of their shoulders, told her they were the boys to get your attention away from the real culprit. Just like Calvin, trying to distract her from something Nate had done—it was in his eyes and careful mouth, his planned shoulders.

"Watch for run," she said. "Calvin gon open it up." The wide receiver dashed hard, drawing the defensive back, and the quarterback handed off. The fullback, thick-legged and short, passed inside and got seven on the run.

"Go head on, boy!" Baby Poppa shouted. Marietta clapped, thinking that nobody ever cheered for Calvin like they did for Nate, nobody ever stood up and shouted, "Great block!" except her and Baby Poppa. Everyone hollered, "What a tackle!" for Nate. She watched Calvin's chest and arms grow like the hood of a cobra she had seen on TV, expanding to shield the quarterback, and then Calvin planted his feet and pushed. The quarterback's wrist flicked beautifully, his socks sagged down his spindle calves, and the ball sailed through the air.

When the other team's quarterback threw a pass late in the game, a desperation bomb, Nate reached up from where he had run to cover the play, and like a magical fish, the ball kissed his chest. Then everyone screamed.

She studied their playbooks at home, fascinated by the arrows and X's, and she smiled at the typed rules and instructions from the coach, who was a round, graying man with light skin, always wearing a rustling, plastic-like jacket. "No girls. Remember, girls are DISTRACTIONS that will hurt your PERFORMANCE. Sex bleeds away STRENGTH and STAMINA you need for each game."

Nate told Baby Poppa, "Man, girls help *me.* I like for em to see me out there, it makes me work harder. Serious."

"Nobody said they couldn't watch you from the stands, boy," Baby Poppa said. "I don't think Coach Terrell limited that."

"Aw, man, girls don't hurt nobody."

"Babies do. You saw Carmen's boy, Robert, had to get married." Baby Poppa frowned at Nate. "You're sixteen—you aren't old enough for a baby. Ask your mother."

She sucked her teeth at him. "I was old enough. But you ain't," she said, looking hard at Baby Poppa. "You got enough trouble in school, Nate. Calvin doing much better than you in everything."

"Everything except girls," he mumbled, and looked up. "Everything except math. Calvin just like to read—that's how come he get through all that other stuff. But he can't add nothing."

"Good. The two of you will have to live together all your lives, since you insist on being two halves of a coin," Baby Poppa said. "And then you won't have to worry about girls."

They came around, though, girls with hair puffed out in beautiful clouds, their eyelashes curling, their feet in wedge shoes that still didn't lift them to the boys' shoulders. Marietta saw them on the stairs in the evenings—with their full hair and the huge bell-bottomed pants around their ankles, the girls looked like people from another country. They smiled and blinked at Nate and Calvin, and Calvin listened while Nate said, "Oh, baby, you know I didn't see you in the hall today." Marietta heard them through the screen and smiled, too.

She and Baby Poppa saw two more games, but the school lost in the playoffs, and Nate and Calvin were angry. "Man, coach need to get a new fullback," they said. "Brian ain't getting it. He need to let Ronnie in there. Just cause he a sophomore, like us. We gon be champs next year."

She still felt nervous, especially in the spring when a friend of the coach hired them at the icehouse. They worked all weekends, after school, and then in the moist heat of summer they started practice again during the mornings. Nate drank pitchers of Kool-Aid, but Calvin had a strange passion for iced tea with a certain number of ice cubes. She and Tiny Momma sat at the table for hours, worrying about the possibility of broken bones, which Tiny Momma predicted as inevitable between the blocks of ice and the coming season. "See? You and Poppa raise em only for play some game, and what if they leg break? What they gon do? No—you better tell em work hard at the icehouse, cause maybe they can find steady work there when they finish school. Big boys like that be fine at the ice house."

The cuts on Nate's knuckles swelled with infection from the mud, and she poured sugar on them like always, packed in the spiderwebs. "Mama, what you gon do when I go to college—pack me some spiders in a jar?" Nate laughed.

College. She pressed the webs into a sticky ball between her fingers. Broken bone—Aint Sister always bathed the limb in vinegar and water, packed creek mud around it for a week or two. Whooping cough—the fiddler crabs, boiled to die for their liquid. Fever, toothache, worms. All the medicines she had forced into their mouths, rubbed on their skins. But their knees, no matter how wide—she thought of cleats flying sideways into the soft inner knees and cracking the kneecaps.

What would happen to them if they couldn't play football? She had kept busy these last two years, trying to keep from thinking about the fact that she had raised two men, huge and fearless, who smiled and waved at white men in cars now and then, who smashed white boys into the grass and raised their fists.

She so big, so black—they huge, they arms blacker from the field. At the icehouse, she had seen an older man, almost as big as the boys, with a drooping stomach and slack jaw. He sat in the shade on the wooden loading dock. Baby Poppa told her the man had spent ten years in prison for rape; he was slow, and somehow a white woman had been in the icehouse alone with him, back in 1938, after which she told her father he had attacked her. He was lucky only to be jailed, not killed. He was even slower when he got out, and he lumbered around the loading area like a shadow, his shoulders so soft and down-slanted next to Calvin's straight, wide ones that she bit her lip.

College. She was already poring over the Street and Smith, which listed all the colleges and universities and ranked their football teams. She and Baby Poppa sifted through the *Sports Illustrated* college issues, debating about coaches and strategies and powerhouses. They didn't mention to Tiny Momma that they looked at any schools outside the state.

"But this is all based on our hopes that they do well in their last two years," Baby Poppa said in the fall, before the season began. "We have no money—we have no say. I think we should keep this quiet for a while, even from the boys."

Marietta nodded. Maybe they would get tired of football, of all the work and practice, and maybe their size wouldn't be enough once their team competed against better squads.

But they came around even that year, just like the girls—a few coaches from Clemson and South Carolina State and Auburn, the schools close by. They had slicked-back hair, large flat ears with long lobes, the grooves of practice in their foreheads and deep creases of sun in the arms and necks. "Nathaniel and Calvin are being watched closely," said the coach from South Carolina State, a light-skinned black man who looked somehow like the white coaches. "They're outstanding, and I'd like to express my interest early. South Carolina State has a tradition of. . ."

She didn't listen. She nodded politely, watched them talk to the boys on the piazza, saw them come to the games; but she didn't really listen. The girls and coaches gathered around the yard where the steps began, where the boys sat sometimes, Nate talking, Calvin watching. She didn't hear anymore, because she thought she had already made up her mind about the college she wanted. Now she had to wait.

They played well all year. Nate broke a city record for intercepted passes, broke another record for tackles. Calvin kept James, the thin quarterback, protected for touchdown throws, but no one kept those records. Marietta told him, "I seen you out there. Baby Poppa did. Them scouts did. Don't worry."

He said nothing about Nate's name and picture everywhere, and she asked him over and over, "You sorry you chose offensive line?"

"Uh-uh," he said. "I'ma get mine later."

Get mine? They had even begun to talk differently, one way around her and each other, another way around the girls and teammates. Another way around Jesse and Joe and the men who always cornered them to talk about the games.

For the state championship, they played a white school. She and Baby Poppa rode with Jesse and Joe in Jesse's long Buick. Columbia—she had never been so far. The windows smeared with the passing scenery, and Joe said, "Man, I use to hate this run when I drove it in the truck. Nothing but crackers on this run."

Baby Poppa said, "This reminds me of how little I leave Charleston. I recognize how varied the scenery is outside the city—but I try to forget Bamberg."

"That where you and your wife come from?" Joe said.

"And where we've never returned," Baby Poppa said.

"What about you, Big Ma?" Joe said. "Where you come from? Jesse told me once you from the islands."

"Uh-uh," she said. "From Pine Garden—not a island, just a stop off the road. But it near the water."

"Oh, yeah, I been there on a run, too," Joe said. "Just a little store, huh, and all kinda fish in there. I bought some shrimp."

"Buy shrimp anywhere, man," Jesse said.

"You ever go back there?" Joe kept on.

Marietta shook her head, and he turned to look at her in the back seat. "Nothing I ain't already see," she said so that he would stop asking. He and Jesse and Baby Poppa started to talk about highways, and she turned to the window to look at the trees whip past. Pine Garden. She let the trees blur into a wall and thought instead about California. University of Southern California. It was so far. It was the best one. How could she send them all that way—what would Tiny Momma say? Baby Poppa would agree—it had the best offensive line in the country, the best place for Calvin to shine. Nate would shine anywhere. She had to wait.

When the players stretched and trotted, spread out over the field in the glaring lights, she wasn't sure if they were the tallest on the field, but when they were lined up at the bench and then standing in the huddles, Nate and Calvin were above the rest. Nate was six-six now, Calvin six-seven. Calvin's waist was wider, his legs bulging at the thigh pads, and Nate's arms were rounded with muscle. She was light-headed, and couldn't breathe, couldn't even concentrate on the plays with the men shouting in her ear. She couldn't tell Nate under her breath to watch for the run, couldn't remind Calvin to drink enough at halftime.

One of the white boys said it just after halftime, when the

score was still 0-0. They all heard it, she and the men, where they sat close to the sideline because they had been too late to move around and get seats higher up where she wanted. They were near the end zone. "Nigger," one of the white boys said to the quarterback. She couldn't see Calvin's face. The white boy, a defensive lineman, said it again after the play was over. "Good fake, nigger," he said to Calvin.

James, the quarterback, set his thin face in a smile. So did Calvin, she saw, as he turned to walk back to the line of scrimmage, and Natty, the wide receiver who lined up closest to Marietta and the men. Baby Poppa and the others were silent. Natty's hair edged out from underneath his helmet like a sponge, the round Afro squashed underneath. She saw Calvin's teeth. James threw a pass to Natty on the next play for seven yards, and Calvin slammed into the white guard, smiling. He was shorter than Calvin, but as wide; Calvin lowered his shoulder on the next play and shot forward, catching the guard in the chest, and Natty caught the short pass in the end zone. Smiling—they all smiled. "Niggers are bigger, and white boys got no heart," Natty sang softly when he and Calvin came to the sidelines.

"Lord have mercy," Baby Poppa whispered. "Mercy on me."

Twenty-one to seven. Nate's knuckles bled, and he had smashed into the quarterback three times; Calvin's pads were black with mud, but she hugged them on the field, the plastic shields resounding and slapping all over against people's shoulders and chests. "Whupping," Nate crowed. "It was a spanking."

"My hand stinging," Calvin said.

After they'd gotten on the bus, she and the men started the long drive home, but she smelled them on her blouse and coat. My boys. Football mud—not fish mud. She listened to Baby Poppa and Jesse and Joe. "Them white boys wasn't too white after they done rolled in the mud like pigs, huh?" Jesse said.

Baby Poppa always stuck to the strategy. "I thought their quarterback would have been decent if he'd had some protection."

"Who gonna protect him from Nate?" Joe hollered. "Only Calvin!"

"Still, he had a fairly accurate arm."

"But he was too worried about his ass!"

"White boys talking bout nigger this and nigger that. They better retire that shit and go home!"

"I know the scouts was there watching Nate."

Marietta said nothing, watching the country darkness fly by. Nate and Calvin, grappling all these years in the field, dancing around each other, each the only one who could force hands open or mouths to laugh. They were going away.

The coaches came like boyfriends, sitting awkwardly in their cars, waiting on the piazza with hands folded and dangling between their legs, soda or Styrofoam cups of coffee perched on the floor beside their shoes. They brought hats, brochures, shirts, and game films. They called on the phone every few minutes until she took the receiver off the hook. The letters piled up in the corner, hundreds of them, until Nate and Calvin stopped opening the envelopes.

Some talked only with Nate, being excruciating polite to Calvin and to her, but relaxing with Nate, their words flowing smoother and their hands flying around the apartment. They took both boys out to eat, and often brought back more food; she found wrappers with see-through flowers of grease everywhere in the kitchen. Then they all sat in the front room again for hours.

She studied the coaches' faces. Most of them had noses that had fallen to fatter, rounded tips; their cheeks were heavy and square to their jaws; their hair showed faint toothmarks from combs and cream. They looked a little like Mr. Ray would now, she imagined, but that didn't frighten her the way she'd expected it would. They were more than careful with everything they said to her, and inside she smiled. She knew they knew about mamas.

Nate and Calvin smiled, sometimes politely if they were bored, sometimes really laughing at a story a coach told; they ate hamburgers or chicken, chewing while their eyes stayed on the coach. She saw by their shoulders and their mouths that they weren't intimidated at all. Nate puffed up a little when they recited his statistics in wonder, and he'd correct them if they got a score or the number of sacks wrong, but he didn't run his mouth. Marietta was proud. For the most part, he and Calvin listened as silently as she did, and Nate always said, "Long as you know me and my brother go together, full ride for him, too. We a package deal."

While the coach was nodding vigorously and saying, "He'd be a great asset to the program, too," Calvin would look over at Marietta and widen his eyes slightly in question. She'd raise her head to let him know he didn't have to worry or recite his own statistics.

Many times the coaches took the boys to the high school to watch game films on the projector, and they came back praising Coach Terrell and what he'd done with such a small program. Coach Terrell only came twice—he had never spoken much to her. She could tell that he didn't like women, mamas, that they usually bothered him like sprained ankles, or holes in a field, or summer flies. "They only get three official school visits," he said, uncomfortable on her couch.

"We're quite aware of the regulations," Baby Poppa said. "The boys haven't narrowed their choices down to three yet."

"What we looking at?" she said.

"Head coaches are coming from Georgia, Penn State, Michigan, they say. Nate likes Penn State's guy, but I know what you have planned."

"The man from USC coming next week," she said. "We gon have to see."

"Where you want to visit?" she asked the boys when they came in that night.

Nate said, "We going to LA, to USC."

She said, "I know. But you can visit two other places. Get you a free trip. Maybe you think I wrong to choose for you."

Nate shrugged. "Anyplace fine with me."

"You choose one, Calvin choose one for visit." She turned back to the sink.

Baby Poppa said, "Do you both think your mother and I are being too firm in our support of Southern California?"

Calvin said, "They want me, they like what I can do, and some of these dudes only want Nate for real."

"You're right," Baby Poppa said carefully. "Historically, USC has groomed great offensive lines, and they nurture their linemen, give them attention. They know you're crucial to their running game. But it's also a school full of rich white kids from California. I'm talking about the possible distractions for both of you. You'll be far from here, maybe lonely, maybe less motivated to work hard. What about you, Marietta?" he said.

"What you ax me?" she said.

"They'll be far away from you. How will you handle that?"

"I be busy," she said harshly. "When I ain't busy?"

He stared at her for a minute.

Nate said, "We know what we gotta do, Poppa. But I ain't sayin girls is a problem. I'ma have to check that out for myself, especially with them California ones in bikinis."

"Yeah, we ain't gon *be* on the beach, Nate, we gon be on the field. All summer, man, daily doubles," Calvin said.

"This is a professional enterprise," Baby Poppa said.

Nate interrupted, "But I heard the girls love to come to practice. I can handle that."

Baby Poppa rolled his eyes. "You've made me feel so much more confident, Nate," he said.

One weekend, there was a crowd of them in the street, awkwardly trying to avoid each other, waiting outside while one sat on the couch, then waiting a few anxious moments to ring the bell after the other had left.

Marietta and Tiny Momma and the boys laughed at the

parade of handshakes and smiles and offers: "Can I run out and bring you something to eat?" Tiny Momma had finally learned not to offer the coaches her cakes and macaroni and rice and chicken, because there were so many men that they ate most of her leftovers.

But two of them were important: the head coach from USC, John Garland, and the linebacker coach from Penn State, a blond man named Jim Hart.

Hart spent hours with Nate, but more and more he talked to Marietta. Baby Poppa came to her in surprise at the bar that Monday night, when she told him that Hart would be back next weekend. "I think he likes you," Baby Poppa said. "He looks at you the way Milton did."

Marietta frowned and said, "Huh. You seeing things." She had brought no magazines, and she rubbed her palms across the table. "Coach Garland spend a lot of time with Calvin, and Calvin like him. I was worry we like the school and they don't like the coach."

"I worry that you'll like the coach and not the school," Baby Poppa said, and she knew he was joking.

"I don't know what you talking about," she said.

But he was right, and when Jim Hart came back the next weekend, she saw that he looked at her face, not just her scarf; he looked at her hands, didn't just smile and turn to the boys for real words.

"Penn State could offer your sons a completely different environment from what they're used to," he said. He was maybe forty, round-faced and tall. "I was a linebacker at Wyoming, the state where I was born," he went on, "and what I loved when I began coaching was the opportunity to see other parts of the country, to see how other people live."

Marietta hesitated. She used her Pine Gardens voice with most of the coaches, partly so they would think she was too ignorant to bother much, and partly so she could talk to Nate and Calvin half-privately. But with Jim Hart her voice became more like Baby Poppa's, the way she often heard it practiced in her head but rarely out loud.

"Where else have you coach?" she said.

"Well, I coached at San Jose State for a while, in California, and then I went to New Mexico State. I came to Penn State four years ago. I think we have the best program, and I think I'll stay. I'm confident that I can offer Calvin and Nate a great opportunity with us."

She smiled at the way he kept tacking on the things he was supposed to say. "You like to travel, huh?"

"Well, I'm single, and I have to recruit, but yeah, I like to come into a city and figure things out, see how people act and talk." He paused. "This has been one of the best trips I've made, because Charleston is not only fascinating, I've had a great time hearing you talk."

"I don't talk too much," she said.

"The South had always made me nervous," he went on quickly, "but you and your neighbors have made me feel right at home. I did want to, uh, let you know that there might be more opportunities for you, too, in Pennsylvania. I mean, Nate has told me that your husband is deceased, and that you work nights. Maybe you could move up to the area with the boys and find a job with better hours."

She looked at his gray eyes, the color of oyster shells, and his round head, with straight hair over his ears. Either he wanted Nate very badly or he *was* being particularly nice to her. She said, "I'm not unhappy here. I want the boys to go where they want."

"Well, I know there are so many more restrictions in the South, on your social life and just the attitudes in general," he said, hurrying over his words.

"Restrictions everywhere," she said.

"But in Pennsylvania things are just less formal, and they're freer," he said.

Marietta smiled again. He said, "I think the boys would really benefit from the climate." She thought, He safe again.

That night, when she lay on the couch, she couldn't help but think of his face, his hand shaking hers for a long time at the door while the boys were off with Coach Garland. Was Hart just trying to get the boys through her? It seemed, in his fumbling words and leaning forward on the cushions that he really thought Pennsylvania would be better for her. He had even given her his phone number at home again, saying, "You can always call me about setting up job prospects. I'd really like to see you in, uh, less restricted circumstances."

But when she tried to picture herself in an apartment in Pennsylvania, alone, with the boys living at the college and her in the snow, maybe this coach or someone else coming to visit her, she couldn't help seeing his cheeks, pale after he had shaved, the pores even and tiny as grains in cooked grits. She saw Maussa then, the haint, short and round, with the cigar between his lips. Had he *loved* the Africa woman? But in love was ownership, moving bodies and spirits around to plant them where men liked. This coach ain't no maussa, but he like for move people round. He not a bad man, but he don't know more than me. She saw the tiny darker hairs between his knuckles when he put his hands on his knees, nervous.

The boys said Coach Garland was nicknamed "The Silver Fox" because of his hair and his smooth words, and she thought the name fit. He saw her only for an hour, the three of them at a coffee shop; he drank black coffee while the boys ate eggs and Marietta listened over her cold tea. And the strangest thing was that she couldn't remember half of what he said, about California or the school or the offensive line, because while she watched his confident lips bare his teeth, his straight silky hair combed high over his beaked nose, she kept feeling sorry for Jim Hart. He called every day, asking if the boys had decided, if she had thought about what he'd said. She watched Calvin duck his head in laughter at Coach Garland's words, and she heard Nate say, "I heard you got plenty of summer jobs out there." Suddenly she wanted them to sign the letters of intent, so that the endless stream of nervous, sweating pale men would stop sitting on her couch, imploring her boys with their eyes; even though at first she had marveled that men who looked like Mr. Ray wouldn't fill her with fear, now she wanted the quiet back in her kitchen.

She asked them several times. "You still go long with it?" she said to Nate. "You sure?"

He was serious now. "Mama, long as me and Calvin go together, it's cool."

"Nate gon shine anywhere," she said, almost to herself, for the hundredth time. "But USC got what Calvin need. The man want both of you, I can tell he serious. Baby Poppa like he staff."

"California. You could come out there, Mama. All kinda jobs," Calvin said.

"Yeah, Coach Hart was talkin bout you could come to Pennsylvania, too," Nate said. "He said he could find you a job, too."

"I done did my job," she said. "Now I gon rest by myself for a change and let them coaches feed you, they want you so bad."

She loved turning away the other coaches who still came, watching their faces fill with gentle instruction and no wariness when they first saw her on the piazza or the couch, sitting down, her hair hidden by the headwrap. They spoke slowly, as if she were a child, and they were sure to mention climate, academics, wholesome campus life, tradition, and meals. After she'd told them briefly and politely that Nate and Calvin were in Los Angeles and she wouldn't consider the schools they were describing, after they smiled and began again patiently, she explained her admiration for USC's offensive line and closed her mouth. Their eyes became smaller, then larger in disbelief—the mouths were crooked when they lost the polite smirk.

"He really got to you," one of them said, disgustedly. "Garland really sold you a line."

She didn't have to smile. "I decide three year ago, before I ever see a coach," she said, and then she added, "Afternoon," as she stood up, looking over their heads or shoulders at the street. Or if it was getting dark, "Evening."

leaving

1983

"Hey, Big Ma, when them boys coming back? Didn't they just go out for some ice?" someone said.

"Mmm-hmm, probly got to showin off that new car. I know they talkin to the guys at the icehouse, cause they use to work there, remember?" Jesse answered.

"Probly buyin some crab. They use to crave some crab when they was little."

"They wasn't *never* little!"

Everyone laughed at Jesse's joke, the people who were left from the crowd that had been shifting in and out all day. The men and boys who had lined the railing along the piazza were down to five or six, framing the doorway to let in dancing fingers of late-afternoon light around their shadows. Carmen and Jean from downstairs sat in borrowed chairs, but most of the other chairs had gone back to apartments with their owners by now, and Marietta was impatient for the rest to leave.

"Yeah," she said, "they use to work there, and they don't get back here soon, I'ma let both of em sleep there. Cool off all this bighead foolish."

She knew as soon as she said it that their faces would shift just a little, their eyes find other eyes and smile. "Big Ma don't never relax," they were thinking. "Uh-uh, she cain't even sit back and enjoy nothin." She knew she couldn't have said anything else. She didn't know how. All the visitors were here for Nate and Calvin, and she rarely talked to more than one person in an entire day. She was aware of every word she said now, in the little quiet.

Jesse fished through an ice chest for another beer, and she heard water slosh against the cans. The sodas and beer in all the tubs and coolers were floating now, floating the way that voices had bobbed tightly in the small front room. In and out the door they had come all day, knocking up against each other the way they did at funerals, weddings, barbecues, and new-baby days. But all the voices, smells of food and hairdress and beer had been in other rooms up and down the street. She had been to some celebrations with Tiny Momma, but no one ever had reason to gather in her place; no one had been encouraged to sit awhile and talk except Tiny Momma and Miss Alberta, who had moved into the apartment next door the year before. They sat beside her at the kitchen table, shelling shrimp and drawing fingernails up the bellies, arguing with everyone.

"Ain't none of em a safe way to go," Tiny Momma said. Miss Alberta nodded her head.

"I can't believe she refusing to fly," Mr. Taylor, another neighbor, said. "Don't you know the newspapers say flying is actually safer than driving on the freeway, Big Ma?" She looked into his wire-rimmed glasses. He was probably only a year younger than she was, and she always felt strange when he called her Big Ma—but his son did, everyone had, for so long now that she forgot her name sometimes.

"But them boys already bought a car to take her back in—you seen that Lincoln," someone said behind her, and she could hear the raised eyebrows in the approving voice. "Black, with a wine-red interior—mmm, mmm, mmm."

"Gon take you days to drive, you know. No tellin who you might run cross, and y'all in that brand-new Lincoln, police *love* to stop you," Jesse said.

"Shoot, won't take no days to get to California with Nate and Calvin drivin!" Joe said. "The Cook twins! I can't believe Nate went first round. Probly got more money on that signing bonus than this whole street make in a lifetime. Two hundred thousand—just for breakin out a pen."

"But them Cook boys, they ain't just cooks, now. They master *chefs*. I ain't playing. Calvin gon chop-block you. And Nate, he fry yo ass every time. Don't nobody get by for free!"

They had been doing this all day. Marietta looked at the clock again. "And how that gon work?" Miss Alberta said.

"Calvin's a offensive lineman, Miss Alberta," one of the boys said. "He gotta block the dudes tryin to get to the quarterback. Or the running back."

"Huh."

"And Nate, he like Lawrence Taylor play for the Giants. Huntin dudes down, man. He sack any quarterback, I don't care who it is."

"Nate playin gainst his own brother?" Her voice rose.

"Naw, Miss Alberta, he don't. . . oh, I'ma show you when the season start. I'ma show you on TV."

"She don't know nothin bout football. Baby Poppa coulda explained it to her," Jesse said. They were all respectfully silent for a moment, and Tiny Momma hummed when she pinched the heads off the shrimp.

He suppose for be here, sit in that folding chair by Joe and argue bout Calvin should be done got more attention. He suppose for puff up stead a me—he done did it, in the field. He they poppa.

She had found him, two years earlier. Nothing had happened that day, nothing! She went over and over it. He hadn't sat sweating and hollering in front of a game with Jesse, slapping his leg if Nate misread a play or Calvin let someone slip past. He hadn't held his neck tense as a dried sunflower, talking about, "This is it, they can't fool around now. They never played anybody competitive in Charleston—they won't make it out there if they don't want it worse now." No Rose Bowl to make his snaky temple veins jump. Their sophomore season was over then—it was spring.

And no cold or headache or pain in his leg. Nothing at work—no angry guests or woman who wanted ice ten times in an hour, no stopped elevator or spills in the lobby.

He just didn't come to the bar. And when she opened the closet door, he lay curled on the floor between his chair and the large mop bucket. The mottled tin so close to his cheek made her scream; he was so small with his arms hunched in to his chest, where his heart had hurt him.

She picked him up and carried him to Mr. Powell's office, where she could lay him on the couch, the leather couch, instead of the hard floor.

Nate and Calvin flew out from California for the burying. Baby Poppa always said he didn't care about a funeral or headstone—"Give me the good stuff while I'm breathing." But Tiny Momma had paid a policy for him, secretly, for over forty years, and the funeral was elaborate, with a marble marker as tall as he was.

His picture watched them from the wall now, the team photo from the junior league, in which he'd stood by the coach, smile even in line with Nate and Calvin. His jacket was creamy-pressed, his hat cocked back on his head, and his face was all sickle moons in the bright sun.

Marietta rinsed the shrimp in the sink, listening for the car. She glanced up at the picture, telling Baby Poppa again, They still have fe make it, they still have fe want it worse. Professional get cut in a second. With all the crowing and hollering the men had done, she knew she couldn't say that to anyone but him.

She felt nervous all the time, but she knew it wasn't just the draft. They would be leaving in a day, all three of them, and she didn't really believe they would go, but she knew she was really seeing Nate's wife in her worry mind.

His wife: they had gotten married last year, during Christmas break, before USC played in the Rose Bowl. "How you get this money for fly out here?" Marietta had demanded of Nate, and he just smiled. "Don't worry, Mama."

Carolanne—that was her name. She had spent the day and a half they were here hugging Nate. When they got back from the courthouse, Marietta had watched Carolanne's long red nails, her arms completely outstretched across Nate's chest, like a kitten climbing a tree trunk. She was very light-skinned, and her eyes were green as a mallard's head. That was all Marietta remembered. That and her little belly—Carolanne was six months pregnant.

The people were just about gone now, some because they'd only come to be polite to Jesse and Tiny Momma or to have a few beers; the last few waited for the boys. She was tired of the voices. She waited for it to be just her and the two women, eating shrimp at the same placemats where they had liver and onions, peach cobbler, oxtail stew in winter. They wouldn't care about football; they wanted to talk about Marietta's grandson, Freeman. Nate's boy.

"I sure wanted to see him," Tiny Momma said again.

"But he only what—fifteen month? It ain't good for them babies to fly, hurts they ears," Miss Alberta said. "Ain't good for nobody to fly."

Marietta looked out the window again. Even the two women—she wanted them to go soon, too, so that the boys could breathe in sleep and she could look at the magazines, think, plan what she should prepare to see. She wanted to lay out the pictures of California she had been collecting from Baby Poppa's magazines, the ones they had fingered all these years.

"Can't sleep good anyway," Nate said, rubbing his back the next morning. He had the floor last night; Calvin would have it tonight.

"You still ain't have for come in that late," she whispered. She didn't want one of the men to hear her and admonish her for scolding famous athletes again.

The men had come back because it was Sunday and the boys had brought more cases of beer and Coke, more fish and shrimp. They leaned against the wall outside in the folding chairs, sat on the rickety wooden railing, putting their feet up on boxes and crates. They hadn't tired, and now they started on the Giants and 49ers and Dolphins.

"Did you *see* it, though, Big Ma?" one of the boys called to her where she stood in the doorway. "You watch the draft on TV?"

"Man, them guys *been* on TV whole lotta times already," Andre, one of the older teenaged boys, said. He squinted at Nate in superiority. "You got two interceptions when you played Oklahoma, huh, Nate? And I seen you guys getting interviewed after the game."

Marietta remembered—she had watched college and pro players act a fool in front of TV cameras for years, talking about, "Hi, Mom!" and dancing or clowning. When the boys were in high school, she had told them she never wanted to see them grinning and entertaining folks like old-time Negroes in the movies. "Just do you job," she said. After the Oklahoma game, they stood shoulder to shoulder and she could hear it in the interviewer's voice—he wanted something funny and colorful from these twins, a new dance or handslap. Stiff as soldiers, fighting laughter, they smiled into the camera, rubbing their shoulders hard. "We just did what we were supposed to do. We did our *job* on them, huh, Calvin?"

Jesse answered everyone, proud. "She seen the highlights at our place. I thought Big Ma was gon cry when she seen Nate go first round."

She felt her smile go deep into her left cheek, so she wouldn't say anything. Jesse always talked about people like he knew them better than they knew themselves. She hadn't cried in front of anyone since her mother died. She was so good at it now that tears didn't even begin to form and drop down behind her eyelids to make her lips shake, the way women's did. Trained, her eyes, and they never betrayed her in public.

But hearing Nate's name three days ago, April 23rd, in the first round, had made her work at it for a moment, to think about the possibility of water rising near her nose and eyebrows. Then she worried about Calvin. He went in the fourth round, and the relief was like a rope had been lifted straight out of her spine.

"Shoot, you guys been in every newspaper around the country—bet you be in *Sports Illustrated* next," Andre said to Nate. She could hear Calvin drop his shoes to the floor behind the bedroom door.

"We was in there, that little section at the back, when we first went to USC," Nate said.

"The Cook twins! High school, college, and both goin to the Rams! Ain't no way," Joe said.

"What are the odds, man?"

"Lucky the Rams needed a star like Nate, man, they defense was rusty. All them veterans need to retire, Nate, they gettin too slow. You gon have to jack it up."

The sharpness of the lemon cake Tiny Momma took out of the oven cut through the room. "Calvin, hurry up!" Marietta shouted at the door. "You two was out too late. We suppose to been gone two hour ago."

"Aw, Big Ma, Nate and Calvin stars and you sound like they still schoolboys." Jesse laughed. "You got celebrities to love now."

"I don't need they heads any bigger," she said. "They still have fe do what they suppose fe do." Nate laughed.

"Big Ma don't give *nobody* a break," Joe said.

"You all stop," Tiny Momma said. "That why them boys done so good, cause she raise em serious. She doin her job."

Miss Alberta fanned herself with a newspaper. "Mama job don't never end," she whispered, and only Marietta heard her.

Calvin dangled his legs out of the car to put on his huge white tennis shoes. She left the women in the apartment and ran her hand down the peeling paint of the railing on the way down the stairs. People were still admiring the Lincoln at the curb. Did she really want to go up the highway today, to see who was still there?

To say goodbye? She pulled on her earrings and straightened her shirt. That was all she wore now—straight-waisted men's shirts, medium, and pants with flat shoes.

"So when *you* gon get married?" Jesse said to Calvin.

"Man, Nate's married enough for *both* of us. Huh, Nate?" Calvin smiled.

"Shut up," Nate said.

"Yeah, and you didn't call Carolanne last night like you was told to. She gon be hot."

"So? We was at Lee's house. She'll live."

"Shoot, you ain't even told her about the car. You two gon have a serious throwdown when we get back."

Nate smiled wide at Marietta. "So? My money. My car. My mama. Carolanne ain't the only woman in my world." Marietta slid into the back seat, the leather cool, hearing Sinbad say those words.

"Where y'all headed?" Jesse asked.

"Mama want to pick up a few things before we go tomorrow," Nate said. "Where we goin, Mama?"

"Out to the highway," she answered. "Go on to the water and then north." The car sped quietly through the neighborhood, and she thought for a minute about taking them by the fish market. But it was just a new beauty salon the last time she'd walked by there, and Sinbad's window was still covered with plywood.

People stared at them from Sunday-morning railings and corners. Nate and Calvin were suddenly silent, and Nate turned on the radio. She realized she hadn't been alone with them at all. "Don't play the music so loud I can't think," she said.

Nate got onto Highway 17. "You know where we going?" she asked.

"Yeah," Calvin said.

"We going for buy some gift for you wife, Nate," she said, watching the trees and water. "She fixing up this place for we live, and I don't have nothing for bring she, no fruit or cake, nothing I can carry cross the country. None of the thing you suppose for bring in a new house."

"Don't worry about that, Mama. She got plenty money to buy whatever she want," Nate said.

"I know—you keep tell me over and over. She cain't buy one a these. She need one for my grandson keep he toy inside. If he got toy."

Calvin shifted in his seat to look at her. "You always sound like you think California is gon kill you. You don't want to come out there?"

"Of course I want to come. Four year a long time and you two only visit in summer. Only see you on TV."

Carolanne make my voice sound wrong like I ain't want fe go. Carolanne. Name frilly and sweet as lemon pie—just what they fe say my name. She ain't like me already, ain't gon like me now. I ain't let Nate go hardship last year and get he some money fast. But he and Calvin stay together, before she. And she ain't like that they beena run out here first thing this week, when they get that bonus check.

"California got water, too," she said to Calvin. "Palmetto, too. Just bigger street, freeway everywhere, but same thing, huh?" She leaned toward the window. "Slow down, Nate."

The gate that said PINE GARDENS was closed, locked. She wondered who was down that road. Nate drove toward the edge of the highway, tires half in the sand, and he raised dust. "Aw, man, on my black car," he said.

Three stands had been rebuilt, but they still sagged, and she saw for the first time the leaves and dirt and pine needles on top of the tin roofs. But it was too early in the season—it must be, because no one sat inside the bare slats. The wood leaned hungrily toward the highway, as if the sand were getting softer under it.

Nate turned into Pearl's lot. Marietta stared at the big Marlboro Man near the open door, and then she got out. She knew whoever was in the store had heard the tires on the gravel.

Rosie sat behind the counter, close to another woman. Her eyes were half-lidded, stranger-cool for a minute, and then she saw Marietta. "Wha-a-a?" she said, the word trailing off high, and Marietta heard the stories about men and children and peach trees.

"Rosie," she said. "Remember my boy? Nate and Calvin?"

"Marietta! No—uh-uh. And they taller than you, look just like you. I don believe it!" Rosie put her arms around Marietta, and the hands barely reached together.

"What you fe do here?" she asked. "You come back?" She stepped to the doorway. "No—look fe that car! Where you get that?"

"Nate and Calvin play football, sign with the Los Angeles Rams. We move out to California tomorrow. They buy the car for take we," she said, feeling strange at all the words tumbling out.

"We been in L.A. four years already," Nate said, holding three dripping sodas over the scarred counter. Calvin tapped at the pig's feet floating in the big jar.

"Wha-a-a? Los Angeles? We beena think about you, Marietta. We wonder. Lil Johnny tell we you don have place, you in the street, but you never come back." Rosie's hair was edged with gray, like frayed cord showing around her forehead under her scarf.

"Tell Johnny the Rams," Marietta said. "He know." She turned to the wall so that they couldn't see that all her eye training was fading and heat was rising behind her cheekbones. Baskets were lined along the wall on a shelf, and she touched each one. Smelling the sweetgrass, feeling the dry rush slip through her fingers—"This what we want, Nate, for you wife. This what I bring she." She took down the smaller ones, with the flexible handles, and then she pointed to the large, rounded ones. "Freeman can put thing in them two."

"Freeman?" Rosie said, her voice changing.

"My gran," Marietta said, turning. "Name after my daddy—Nate think of it."

"Girl, get in here," Rosie called out the door, and a child ran inside, stopping when she saw the tall men. She was red-brown, with touches of light dust in her braids, and Marietta thought of the hands that had tried to pat the dust from her head, slapping when she came back to the stand.

"This is my baby gran, and my daughter-in-law, Tonette," Rosie said. The younger woman nodded, and the girl hid her face in her mother's knees. "I got four gran now. Lil Johnny work with he daddy on the boat, build he family place by Laha."

"Laha fine?" Marietta said, placing baskets on the counter.

"Laha fine, Jerry, all she kids okay."

"She still work fe Mr. Ray?"

Rosie laughed. "Girl, Mr. Ray *been* done go—that house all close up again. Don nobody go by there. Nobody in the tree now since you gone." Rosie looked at her and smiled. "Marietta always in the tree."

Marietta put her tongue behind her teeth. "I gone farther now—California."

"California," Rosie said, shaking her head. "What you fe work?"

Marietta felt the defensiveness flash into her mouth anyway, felt like a child again. She looked at the little girl near her mother's lap. "I ain't have fe do nothing. Them two make so much money play football. . ."

"Wha-a-a? I know I cain just do nothin. And ain likely fe find out!" Rosie laughed toward Tonette, and Marietta didn't know how she was losing, but every time Rosie spoke, she felt like she was disappearing; when Rosie said "Marietta" it sounded strange. No one in Charleston called her that. She was Big Ma.

"I guess you see Pearl beena pass," Rosie went on. "She near you mama."

"We go fe see em now," Marietta said. "We gon take these."

Rosie looked at all the baskets. "You want fe *buy* these? You ain't make no basket yourself? You ever was restless too much fe make basket."

"They gift."

"Then take em, huh? You ain't have fe pay," Rosie said sharply, stacking the smaller ones inside each other.

Calvin pulled out a hundred-dollar bill, and Nate shoved him. He put five twenties on the counter and scooped up the baskets. "We better go, Mama," he said.

She felt a rush of warmth when they stepped outside; with all the people surrounding them in the apartment, she'd been afraid to talk to the boys, afraid they had forgotten her. She'd thought it was gone, the way they could stand near her as children and know what she felt, sense her fear. The car slid past the houses, past the huge Angel Oak, and she said, "Right here."

She bent at the graves, her mother's first, and left the blue dishes she had bought. She left new gold hoops for Aint Sister. And then she opened the Mason jar of pennies and bits of blue glass, every piece of sapphire or aqua or turquoise glass or shard she had picked up since she went to Charleston, all the sharp pieces the boys had carried out from the vacant lot; she scattered them over her mother's leaves and dusty plastic flowers.

The stone was there—half covered with twigs and leaves. She knew no one had touched it. They think haint move it here, and haint be vex if they put finger on it. Mm-hmm—I haint, I be vex. She lifted the stone for the Africa woman and put new gold hoops underneath, in the wet black dirt.

The car wouldn't go any farther up the lane than Pinkie's, and no one came out onto her front step. "Come on," she told the boys, and they ducked into the moss-dangled tunnel.

"Mama, you crazy?" Nate said, but she led them to the bare spot where Aint Sister's house had been. Brick dust and triangular chunks of pale brown mud were in a pile; they had broken the chimney when they took the house.

Her mother's house was nearly hidden in a tangle of vines. The pump was gone, but plants hadn't covered a small patch of ground where she'd always dumped the wash water. "All that bleach and pee from you diaper," she said, "nothing grow there." She knew they couldn't get through any of her old paths to the water, so when they started back down the road, she closed her eyes to see it, the shine and slap of water near her feet.

They wouldn't let her pack. "You don't need none a this, Mama, we get everything new. No, you can't take that chair. I'm tellin you, Carolanne gon take you shoppin everywhere." Nate put everything back in its place.

"Leave it for whoever gon rent this place," Calvin said.

"Who gon rent this place?" Tiny Momma muttered. "Somebody I don't know, cain't even borrow a egg if I needs one."

"It's only me leave, not everybody else on the block got egg," Marietta said gently. "You got Miss Alberta borrow egg."

"Shoot, she no more able to walk to the store half the time as me. Don't eat nothin, pick like a bird. How I gon make a whole cake? Who gon eat it?" Tiny Momma's hands were small as biscuits, her fingers short, against the empty boxes. "You two ain't even gon let you mama take her pots?"

Tiny Momma's long braid was loose. Marietta had braided that spider-web-soft hair when Tiny Momma had pneumonia and couldn't get out of bed for a month. She had combed the silky, matted hair until the head swayed in sleep.

Marietta moved to the wall to take down the photos, and Tiny Momma said, "Baby Poppa the one got em started." She watched Marietta handle the photo of Freeman smiling over a teddy bear, of Nate and Calvin in their high school and college uniforms, but she waited to hold the one of Baby Poppa in the team picture. Marietta remembered that when he'd told the officials he was their father the coaches looked at this short red man, bent at the back from years of work. "They didn't say anything," Baby Poppa had crowed again and again. "What could they say? You too old to have kids?" She touched his small, glossy face.

"Why she want to take pots?" Nate came back into the apartment to challenge Tiny Momma. "She should be glad to leave em behind."

"Cause she *know* these pots. She know just how they gon cook some-thin. You buy them new pots they got in the store now, them cheap cute things, you don't know they gon burn you food till after they been done ruined it."

Marietta said, "He don't have to know nothing bout cook, just bring the food to him and he eat." She wiped the bottoms of the cast-iron frying pan and the rice pot. Corn bobbing like rafts; piles of greens simmered to a tight web of softness, laced with ham; oxtails that Tiny Momma stirred with turnips and potatoes for coughing boys.

"She takin them pots," Tiny Momma said, lifting her chin. She rubbed the oilcloth, Marietta saw, since there were no beans to snap, nothing to peel. Who else would ever know her like Tiny Momma? Know about the pots, the steam in your lungs that meant you were feeding your boys all by yourself? Who in California would sit at the table even when there was nothing to do and not much to tell? She thought of Rosie and the daughter--in-law. Would she and the fingernailed, green-eyed girl sit somewhere, their voices so slow and regular that Freeman would fall asleep as if they were ticking clocks? She felt a sharp twist in her chest—Aint Sister dead and Marietta never knowing that she had been a Tiny Momma to everyone, to her own mother.

She reached into a cupboard and got down the jars of tea, the spider, and put them with Rosie's baskets into a box. "You think you gon get sick in California?" Tiny Momma smiled. "You might have to drink some a that tea, huh?"

Marietta nodded. Why I take Pine Garden with me? That all I have for take, after twenty year in Charleston? Take old Pine Garden to California? She hesitated, then went to the closet to get the wooden box. Now it held dust, one photo, shells, and the birth certificates Coach Terrell had gotten for the boys in high school. He had gone to someone in the government to say that the originals had been lost. She put the wooden box in, then a pile of magazines she had culled carefully. She said, "I'm finish now."

Just when the sun came up, when fog still wafted along the piazzas, Nate and Calvin put the boxes in the trunk, and Marietta carried out a bag of biscuits, pound cake, and chicken. "I don't know if I want everybody lookin at us go," Calvin said, sounding uncomfortable. "Time for just get on the road."

"How you know they ain't want say goodbye for *me?*" Marietta said, putting her hand on his shoulder.

But when Jesse and Joe and the rest stood against railings, sleepy, rubbing hair and the skin over their nipples, they called out to Nate and Calvin. Miss Alberta stood in her doorway, and Tiny Momma sat on the top step, wrapped in a blanket like a child. "Y'all take the interstates all the way cross," Joe said. "Don't get on no little highways."

"Man, nothing gon happen," Nate said. "If a cop pull us over, we just tell him we play for the Rams, like we tell em in L.A."

"Shit, boy, you ain't in no L.A.," Joe said. "Just stay on the interstate. You won't see nothin, but nothin won't see you, neither."

Tiny Momma called, "They mama take care of em. Go on. Longer you stay, harder it is for me to see you."

Marietta closed the door, the press of Tiny Momma's elbows still tingling in her sides, the push of the fingertips like dimples in her palms. The windows went down silently, startling her, and Nate shouted, "We gone!"

He pushed the buttons to raise them back up when they headed toward the highway. "When it get hot, we got air-conditioning, and this antenna get every station we need to hear. Just sit back and chill, Mama."

His voice had changed already. Two languages. "You two give Tiny Momma some money?" she said sharply.

"We gave her two grand, Mama," Calvin said.

"How much?"

"Two thousand. I told her we'd send a thousand a month."

Marietta said, "You sure you don't want she come to California, help Carolanne with the baby?"

"Mama, we ax her over and over. She don't want to leave Baby Poppa," Nate said.

Tiny Momma visited his grave every afternoon before the sun went too low, sitting there to talk to him for a few minutes, weaving words around the wrought iron and trees in the cemetery. Marietta had hidden a whistle and the picture of Mean Joe Greene she had torn from *Sports Illustrated* on his grave, in the grass beside the headstone. She knew Tiny Momma would find them soon, but Tiny Momma didn't believe in leaving things for spirits.

"We can take 26 and then 20 to Atlanta," Calvin said, looking at the map. "Like Joe said, interstate all the way."

"We gotta see what's the fastest, man. I ain't goin out of my way just to stay on no interstate, it could be a whole lotta miles wasted," Nate said.

"Mama, why you bring all this food?" Calvin said, taking the biscuit she handed him. "It ain't like we don't have money to stop and eat."

"If I could eat anything this time a morning, I want biscuits. Tiny Momma biscuit," she said.

"How we gon take this woman to L.A.?" Nate laughed, and the car swerved into the fast lane.

"She think she gon take *us,*" Calvin said, laughing back.

They ate while driving, switched, and Marietta fell asleep, woke to hear them speaking the foreign language. Minicamp, condos, Nordstrom's.

"You want to drive all night, man?" Nate said.

"We still three niggers in a new Lincoln, huh," Calvin told him.

"Do that mean stop or keep going, bro?" Nate tapped the steering wheel. While dark settled around the windows, they pulled off at a small store. "Texas look *too* long," Calvin said. "The sign said Birmingham ten miles away—we gotta decide."

"This 20 go through too much a Mississippi for me. Shit, let's take the little one up to Memphis and go catch 40." They went inside and brought back six-packs of Coke and candy bars that looked like twigs in their huge hands. Nate peered in at her. "Hey, Mama, you sleeping?"

She nodded, closed her eyes again, listened to the cars tearing past. Birmingham—where Mr. Ray had a house.

The smaller highway was more dipping and curved. She stayed settled against the seat and watched the moon rise. Why did it look so different, sitting at the top of the windshield between the boys? They couldn't be that far away yet, that the moon would change into this strange, glowing yellow—too gold, like cat eyes in the night. There was a ring around it. . . how far away were they?

She was frightened for the first time, trying to read the passing highway signs that flashed by too quickly. Not moving, she watched the moon shift to her side window when Nate followed a curve around a hill—now it was white again, round. She was frightened of herself. What was she seeing? Aint Sister or her mother, trying to tell her something? A cat-eye moon turned bone-clean.

Again, Nate turned the wheel slightly, and the moon slowly swung back to the windshield. This time she *saw* it change, colored by something in the glass, a bar of color in the upper half. But she stayed silent, closed her eyes again to calm her heart.

"Feel weird to see Mama sleep, huh?" Nate said after a long time. She'd heard his shoulder on the leather when he turned in his seat to look at her.

"Yeah," Calvin said. "What you think about Mason? Can he hang?"

Their voices were nervous. "He got traded by the Seahawks, right? I don't know—blood got the heart, like Rock say, but do he got the wheels?"

"You scared, Nate?"

"About what?"

"Camp, fool."

"Hilarious, Calvin. Shit, we best not get scared bout no rookie camp. July gon be a lot worse."

"So?"

"Yeah, I'm scared, okay?" Nate sucked his teeth. "Coach gon be lookin at us hard."

"You see Johnson gon be there. Remember him when we played Notre Dame?"

"Yeah." She heard Nate turn to look at her again. "The condo should be fixed up, I guess. Carolanne said escrow was fixing to close, or whatever it's called." Marietta let out a slow breath and thought of Carolanne and the baby. Freeman. His head so big for his body in the pictures.

"Man, you scared to death," Nate said. "You *always* been scary. Remember you calling me into the bathroom when we first got to Charleston, talking bout, 'Nate, man, I broke the toilet.' First night!"

"Shut up, I was only three or something."

"Nate, look I make one too big.'" Nate imitated. "It gon break the. . ."

"Oh, man, you scared, too," Calvin whispered. "Man, why Mama don't want to fly?" He rattled the map. "Oklahoma look long, too. This ain't like when we was on the plane with the team."

"Okay," Nate said harshly. "Let's go over the plays. Remember that sweep they kept running, the one we seen on the video? Who I gotta pull? Come on, think. . ."

The tires sang below her.

california

anaheim hills

Along this wall, she saw patches of green. The brown cinder blocks must have had narrow gaps somewhere because, when she came closer, every ten feet or so there was a springy vine, a wild ivy or maybe a grape, tumbling out of a crack. But they were so regularly spaced—how had someone planted seeds in the cement?

The bending plants, pouring down the wall like little waterfalls, were the only green Marietta had seen since she left the gate of the condominium complex. She looked away from the shady side of the wall to the hills all around her. This was the farthest she'd ever walked, and she was at the edge of the developed land. Red tile roofs, white stucco walls like all the other houses and condos, covered the hills in wide crescents.

"Tracks," she said to herself. That was what she had heard Carolanne call them, the curve on curve of houses laid out behind walls. Covering the hills like big smiles, she thought, red lips and white, white teeth. Mouths laughing forever. Baby Poppa saying, "Look at those girls when your sons come home to visit—every mouth for miles gets to grinning."

The land was gold where it had been left bare, the grass burned pale or gone in the vacant lots where she walked and the dirt had been leveled for new houses. And the sky was white here in California, already no-color from the heat and it was only the end of May. Sky so bright from the first minute of day, before 6 A.M., not like Pine Gardens, where even on the longest, hottest days the oaks and their long moss curls kept the light spotted and deep. She reached out and ran her hand along this rough wall, touching the vines. This must be an older track, because the street was slightly grayed, like the sun had been working it for a while. Not like the deep black asphalt of the brand-new complex where they lived. Tendrils brushed her fingers; where did the vines find water in the walls?

There surely wasn't water anywhere else, only from sprinklers. She knew by the way the gentle slope went before her that the depression ahead wasn't a river, the way it would be at home, but the freeway again. The same place she had ended up last week, walking down a different road next to another track. She could hear the traffic-wind, and quickly she came to the end of the wall and the hard-packed dirt that was everywhere past the sidewalk. At the chainlink fence lining the banks of the freeway, she watched the cars swim slowly past her. Six-thirty—morning rush hour, Carolanne said. The tips of dried weeds tangled in the wire near her feet, rustling like autumn cornstalks when she nudged them.

"Don't think you can go out this early and nobody'll see you," Carolanne had told her pointedly when she'd seen Marietta come back from a walk one morning. She'd looked at Marietta's dusty black shoes, her shirt. "Rush-hour people are out before six."

Along the curve of fence, she kept on until she saw one of the green freeway signs, huge because it was so close. BEACHES—an arrow pointed down toward the left lanes. LOS ANGELES—another pointed to the right lanes.

Nate and Calvin had taken her to Los Angeles one day and the beach the next. L.A. was a too-fast jumble of buildings to her, because she was still tired and dazed from the long drive across the country, but they wanted to show her the university and the dorms where they'd lived.

But Newport Beach—the blue and sand of this ocean, the huge waves—was a surprise. Nate wore his practice jersey, LOS ANGELES RAMS across the front, and he smiled big as a banana when a blond kid walking close to the water shouted, "Daddy, that's Nate and Calvin Cook! They got drafted by the Rams and I saw them on TV!"

Marietta had tried to imagine fishing there, but the broad expanse of sand was covered with towels and people and umbrellas; no reeds or grasses where fish could hide, no point jutting out into the water, no place to see green until they drove to Balboa, a word Nate liked to roll around his tongue. "It's private, see all the houses, Mama? I'm a have to get you one, oh, next year, most def," he had said.

"You best worry bout this year, fool," Calvin had said.

"Don't let your mouth write a check your behind can't cash," Carolanne had said sharply behind them. Little Freeman slept, his head lolling on her shoulder.

Following the line of traffic, the car roofs stacked together tight as Freeman's toy trains, only gave her a headache. All the exhaust made dancing wavers in the air. At the street that led back up the hill, she turned.

Hadn't been here but a month and already she was out of walks. She'd been walking in the space of time after the boys left for the field and before Carolanne and Freeman woke up. The boys had to run and work out early, before the heat and smog filled the air. Every morning, Calvin dressed in his sweats at five-thirty, and when she heard his feet thud on the carpet, she got up to make him biscuits and grits. "Mama, I ain't eating till we get back," he said. "Come on, now."

"You best get use to good food again, not that McDonald food. How you muscle gon work on air and grease?" She handed him a plate wrapped in foil, for Nate. "Take this and I see you when you back."

He would walk next door, pound for a minute, and when she looked outside in the gray dark, she could see Nate put the food in his mouth as he leaned into the dashboard light.

Jump around like crickets in these new condominium rooms, run and lift weight in the morning, then don't know what for do rest a the day. Talking bout rookie mini-camp over but official training camp start in July—that almost two month away.

A scratch of tires, quick as a burp, squealed again and again ahead of her. The line of cars waited to get out of the walls. Only one street led into the square of houses, and each car rushed through the stop sign, slowing just a second so the drivers could stare at her and past her; then they swerved out to join the line snaking up the hill to the main road and the freeway.

They turned away from her quickly. She tensed, made herself breathe. She'd forgotten about them for a while. Her clothes, her back. Damn, that woman big. Damn, that woman black. Is that a *woman?* The knock on the condo door—Uh, excuse me, I'm looking for the lady of the house. Oh, the owner? She held her shoulders tight, breathed, until she crossed between two cars. The first time she'd walked—Uh, need a lift, buddy? someone had said behind her. When she turned, a security guard leaned out his car window, growing a sunset across his cheeks. "Sorry, uh, sorry. Are you lost, ma'am?"

Her clothes were wrong. Already, through the open patio doors of their adjoining balconies, she'd heard Carolanne say on the phone, "We look black enough, okay? It ain't like there's a whole lot of us in the complex—try none. And what's she gonna wear? She ain't fitting into no Spiegel's. I *gave* her the catalog, okay?"

That first week she'd lived here—when Carolanne had tried to smile and not study her, when she didn't know if she could just open their door or if she had to knock—she'd stood outside, hearing Freeman's cries after the boys had left, and pushed the door open. She had seen the way Carolanne looked at her clothes, her scarf, but she didn't know what Carolanne was trying to tell her.

"Where you going, anyway?"

"Just walk, what wrong with the baby?"

"He's had diarrhea."

"I stop at the store when I walk for some more rice—you can give he rice water."

"There's no store around here you can walk to—this is Anaheim Hills." Carolanne squinted at her. "You can't drive, really? You're exercise walking?"

Marietta felt the air on her palms. She carried nothing in her hands, she had finally realized, no weights to swing or tiny radio with headphones or little white towel. By nine or ten each morning, when she watched out her window, she could see the other women from the condos walking, usually in pairs, wearing pink or yellow or lavender sweatsuits, white shoes, white headbands or visors. They swung their arms and weights, their feet round and hard on the pavement. They were dressed right; she looked like she was headed to a store or cemetery or house that needed cleaning. "Great workout, huh!" one had called to her, and she thought, Carry you some grocery, two baby, and a basket of peach fe exercise. Walk to the store—two mile.

But there was no store here. Squares and circles of streets inside the walls, and she'd gotten lost in one that first week, a maze of white stucco fronts and square-closed garages all the same, staring like boxes on the game shows Carolanne watched sometimes. Tiny trees like feather dusters in planters along the walls. She was almost home now, back to the huge sign that said "EDGEWILD OAKS—LUXURY CONDOMINIUMS IN THE ANAHEIM HILLS."

She had forgotten about these two trees. The huge gnarled oaks and branches that reached out past their fenced-in planter—one on each side of the guard gate where she had to nod each time to the eyes. A woman came out of the section of cobblestone road between the two trees. "Aren't they beautiful?" she said when she saw Marietta and smiled. She wore a purple sweatsuit and purple hoop earrings. "I'm always so happy to see they left them here."

"I never knew oak trees live in California," Marietta murmured.

"California live oaks," the woman said. "Do you work in the neighborhood?" She smiled again and stretched her arms behind her.

"No. I live here with my son."

"Oh! Where are you from?" The woman's voice was southern-soft.

"South Carolina."

"I'm from Georgia!" she said. "I didn't expect oaks, either." She smiled once more and began to walk quickly, her arms pumping like she was boxing with the air.

"She too evil for me stay over there," Nate said, sitting on the black leather couch with Calvin. He had brought his cherry Kool-Aid with him, in a plastic bottle that he tilted to his mouth for long swallows. "She don't want this stuff around, talking bout, 'Why you can't drink somethin cept sugar water? Poor people drink Kool-Aid. You got money—buy them Perrier or somethin.'" He unscrewed his face from the imitation. "Them Perrier taste like bubble spit. She gettin on my nerves."

"Kool-Aid make you tongue all red, like a dog from hell," Calvin said, and Nate tried to touch his chin with it.

"L-l-l-aahh," he gargled. "So?"

"Maybe she just tire from run around in this heat," Marietta said. "She been had for take the baby day care and go to she dance class."

"Ain't nobody said she gotta take Freeman down there. Place cost big money, and you said you want for watch him anyway. Don't ax me all the scientific reason she gotta have him in day care, cause I don't even want for think about it. Now she fixin for go shopping and want me come. Uh-uh."

Calvin changed channels on the huge television with the remote control, switching back and forth, driving her crazy. Sixty-eight channels, and he and Nate would sit there for hours, blip zip blip, sports channels and music videos and shooting, loud cheers and then high laughter flying around the room until they found something they liked.

"Man, go get me a towel," Nate said. "You couch sticky as hell less I put on long pants and long sleeve."

Calvin raised his eyebrows, not looking away from the guitar player and the girls in black underwear. Marietta saw a wild wind blow the girls' long hair. "What you talk bout '*Get* me'? I look like you valet? Heat made you foolish? You ain't taken no shower, man. This real leather."

"And real sticky. Now you sound like Carolanne, too. Take a shower—go clean up. You all funky. Hell, she know we gon go back out later and lift weights, get all sweaty again. I ain't takin no two shower a day—both y'all crazy." They could hear his arms peel away from the cushion.

"Leather ain't practical," Marietta said, getting up to check the chicken frying in the kitchen. Calvin liked wings and drumsticks for snacks.

"But it look *good,* don't it?" Calvin called to her, and she smiled.

She turned the spitting chicken and moved the paper bag holding the flour and spices. Cook some okra later, if she could get Carolanne to bring some from the store. She go to the store every day, seem like. The vegetables from the big stores were waxy and too hard, but Marietta hadn't seen a fresh vegetable or fruit stand anywhere, on all the streets and freeways they'd driven.

She went next door and knocked. Carolanne opened the door after a few minutes, but she held the edge against her. "I'm not dressed," she said. Her eyes were small and bare, tight like she'd been asleep.

"I just want to know you going to the store," Marietta said. "I need some okra."

"I'll be over in a while," Carolanne said, already pushing on the door. "Tell Nate he has to come because we're going to look for more furniture for you."

Marietta didn't say anything to Nate when she was back in the kitchen. He and Calvin lay sprawled on the couch, watching the television and laughing at the music videos. Nate had been complaining about Carolanne for days; she had heard them shouting through the screens, the walls. Maybe Carolanne was angry because Nate spent his time over here, even brought Freeman to eat because Carolanne didn't want to cook much. Too hot, she said, and she did seem to be suffering from the heat, for some reason, her face puffy and movements slow. Marietta thought Carolanne should be used to the heat, she'd been born in Los Angeles and lived all her life here, but even Calvin told her that Carolanne didn't seem right. "She tripping" was all Nate would say.

The boys' voices echoed off the mostly bare walls, hollered above the television, and she shook her head. How were they planning to last until July? Everything had moved so fast since the day of the draft, and now time was stalled, Nate and Calvin like fish much too small for the glass bowl someone had put them in.

And she felt restless herself, cooking whenever she could, the boys eating it all right away. Nate kept saying he had to get bigger before camp started. They talked to their agent on the phone nearly every day; he took care of all the money, the contracts, and when she heard the words Calvin repeated into the phone, she knew everything had shifted big-time. It would never be like before—she could study all the sports magazines, their playbooks from the coaches, but she couldn't plan anything for them now. Carolanne had picked out the condominiums, the little potted plants on the patios. She loved to decorate, she said. And Freeman, the grandboy, still wouldn't let his Big Ma carry him or hug him often because he didn't know her yet. He seemed afraid of her height, her headscarf, which he stared at, and he always buried his face in his mother's legs if Marietta tried to get him to say, "Big Ma," or pick up a toy and hand it to her.

She heard Nate and Carolanne's telephone, piercing through the walls. No *ringing* phones here, like she was used to, with a bell sound. Carolanne's phone squealed like Jesse's wheezing brakes back in Charleston, insistent and then stopping abruptly, mad. No faint echo of metal. Nate and Calvin stopped talking, and the phone creaked again. "Answering machine a get it," Nate said. "If it's D.J. and them and Carolanne don't pick it up, they call over here."

The squeal stopped, and then Calvin's phone burbled. His was an electric bubble, like nothing she could picture in her head, and on the second sound, Calvin picked it up. They would go out and run the street, or the freeways, she guessed, with some of the other rookies who were just as bored, or with Rock Jones, the second-year defensive back. Like stray dogs out to see what they were missing.

Nate stuck his head back in the door. "Now she sleep again, Mama," he said. "Something ain't right, like she sick but not really. You gon check on her?"

She stood in the still-shady spot between their doors. The sun beat hard on the other side of the buildings. Nate and Calvin slammed car doors, and she heard the loud stereo vibrate against the metal and glass when they left the garage below her. She listened at Carolanne's kitchen window, which looked out at the valley between buildings, but she heard no talking, no television.

The chicken was cooling on the counter. She wiped the grease from around the burners, washed the dishes, and stood in the doorway again, not sure what to do. The air was silent except for the low, faint hum of all the huge boxes outside that controlled the air-conditioning, the metal things that stood next to each building, hidden by little walls and bushes. No yard work to do; the landscaping, as Carolanne called it, was taken care of by the condominium people.

Marietta went back into the shadowy darkness of the living room, where the blinds were drawn on the sliding glass door. The air felt suddenly too cool and stale to her; she had liked being *cold* a few times in this place, where she could turn the air up that high, but now she felt as if she couldn't breathe. No screen doors here, either, so you were either inside or outside, or in the car, where the air pushed against your face from the dashboard, too. Nothing between these doors to let you listen, nothing to let you hear footsteps of someone visiting.

The living room was bare except for the huge black couch, a black reclining chair, a shelf-like stack of black-stained wood holding the stereo against one wall, and a beautiful wooden box Carolanne had bought for Calvin's cassette tapes and videos. Gleaming ebony shone under the coat of varnish, the corners were rounded and bent as if by magic, and Marietta liked to touch the drawers that slid smooth as oil into water.

"He was just going to let them lay around all sloppy or put them in a shoebox," Carolanne had told her. "Men are slobs. That's why you have to think about every piece you buy when you're decorating—so it won't look sloppy, so it'll work together."

Marietta breathed in the smell of chicken and opened the cream-colored blinds to get to the glass door. The walls were creamy, too, but Carolanne was working on something—"black for Calvin's okay, but we need something feminine for you," she said. "I saw some things in a magazine—I could show you."

Out on these balconies, stretching in a curved line all around her, cutting each condominium in half, Marietta had never seen anyone else. Maybe she came out at the wrong times. A few people had plants and wicker or white metal chairs behind the wooden railings, but most of the balconies were bare. It was different from Charleston, where people turned balconies into jungles of green leaves and hanging stems, where clothes dangled in the wind and people sat outside to shell peanuts, drink iced tea.

She pulled one of the dinette chairs outside and sat in the sail-shaped corner of shade that was beginning to creep onto the stucco. The stucco was sandy-colored, like the shoulder of the highway—she rubbed her feet across the grainy hardness. All this time she'd known she would leave, been waiting to leave and imagining the place they would end up, she and the boys. Now Charleston, not just Tiny Momma and the others, but the railings and the river, and even Pine Gardens, kept appearing in her mind; they flashed like someone showing off photos to friends.

She put up her feet close to the railing and looked at the center strip of landscaping and the balconies facing her. Too hot for most people to come out in the middle of the day. But no one came out in the evening either, no kids, no dogs. People came home from work, she heard their cars growling in the garages below, but then they seemed to disappear straight from the garages, inside until morning.

She had really come out here to see the stream, she knew. She wanted to walk down the center piece of grass and sit beside it, put her feet in the water, and walk on the white rocks that lined the streambed. It was too blue, of course, and she'd had to study for a while to figure out that the streambed was painted, a pale sky shade. But flowers surrounded the water, growing near the rocks, the dead ones pulled out and replaced as soon as she'd noticed them wilting. When she was a child, she would have thought it was magic, the trickling and the perfect white rocks like giant eggs. She imagined lying near them, flowers against her arms, ignoring the baskets and peaches waiting for her.

But she'd never seen anyone touch the water or walk near it. She wondered if Freeman wanted to wade in it; Carolanne's blinds were always closed on the sliding glass door. Rubbing her fingers across the stucco bumps beside her, she closed her eyes to listen for Carolanne's movement behind the glass a few feet away.

The first thing she saw was the hand and long red nails around the corner, and then Carolanne. "Why you out here in the heat? You got the air-conditioning on."

Marietta shook her head. "I still don't see how you go long with them nails."

"Like I said, the hardest thing is dialing. You've gotta have pushbutton phones."

"I bet you do," Marietta said. She smiled at the peach-colored forehead, remembering all the bleaching cremes when she saw how pale the gold skin was under the hair rising black and feathery away from it. Carolanne's eyes were gold, today, and the powder under her brows was sparkling purple.

"Air-condition make my nose stop up."

"We could get some Mentholatum from the store," Carolanne said. "Freeman has a stuffy nose, too. Again."

Inside, she said she shouldn't, but Carolanne ate two of the chicken wings. Marietta peeled potatoes and gouged out the eyes with her thumbnail. Carolanne grasped her hand and looked at the hard, thick nails.

"Look at this—I have to paint mine with all that strengthening stuff or get mine wrapped, and you just grow these."

"They useful sometime."

"They have really good potato salad in the deli section at Pavilions. Just pick some up when we're there," Carolanne said.

"I don't need to save no time," Marietta said. "Go on and get ready."

The potatoes were boiled by the time Carolanne came back with different clothes, redder lips. She looked at the cream carpet and black furniture again while Marietta put on her shoes.

"I thought we could try purple and green, you know? We need to go to Pier 1 and get some stuff for color."

She whipped her small car out of the security gate without looking at the guard. "Don't you want to learn how to drive?"

Marietta said, "Maybe. But I rather learn in the Lincoln, case somebody hit me."

"You won't have an accident. Calvin's a good driver." Carolanne sped down the ramp and onto the freeway. "I thought we could hit Pier 1 first, then get the food and stuff, and pick up Freeman. My girlfriend called and said something good's on Oprah. Cross dressers—guys wearing ladies' underwear."

"You watch some crazy things on that show," Marietta said.

She did want to learn to drive, she had decided on the long trip with the boys. But the way Carolanne drove every day made her dizzy. Carolanne circled around tight and impatient in the malls and store parking lots, looking for a space, getting angry when somebody dumped packages and didn't start her car. "Why people so damn slow all the time?" she said, and in the clog of cars on the main streets near the shopping centers, she rocked impatiently. "I hate this mall," she said.

People crowded the stores no matter what time they went. Marietta walked beside Carolanne into the jungle cool of the mall; her skin tingled at the cool, hot, cool—car, parking lot, store—over and over. In Pier 1, Carolanne slowed down, considering bright purple pillows and holding them out for Marietta.

"The couch?" she asked. "They'll just throw them on the floor, but that's okay. And see this green vase? Look."

Marietta lingered at the wall of baskets—every size, from matchbox squares to huge clothes hampers. And all colors, weaves, materials, but when she examined them closely, the sheaves and twine and straw were usually loose and very simple. The patterns were painted on, the colored straw dyed green and red and yellow. She ran her fingers down the rough weave of a trashbasket, thinking that Aint Sister would snort. Made in China—Made in Taiwan—Made in Philippines. Marietta turned when Carolanne called her.

"How about brass?" Carolanne said, holding up candlesticks and bowls to catch the light. They were etched with tiny marks and patterns.

"Those thing too beautiful," Marietta said, surprised.

They bought the brass decorations, several pillows, and a wicker trunk with brass fittings. "I need something for my bedroom, for keep picture and thing," Marietta said.

"Didn't you want some baskets?"

"No—look how much we spend already."

"But you gave me all the ones you brought with you from South Carolina."

"They was for you," Marietta said. "We need for go on to the store."

After the riot of colors and touching at Pier 1, she was already tired of shopping, and the huge supermarket was cold and confusing as ever; she hated the smell, like a refrigerator that had been washed with mop water already cloudy from floor dirt.

The carts fought and women stared and everything was too hard to distinguish—there were walls of shampoo, rows and rows of cereal boxes and cans. Baking soda was near chocolate, grits were by the cereal, and rice was in with the spaghetti. She stood, bewildered, by the medicine section, where tiny bottles and boxes were lined up so close the antlike script ran together. Carolanne grabbed the bright green jar of Mentholatum and said, "You see those new cards they have—for kids! Like 'I'm proud of you' and 'Here's a hug.' When Freeman can read, I'ma start buying those."

He came staggering to them in the bright room of the daycare center, still walking uncertainly, like Nate and Calvin that summer when they sometimes raised puffs of dust with their behinds. "Doggie," he said to Marietta, pointing at the wall where posters of cats and dogs and lions hung. Then he wandered back to the group of children playing on the carpet; his brown face bobbed into the heads immediately. The other children were all white or Asian, and his head was the only one with curls. He looked up for a second and Carolanne said, "It's like he doesn't even care that we're here."

"No," Marietta said. She remembered those checking looks and then the seeming disinterest. "You walk out, he start for cry. He know where we are."

"Where's the truck?" Carolanne said in the car, and he pointed out the window. "Good boy! You are so smart."

"Where tree?" Marietta asked, and he jabbed a finger toward the palm.

They brought the trunk and bags to Marietta's first, and Freeman ran to swim on the black couch he loved. He rubbed his cheek against the cool leather until Marietta carried the trunk into the living room, and then he stood peering into it while she moved her wooden box from a kitchen cupboard to the place of honor in the trunk.

She had kept all her things in the kitchen cupboard because she couldn't think of a better place. Carolanne saw the spider and the jars of tea, turning them curiously in the harsh fluorescent light. She said, "I'll be right back," and in a moment she came from her place carrying a small table. She put it in the corner near the sliding glass door and arranged the jars on it, then stood back. "I can't use this table cause Freeman always messes with it," she said. "Look—this can go here." She took the spider and put it on the edge of the marble fireplace. "These colors are great."

Marietta looked at them and quickly walked over to move

them back to the cupboard. "This tea—for me drink, maybe I get sick," she said. "And spider for cook outside, over fire. Who gon make a fire in there?"

Carolanne said, "This is great stuff—look, you're supposed to *display* collections of antiques like this."

"It just medicine," Marietta said, holding the jars. "I don't see you display no Mentholatum and aspirin." She heard her voice hard, and she saw Carolanne's mouth twitch into her cheek. She was hurt.

"Nate said you've had that stuff all his life and he's never seen you drink it," Carolanne said.

Marietta couldn't stop. "Maybe he didn't see me every minute I been alive."

"Whatever," Carolanne said, angry, and she pulled Freeman up from the trunk, where he was half-fallen inside. "Leave that stuff alone. We have to go home now."

Marietta sat on the couch when they had left, looking out the huge sheet of glass. No reprimands from Aint Sister, no humming complaints from Rosie or Pinkie or Tiny Momma—no questions about what she wasn't doing or cooking or watching. She went to the trunk and opened the wooden box, took out the picture of her father. Freeman. Another Freeman next door. She held the shell Calvin had brought from Pine Gardens to Charleston, all those years ago. Go knock, she thought. Take she something. But don't tell she what for do. Just help. She try she own way.

In Carolanne's living room, she said, "I don't mean for say something so hard," and Carolanne nodded. Freeman let Marietta hold him long enough to smell his hair and neck before he got down, carrying the shell. She watched his round face, not as dark as Nate's, much darker than Carolanne's. He had Nate's large black-shined eyes and eyebrows, and Carolanne's delicate mouth. His arms were padded around the elbows when he knocked into her, pulling out the cars and bears and trucks from his toy chest to bring them to her and then take them back. Rosie's large basket held plastic blocks, and the smaller baskets were on the counter separating the kitchen from the dining area; they were filled with the peppermints Nate liked.

Carolanne got a bottle of bubbly water from the kitchen and sat on the couch. "I wonder when he'll listen for the ocean," she said, watching Freeman put the shell into a truckbed and move it to a bowl. Marietta smiled. "I have to change these shoes," Carolanne said, and went to her bedroom.

Marietta listened to the television and Freeman's chattering at the bears and trucks. Carolanne's living room was peach-colored, with paintings of deserts and huge flowers; she had put tall vases filled with plumes of fluffy grass and stark branches in the corners. The dining-room table had a pale green vase in the center, filled with white flowers.

"Go take that in your room and play," Carolanne said, coming back to collapse into one of the armchairs. Freeman had gotten the xylophone. "Go on, you make too much noise with that." He got a grasp on it and went obediently to his bedroom.

Marietta waited for the phone to ring as Oprah came out into the audience. Every day Calvin's friend Tiana, who was still in college, one-rang Carolanne, who called her back long distance, and they watched the show together. Long pauses and then, "Gi-i-rl, you hear what he said?"

Marietta went into the bathroom and closed the door. Freeman's plinking still came through. When she sat on the toilet, a shard of deep blue, like a piece of the glass she had always looked for, caught her eye. In the wastebasket, a white plastic wand had blue staining the tip. She leaned down to pull it out, then found a small box. Home pregnancy test. Results in minutes. Turns blue if positive.

Carolanne appeared at the door with Nate a few days later, carrying a stack of large baskets shaped like buckets; Nate held two trees, which she put inside the baskets and placed near the couch. "Here's more," she said, bringing in some of the dark green and purple baskets Marietta had touched. "I saw you looking at them, spending a lot of time over there," Carolanne said, smiling. "You should always get what you want."

She couldn't ask Nate if he knew. Of course he didn't know. She couldn't make herself ask Carolanne about what she'd seen, either. The boys stayed in Calvin's living room most of the days, and Carolanne slept, grew angry when Freeman whined and stiffened and cried in the car seat and the stroller at the mall. But she went to aerobics class every day, and her belly was shined tight in the leotard she wore.

Maybe the shouting she heard from their place, drifting

through the walls and screens, and the way Nate spent hours with the other players, had nothing to do with Carolanne. It had to be because both of the boys were so nervous—obsessed with workouts, running sprints, and blocking, studying plays and tapes, and it seemed as if Nate didn't want to talk about anything else. "Preseason," he said over and over. Maybe Carolanne feel neglect, maybe she tell he and he ain't excited. But how I ax Nate?

Almost every afternoon, their friends came before weight lifting, several huge men ducking in the doorway to greet Calvin and Nate. She couldn't believe she was cooking for four or five men with necks so thick they could probably swallow whole fish; why was she cutting it into pieces to fry it?

"Where you live?" she asked the one they called Rock, the smallest.

"Me and Marcus stay in Santa Ana, Miz Cook," he said. "We got an apartment."

"Just you two?"

"Yeah."

"How I know that—how I guess nobody there for cook?" she asked, rolling her eyes. She liked him. "And you?" She turned to the one they had introduced as Incredible Bulk. His real name was Jeffrey, and she liked that; he was light, with a round head and clean face. He looked like a Jeffrey, so that was what she called him. "Jeffrey, where you live?"

"I live with my dad, in L.A. I have a brother in San Francisco, and my sister's in San Diego." He was so polite and careful that she smiled.

"And you gotta come visit Calvin," she said, "when you hungry."

"I like fish, ma'am."

"Miz Cook," Rock said. "My uncle lives in Rio Seco, and he go fishin all the time. Maybe sometime you and Calvin can drive out there with me, if you like to catch something."

"Well, I have for catch a shark if I feed all you."

"You can't eat shark, man," Jeffrey said.

"We use to watch guys throw sharks on the dock every day, man," Nate told him. "Do whatever you want with em."

"I forgot, you two are swamp boys," Rock said. "Talkin that secret talk when you don't want me to dig what you saying to each other. Hmmm."

They ate on the couch or the carpet, watching kung fu videos or game tapes or ESPN. She brought them plates, and then she sat at the dining-room table alone, listening. She really didn't mind all the cooking, because she liked to listen to them talk. She tried to decipher the language, careful with the context like when she had stared at the pictures and words of the magazine under the tree. At first, she couldn't understand half of what they said, especially Rock and Jeffrey, who spoke some kind of California language.

"Oh, man, we livin large. We can *choose* the ride, the crib. Females for me and Calvin, and look but don't touch for my man Nate. Homeboy tied down in the desert with rope, and the ants are on they way." Rock patted Nate's shoulder, and Nate backhanded him in the chest, but he said nothing about another baby. Marietta knew he didn't know.

"Shut up, man, we ain't livin no large yet. We ain't made the cut. August 29—roster time. Then I'ma talk smack, okay?" Nate stared at the screen.

Where had he learned to talk like this? His voice was still soft, but the words were fast. Marietta didn't look at them; she watched for bones in the fish, chewing softly so she could hear.

"You talkin *too* much yang, Nate, man. I heard Wilson jammin you up yesterday," Rock said.

"Shit, he been around forever," Jeffrey said.

"Yeah, and he was saying, '*Nate* think he *great,* talking bout *fate,* but when he go up against me, we talking *checkmate.*'" Rock laughed.

"Why blood always smackin in rhyme like that?" Nate said.

"That's his personality, you know, he get plenty pub for that. See him in the paper all the time—fans eat it up."

Nate stood up and paced. "Well, damn, that's all I'm tryin to do. Stand out so coach notice me. I'ma be the linebacker give everybody trouble. Trouble Man. Y'all call me that. I like that." He sang in a high voice like Marvin Gaye, from a record people had played back in Charleston, Marietta remembered. "I come up hard, baby, but never cool; I didn't make it, baby, playin by the rules. Come up hard, baby, I had to fight; checkin trouble, sugar, with all my might."

"Listen at blood!" Rock laughed. "Little old voice out them big-ass lungs."

"Hey, I come up serious hard, man," Nate said.

"Shit, man," Jeffrey frowned. "You didn't live in the jungle."

"Shut up, Bulk, you said you from L.A.," Calvin said.

"Yeah, my hood called the Jungle. Like you two boys never seen."

Nate said, "Yeah, well, we from the woods, man. Like you never. . ."

Calvin interrupted them. "Man, don't none a that count if we can't make it on the field. I think y'all better slow down with talkin big smack till we catch up to the plays."

"Aw, brother, you *always* been scary," Nate said. "Remember. . ." Marietta clicked her glass hard on the table when she stood up, embarrassed now, and they stopped when they heard.

"I didn't move here to California for do day work," she said.

"Excuse me, Miz Cook?" Rock said, and she had to shake her head. He didn't understand her language.

"'Day work' mean 'maid.' You all pick up you dish, cause I ain't get pay for that. And don't forget you glass on the floor."

But sometimes she heard Nate and Calvin talk like gone time, like Pine Gardens. They spoke like children when they wanted to hide something from the other players, and the past was a secret code. "He long-eye at the track," Calvin said. "Wilson."

"What?" Nate said softly.

"Somebody sweetmouth you today. You ear was close. You gon know who talk fe you, fast-fast. Sweetmouth fe you too much."

"So?"

"Coach see. Wilson beena hot the fight—better for he, not you, cause you fe get bighead. Use you vex, man—vex help you fe beat he August."

"What the hell you saying, Calvin?" Rock would frown. "Speak English, man, you in America."

"Yeah, Rock," Calvin smiled. "We in America, living large. Living *big* large, for now."

Freeman spoke his own language, too. After Nate and Calvin returned from weight lifting in the evening, Marietta went next door to give her grandson a bath. That was one thing Carolanne let her do, because she said Freeman whined and got water all over her clothes.

Before the bath, he had free run of the living room, just like the boys had roamed the yard frantically as dark fell, knowing their day was almost finished. "Ah-in," Freeman said, touching Calvin. That was as close as he could get to the name. His only clearly pronounced words were "Daddy," "doggie," "duck," and "ot-ot," for food that he wasn't supposed to touch yet because it was still steaming.

Marietta could hold him now, but she had no name. Nate kept telling Carolanne that his gran should be watching him, because she'd keep the best eye on him, probably better than the day care, where there were so many kids, but Carolanne shook her head.

"He's seventeen months. He needs structured playtime, that's what all the books say. He needs organized activities with other kids, so he can get used to social situations. He sees Gramma every night." Carolanne didn't have a name for her, either. She was Big Ma around Freeman, but when she and Marietta were shopping, she said, "You need some milk? Uh, here, you passed the toothpaste."

Structure play, Marietta thought. I send he out in the yard with some pot and pan and spoon. He find out what for play he ownself. But ain't no yard, and ain't none of you pot and pan you let near no ground. Flower and gold all round the edge—they too fancy.

She had kept Freeman one afternoon when he had a cold, while Carolanne went to aerobics. Marietta looked at the blouse she wore over her leotard. "It's too cold in the studio," Carolanne said. And when she had come in the door unexpectedly, Freeman was shrieking with laughter while Marietta danced a headless whole chicken toward him. "Chicken gon get you!" Marietta said, and then with the other hand made the trout wiggle-swim in the air at him. "Fish get you, too!"

"My God," Carolanne said. "He's gonna have nightmares about seeing animals and then eating them." The rise of her lip made Marietta as hot as she had been near the women who were silent while she cleaned around them all those years.

Nowhere for walk, get a ice cream. No fish in the creek, I mean the landscape. She said nothing, just watched as Carolanne said, "Show him that book, Nate, the one he likes you to read. The doggie one."

"Mr. Thomas took his dog Walter for a walk in the park every day," Nate read, and Marietta looked over his shoulder at the big, shaggy dog with his tongue hanging out.

"Where the doggie, Freeman?" Carolanne said. "Show me doggie."

"Oh, da," Freeman said, pointing at the window. He had seen dogs being walked in the street.

"No, baby, in the book. Where the doggie?"

He stared at the book, but didn't point. "Shoot, he tired," Nate said. "Me, too."

"No, he never picks out the dogs in his books," Carolanne said. "He always does at the wall in day care. See, this isn't a learning situation for him, it's a play thing. That's why I like the day-care center."

Marietta looked at the shaggy dog again, but all she said was "Come for take bath, Freeman. Time give Mama some rest before you go bed." In the tub, he poured water into her palms, watching it disappear. Kneeling, she soaped him all over, and when she ran her hands down him to wipe off the excess bubbles, she thought there was nothing smoother in the world than a baby's back, with no spine showing, no muscle, nothing but a blind fall of skin, straight as could be.

Calvin and Nate showed their backs when they watched TV with Rock and Jeffrey, shirtless or in tank tops, and their muscles fascinated her, almost frightened her. Their skin stretched tight over miniature pillows, at their shoulders, their biceps, even their backs when they leaned past the coffee table. Rock not so big—he a defensive back, she thought. Like me. But look them other boy. Lift weight every day, till they got stretch mark like a woman. The broken lines of paler skin webbed out from their armpits; she imagined hard bags of grits, packets of rice, growing under their skin. Laha's Jerry and Big Johnny had flat arms until they strained with a shovel or an ax, and then their muscles were ropy-long. But Nate's arms bulged even while he sat and worried about weight lifting.

"I gotta get up to four twenty-five today, man. I gotta bench four twenty-five. I gotta get bulked up. I been eating and lifting forever—it takes too long."

"You ain't the Incredible Bulk, man," Rock said.

"Yeah, I had to *sacrifice* to get this way, homeboy. I could help you out, but you don't want to. . ." Jeffrey said.

"I ain't gotta be *you,* man," Nate said. "I just gotta weigh two-eighty in August. Coach said that's what he wants. He keep talking bout college was only twelve games a season, and we got twenty." Nate stuffed meat and rice into his mouth, three and four times a day, whole plates of whatever Marietta gave him, and he grumbled, "All Carolanne want to do is buy something from the deli or make one a them Lean Cuisines. I gotta get bulked, I told her."

"You pacing round here losing weight from worry," Marietta told him.

"That don't have nothin to do with weight, Mama," he said. "It's hard."

Rock came over almost every day before lunch and scared them about next month's training camp; it was late June now, and they listened to him over chickens and regiments of glasses.

"Naw, man, double-days gon kick you *ass*—just like they suppose to. And the *veteranos* gon kick you ass at night. They get you on the field and they get you in the dorm. Last year they dogged Leroy, man, they put cold spaghetti in his bed, like worms, and then somebody locked him in our room so he was late to practice. Coach was hot."

They paced around after lunch and Nate said, "I can't be thinkin so much. Let's hit the flicks." They would all go to the movies, leaving her with the television.

She washed the dishes to the endless talking of soap operas. In Charleston, she had half listened to the soaps with Tiny Momma on days off, but her eyes had really been on the bowl of peas or the hole in the jeans. On a cleaning job, there was often a TV in the kitchen with the housekeeper and one somewhere else for the woman of the house, but Marietta caught only scattered sobs and shouting between rooms while she worked.

She sat on the black leather, careful to pull a shirt behind her, and stared at the glitter of the women's eyes and lips, their hair standing away from their faces stiffly. The men's hair was careful and thick, too, their chins pointing at the women. She concentrated. Things seemed slower and louder than she remembered from her glimpses, and their mouths moved so much more than anyone's she knew, but she put her feet up and rested her hands on her stomach. The couple on the screen began to kiss, their mouths wide against each other; they moved through the room and fell onto the bed, and the pink satin straps fell from her neck when she arched back for his lips. Marietta looked out the sliding glass door. Tiny Momma and Miss Alberta always loved this part.

Maybe she should call Tiny Momma. The phone rang and rang—it was already five o'clock there. Tiny Momma was probably at the store, now that the heat had faded a bit.

Carolanne was getting her nails done before she went to get Freeman.

Marietta tried to force herself to relax, keep her hands still. She looked at her own nails again. The women on TV had colored, carefully pointed nails like Carolanne's. She saw Carolanne's nails on Nate's arms, back in Charleston that first time; she saw the glossy drops on the bare back of the man on the screen. When she turned the channel with the remote, she saw more soaps, more lips, and on MTV the colors changed suddenly to bluish-gray and white—shadowed forms, but they were still man and woman tangled in sheets, then an alley, then writhing in the back seat of a car.

She smelled Sinbad's cologne in the back of her throat. Milt's palms, wood and oil and bergamot hairdress, passing her face to hold the back of her head when he kissed her. The car—the close air—teeth on her ear and lips in Sinbad's bed.

She stared at the couple, their pale skin in the moonlight, turned them to more lush-haired actors, to ESPN. A soccer game.

Carolanne's nails in Nate's short hair when she bent over him on the couch—Marietta shook her head and stood in the space between the condo doors to listen for Carolanne's car.

She paced, and the boys paced, too. She had fed them fish, always fish, but this fish she bought from the store in the plastic wrap and Styrofoam trays didn't seem to calm them, stop them from twisting around the room like they had swirled in her belly. She went to the fish counter at the big supermarket and bought red snapper from the ice, piles of not-fresh shrimp, but Nate grew more and more unpredictable. He snapped at Calvin, at Carolanne, and Marietta thought, She beena tell he bout the baby.

If a baby in there. Carolanne's stomach was only slightly pouched, just a bend, and Marietta thought that could be Freeman's seat from when he was born, the little shelf women kept near their hips for their just-walking babies. Aerobics, dance lessons, her eyes still brilliant green sometimes and gold others, but always bright. Maybe there wasn't a baby.

But Nate threw a chair at the wall one night; Calvin was gone somewhere with Rock, and Marietta was on the couch, napping, when she heard the crash of something against the plaster. She ran next door, thinking something had fallen—was Freeman all right?—but Nate answered the door.

"Sorry, Mama, soon as I do it I know I scare you." He tried to put his arms around Carolanne, who was crying, and said, "I got too much on my mind."

Carolanne pulled away from him and snapped, "You gon have a lot of blood on your head you do that again, cause I'll knock your ass out when you sleep. I don't play that shit, nigger. Don't you ever do that shit in front of my son."

Marietta had never heard Carolanne's voice like that, that language, and she went out onto her balcony even after Calvin came home. She couldn't sleep well at night anyway, not in that big bed. She was used to warm, noisy naps on a couch, with voices through the window.

She could see all the lights on the hills across the freeway. Gold street lights, silver house lights—they flickered in the heat, and then red tail-lights were blinking rubies when a car headed up the streets. She couldn't do anything for Nate. What could she give Carolanne? All day, she made work for herself, saying she didn't like the harsh-chalky smell of the dishes when they came out of the dishwasher, so she washed them herself, dried and put them away. She crocheted like Tiny Momma had finally taught her, and she tried to read Carolanne's magazines—fashion and decorating and cooking. But when she had finished a blanket for the leather couch, to keep Nate from sticking, she saw that there was nothing crocheted in the kind of decor Carolanne had told her would be perfect for the condo. Nothing so homemade, or so yellow.

She sat with her feet up on the balcony railing, listening to the stream. I be thirty-nine in August, when preseason game start. Near forty year old.

She tried to watch Oprah and Phil with Carolanne, tried to make conversation. The baby with water on the brain, the women who had been raped, the men who cheated on their wives and mistresses—after someone spoke, applause like clicking marbles, before each commercial, after each commercial, the people clapping like machines. No girls came over to talk to Carolanne; she talked on the phone with Tiana, she called her aunt and sister in L.A. often.

Nate said Carolanne's mother had died when she was young. Carolanne painted her fingernails, cut out recipes, looked at the shopping channel, and pushed buttons on the phone. She told Marietta that Nate was angrier every day, refusing to do anything she asked. "He doesn't want to change. He wants his life-style to stay just the same, hang out with the boys, dress like a slob, play with Freeman for three minutes, and then watch ESPN. That's not a life-style."

When Carolanne slapped Freeman's hand lightly to make him stop pulling the leaves from the plants in the living room, he smiled as she lectured him. Nate popped him hard, and he wailed, ran in circles. "Yeah, do it the old way, Nate," Carolanne hissed. "Don't explain what he's doing wrong—just hit him and tell him 'Because.'"

Marietta couldn't watch. One night she told them, "You all come over here for eat tonight. Them boys be gone for training camp soon. I make something special."

When they were sitting at the smoked-glass table in the dining room, she put down four large dishes and turned to Carolanne. They all looked at the bowls—grits, rice, tomatoes, watermelon.

"Okay. This it—remember, Nate? Carolanne don't know. This it. Winter the white one. Summer the red one. All we have for eat sometime, maybe a week, maybe two. Calvin? You remember?"

"So?" Nate said. "Pass the rice."

"So you all worry every day bout you should be buy this, you gotta have that, all you three worry every minute. Have for go shopping, buy a new tape and new shirt. Carolanne don't know what for do with sheself, think so hard how she spend some money today. You make yourself crazy, Carolanne. Always talk bout life-style." Carolanne opened her mouth, her forehead angry, but Marietta said, "I finish. I just want recall for you how we come up."

She left, relieved and ashamed, and walked around the cars in the garage below the condos. She hadn't learned to drive yet. Maybe Calvin could teach her someday. A woman drove past and looked at her, eyes wide, and she went back inside the garage to sit inside the cool front seat of the Lincoln.

She didn't go next door for a few days, because she didn't know what to say to Carolanne. She waited for Nate to tell her something, but he only asked for more chicken. Calvin let Rock in, and Marietta said, "Well, Mr. Rock, I think we need you for take us."

"Excuse me, Miz Cook?"

"That all you ever say for me," Marietta said. "I speak clear now. My boy too worry every day. You make em worry. I think you all need for take a day off tomorrow and we go where you say you uncle and them fish. Where that place?"

"Rio Seco. I don't know, tomorrow's Saturday. Y'all think you can hang fishin in the city instead a the swamp?" Rock laughed.

Nate shrugged, but Calvin said, "I know I need a break."

"Jammin," Rock said. "You can follow me in the Lincoln."

"We gon take Freeman, Nate," Marietta said. But when she went early the next morning to get him, nodding carefully to Carolanne, she saw that Nate hadn't told her.

"Where you guys going?" Carolanne said, looking at their clothes.

"We give you a break day. We gon go fish with Rock," Marietta said. Nate picked up Freeman and walked toward the open door.

"Uh-uh, don't even trip like that," Carolanne said. "He ain't goin nowhere by no water in this heat, get burned black and he can't even swim."

"He need some color," Nate said. "You raise him like a sissy, won't let me do nothin. He goin fishin."

After Freeman's feet swung clear of the doorway, Carolanne turned to Marietta. "I don't know why you want to do this shit. You didn't want Nate to marry me in the first place, and now you want to break us up."

Marietta breathed deep. "I ain't do nothing. You two doing it. I didn't even know you and Nate was gon get marry when you come to Charleston."

"You wouldn't let him go hardship when we needed the money, you made him stay his senior year. Go ahead—catch some damn fish. I don't want to see none a you anyway." Carolanne slammed the bedroom door.

"Let's go, man," Rock said.

"I gotta wait for Bulk," Nate said.

"Bulk ain't comin, he ain't never seen a lake in his life," Rock said.

"No, he just comin by cause I have to give him somethin," Nate said, and they sat on the couch for a few minutes while Marietta changed Freeman's diaper.

When Jeffrey came in, Nate smiled and the others joked with him. Then Nate said, "Uh, come in the bedroom, man, you gotta see Calvin's new suit," and Jeffrey followed him, saying, "Yeah, Calvin, I heard you tryin to get *live* with the double-breasted." But something was too careful about Nate's eyes. His words were practiced, and she knew he was hiding something.

Calvin bounced his knee nervously and then said, "I'ma tell him we gotta go."

They were waiting in the Lincoln when Jeffrey drove away. "Just get in here and I'll drive," Nate said to Rock.

"Naw, man," Rock complained, but Calvin said, "I'll sit in the back, man, let's get on the road."

They headed the opposite way from Los Angeles, winding through steep hills, and she thought again that the California she had always seen in the magazines wasn't here. The slopes were brown and gold, and then they crossed over a riverbed. She looked down and saw a wide, sandy stripe with a thin, silver streak of water slicing down the center.

"That's the Santa Ana River," Rock said proudly.

"That ain't no river!" Nate said. "That some rain running down a gutter."

"Shut up, man, it's the only river around here. The L.A. River is in concrete and shit—this is a real river," Rock said. Calvin and Marietta laughed, too.

"We gotta go by and get my uncle," Rock went on. "He gon talk to you all day about our defense, Nate. Get off here and turn left."

They drove among warehouses and railroad tracks and suddenly they were in a neighborhood of black faces, small wooden houses with palm trees lining the streets and geraniums growing into the fences. Marietta felt her heart quicken, seeing an old truck like Big Johnny's and shirts hanging on a backyard line.

"We in the ghetto now," Rock said.

"Shit, you call *this* a ghetto?" Nate said. "Huh."

"Palm tree bigger here," Marietta murmured to Calvin, and at a house with cars parked on the dirt yard and tangles of engines around the edges, Rock told Nate to stop. A man with a long nose and freckles on his reddish skin sat with several other men on folding chairs in the yard.

"Can't you tell which one is my uncle?" Rock said. "I told you his name."

"Red Man," Calvin said. "Yeah, I can tell."

The uncle began asking Nate about the defense, the blitzes, and passing offense they might see in Cincinnati for the first exhibition game, but Calvin and Nate wanted to look at the old blunt-nosed truck parked the narrow side yard.

"Mama, didn't you use to tell us Big Johnny had a truck like that?" Nate said. "I saw it when we went back that last day before we left. I remember that big old hood, I guess. What is it, anyhow?"

"That's a '47 Chevy," one of the other men said. "Been here in Red Man's side yard since '48." They all laughed.

"Shut up, nigger, I wasn't even here in '48," Red Man shouted. Everyone started to talk then, and it was an hour before they even suggested going to the lake. Marietta circled the yard to follow Freeman, keeping him away from rusted radiators, watching the way the men listened to Nate and Calvin.

Finally, Rock got into his uncle's car, but Red Man wanted to sit with Nate and Calvin to hear more about the season. They floated down the street in the Lincoln, and at the corner stop sign she saw an old white house sitting across the street, past a long dirt yard and a wallow of dried mud; the windows were covered with plywood, just like the House in Pine Gardens, but this one was only ordinary sized.

"They was sellin that rock cocaine in there," Red Man said. "Po-lice come and got em last week, closed up the house. An old woman use to live there, when I first moved to Rico Seco, but I don't know who own it now. Use to be a pretty little house. She had the best plum tree on the Westside."

Marietta had heard about "rock houses" on the news, and she said, "Who was selling it?"

"Boys, just these dumb-ass boys from the neighborhood," Red Man said. "Three of em. One was my partner's son. Use to play basketball. They all downtown now."

Nate continued through the neighborhood and then across a deep ravine, dry at the bottom. She couldn't believe there was enough water in this place for a lake, but she kept telling Freeman, "We gon see fish and duck." They came around a curving road and she glimpsed the blue.

Close up, it was greenish brown, murky as the creeks beside the rice fields. It was a man-made lake, with bare, hard-packed dirt leading to a sharp edge and the abrupt start of the water. The ducks were so lazy and well fed that they paddled past the bread kids threw near Marietta, and Freeman ran after them, pointing, shouting, "Duck-duck! Duck-duck!"

The catfish were stocked by the county, Red Man said, but they were mean as ever, and he pointed to the regular line of men around the lake. Most of them were black or brown, she saw, and a few older white men. Loud cars drove around the lake with their stereos pounding, but the fingerlings rose and snapped at the gnats near the surface of the water when dusk came, and Marietta, Calvin, and Red Man still threw out their lines. Nate and Rock sat in beach chairs nearby, talking, and Freeman was covered with sticky ice cream from the cone Nate bought him when the tinkling truck passed.

Calvin said, "We ain't caught but a few bluegill. I ain't seen no one get a cat."

Marietta just smiled, sitting in the folding chair Red Man had brought, watching the silver moments of leaping fish, listening to the men's laughter. All day, she'd meant to take Nate aside and talk to him about what she knew wasn't right, find out why he couldn't calm himself and concentrate on next month, ask him what was wrong with him and Carolanne. She felt comfortable, away from the condo that didn't belong to her, and she watched him for the right time, but he seemed to see her eyes and stay with Rock and Red Man. She smelled the water over and over, willing him to remember the sound of tiny things hitting the surface and the bubbles rising slowly from hiding crayfish at the water's edge, hoping he would stop talking and listen.

soul gardens

july

Her legs tingled from sitting on the leather couch. She watched the soap operas, the people who moved their mouths so much more than they needed to for each word. She tried to listen to Oprah, but the clapping prickled into her ears until she turned off the television. She heard Carolanne's door open and close. Nate and Calvin only came home every two days or so, for an hour in the evening if there was no meeting. They had been at training camp for ten days, living with the other players in the Ram's compound twenty minutes' drive from the condominiums.

She slept on the couch, covered with the blanket she had made, and the telephone rang, startling her. When she said, "Hello?" a man's deep, strange voice said, "Hello. I have a very important message for you concerning financial security."

"I'm not interest today," she began, but he kept talking while she spoke. She stopped, tried again, and the voice kept on until she hung up, angry.

She thought she'd better tell Carolanne, because whoever called Calvin would probably call Nate, too, and Carolanne could tell Calvin whatever it was that the man had been saying. Maybe the phone was broken and he couldn't hear her trying to talk—the message could be important.

She hadn't been next door for days, ever since the fishing trip when they'd come back so late and Carolanne wouldn't leave her bedroom. Now she knocked and Carolanne answered, wearing shorts and a big T-shirt. "Excuse me, Carolanne," Marietta said. "Some man call for Calvin, talk about some financial thing, and when I try tell he no, he keep talking. Maybe you should come listen to the phone."

Carolanne looked puzzled for a moment and said, "He wouldn't stop talking?"

"Uh-uh. Didn't even hear me, seem."

Carolanne puffed air through her nose. "Yeah, cause he was a machine. Didn't he sound funny to you? Like he wasn't real?"

Marietta chewed on her cheek, embarrassed. "What?"

"They have machines, and when you say something, they click on. It's a computer. You didn't know that?" She sounded derisive, like she was talking to a child.

"How I know? Calvin always answer the phone."

"Well, if you don't want to answer it, put on your machine." When Carolanne began to disappear behind her closing door, Marietta said quickly, "How Freeman?"

"He's fine. He comes up the stairs and points to your door all the time. But we don't want to bother you, or eat the wrong kind of food or anything." She closed the door further.

Marietta said, "I feel bad what you think, that I want you and Nate fight." She stopped, moving closer to the crack. "I think you good for Nate."

Carolanne said, "You don't know nothing about me." She closed the door.

The answering machine filled the house with clicks and whirring and then Calvin's disembodied voice, too high and metallic, floating from the table every time the phone rang. People called to sell them mini-blinds, carpet-cleaning systems, and home security. She turned off the machine and unplugged the telephone. Lemon cake—she smelled it baking, washed the bowl of sticky batter, and thought she'd made it almost to force tears from her eyes. I ain't no Tiny Momma. I need for go. Nothing I do right, now.

But Carolanne knocked after a few hours, Freeman beside her leg. "I want you to come over for dinner tonight," she said harshly. "I made something special, just like you did for me. Five o'clock, okay?" She turned her face to Freeman. "You want to visit?"

"Dig Ma," he said, pointing.

Marietta sat, tight between her shoulder blades, at Carolanne's bleached-wood table. "Just two courses here," Carolanne said, and she placed a pitcher on the table near Freeman. Thick cut glass, with pink liquid. And a platter edged with roses and gold. A raft of hot dogs sat square in the middle.

"You gave me red and white. Well, here's pink. Yeah, you

trying to teach me some kind a lesson with that little dinner. We had pink a lot at my house, okay? This is strawberry Kool-Aid. But taste it—I made it like my auntie does. Stretch that bit a sugar far as it'll go. And I always had to cook the hot dogs—see, you know when they're done cause they split open. I was about seven, so that was the only way I could tell." Marietta was silent, watching the liquid seep into a pool around the hot dogs.

"Look, I even went out and *bought* the pitcher and the plate, just for this occasion," Carolanne said, louder. "And I wore a color-coordinated outfit just for you. Pink everything." Her dress was pale, and her lips had been colored rosy.

Marietta said, "When you plan for tell Nate you having a baby?"

Carolanne didn't look scared or surprised. She only said, "Come on, I have to take you someplace. Here, baby." She picked up Freeman and held him at her stomach. "We have to go quick, cause it'll get dark in a few hours."

"I ain't feel like shopping," Marietta said. "When you gon tell him?"

"We have to drive," Carolanne said. "And I'll tell you."

She talked in a steady stream after they passed under the sign that pointed the way to Los Angeles. "I'm just gon say it all. I was twenty when I had Freeman, okay? All my girlfriends from the Gardens *been* had babies. I was late."

"The Gardens?" Marietta interrupted.

"I'm from the Gardens. That's where we goin now, we gon pay my house a visit. So—I was twenty, and all the white girls at USC looked at me like I was contagious and shit. I couldn't stay in the dorms with them tripping like that. Ignorant nigger bitch from the ghetto—them damn girls never even had a hickey on their necks, them Polo shirts all buttoned up cute and lookin at me like *I* would give them a baby. The girls in the Gardens talkin, It's about time—I was a sidity bitch thought I was too good cause I went to SC."

She paused. Freeman nodded asleep in the car seat behind them. "Okay. I knew what I was doing—I knew I was fixing to get pregnant. I wanted Nate bad. He could pick me up like I wasn't nothing but a baby. Once he carried me across this lawn at school, after a dance, because it was wet and I had on leather shoes. He was always laughing, and he was gon *get* him some money."

"Carolanne," Marietta said. "You can't hide no baby. You have for tell Nate."

"Listen," she said. "You see how he is. He's so nervous and jumpy, throwing shit around, acting like I've never seen. I'm only three, maybe three and a half months. They got five preseason games and then the final roster cuts, all in August. It'd be crazy as hell to tell him now—he'd go off, get even more nervous. I'ma wait till after final roster cuts."

"How Nate not gon know you pregnant?" Marietta said, disbelieving.

Carolanne smiled. "Look at me. My aerobics instructor only gained fifteen pounds with her first baby. If you keep in shape. . . and Nate hasn't been trying anything with me anyway. It's like he's too nervous even to fuck—excuse me. But he ain't touched me. Anyway, we've been fighting too much, and he's glad to be in camp."

Marietta looked out the window; first, her mind flashed with images of Nate above Carolanne, his fingers clenched on the sheet, her nails at his back. She shook her head, embarrassed. Nate think something wrong with Carolanne, she tell me something wrong with Nate. Both of em sneak around like child hide cigarette in he jacket. She felt Carolanne's breath float toward her across the seat, and she focused out the window. They had left the freeway and were heading down wide, long boulevards now. Everywhere the faces were black, like Red Man's neighborhood, but here were only storefronts with iron bars much more square and dense than the gates in Charleston. Heat rose up and shimmered over railroad tracks and asphalt, and sometimes she saw houses that were small, stucco boxes with more black bars lined up over windows and doors. No bushes, no grass, no trees—just the shine of the evening sun off windows and metal and signs. "Where the Gardens?" Marietta asked, confused.

"We just got to Watts—we'll see Gardens in a minute," Carolanne said. "Ha, yeah. Every damn one a these projects is named after some garden. You got Nickerson Gardens, Imperial Gardens. Here we are—my lovely home—Soul Gardens."

They drove into a fenced collection of brick buildings. A sign said SOLANO GARDENS but Carolanne pointed to the low wall surrounding the huge trash dumpsters. Painted writing was slanted so crazily that Marietta squinted at it. "That says 'Soul Gardens'," Carolanne said. "You can't read it, huh?"

There had been a strip of lawn around the edge of each building, but it was dry-tufted and bald in places, like a sick dog. People sat outside on the asphalt in chairs and stared hard at Carolanne's car. A group of men sat with their legs sprawling out of open car doors, and when Marietta looked at them, two got up and stared harder, their faces blank until Carolanne leaned out the window and said, "Hey, girl," to a woman with a plastic shower cap on her hair, standing near the hood of the car.

"Carolanne, what you doin here?" the young woman said, smiling and coming toward them.

"Came to visit Auntie," Carolanne said.

"You don't never visit her," the woman said accusingly, and then she leaned into the car. "Look how big he gotten! He so pretty, look at them eyelashes."

"I know," Carolanne said. "They definitely mine, huh? This my mother-in-law, Niecie. Marietta Cook."

Marietta nodded, uncomfortable with the people staring.

"How you doin?" Niecie said.

"Well, let me get on over there," Carolanne said. "I see you in a while."

"All right then," Niecie said, backing away from the window.

Carolanne's car cruised slowly around the buildings. "You right," Marietta said. "I don't see much garden."

"The city men won't come to water the grass, cause of the shooting. And every time they hire a maintenance man, first time he try to scrub off the graffiti, they kick his natural ass."

She carried Freeman from the car and he began to wake up when they reached a closed door. Carolanne knocked. "It's only me, Auntie. Carolanne."

A girl about five opened it. "Hi, Auntie Carol," she said, but she stared at Marietta.

"What you talkin bout, 'It's only me,'" came a voice from the dim room. "You ain't been here for weeks, how I know who the hell 'me' suppose to be?"

A very short, plump woman sat deep inside the brown couch; the carpet was brown, the curtains were closed, and the room so dark that she seemed even pinker to Marietta, and her legs were almost hidden in the cushions. Her hair was braided in cornrows that stopped at her neck.

"Hi, Auntie," Carolanne said, trying to put Freeman down, but he whined to stay in her arms. "This my mother-in-law, Marietta Cook. My Auntie Mary, who raised me to be so good." She smiled.

Marietta said, "Nice to meet you," and the woman said, "Same here." Marietta sat on the folding chair by the door, the metal warm under her pants.

"Come here, baby," Mary said to Freeman, but he pushed his face into Carolanne's neck, and she said around his cheek, "He sleepy. We can't stay too long."

"Surprise, surprise," Mary said. Her voice was deep and dry, hoarse as Marietta's when she hadn't spoken. But three other children lay on the carpet, watching TV and not looking up. Only the little girl stood near Marietta, watching her. "Carolanne have to be runnin around, doin a lotta shoppin," Mary said to Marietta. "And ain't no shoppin round here."

"I seen Niecie," Carolanne interrupted.

"She just had her a boy. Last week."

"I didn't even remember she was pregnant," Carolanne said lightly.

"He was only four pounds, but they gon let her take him home Friday."

"I just seen her drinking that Bacardi with Darrell and them. She crazy to do that to a baby."

"She didn't tell nobody she was pregnant," Mary said. "We just thought she was getting big off all that beer. She hide it good as you did. Huh."

"So she got two boys and a girl now."

"Mmm-hmm."

"What she name him?"

"Ain't even name him yet. They lookin for his daddy, cause she need to know how to spell his name. Some nigger name Doshio or somethin. His mama Japanese."

"Yeah, I know who he is."

"So Freeman go to you?" Mary said suddenly to Marietta.

"You mean he let me hold him?" Marietta said carefully.

"Uh-huh. He so sometimey, he only let me get him a coupla times. I bet he go to you cause he *see* you all the time. He comfortable with you."

"Oh, Auntie, don't start. My mother-in-law live next door, okay? I can't be driving out here all the time, you know that. I gotta take care of my business, my house." Carolanne sounded like she had said this so many times that she let her voice trail off while she looked at the TV for a moment, swaying with Freeman automatically.

"So, Quita called and said you guys needed clothes for school," she said, looking at the floor, and the kids raised their heads.

"Yeah, I need shoes," one of the girls said.

"I want some Nikes," the boy said.

"You know I like to buy they clothes, so I brought somethin,"

Carolanne said, turning to the couch. She went into her purse and took out an envelope, and her aunt put it under her thigh without even looking inside.

"That's nice of you," she said. "Them clothes is ridiculous. Same price as grown folks' clothes."

"I know. Well, we didn't have no dinner yet, so I better be takin this cranky boy on back."

Mary said, "Yeah, well, if you had called, I coulda fix somethin for you to eat. But probably nothin fancy." She leaned her head back on the couch and lifted her chin at Carolanne.

"Whatever," Carolanne said. "I'ma come by the first of September and see what clothes y'all bought. If they need somethin else, if the shoes too much, call and let me know." She looked at Marietta. "You ready, uh, so we can eat?"

In the car, she said, "We stay here even *close* to dark and Nate find out, he'll swallow the car keys or some shit like that." She drove back down the maze of buildings, waving a couple of times, but she didn't stop. At the street light, Marietta heard the rush of cars passing the project.

"This is a noisy street," she said, for something to say. She saw the woman on the couch, sunk deep like she never left the recess of the dark material, saw her eyes hard and angry at her and Carolanne. The asphalt, the wrought-iron bars, the large black dumpsters and black writing all made it seem as if dark were already falling here. Marietta thought of the projects in Charleston, the ones they'd built long after she came—always women and kids in the doorways. No porches. Gardens?

"Yeah," Carolanne said. "When I was first pregnant with Freeman, I used to sit on the couch, three-thirty, four in the morning, cars going by. Eat a whole box of cereal—Cap'n Crunch, Cocoa Puffs, anything crunchy. Just throw it down, dry, no milk. Whole handfuls, and I be lookin at the cars, seein people stop and buy some rock, come home from work, whatever. We lived upstairs then, before Auntie moved. I'd wait till a car go by so she wouldn't hear me eating all the kids' cereal and start hollerin. All them kids in there my sister's, I mean, my cousin's. They'd all be crashed on the floor, dead sleep, wouldn't nobody hear me eatin but Auntie."

"You knew you was getting pregnant," Marietta said. "Why you do it? You was in school, smart, why you didn't wait?"

"You didn't wait. Auntie didn't wait."

"No, I don't even know you auntie, but I know it wasn't nothin like that for us," Marietta said. "Uh-uh, you had school."

"Yeah, what was I gonna do? Major in English and be a teacher? Right." Carolanne's voice changed. "Major in Business and try to be the one nigger they need? Major in Chemistry—I can't hang with all that math. Work my ass off so I can get some job? Nuh-uh. I wanted a rich boy. Don't know how I got with Nate, shit, I wanted some rich boy from back East who didn't know nothin bout Watts. Cause anybody from L.A., shit, you talkin bout a serious attitude they find out my address, don't matter what I major in. And Nate asked me to dance at this party, and I heard that voice, I knew he wasn't from here. I don't know. He just bogarted his way into my life."

"Bogart?"

"Just went on ahead, outta turn, did things his way. He kept callin, teasin me. Wait. I'ma show you." She was quiet until they stopped at a few more lights on the avenue, and Freeman cried. "Hungry boy, wait a minute," she said. She pointed at a car turning quickly ahead of everyone when the light switched green. "There, he did it, see?" Carolanne said. "He just bogarted."

When they were back in Anaheim, Carolanne stopped at Taco Bell and bought some burritos. She handed the bag to Marietta and said, "Let's go home and eat."

Marietta looked down into the bag, where the burritos were wrapped in paper, lying side by side. She stared until the memory came to her—Nate and Calvin rolled tight as the burritos in thin blankets to keep their arms and legs from flailing when they were just born; Aint Sister had swaddled them so she could hold them both while they nursed.

Carolanne microwaved the burritos and some leftover chicken, staring at the clean stove. "I remember Auntie Mary's mama, Gramma Rose, always talking bout, 'I been in sorrow's kitchen *too* long.' I always thought, nuh-uh, not *me.* I ain't planning to be in *nobody's* kitchen." Marietta stood near the humming, glowing box that made her nervous, remembering Sinbad's voice. Sorrow's kitchen. The microwave beeped insistently and Carolanne jerked away from the stove.

Freeman sucked white strings of chicken meat into his mouth. Marietta looked at Carolanne's tired face: all the colors seemed stark, the red cheeks, gold forehead, the purple shadow melted to dark creases in her eyelids. "I think you best tell him," Marietta said. "Maybe he calm down."

"I don't think so. I want to wait. They said they might come by tonight, you know. And don't tell him we went to the Gardens. He hates it when I go."

"I give Freeman a bath," Marietta said.

"Thanks."

She poured water on his head, over his tightly scrunched eyes, and thought maybe Carolanne was right. This was different from feeding Nate and Calvin, giving them peach pits to play with. Maybe Freeman need more than play and go outside and feed chicken. Maybe I don't know nothing bout raise child now.

Nate and Calvin came a while later, but Freeman was still awake, because he'd napped too long in the car and wasn't sleepy now. While Nate sat on the couch, looking tired, telling Marietta and Carolanne about the smog that seemed worse on the practice field today, Freeman pushed at his knees and then cried to be held. Nate picked him up and Freeman lifted Nate's T-shirt to poke at the blacker skin of his nipples.

"Quit," Nate said. "You always doing that. I told you it tickle."

Freeman thought that was funny, and he leaned forward and bit Nate's left nipple. "Shit," Nate shouted. "I thought you said he wasn't doin this no more!"

"That hurts, man," Calvin told Freeman, who smiled.

"Nate," Carolanne said, and then Nate leaned forward and bit Freeman on the arm, hard enough to leave faint toothmarks.

Freeman screamed, taking in a long breath and then screaming again. Carolanne rushed over and pulled him away from Nate's chest. "What the *fuck* are you doing?" she yelled.

"Teach him don't do that shit."

"What you teachin him? No—you teaching him that if you bigger, it's okay to bite or hit. We talked about this, Nate!"

Marietta took Freeman from Carolanne's hands and went into the bedroom. "You gon have fe cry, sweetie," she said to his twisted face over the crib bars. She was frightened. "You need fe go sleep now."

Hurrying back to the living room, she saw Calvin stand up and go to the sliding glass door. "I ain't even in the mood," Nate shouted. "I come home for a fuckin hour and I want some rest."

"I don't care. That was two seconds that could traumatize him."

"I'ma show him how it feel," Nate shouted, louder. "He don't like it, either."

"You're showing him that the biggest person gets to do whatever he wants." Carolanne went closer to the TV, because Nate sat back down and stared at the screen.

Marietta said, "Carolanne," but she didn't look away from Nate's face, the gap showing where his mouth hung open slightly.

"He do," Nate said. "Get to do whatever the fuck he want."

"Not here he don't. Don't look past me at the damn TV."

"Nate, man, let's get on back. We got a hundred-dollar fine if we late," Calvin said.

Carolanne went to the couch and pushed Nate's shoulder. "I said don't look at the damn TV when I'm trying to tell you somethin."

In the moment of quiet, they could hear the thin thread of Freeman's crying, and Marietta remembered her pulsing breasts, the boys' unending squalls out the window. "Goddamnit," Nate said, leaping up from the couch. "This my fuckin house, I'm working my black ass off for pay these bill, and you in my face every minute! I feel like bit you to stop you damn mouth!"

"Carolanne, leave he be, he ain't right," Calvin said, moving between them.

Nate spun around the room, so big and wide he knocked into the ficus tree by the couch. "What in hell we got fucking tree for in the house?" He picked up the pot and threw it at the wall; the leaves brushed soft against the wallpaper, but the black dirt rustled down to the carpet.

"Quit, Nate—see, man, that shit Bulk give you make you crazy!" Calvin shouted, and he slipped around Nate to hold his arms.

"This ain't you house, nigger, let me go," Nate yelled. "Let go."

Carolanne's mouth opened wide. "What?" She curled her fingernails and Marietta put her hands on Carolanne's shoulders to hold her, too. "What the fuck—you takin something? You on something? Nigger, don't you fuck up *my* life! Shit! *Shit!* All them times I had some dude flash something in my face, smoke somethin—you fuckin with my whole *life!*" She cried like Freeman, mouth stretching wide, black at the corners of her eyes, and she tried to get past Marietta. "I go back and ain't nobody around, they all dead or wackheads, and you want to fuck with *my* life." She broke away from Marietta and slapped Nate.

"Hold he now, Calvin," Marietta said, and she couldn't believe how calm her voice was. "Don't let he go."

She let Carolanne hit him in the chest until one of her nails caught in his skin and drew a line of blood like magic quick along his neck; red welling in a perfect line, thick and content, not spreading. They all stopped, heard Freeman howl, and Nate shouted at Marietta, looking straight at her, "Who got the advantage, Mama? Why you let she hurt me?"

Marietta ran for the bedroom and caught Freeman shaking in her arms. She slammed the door and sat with him in the rocking chair while he stuttered breath into her shirt until the front door closed.

She waited for Calvin the next night He stirred a rain of sugar into his iced tea, clicking the ice cubes together. "Nate stay with Bulk and them tonight," he said. "They goin over plays."

"Okay."

He stirred and stirred, looking into the glass that he always held far from him, with almost-straight arms. "Mama, you remember when it hailed?"

"No."

"I was about four. You know you can remember just a picture, not no whole thing but you just see one picture, that all you remember bout something?"

"I don't know, Calvin."

"We was in the field. Me and Nate was playing and little piece of white, like dots, start falling around me, all around. Come down through the tree. Every time I put sugar in my iced tea, look like that hail, fall down by the ice cube. I remember that sound."

She pushed her fingers along the smoked glass, the thick edge.

"I know you remember when I use to cut myself," he said.

"I do. That one hard forgetting."

He rattled the ice. "Nate taking steroids."

"What you mean?"

"You seen articles bout em, in the magazines."

"He taking pill?"

"He take pills and he have Bulk give he shot. He think he need the size for go up against the others."

"That why he so crazy?"

"Yeah, steroid mess with he mind."

She sat, not knowing what to say. Fish—blood—nothing worked. She saw Calvin's heart the way it had always been, a sponge, and Nate's—she had begun to see it square-sectioned, hard-curved: a turtle shell.

Calvin said, "When I ax he one time, Nate don't remember no hail. He remember you whup him bout Timmy, and he remember Willie catch a snake. Like we was in two different states or something. Last night, that was all he talk bout—you whup him for Timmy, and you whup him in the back, behind the house in Charleston. He say, 'Who got the advantage, man?'"

Marietta put her palms on either side of her head. "Camp gon be over in a week, huh?" she asked. Calvin nodded. She pressed hard on her scarf. "And you two gon to Ohio then, for that first game." She looked at Calvin's nicked fingers and arms.

"I need you take me somewhere, when you come home tomorrow night," she said, her eyes closed. "Someplace close. You gon teach me how for drive right quick."

rio seco

august

The ball of her foot against the gas pedal, her finger bones hard on the steering wheel—tiny movements and feeling the response, then heavier or lighter touching the brake: it was only paying attention to what the little motions did, just like hoeing or peeling peaches. Varying the pressure of her thumb against the knife blade and pulling the skin, slicing the hoe blade as close to the rice plants as she could—she pressed the gas pedal and felt the car's movement.

Calvin had taken her to the empty parking lot of a medical clinic a few miles from the condominium, but he only had an hour or so before he had to get back to camp. Marietta hadn't seen Nate since the night of the fighting. She heard Calvin nervous, watching her cross the black asphalt and white parking lines. "I can't teach you nothing in the dark, Mama," he said. "Why you can't wait till preseason's over and we come home?"

She shook her head, concentrating on the wheels underneath her, imagining what they did when she turned the circle in her hands. "Tomorrow you ax Rock follow you home and take you back to camp. You leave the car. You all gon go to Ohio on Friday for the game."

"Uh-uh, Mama, you only been practicing three nights. Where you need for go Carolanne can't take you?"

"Boy, I'm a grown woman. Don't be ax me where I have fe go." She heard the wheels popping over the grit in the asphalt and remembered all the long cars pulling off the highway toward her.

Where was she going now? She was just driving, doing what all these other people did day and night, floating along the freeway. Not like she and Carolanne did during the day, with the windows up and the gray-smelling conditioned air cold against her face; not cutting sharp around the corners of filled parking lots, hearing, "Are you leaving now or what?" and "Damn, fool, watch where you going!" Not stopping again and again, pushing through thick glass doors, sitting at a gas station while someone silently filled the tank and Marietta ached in her seat with the idleness of her hands; a card was handed through the window, Carolanne signed it, and the accountant Marietta had never seen paid all the bills every month. Carolanne collected the receipts, thin as onionskins, and Marietta stared at the plastic bags from the malls; she could see the Styrofoam trays holding meat and fish, the clothes pressing against shoes and scarves, the sharp box corners pressing through the filmy bags, thin-white as the membrane under the shell of a hard-cooked egg.

No. She floated alone now, the last few nights, the windows silently disappearing into their long slits, and the air that was heated and misty-full of smog all day turned cool and invisible in the dark. The hills were black, and she couldn't see the burned tufts of grass or the lack of trees. She couldn't imagine ever liking this landscape, ever being able to tell Nate what to do. His face, smooth as hers, but his mouth wider, smiling and boasting and one side curling in scorn at what someone told him about another player; his arms wide as branches, his fingers with dirty white web traces of the tape from practice and games. No spiderwebs to press into torn flesh.

His face flopped onto the hand bound with her webs, when he was in high school and sitting at the kitchen table, complaining, "Man, I *hate* all this reading. I can't tell when I ever be finish. I can't see nothing. I gotta *see* something. Give me some wood for chop so I can see when I be finish. Give me all that ice for load. So I learn the name of these dude, all them president and whoever? What I'ma do with that?" And Calvin laughing—because Marietta tried to make him read, and no one made Nate know the names in class. No one at school cared whether he read the books or not.

She drove on the wide freeway, eight lanes, cars weaving and dodging all around her. She felt Nate's tiny hands on her shirt, trying to drag her to what he wanted her to see in the yard; he couldn't believe she was too big for him to move. No fish and crab and shrimp to make him stop kicking in her belly; no rocking in the night or helping him with his belt or telling him that the offensive guard was pulling him inside too often.

Mama job never finish—but she heard the awful ping and racket of marbles into the shell-like sink and over her feet. Mama keep she job too long. Could she help anyone now? Carolanne had Oprah and Phil; Nate and Calvin had each other. Freeman? The new baby? Was he turning and turning yet, in Carolanne's water?

She braced for the rush of cars passing, split around her; she seemed suspended in the middle lane. She pressed down harder and the speedometer said 60. The windows and faces passing her glowed faintly green or red or silver, and she started to cry, her breasts and shoulders shaking with the force of her sobs.

Never in front of anyone, all those years, she wouldn't cry, and here she cried in front of a hundred people, a thousand, all these windows and faces—but no one looked, no one saw inside the dark-tinted windows. The road blurred as if rain were pouring down the windshield and she pulled over to the shoulder and put her forehead against the steering wheel, roaring so hard she felt everything leave her lungs, her chest. She was as lonely as she'd been everywhere else—Pine Gardens, Charleston, here in the condominium, in the wide new bed, in the rooms silent while Calvin was at camp.

She had cried sometimes in each of those places, in a dark room, but never in front of Aint Sister or Tiny Momma. All those Saturdays on the piazza or in Baby Poppa's living room, watching Calvin smash his chest into someone and seeing cleats fly into his calf; seeing Nate's lowered head and spread-wide arms knock a white boy ten yards, seeing Nate's face, his fist, the way the camera went in close, when she was afraid of his huge eyes and the palms slapping him with joy. But then the announcers' voices would say, "That's the intensity level Nate Cook needs, he's a wild man out there against Ohio State."

Her shirt front was cold with tears now. The boys—she'd had to be so hard, fearless and tearless as a man all those years so they wouldn't challenge her or question her or pity her. And Tiny Momma, Baby Poppa—no one saw her crack or wet her face, so that no one could get a hand over her by using one to comfort her.

But a hand—was she crying for that, too? She drew a breath in shame: A man's hand on her back, long fingers laid out in that curve above her hips, Sinbad's chest much harder than her own arm under her cheek, his lips mistakenly touching her forehead when he turned in his sleep. Carolanne slept on Nate's chest, her skin gold and young, no veins growing up the backs of her hands and wrists. Nate would catch her shoulders in the bend of his elbow for a minute, then her neck. On television, men put thumbs under the women's chins to tilt up the pale faces, rested thumbs in the hollow dimples by their kneecaps under restaurant tables.

Why did the air from the dashboard rise now and make her see this, too—Sinbad's hands, Milt's, Nate's arms holding Carolanne's hair hard against the pillows? He was grown, a husband.

She couldn't help. She didn't know anything about investments or training camp or the right publicity. She didn't know how to work the microwave or help with fingernails or shout instructions to soap-opera actresses. She didn't know about structured playtime or socialization or educational toys. Her cheeks began to dry, taut. She had thought all these weeks that she would make Carolanne sit with her at a table and peel peaches, snap beans, slide the veins from shrimp; ever since she found the blue-tipped wand in the trash, she thought she would help Carolanne see that the delicate motions, done over and over, let you think, let you feed salty-sweet fish and cobbler swimming in thick juice to Nate so that you could speak to him. Carolanne had too much time to think, so she filled her days—she had no time for slow thinking and peach juice running ticklish down her wrists any more than Marietta had had time to sit in the humming dust and coil sweetgrass.

Cars shot past her, snatching at the air from the open window like a vacuum hose. Sucking hard, letting go, the cars' headlights disappeared, then someone pulled behind her slowly. Inside the car the brighter beams were blinding, blue-white as lightning.

Marietta gripped the steering wheel. Should she start the car and drive away? She heard the police radio and the feet approaching her door.

"Uh, is there a problem here?" the officer said warily from behind the door. "Do you have car trouble?"

"No, sir," she said.

"Please bring both your hands outside the car, sir," he said harshly. "Show me your hands!"

She pushed her hands into the air. His face came into view and she whispered, "I just stop cause I have something in my eye, sir."

"Ma'am, uh, I'm sorry, ma'am. Have you been drinking?" His reddish mustache curled around his mouth.

"No, sir. I have something in my eye, a bug fly in my window, and I get it out now."

"Can I see your license, ma'am?" He peered into the car.

"My son just teach me how for drive this week."

"You don't have a license?"

"No, sir. My son don't have time for take me to get one. He got a game." She remembered Nate saying, "I just tell em I play with the *Rams,* man!" She said, "First game of the preseason tomorrow, and my sons go to Ohio. Nate and Calvin Cook, play for the Rams."

"What?" He looked hard at her.

She said, "This Calvin's car. I just move here from Charleston, and he teach me to drive this week. I get a license soon as he get back from Canton, Ohio. Hall of Fame game."

"You're not kidding, huh? The Cook twins. What does Nate drive?"

She took in a small bit of air. "He drive a BMW, sir. I don't remember the number. He wife got a Supra."

"And Calvin bought this big gas hog? You know, I can only tell em apart when Nate smiles, cause of that tooth."

"Yes, sir."

"Who do they play tomorrow—Cleveland?"

"Cincinnati, sir."

"Yeah. I didn't remember cause I don't have the day off. Well, Miz Cook, you know you can't stop the car on the freeway except in emergency situations. It's illegal. I think your son better get you a driver's handbook. I'm not going to give you a citation, but I think you should drive real carefully on your way home. Where do you live?"

"Anaheim Hills."

"Must be nice. Well, you're almost to Rico Seco," he said. "Remember, no stopping on the freeway shoulder. And tell Calvin and Nate good luck on the season."

Marietta started the Lincoln again and waited, but he stayed behind her until she pulled onto the freeway. Rio Seco. She drove off carefully and found the next exit ramp, then stopped on the bridge overlooking the freeway. She would have to get back on, going west, to get home. No stopping on the road, no stopping on the freeway. She had gotten lost in a track that first week and sat down on a curb to rest in the heat, and people stared hard; a security guard in a car cruised past. She couldn't sit by the too-blue stream in the landscaping. No fish swam there.

She pointed the car back down the on ramp. She knew where she wanted to go, but it would have to wait until daylight, after the game tomorrow. She tried to remember the street, the one she had seen with a row of palms on each side, long sprays of misty yellow hanging from each tree, dangling almost as low as the gray moss from oaks.

The weather was wrong for football. She paced out to Carolanne's balcony, where the sun was white-hot on the stucco, then went back inside the living room, where Carolanne sat on the couch looking at a catalog, and Freeman tried to push his stroller across the carpet. Marietta sat on the other end of the couch and listened to the pregame show. This room seemed too light, not the darkened cave that Baby Poppa liked when he watched football.

When they'd played college games on television, she had loved to watch close to the screen, to see the movement and faces. She didn't like to talk, to hear anything but the grunts and yardage, so sometimes she went inside to sit with Tiny Momma. Then she could stare at the vulnerable, smooth necks of the wide receivers, the skin that showed between helmet and name. On Nate and Calvin nothing showed—their necks were so thick and close to their huge shoulders now, the stabilizing collars sealing all skin off.

She thought she'd go next door and watch the game alone now, but Freeman came and pulled on her hand to make her come and see that the stroller was caught on a corner in the hallway.

"Gotta be some rule that says if you're a sportscaster you have to wear a nasty polyester suit coat," Carolanne said, looking at the announcers. "Could we start the game now, huh, guys?"

Nate and Calvin were on the sidelines, their hands, forearms, knuckles covered with white tape. Only their eyes—the TV cameras loved to show Nate's face. She could see just his eyes above the face mask. "Look at that fearsome gaze," an announcer said. "Are we gonna see Nate Cook in action today?"

His mouthpiece made his lips carve hard, and when he leaned forward, his face was a mask of concentration. Marietta saw Nate, saw the Africa woman, saw her father's face. Her face. Chemicals in he blood, under he bone.

Calvin wasn't starting; she knew that the offensive tackle, Matt Frazier, was coming off one of his best seasons. But she might see him anyway, she thought, because the exhibition season was really just testing for the rookies, seeing what they could do before the regular season and the scores that mattered. The Bengals kicked off, and Carolanne said, "Here we go. Smash and grab that money, guys."

Freeman hummed and sang, pushed the stroller against Marietta's knees after she moved the coffee table closer to Carolanne, who looked up from the catalog during plays and ignored the talk and the statistics flashing on the screen. "The Rams' cheerleaders are dogs," she said.

Marietta watched the first series carefully. The Rams' quarterback was blond and flat-nosed, his stomach and legs squarer than those of the round-bellied offensive linemen. He planted back like they all did and threw, but the ball dropped a foot in front of the praying fingertips of Leroy Sims, the wide receiver. Marietta had been reading every football article in the *Los Angeles Times* for weeks; she had memorized all the players' names and numbers.

They punted, and she saw Nate run onto the field. "Nate Cook, first-round draft choice of the Rams, is starting at that outside linebacker slot left open by the retirement of Corcoran," the announcer said. "This guy's got competition for the job, but he's supposed to be a wild man on the pass rush, so we'll see what he does against that Bengal offensive line."

"There Daddy," Carolanne said to Freeman. "All muscle and no brain by now. Shit."

"Freeman," Marietta said, "there he go." Nate's uniform was sapphire blue and carp gold. He dug his knuckles into the grass and froze. The Bengal quarterback's mouth moved and then they all sprang forward; Nate crashed off the chest of the offensive tackle and slid around, but the running back was already down under two others.

"Thrills and chills," Carolanne said. "Only five thousand fifty-five tackles to go. Lucky he doesn't have to think too hard, since he's fucked up his head."

"Carolanne." It was the first time Marietta had ever called her name. "They got plays to remember. Plenty for think about."

Carolanne raised her eyebrows. "Nate just goes by instinct. Smell it and try to kill it."

"You know that ain't the whole thing," Marietta said, watching him line up again.

The game was conservative, as the first ones usually were. Nate made two tackles by halftime, and he walked away quickly after each one, no punching the air. She saw Calvin on the sidelines once, but then the third quarter was almost through, and the score was only 3-0. The Bengals hit their field goal, and the Ram kicker was short from forty-nine yards out.

On the first play of the fourth quarter, the Bengal quarterback dropped back, looking, and Nate shot through the line to wrap his arms around the quarterback like Marietta with a huge towel around a wet Freeman after the bath. His arms hid the quarterback's helmet, and the ball squeezed downfield. The other outside linebacker, Sharpe, scooped up the ball and lumbered for the goal line, but two Bengals caught him at the twelve-yard line. Nate was slapping and slapped so hard that the announcers laughed. "Whoa, after a celebration like that, I don't think Jones, the safety, is gonna be able to play! Did you see Cook hit him? That's how he hits when he's happy."

When the camera lingered on the faces lined up at the Rams' bench, she waited. Winks. If Nate and Calvin saw the camera on them, no waves or mouthing, just their joke for her—winks. The white, pink, gold, and light-brown faces of the players wore streaks of black paint under the eyes. Nate used to boast, "You better put that black all over you whole face, man, so you can be bad as *me.* I'm natural, built-in black—but you could be a imitation."

The Rams never scored; the fullback, Lonnie Brigham, went head into the wall of Bengals twice, and when Coach Roberts gave the signal to go for it on fourth and three, the pass to the tight end was deflected.

But it was preseason. Nate had announced himself. Calvin had stood on the sidelines, but she knew they would try him before the regular season began.

While the announcers talked and Freeman lay in her lap, Carolanne wrote in orders on the catalog form. Marietta said, "What you think? Nate do fine."

"Yeah," Carolanne said. "That ain't gon make him feel better."

"The first game."

"Nate's so freaked over making a big rep for himself he's not gon be better after one game. You know him better than I do."

Marietta thought about high school, when he and Calvin had been so much bigger than the other boys. And college—no, she hadn't seen them during those seasons, just read the articles they mailed and watched them on the screen now and then. She said, "I don't know why Nate think he have for take steroid. He use to believe he great, just cause he love football so much."

Carolanne snorted. "Welcome to life in L.A.—you gotta be better than that."

"Steroid make he not want no touching—from you?" Marietta asked.

Carolanne shrugged. Marietta had gotten out the magazine articles about steroid use among track stars, weight lifters, football players. Their oiled, stretched skin—their eyes and hard smiles. The articles detailed the acne, breast growth, rage, and paranoia until she put them on the carpet and buried her face in her hands. No Baby Poppa across from her to ask for help, no pictures of Mean Joe Greene to study, nothing to plan. Nate was *grown*.

"What you gon do about he?" she asked Carolanne softly. "You think he still take em?"

Carolanne shrugged again. "What I'ma do? Ground him? Take away his privileges? Call his mama?" She picked up the phone and pushed the buttons, her nails clicking the plastic. "Hello; can I speak to Bonnie? Hi. It's Carolanne Cook. Yeah, I saw the game. Mr. Sharpe was very sharp. I know. Yeah. Well, I remember you asked if I wanted to go to lunch with some of the other wives, and I talked to Tina Brigham. They just moved here from Michigan, that's where he's from. . ."

Marietta knew the phone would ring next door. She went and laid Freeman in his crib, but he stirred and cried at the sight of the bars, the way he had ever since Nate and Carolanne fought. He wouldn't stay in the crib at all. She took him next door just as the phone burbled, and she said, "Hello?" in case it wasn't them.

"I love it when they give me play action, Mama!" Nate laughed loudly. "What you think?"

"I think you need fe talk you wife," she said. "Put Calvin on the phone."

"Mama, come on," he said.

"Nate, I ain't talk with you till you go long and put thing right," she said. She wouldn't tell him how he looked slanting. She wouldn't ask him how the arms of the offensive tackle had looked. She heard him put the phone down.

She had read it in a magazine when the boys were still in junior high, how a linebacker studied the hands and arms of the guard opposite him. When the full weight was on the flesh and it bulged with the effort of holding up the man, the linebacker knew he would rush forward and block, for a running play; when the arms were more relaxed, holding back, the guard would be dropping back to protect the quarterback. She had told Nate, and sometimes it worked.

All those games, in college, they had called and the sounds were loud around their voices, Nate cutting through to say, "Yeah, them arms give up some big secret, Mama!" Calvin would shout, "He wasn't as bad as Nate, Mama, that dude wasn't about nothing to hold."

"Mama," Calvin said now. "Nothin for tell you."

"Say how it feel to play in you first pro game," she said. "I'm so proud. Tell me what you think."

When the sun went down, there were no clouds to hold the pink or red, or trees to catch the goodbye colors—the huge sky was a flat blank behind the roofs, and then the blue turned dark.

Inside, Freeman slept on the couch. She didn't want to try the crib again. Carolanne had gone out somewhere, leaving him in Marietta's care.

Marietta sat on the couch and looked through Carolanne's magazines and catalogs, stopping at the order form to see what she had checked during the game.

Bionaire 700. "Bring mountaintop freshness indoors. The Bionaire 700 will clean and rejuvenate stale air with a filtering system that removes particulate pollutants as small as .01 microns. And the unique negative ion generator not only precipitates any remaining particles, it generates millions of negative ions to reproduce the effect of stimulating, fresh mountain air. $149.95."

She tried to read it again, with the sounds of Freeman's gargling little snore and the clicking of kitchen things in the background. Negative ions. Precipitate. She thought precipitation was rain—Baby Poppa had loved that word. She looked at the clock. It was only seven-thirty. She dialed Charleston.

Once a week, she called Tiny Momma, told her what the boys were eating and what Freeman could say and do. She had only said that Carolanne was pretty, small, and had hands as delicate as Tiny Momma's. But Tiny Momma's voice was a muffled whisper from the old phone that sat on a crocheted doily in her living room, and it almost hurt more to hear the faraway words than to see Tiny Momma in her imagination.

Tiny Momma and Miss Alberta never really watched the games, not like they concentrated on the soap operas; the screen flashed and the announcers grew excited, but they sat at the table, hands busy, until someone said, "See him—he gone!" Then they would peer at the TV and try to follow the pointing fingers of Jesse's son or one of the other boys.

"Hello?"

"It's me, Tiny Momma."

"Chile, I knew you was gon call. I been waiting on you. How that baby?"

Marietta started, thinking that she had told Tiny Momma about Carolanne's hard-to-tell belly, but she realized that Freeman was the baby. "He sleep right here by me. He mama go out for a bit, and she gon take a fit when she come home and he ain't in the crib."

"Gramma meant to spoil babies! I know she hate me if I there."

"I wish you was here. Why you don't come for stay? We get a big house for you fill up with crochet." Marietta was embarrassed at how lonely her voice was until she remembered that Tiny Momma had seen her sick, sweating, sleeping.

"Now you know I love to come and see California, but who gon take care Baby Poppa and Alberta?" Marietta could smell the tea, the cooking smells in the close room, the woolly breath of the yarn balls everywhere. No—no cemetery anywhere near here. Tiny Momma had to wash his headstone, bring him flowers, tell him everything. And Miss Alberta waited for her to come back to the table even now.

Tiny Momma said, "I watch them two—I know Nate do what he like to do cause I hear Jesse and them hoopin and hollerin all up and down the piazza. That's how I always know—they yellin bout Nate—so I can get over there to the TV in time when they show it again."

"They give you three replay this time, huh?" Marietta smiled.

"Yeah. That white boy get squeeze just like a sausage from Nate. And Calvin just biding his time?"

"He patient. Nate the one can't wait." Marietta stopped.

"Mmm-hmm." Tiny Momma paused, too; Marietta heard the hiss of her lips drawing in tea. "Miss Alberta done taken a cold. She restin now."

She couldn't tell Tiny Momma bout the drugs, not even about Carolanne's baby. She swallowed spit, imagining it was cinnamon tea, and said, "Calvin done tell me Nate eat four dinner before that game. Just so he get energy for face them other player."

When she had hung up, she heard Freeman stir and cry. He probably would have gone right back to sleep, but she arranged him on her lap, his hot, straight back under her hand, his lips crushed to her pants. She would have to listen for the growl of Carolanne's car underneath her, in the garage.

Precipitate a particle. Turning back to the catalog, she felt more helpless than ever. Tiny Momma couldn't tell her. Nate hadn't called Carolanne, and Marietta wondered where she had gone. Maybe to Soul Gardens; maybe to visit one of the wives she had called. Carolanne had only said, "I'm gone on a run, like Nate and Calvin say. I'll be back in a while."

Zone of calm. Carolanne had put an X next to the picture of a small thing that looked like a radio. "Today the volume of civilization seriously interferes with our abilities to relax, read, sleep, and concentrate at optimum levels of efficiency. The new

Marsona Sound Conditioner electrically synthesizes a variety of pleasing natural sounds that mask and reduce the annoyance of unwanted noise pollution. You control the volume, rhythm, and wave pattern of ocean surf, summer rain, mountain waterfalls, and the seeming nearness or distance of the source. $139.95."

Carolanne had ordered one of each and added up the total in the box. She had written in the numbers next to VISA and signed her name. Marietta kept her palm on Freeman's behind and read this one again. Ocean surf. Summer rain. She saw her porch, the shutters that kept out wind, the newspaper flapping with air blowing through.

What was in breath, the breath everyone always said not to let leave an empty house? Don let fire out, Aint Sister growled. Bad luck for lose ember.

She stared at the beige-slatted blinds, imagined the window Carolanne had looked out when she was pregnant, the wide avenue and people standing in doorways. Noise pollution—you don't know what she need.

"When you gon go to the doctor?" Marietta asked.

Carolanne shrugged. "You read all them magazine," Marietta went on. "They all talk bout go to a doctor soon as you know you pregnant."

"I didn't have no money to go with Freeman," Carolanne said. "He was fine. I'm only four months or something. I take vitamins." She glanced at Marietta. "I didn't even know you looked at the magazines."

"I look at that catalog last night. Them thing expensive."

"Oh, the *Lifestyle Resource?* Yeah, I want to put those things in Freeman's room. I thought they'd be good, maybe help him sleep in his crib."

"They gon be back tonight, you know," Marietta said. "You and Nate need for have a serious talk." Carolanne only nodded. "You ain't tell he bout the baby?"

Carolanne snapped, "He ain't told me bout his drug habit." She sighed. "I'm waiting till roster cuts, remember? But I promise I'll go to the doctor next week. What do you want to fix for dinner? What should we get?"

Marietta played on the xylophone with Freeman while Carolanne watched Oprah. A parade of people who had lost weight—their before videos were shown and then they strode onto the stage, thinner, with more makeup and their hair closer to their heads, or puffed out bigger than it had been. Constant applause like rain on a tin roof. Light Scent Downy Dryer Sheets—make your clothes smell like you hung them outside. Lysol Fresh Scent—so no one will know that you had fish.

She looked at Carolanne's pink-gold cheeks and her hands busy putting toys away, cleaning off the countertop, vacuuming after the show was over. "They're gonna want a snack," Carolanne said. "Are you sure you don't want to make something? They like your cooking a lot better than mine."

Marietta shook her head. "You two need for talk, not chew."

"I got it, huh?"

Freeman ate macaroni, and Marietta thought of how tomorrow she would drive to the palm trees she kept seeing in her mind. But she wouldn't tell the boys or Carolanne what she was thinking about doing until she was sure.

The music thrummed into the garage below and Carolanne didn't look nervous. She flicked nail polish onto the very tips of her fingernails, where a faint edge of white had worn.

Calvin came in first. "Hey, I don't smell nothing! Don't you got something for two starving travelers? We been wait all this time for real food, Mama."

"We too tire for cook," Marietta said, hugging him. "Just watch that game take all our energy."

Nate came around him and Freeman yelled, "Daddy!" He ran with hands wide to catch Nate's knees. Nate swung him up and said, "You been on my couch? I came to get you, boy!" Freeman screamed into his neck and kicked with joy. Nate's tongue showed pink in the tiny triangle between his front teeth. "Okay," he said. "I'ma say sorry for how I been, but you seen them boys I went up against, Mama. You seen how big they was."

"You ain't apologize for me," Marietta said, angry at his wide, I-told-you eyes. "Go in the bedroom and talk you wife. I ain't live here with you—don't sorry for me. Go on." She stepped forward and took the squealing Freeman, whose laughter turned immediately to cries of anger. "Come on see you crazy uncle," Marietta said, and Calvin grabbed his waist to fly him around the room.

"You impatient?" she said to Calvin when Nate had led Carolanne into the bedroom.

He shrugged. "Yeah. Feel like they just take me for maybe, if somebody get hurt."

"No. But you can't hope for somebody go down so you go up."

"Yeah, I can. I ain't suppose to, but I do," he said, tickling Freeman. "Frazier ain't go nowhere. He a boulder."

"Like Bruce, the one Nate look at for Denver." She raised her chin.

"Yeah, Bill Bruce. Nate looking at three hundred pound of NFL."

"So you gon do it, too?" she said harshly. "Take them drug?"

"I always like for lift weight, Mama, I'm cool," Calvin said defensively. "I ain't worry bout my size. Just a chance."

"Denver only five day from now. How you all be rest by then?" she said.

"I don't know. Seem like they say it be hell for four more week, then let up, so we can get through. They gon test me least one time, I figure."

Carolanne came out first, her lips hard and small. "Naw—I ain't finish," Nate said loudly from the doorway.

"Yeah, you are," Carolanne shouted. "You ain't said nothin new." Freeman trembled and held Marietta's knee.

"How Jeffrey?" Marietta said to Nate, folding her arms.

"He okay, talkin big smack," Nate said. "He ain't have to look at Bill Bruce on Friday."

"But we have fe look at *you* every day, long time," Marietta said.

"Hey, I did something y'all don't like. I got results, right?" Nate said, raising his chin, too. "Come on, Mama. Let's go over Calvin's and get this finish."

They went next door. Across the cool, glossy table from him, Marietta hesitated. His face was hard. None of this furniture was hers, none of these walls—she wasn't scolding him in her house.

"Go head, Mama," Nate said. "You make we do everything for football—you study the playbook, make we lift, all that. Whatever it take, you always beena tell we—don't complain."

"This ain't in those limits," she said, almost without thinking. Baby Poppa—he say that at the hotel all the time.

"Yeah, it is. Look at them guys we up against, Mama."

She considered, staring at his knuckles. "Okay—maybe within the limit for football. For the game. But not for you family. I read bout them player gotta throw chair through the wall and break thing. . ."

Nate interrupted her. "You gotta do that to get up for the game—get pumped."

"No—you got a baby. You can't."

"I ain't plan on no baby," he said. "Somebody else did."

"I ain't plan on *you,"* she said.

"You was marry already, you didn't know we daddy die."

Marietta almost bent over the table with the fingers of pain in her heart. She couldn't tell him. "Why you marry she then?" she said, as hard as she could.

Nate clenched his hands on the glass. "She so little and she been a talk so much smack, like she didn't care if I ever look for she again. . ." he said, and then he stopped.

Marietta imagined Carolanne watching him, seeing what he would do, what he wanted. Her eyes and smile—her fingers on his arm. Her back when she turned. "What you fe do she never look at you now—she leave and take Freeman? You gon chase she out, crazy from them steroid."

Nate let his head fall back against the tall chair Calvin loved.

His neck was full and thick, no scars, no lines. "How I gon make it then? I gotta have edge over Bruce and them. I gotta make the cut."

"Be lonely you make the cut and lose you family. Lose me, too. Cause that my blood now—you choose for me when you marry she."

"What if I can handle it, if I act better?"

"What if you don't?" She saw him weighing it.

"I can't say what I'ma do later in the season," he said finally, slowly. "I'll quit for now. But I gotta keep my power."

"And I gotta keep you safe," she said, standing up. He said nothing when she went back inside ahead of him.

"Well," she said to Calvin. "You tell Rock I look for he, go see he uncle sometime and fish."

"What you talk bout fish?" Calvin said, studying her face and Nate's. "That little place?"

"Fish in that lake probably so full a poison you shouldn't eat em anyway," Nate said, laughing, but looking at Carolanne. "Look what they did to Rock."

"Come on," Calvin said. "Me and Nate got another hour. Let's go get ice cream."

Marietta looked long at Carolanne, but she only shook her head slightly and picked up Freeman. "Come on, baby, you daddy treatin," Carolanne said, narrowing her eyes at Nate. "He buying whatever you want."

The Denver game wasn't televised, so Marietta waited in Calvin's silent living room for the highlights and score reports between the New Orleans-San Francisco quarters. The Rams were down

7–0, but then Brigham ran seventeen yards for a touchdown, and Rock intercepted a pass to set up another touchdown. That was it, until the sports wrapup late that night.

All these preseason game quiet, she thought. No big score. She wondered if Calvin had played, and waited for the phone to ring.

They didn't call until just before the news, and Nate said, "Bruce smother me. I didn't even breathe, I didn't do shit."

"Watch you mouth," she said. "Calvin play?"

"He did the last seven downs of the last quarter. He did okay. I got killed."

She watched the highlights. All the announcer said was "First-round draft pick Nate Cook, who forced a fumble in Cincinnati last week, was silent today. We didn't hear his name called once, John."

"No, Phil, Bill Bruce pretty much took a nap on him today. But Jeff Foster, last year's big draft choice at nose tackle, really gave Bronco running back Mark Roberts a hard time. Look at this guy slide off center. Wow."

"The big story, of course, was the interception. . ."

Carolanne took a blood test that day, and she said she would take one more next week, the day before the first home game against the Chargers.

"Then I have to see the doctor to evaluate the tests. And I can tell Nate a couple of weeks after that, okay? I'll know the due date and everything."

"Would you like to come in with her and listen for the heartbeat?" the nurse asked. She was Marietta's age, smiling and blonde. "When we had our kids, they didn't have all this sensitive sound equipment. I bet all your doctor had was a stethoscope."

"No," Marietta said, following Carolanne into the room. She saw Aint Sister's small hands on her belly, tracing and feeling. "Not even that."

Carolanne was silent, watching the woman smear thick gel on her belly; Marietta was amazed at how small the hill was. Maybe it was because Carolanne was lying down. The skin was pale as lemonade.

An Asian man whose hair shone blueblack in the harsh light of the room walked in quickly. Marietta thought the thick hair was beautiful, straight and glinting when he bent over a clipboard.

"Carolanne Cook," he said pleasantly. "I'm Doctor Yee. You've had two blood tests, the HCG and the diabetes screening, right?"

"Yes," Carolanne said. "Last week and this week."

"Ten days apart," Doctor Yee said. "And from the date of your last period, you estimate that you're how far along?"

"Almost five months," she answered.

"Is this your mother?" he said, turning abruptly to Marietta.

"My mother-in-law," Carolanne said quickly.

"Well, what do we hear?" Dr. Yee began moving the wand over Carolanne's skin, pressing hard and looking away at the wall. His eyes were unfocused while he concentrated. The moans and sliding noises coming out of the speaker made Marietta shiver.

"A faint little beat in there," he said suddenly, putting down the wand. "But you didn't hear it, did you, Mrs. Cook?" He looked down at Carolanne.

"No, I didn't hear anything," she said. "Is the machine broken?"

"How much have you been eating, Carolanne? Have you been overly concerned with your diet during this pregnancy?"

"Excuse me?" Carolanne's cheeks turned deeper red under her makeup.

"How much weight did you gain with your first child?" Dr. Yee sat down on the tiny stool near her.

"About thirty-five pounds. Thirty-eight. My aunt said that was too much."

"Well, Carolanne, your HCG levels in the blood test don't look good. They're not going up like they should be, and that means your baby isn't really developing. HCGs are the measure. . ."

Carolanne said, "I know what they are, I've read plenty of books."

"Well, certainly you've read then that trying to limit your weight gain isn't always best for the baby. We've revised earlier recommendations to suggest that women gain up to thirty-five pounds."

"My aerobics instructor only gained fourteen. Mariel Hemingway only gained nineteen." Carolanne tried to sit up.

"No, no, lie back and relax. Would you jump off a cliff if *they* did?" He smiled slightly. "I'm not saying anything for sure about the baby's progress. But I'm very concerned. Of course all body types are different, and you're very slim. But I want you to eat more this week and relax. I'll want another blood test next week and we'll check on this temperamental machine. Don't panic—just concentrate on the baby. I know it's difficult. Have your mother-in-law take that toddler off your hands for a time." He smiled at Marietta. "I'm not trying to scare you, Carolanne, but if things aren't better next week, we might be in serious trouble."

In the car, Marietta stared at Carolanne, horrified. "What you do to that baby? You try for get shed of it?"

"Please, Mama," Carolanne said quickly, just like Nate did, and they both stopped, hearing the word. "No. I just need to slow down, like he said." She held her lips tightly together, trying not to cry, but her eyes were swimming-pink and her chin shook. "I don't want anything to happen to the baby."

"Let me drive," Marietta said, and Carolanne came around to the passenger side, holding the tears until she sat and closed the door. She looked around the parking lot and said, "Can we just go straight home?"

Freeman would be at day care for another three hours. Marietta made a glass of iced tea for Carolanne and she said, "Uh-uh, I can't have caffeine. I keep that in the refrigerator for Calvin. Hand me some 7-Up, please."

"You want the TV on?"

"It's too early for the soaps." Carolanne sipped the soda and flipped the pages of a decorating magazine. "Look, did you see this wardrobe? Well, it used to be for clothes, but now you can put your TV and stereo in there, to keep them out of view. Look at the carving on this one."

"Carolanne," Marietta said, sitting in the chair, "what that baby want?"

Carolanne put the magazine in her lap. "What you mean?"

"What it want? What you crave?" Marietta clicked her thumb

and fingernails together nervously. "You have for feed that baby what it want."

She heard Aint Sister telling Rosie, "If he want egg, go on give he egg. Here." And Tiny Momma saying, "I cain't even look at no watermelon. People say my mama big with me in summer and ate watermelon all day. I never had no taste for it myself."

"They say you don't give a baby what he want, that what he crave. What you give he too much, he gon hate. What he want?"

Carolanne looked at her fingernails. "What did Nate and Calvin want?"

"Fish. Make me feel they want fish. But you see em now."

"Yeah, but you lived by the water. Everybody ate fish. That wasn't too weird."

Marietta paused. She saw Nate strutting by the river in Charleston, showing off at Newport Beach. He surprised people by wading out into the surf. And Calvin, fishing down at the river all day with other boys, quiet. Talking to Rock about fishing in Rio Seco. "What Freeman beena want—crunch something?"

Carolanne smiled. "Cap'n Crunch." Her lips went back straight. "But I don't feel nothing this one craves."

"You ain't listen."

"You think I don't do anything right, okay?" Carolanne began to sob. "And you don't know anything about it." She buried her face in her hands, those claw nails resting by her hair, climbing up into the fine strands at her forehead, and Marietta thought, Baby ax for blood, don't give he fingernail polish. Listen.

She moved quickly to put her arms around Carolanne, but Carolanne didn't stop trembling. "Listen that baby, listen hard."

Carolanne raised her face, the separate colors so close, not blending but patches of cheek, stark rose, eyes too green, and her tipped-red hands pushed into her stomach. "I don't know," she whispered. "I'm scared that if I don't do it right, this whole thing, Nate and the house and everything, if I don't do what I'm *supposed* to, I'll be back where I started."

Marietta's heart jumped at the fear in her voice, real terror—of storms that took houses and boats away, of dogs, of white men in cars racing down the highway. Water seeping into graves, feet pressing muddy rice. She smelled the waxy lipstick near her nose when she pulled Carolanne back, smelled the perfume and sharp hairspray and salty tears.

Freeman kept clinging to Carolanne that night, refusing to be put down in his crib. Carolanne sat on the couch with him on her chest, watched one half-hour show—the kind Marietta hated, with wooden kitchens crowded with laughing families who were always eating. Then Carolanne got up to take him nodding to the crib, but he screamed again.

"I can't hold you all night!" she said. "I got one in here already—I can't breathe with both of em pushing me!"

Marietta took him next door, lying on the bed with him draped over her heart. His fingers cupped her chin, pressed reflexively now and then to be sure she was there. When sleep deepened, his hair grew damp and heated under her chin, and she remembered Calvin—the holding, the razor cuts on his arms. This my blood. She stared at the dark walls. This Cook blood—he daddy mess up he own blood with them drug. He mama trying thin she blood out, starve. What I gon do?

Nothing. Nothing I can do. They grown now—but this one ain't.

She could go back to Charleston and take Freeman with her—but what would she do for work? She could have them send money—but another apartment, a house? She couldn't go back to the hotel to work—the boys wouldn't let her. She didn't like doing nothing here. No—in Charleston she wouldn't be able to see all the Rams' games, watch the players. She liked Rock and Jeffrey and the others, even if they sometimes frightened her and Jeffrey pressured Nate. But he hadn't forced Nate to do anything. Nate chose.

Fish wasn't curing him. She tucked her chin into the moist hollow of Freeman's neck. The boys had begun to pull away so soon back then; they'd pushed her chin out with shrugging, turning shoulders. She missed the heat of a baby's sleep, the patting, directing hands and cocked heads. My blood—my granbaby. I keep a eye for he now.

She took him in the car with her in the morning. "Mama rest today," she told him, and they drove on the freeway to Rio Seco. "Dig duck!" he shouted at the long truck beside them.

Could Carolanne handle Freeman and Nate and the new baby? Maybe she'd take Freeman for a few months, until they settled down. She passed over the river, thin as a stream of rainwater leaving the yard, and then she drove slowly through the streets until she saw the dark faces again. What you want? she thought, listening to Freeman saying, "Dig duck. Man. Go bye-

bye." She slowed the car to see the geraniums brick-red like the ones growing in tomato cans on Charleston piazzas; cloudy gray-green collards marched on their thick stems in side yards, along fences. And one yard outlined with shells, all along the edges of the grass, large clamshells stuck point down.

She turned onto Picasso Street and found Red Man, Rock's uncle, sitting in his yard with two other men. "They gon remember we?" she asked Freeman, pulling to the curb and rolling down the window. "Hello," she called. "You remember, Nate and Calvin Cook mama?"

Red Man's wife, Mary, brought a Pepsi and Marietta sat next to her on the long couch in front of the porch. "Mary, you got any more plums?" the man with the baseball cap said, and she got up and brought a bowl of deep purple plums, nudging each other in their ripeness. "These is the last ones," she said. "Boys went to that board-up house in the lot to get em. She always did have the best plum tree, except for yours, Lanier."

"Mine finish up," the older man with the big-knuckled hands said. "Hey," he called to Freeman. "Where you think you going?" Freeman ran away from the parked truck he was headed to and buried his face in Marietta's lap.

"He look more like his mama round the face," Red Man said. "But he got Nate's forehead."

Marietta nodded. "Red Man didn't lose his manners, cause he never had any," the man with the cap said. "I'm Roscoe Wiley. I assume you're Mrs. Cook, the famed Rams' mother?"

He came and shook her hand. He was a little older than she, Marietta thought, with smooth dark skin reddish-brown underneath and wide lips, the kind that had a definite outline to edge them. "Roscoe is our resident street poet and big mouth," Red Man said. "That's all you need to know."

"If his mouth big, yours must be. . ." Lanier started, and Red Man shouted, "Naw, we ain't talkin bout me, we gotta talk about the game!"

In their crowing over Nate's sack, she heard Jesse and Baby Poppa, everyone who gathered around a TV to watch football with beer in hand and particular men to cheer. "Shoot," Roscoe told her. "Football is a religion with these fools—don't you know Red Man's family considers Super Bowl Sunday a holiday, right up there with Christmas? They have fifty-sixty people crowding in here every January. I can hear em all the way down the street at my house, so I usually just give up and come over, too."

"You come over for the chitlins, nigger, cause you too lazy to fix em your own self," Red Man said, and they all laughed again. "Yeah, but this preseason getting longer and longer every year," he went on. "More money for the networks. No, I gotta wait till September 5. Regular season, Monday Night Football. Then we gon see the real thing. Pardon me," he turned to Marietta, "no offense, I don't mean Nate can't do it then, I just mean. . ."

"He just mean he impatient," Mary said.

"So where you all sit in Angel Stadium tomorrow?" he asked Marietta.

"I don't know," she said. "High up so I can see something, I hope. I don't like being too close to the sideline and all I see Calvin and Nate back."

"Oh, Lord," Red Man shouted. "She knows her football! She

ain't sittin down there by the bench worryin bout her boys, she wants to see the plays. We gon get along fine, uh," and in the awkward pause, she knew no one was sure what to call her. She was younger than them; not Mrs. Cook. But she was Nate and Calvin's mother. She wasn't Big Ma here.

"Marietta," she said. "I hope you all call me Marietta."

After she left them, promising to bring the boys back, she looked for the street. Passing the blind-windowed rock house, she turned down the next street, Pablo, but she didn't see the palms. She tried to recall where they had driven, and headed down the avenue. Looking down the side streets, she finally saw them, near where they had turned off to get back on the freeway.

Short palm trees, almost squat as pineapples, but the pendants of misty flowers were still dangling there, and she and Freeman got out of the car to touch them. Could they be tiny dates? She had read about date palms in California. Down the narrow street, the pale yellow sprays of flowers swayed a little in the breeze, and she let Freeman run up and down the sidewalk underneath them until she worried that Carolanne might think they had run away.

It was dark when she neared the security-guard booth, and Freeman was asleep in his car seat, his head flopped at an impossible angle. Marietta carried him up the stairs to Carolanne's door and saw that the lights were off. She was worried; Carolanne had asked her to take him, but she should be awake now. Marietta fumbled with the key to her own door while Freeman's head slid down her shoulder, and she stood in the dark hall, trying to see. She smelled something unfamiliar, and when she passed into the living room, the lights clicked on and Carolanne stood there with a cake. "Happy birthday, Mama. Here, give me the baby. And listen." She turned on the answering machine and took Freeman into Marietta's bedroom.

Nate's deep voice said, "Happy birthday, Mama. You think we forget, huh? Coach said ain't no way nobody leave night before the game. But we leave you present with Carolanne. I hope I give you a better attitude for you birthday, Mama." She smiled when Carolanne came back into the room. Nate sounded like a little boy promising he wouldn't lick the frosting if you left him alone with the cake.

"You thirty-nine, Mama. Yeah, try to deny it, but you a old woman. Don't pop me, ouch!" Calvin laughed into the telephone. "We gotta stay here, but we wish you happy birthday. Save some cake for we, huh?" Nate must have grabbed the phone—"Calvin droolin all over me, Mama. Don't eat all the cake or I'ma drown!"

The tape clicked off. Marietta sat on the couch, laughing. "I can't believe this. California. Lord God," she said, as Carolanne handed her a large package.

Marietta took the wrapping paper off carefully. She held three soft, already-buttoned shirts in African print. Yellow and red and black and green—not jungle trees and parrots like shirts she saw men wearing at football games, but subtle, small geometric designs. Inside the collar of each shirt was a headwrap in matching print. Carolanne held up one of the shirts to her chest.

"This lady in the project made them for me. Soul Gardens fashion. I told her about your headwraps and she said these were a good size. Here, try."

Marietta went into the bedroom, quiet in the dark of Freeman's breathing, and came out wearing the shirt with the most red; she tied the scarf tight at the back of her head. Carolanne touched her earrings. "You look like a queen," she said. "Except you're wearing pants." She handed Marietta a smaller package. "This one's from Nate and Calvin."

The tiny box held a gold chain with a football pendant outlined in diamonds. She fastened it around her neck, and Carolanne said, "Well, it looks kind of funny with the African print, but what the hell. I suggested earrings, but Nate said you never take those hoops off."

"Diamond. Them two crazy." She let it fall heavy on her collarbone.

"I know. I didn't see it till now—they went by themselves. Well, here's Freeman's present. Actually, this one was hardest to get, cause we had to stand in line at the DMV forever. But he carried it all the way out to the car." She handed Marietta a California driver's handbook and an application for a license. "Calvin said you didn't know how to drive yet, and I told him he didn't know shit."

The sun beat down on them when they found their seats, near the other wives and friends of the players. Carolanne waved and went over to talk to two women with black sunglasses and long, blond hair. She wore a pink sundress and pink sandals, and her sunglasses were black, too. Marietta tried to keep Freeman from sliding out of his seat, watching the players warm up on the field.

"There Daddy," she told him. "Look." Nate stretched and talked to Rock and Bulk. Freeman waved.

Marietta felt a trickle of sweat down her back, and a tickle of fright—this was where she had always wanted to be, and now she watched the boys in their spiraled helmets, their clamshell knees hidden and thousands of other people watching them, too. She said, "Baby Poppa, keep a eye on em," into Freeman's hair.

She had packed food, telling Carolanne, "I don't think you gon want no hot dog, even if somebody else have for cook it and it ain't split. I don't think that what the baby crave, huh?" She put fruit juice, cookies, fried chicken and cheese and crackers into a bag and said, "Don't worry—I carry it so you ain't look country. You just have for eat it."

The crowd settled, all the shirts falling into their seats before the kickoff, and Marietta swept her eyes over the bobbing heads and slashes of black that were hundreds of sunglasses swaying and then still when the ball flew into the air. Then she watched Nate lean on his knuckles to wait.

The Rams blitzed several times, but the Chargers were ready for Nate, and the right tackle had help blocking him. He struggled to swing around the outside, but the quarterback got off pass after pass. The Chargers scored on the third series, and Nate stalked the sidelines, throwing his paper cup down angrily. Calvin came over and touched his helmet to Nate's when they talked.

The little wide receiver, Leroy Sims, was one of Marietta's

favorites. She loved to see him in motion, making that sharp-cornered turn and suddenly sprinting downfield, slanting across, feet flying so high they might have hit him in the butt each step. When he caught a thirty-one-yard pass that soared into the bowl of his palms, she didn't stand up and scream with the others; she sat still, wondering at the beauty of the game far from the hugging crashes of her boys. Then it was Nate's turn to twist and try again.

He made two of the tackles she loved best, the clean leap at the waist of the fullback—Nate flat in the air and the reassuring sound of the fullback falling but big enough so he could handle it. She was afraid of the grabs to flying feet, of the tackles and blocks that looked like glancing blows but sent someone off balance into the benches. And Calvin came in during the last few plays of the second quarter, with Letey, the quarterback, handing off to Brigham way back at the forty-yard line. Calvin thrust his chest into the linebacker's and slid with him, dancing until Brigham was down. When he ran off the field at halftime, she saw his jersey tight around his huge arms, the excess gathered into a little ball in his armpits and secured with tape. He had told her that was to prevent hands from grabbing at his jersey. They were too far away to see her.

Carolanne stood up to take Freeman over and play with Brigham's son. She told Marietta, "I'll try to pay attention, but excuse me if I'm not obsessed, okay?"

Marietta sat alone and watched the people mill around her, laughing, drinking beer. Two men fought, and people stared, rushed over to see. She was watching the litter around the benches, thinking of Baby Poppa, and someone said beside her, "Excuse me, ma'am."

A middle-aged white man bent down to speak to her. "Is this your first football game?" he said, his words very slow and careful.

"No," she said before she could think, she was so surprised.

"Oh, well, I was just watching you, and wondering what you think of American football. You're from Africa, right?" She tried to look into the eyes without looking; he swayed, held a beer cup, and the cheeks were red.

"No, I'm not from Africa," she said, and then she thought, don't tell he bout the boys, he be ax a hundred question. Africa?

"Oh, I saw your outfit and I guess I thought you were like a visitor from another country or something. Well, sorry—hey, you got great seats." He turned and stumbled back up the steps to the higher rows.

She felt the football pendant stick to her skin; it had worked its way inside her shirt. She fingered it, feeling eyes on the back of her headwrap, and she lifted her chin. Africa woman. Huh. I only a haint. Haint move a rock. The gold on the football was warm. August 11—she had really forgotten that yesterday was her birthday. The only thing she had remembered was the date of Carolanne's doctor appointment. The bag of food sat below the seat, spotted with grease from the chicken.

When Carolanne came back, Marietta looked at the small belly underneath the pink knit dress. Rosie—her baby, the one after Lil Johnny, had died in the sixth month; it stopped moving, and Aint Sister knew, told Rosie, but she had to carry it, riding inside her heavy and still, for two more months until Aint Sister went in the middle of the night to help with the labor that pushed out the motionless form.

Marietta handed the sack to Carolanne and said, "Sit down and eat something, now. Stop flitting around."

Carolanne said, "Who was that white dude? Was he rapping to you or what?" She took a piece of chicken, and Freeman took a cookie.

"He want to know was I from Africa," Marietta said.

"What? Why?"

"How I look."

"I know that—I mean what was he gonna do if you were? Start talking Swahili?"

Marietta shook her head. "Hush up and eat," she said, smiling.

The second half was long, and she began to miss Baby Poppa more, realizing that this was the first game where she'd sat in bleachers, in a stadium, for four years. All this time she'd waited to watch Nate and Calvin play pro ball, but she missed Baby Poppa and the cool night air. She looked around carefully a few times and people looked back at her; they were mostly white people like the ones back in Charleston, because these were such expensive seats, she knew.

Nate broke free and chased the quarterback with curved arms, but Marietta knew he would do that again and again, the way he had for years now, and the quarterback would get the pass off or not, but he would fall. No one scrambled fast enough to escape Nate. The ball shot out in a straight line to the full-back, for only three yards. Nate covered the quarterback on the ground, and Marietta thought, He gon do he job. Calvin, too. Roster cuts—that what they all wait for, Carolanne, too. People say first-round draft pick gon make the cut no matter what. If Calvin ain't do nothing wrong, ain't fall or read block wrong, he make it. Mama job never done. I beena tell Carolanne, Freeman don eat more than that? Don he sleep now? Don you put some garlic salt on that chicken first? Don forget Nate like pepper on he egg.

Rock spun the wide receivers around, Nate's shoulder drove the fullback to the waiting chest of Jeffrey, and Letey handed the ball to Brigham twice, until he scored. Beer ran beneath her feet, Freeman fell asleep on her shoulder, and Carolanne laughed with the other wives, their lips fuchsia and apple and lush.

How could she miss watching them on TV? The precise square of the game was all she had to concentrate on then—the grass, bounded by lines of coaches, players, and the edges of the screen. The crowd's roars and constant shouts turned into wind blowing through high pines. She didn't have to endure stares and stepping over bare tanned legs to get to her seat. No beer running under her shoes, no one wondering who she was. TV. Listening to men laugh and holler at the players, watching the plays form and scatter, someone handing her a plate of rice or a slice of cake.

They didn't have to call. She watched *Star Search* with Carolanne, wondering how to tell her about the plan. Carolanne said, "Look at her, I could do so much better than that. She can't even talk."

"Martina Smith, celebrity spokes model," Marietta heard the man say, and she frowned.

"What she suppose to doing? Walk and smile at the same time?" she asked Carolanne.

"Look, she's so stiff." Carolanne sucked her teeth just like Rosie.

"Celebrity spoke model. Them word don't have nothing to do with each other," Marietta said.

"She's supposed to represent products, be an announcer, do commercials or game shows or whatever," Carolanne said. "If she has a brain, she could do a lot of stuff. But you can tell she doesn't. All she has is legs half as tall as me. Shit." She took a drink of juice. "See, I had decided to major in public relations at school. I could have. . . well, I sure as hell ain't tall enough to be a model." The shimmering dress turned and walked back down the runway to applause.

She so big—is that a woman? Blueblack. She looked at Carolanne's tiny feet, her collarbone showing in the neck of the scooped-out T-shirt she wore. All she life, people tell she how little and cute and light. I wild in the tree, big for a man. "What that baby want?" Marietta asked. "What he tell you?"

"Why you keep saying 'he'?" Carolanne asked.

"Just a habit."

Carolanne sighed. "He's thirsty. He wants juice all the time."

"That ain't enough."

"I know."

Marietta said carefully, "What you aintie think?"

"How you know she already knew?"

"Cause she you aintie."

"She said at least I don't bring my kid for her to babysit and she gave all the baby clothes to Niecie, so don't ask for none. I don't know what she think." Carolanne rubbed her eyes. "She said, 'Carolanne don't never come by here—baby be grown next time we see her.' She was mad cause I spent more time talking to the lady made your shirts than I did listening to her."

Marietta didn't say anything, and Carolanne snapped, "I know it ain't that far, okay?"

"I ain't tell you nothing, Carolanne. Listen. I leave my home, my aintie, and didn't go but half as far. Didn't go back for so long. I didn't have no car, no way to go, but I ain't made no way causc I didn't want to, either."

Carolanne said, "I don't have nothing to say to people, all I see in their eyes is dollar signs. I can't hang."

"No matter who you think you are now, you ain't that person when you home. You still a child, do the same thing wrong, huh?" Carolanne nodded. "Hear the same thing people remember bout you then. Now you got a boy—maybe two. I got two. We gon do the same thing to them—always remember what they ain't want for hear."

"No," Carolanne said.

"We have for do that." Marietta smiled. "Ain't no other way." She took off her shoes and said, "I'm fixing to go."

"You tired already?"

"No. I mean I fixing to leave here. I'ma ax Calvin how the money is and I want look for a house. I think I go to Rio Seco."

"What?"

"You and Nate a family now. You come and visit. But I thought I keep Freeman for you, for a few month, since you getting close to you time with the baby. You need for spend this time with Nate—nobody else. And Calvin need for find he a girl—he ain't gon do that with me over there. He need find somebody else cook for he now." She put her hand on Carolanne's arm. "You listen to that baby better if I don't be in you ear all the time."

"You just started talking to me about a week ago—now you think I don't want to hear?" Carolanne said. "I never said that."

"No, you never say it. But look these condo—I ain't never comfortable here. I gon look for a house. And we keep that secret along with you baby secret till roster cut, long as you still determine for do that." Carolanne nodded.

"Aren't you worried about Calvin making the cut?" Carolanne asked. "Nate says Calvin's all nervous."

"Nate nervous, too, huh? But I think they both be okay. They go train Calvin. Nate the one need for keep he head small. You gotta keep he off that stuff."

Carolanne ran the pad of her thumb over her nails. "If he can."

"You keep a eye," Marietta said.

She had planned to go back to Rio Seco the next day, and Carolanne had collected for her some section of the newspaper that featured new homes. "I can't believe you like *Rio Seco,* all out in the country, nothing to do," Carolanne said. "But look, they have five model homes open in this tract, Hampton Hills, and three models in Regency Estates. These are great floor plans."

"Them house look huge," Marietta said. "Big as a barn."

"Well, I was thinking I would come and look with you. We got this new baby coming, we might want more room, cause I don't want Freeman to have to share for long."

"You ain't want for live in Rio Seco," Marietta said, teasing her. "Rock say it 'backwood' for L.A. people."

"I'm just talking about floor plans," Carolanne said absently. "Nate was too conservative when he told me only look for two bedrooms."

But Nate called a few minutes later from training camp. He said something that made Carolanne hand the phone to Marietta and run into the bathroom.

"Mama, *Sports Illustrated* call over here. They want for do some kind a pictures, you and me and Calvin. I guess Carolanne, too. Some story bout twin."

The photographer wanted to meet them in L.A. the next day, and Carolanne was lost for hours, locked in the bathroom, coming out only to call Tiana and Sandi Letey and Tina Brigham. Marietta followed her to the mirror before lunch, watching Carolanne concentrate and stroke the mallard-green shine close to her lashes, then spread gold under her brows. She brushed the curling lashes until they were clotted thick and black, then combed out the clots.

Marietta made her sit at the table to eat lunch. "You better worry bout what the doctor say on Friday," she told Carolanne. "You look fine."

"My hair's disaster. What are you gonna do with yours?" Carolanne tilted her head. "You know, I ain't never seen your hair."

"Ain't much for see." Marietta got up to wash the dishes. She watched TV alone on the black leather couch for an hour, thinking that the only black women she saw in magazines or on TV who looked normal were mothers.

"It's a portrait," the photographer said. "Formal, really, because we're not concentrating on the sport as much as the family, the faces. I'd like you guys to take off your shirts, and the ladies can wear these tube tops." He fingered his beard and looked at Carolanne. "Actually, I'd like to try a couple of shots with just Mrs. Cook and the guys. I mean, your mother, Nate."

Skin no one had ever seen. Her mother, Aint Sister, pouring water on her in the zinc washtub, and never anyone again. Sinbad in the dark. The circle of tight material fit around her chest, and her collarbone was hot in the light where they stood in front of a black sheet of material. She remembered the mirrors in the huge bathrooms in Charleston—the mirrors in Carolanne's bathroom, bedroom. Nate and Calvin teased her about her shoulders and she said, "Hush and look for the camera."

The photographer smiled and said, "No, that's very natural. Go ahead."

Just like cry. You don do it in front of nobody you know, then you gon cry in public on the freeway. Ain't feel no eye on you skin since Sinbad and let the whole country see you old self.

Carolanne sat at the makeup table, angry. Her lips were pressed in a small oval, Marietta saw. The photographer told them he wanted to play with the light now, and they could see the makeup artist.

A thin Asian man with hair that stood up in a frozen wave

rested his bent little finger on her cheek and brushed something on her eyes. The furry brush felt like a mouth, tiny lips on her eyes and then her own lips. "You have gorgeous skin," he said. "You'll never have a wrinkle, I'll bet. I'm not going to do much here. What about your hair?"

He began to untie the scarf and she froze. Her cheeks were darker than ever against his pale elbows while he pulled off the headwrap and she watched in the mirror. "Oh, you've got it cropped close. That'll look great with Nate and Calvin. I thought you had it straightened. Let me just pick it out even and you're done." He patted and combed. "It smells good—what have you been using on it?"

"Almond oil," she said. She had borrowed Tiny Momma's small bottle years ago and loved the smell.

"Nice." He hung his face over her head in the mirror. "Okay?"

She stared. "One thing—my eyebrow. Eyebrows."

He raised his own. "Thicker, a little bit? Darker?" The kissing brush tickled her there, like breath, and he smiled when she did.

In the other room, the photographer stood uncomfortably near his camera. "Naw, man," Nate was saying, arms folded. "I gotta have my wife in here, too. She ready to go. She done did her own makeup."

"Well, we're really looking at twins and their parents, really just one parent, the one that encouraged sports. We've got hockey players and their mom, two tennis players and their dad."

"Look at my wife. She the one use to get photograph," Nate said.

"I did modeling work for the USC catalog and other places,"

Carolanne said. Her hair rose in a perfect shell-like dip over her forehead.

"Well, we'll do some of both," the photographer said, smiling. "Let's get you all in there first, then just the guys, then the guys and Mrs. Cook."

"We both Mrs. Cook," Marietta said, standing on the chair behind the boys as he gently pushed her shoulders down.

He didn't say "Smile" or "Cheese" but just "Lift your chin, Carolanne," and "Not that far, Calvin." The silver lights were hot on Marietta's shoulders, and she looked down to see Nate's and Calvin's huge rounded shoulders just below her, the black skin marked and raised in a few places. Nate had a crescent scar from a broken bottle on the outside of his biceps, and she tried to look down further to see Calvin's forearms, to see if the thin hairline scars still remained on his wrists and inside his elbows.

"Uh, Mrs. Cook, you have to look *up,*" the photographer said, and the light blinded her.

"These are the best ones to see—Hampton Hills, Fox Run, and this one called Palm Lakes," Carolanne said. She held the newspaper ads and the photos of the model homes with her on the front seat of the Lincoln, and she read directions to Marietta after they had passed the off ramp to the Westside. I let she look, Marietta thought. She still vex from the photographer, look for them picture every day in the mail and talk bout "Fool *better* choose the right ones." I go long here first.

But the hills south of Rio Seco, the flat, recently bulldozed land looked very familiar, and the block wall surrounding Fox Run was just as high and blank. The model homes were inside, and then empty, barely finished houses stood on bare lots where weeds had sprung up. "Ain't been no fox round here for long time," Marietta said to Carolanne. "No—no need for even show me this."

Carolanne rattled the newspaper. "I really like this floor plan."

Marietta said, "Go on back. You look another day. I choose a house. I show you where it is."

"Wait—you didn't see Palm Lakes," Carolanne said. "I thought this one would be perfect, cause of the water. It's right over the hill."

When they came over the top of the slope and Marietta saw a huge tract of houses surrounding a blue, circular lake, with a golf course off to one side, she laughed. She stopped the car on the side of the road and said, "That ain't no lake. That landscape." She saw the toothbrush trees scattered around in a pattern, the cement paths leading to the water, and no one anywhere on the grass. "Oh, Carolanne."

She drove to the Westside, not to the house, but around the lake, and Carolanne said, "Yeah, right. A city park. You want to bring Freeman here so he can watch people sell dope and make out all over the grass."

"Ain't nobody sell nothing to me, and ain't nobody bother Rock uncle. We fish, and Freeman play. You gon have for think, Carolanne." Marietta circled the lake and watched the old men play dominoes, the Vietnamese men wading in the shallows looking for the tiny clamshells they put in burlap bags. Then she drove to the neighborhood, and stopped in front of the house.

"No—I ain't even looking," Carolanne said. "A repo. You got all this money and you want to live in the ghetto in some repo. I don't believe you."

Marietta laughed again. "This ain't no ghetto—these people got yard, buy they house, got car and truck. This ain't Soul Garden. This ain't Pine Garden. And you gon have for believe me."

"Freeman's tired—he wants to get out and walk. Let's get on the road. I saw a mall off the freeway, and I have to get something," was all Carolanne said, and Marietta nodded. She know. She gon give he to me for a time. She know. But I take she shopping.

In the department store, Carolanne hurried into the baby section and bought bottles that turned different colors when they were heated—"I saw these in a magazine, you can tell if the milk's too hot without even testing it"—and a bassinet that rocked by itself when you pushed a button. "Freeman never had a bassinet," she told Marietta when it was in the trunk.

The doctor shook his head and apologized. The lab had given him the results of the first blood test twice, he said, and that was why he'd thought maybe the baby was dead. Now the HCG levels were progressing, and even though the machine still wavered eerily and spit at them from the speaker, Marietta heard the tapping heartbeat.

Carolanne was triumphant at home. "I grew up on Kool-Aid and smoke," she said. "I know what I'm doing."

"I hope so," Marietta said. "Cause you promise you tell Nate next week."

Carolanne had gotten the envelope of photographs yesterday, the proof sheets from the *Sports Illustrated* session. There was no letter saying which ones would be used. In some of the pictures no one smiled, and Marietta looked hard at their faces, she and the boys' dark cheeks angled to the sides in the harsh light, all shadows and reflection of their straight-set mouths. Carolanne was a silvery flower floating on Nate's wide chest, her brows and eyes and mouth round and surprised. Carolanne bent close, studying the photos for hours.

The Houston game was the last one of the exhibition season, and again Marietta saw only the highlights on the late night news. The boys called, said they would be coming home for a week, until final roster cuts.

But she didn't stay in the condominiums to wait with them; she took Freeman with her to the little lake in Rio Seco. They didn't fish; they walked around the still water and plucked long reeds from the swampy area where water trickled from a pipe into the lake and the mud was wet-black. "Duck-duck," Freeman called to the geese, and he ran to pick up the dried strands of grass she pointed to.

She sat on a scarred picnic bench, playing with the grass. You want run again. Almost forty year old and you still want run, out here now. Every time, you leave. She saw the geese crash into the water, and Freeman ran after a ball kicked by a small boy who shouted in another language. She was pulling the strands of grass, bending them into a circle, and then she realized that, without thinking, she was trying to fashion them into a round, weave them together to make a tiny coil—the beginning. Her fingers were clumsy, used to mops and brooms and sponges, and it was hard to hold the awkward packet of grass, but she bent the blades as carefully as she could and Freeman pushed his nose close to see what she was doing.

the westside

october

When wasps began to hover and own the eaves at Red Man's house, his daughter was sent to Marietta's, and she came in an hour or so with her long, fat branch-stick and a torch of rolled newspapers. All the boys playing on Picasso Street would say, "There go Nate and Calvin Cook mama! They play on the Rams! But I bet she still holler at em—she look mean."

Red Man saw her tall shadow on the porch and said, "Hey, Marietta, they over in the side yard again. Can't nobody get near the Cadillac to fix it. I heard you like to fish with that stuff. How them catfish down to the lake?"

"Waiting for me, I hope," she said.

The boys kept a distance from her in the side yard, close to the wasps. "Why she ain't scared?" they whispered to each other, looking around the corner of the house, stucco brushing their cheeks. "Cause she so big and black. Look. I bet if them wasp bite her, she ain't feel it."

She heard their thin whispers, smiled to herself when she lit the newspaper for a moment, then blew out the quick flames. The smoke rose into the eaves and the wasps hung, stunned, for a second before they sped away; they flew fast, not lazy and taunting like they did when the boys came near.

Marietta knocked the papery nest down with her stick. She put it in a sack, tapped the ash from her torch, and walked back to the front yard. Freeman waited with Roscoe and Red Man. He had gone inside for a cookie from Mary, because he was afraid of the wasps.

Roscoe said, "We finished for the day. I'ma go get my granddaughter from Mrs. Rollins, see how these two play with each other. She's turning four next month."

It was Friday, and the crowd of small boys had just gotten out of school. They ran up and down the street, watching for cars, barely stepping out of the way. Red Man's huge truck was parked in the yard; it was piled to the top of the gates with branches and clippings and trash. Red Man and Roscoe did gardening, tree trimming, hauling, and cleanup.

"Still hot for October, huh?" Red Man said. "I think that's why them wasps keep hanging around." He paused and then said, "It's a bye week, and they ain't got a game till next Sunday, huh?"

She knew he didn't like to ask about Calvin and Nate directly, since she lived down the street now. The men were sometimes afraid to mention the Rams or the boys until she did, and it had taken her some figuring to guess that they didn't want her to think they expected tickets or favors or explanations. She hadn't raised Nate and Calvin in the neighborhood, and so these men didn't own them. She listened for their hesitation and tried to answer right.

"They ready for a break," she said, "but this the second week of October, ain't it? They play in Chicago on Sunday, and next week they bye time."

"You knew that," Mary said to Red Man. She turned to Marietta. "How he eatin today?"

Freeman had left half the cookie on Marietta's leg. "He picky," she said. "And he mama don't like when he sleep in thc bed with me. Granma never do right, huh?"

Roscoe walked down the sidewalk with Hollie, his granddaughter, and Mary said, "But not with him, cause he the only one got that girl. Her daddy runnin the streets. Roscoe do a good job with her."

Hollie adjusted the barrettes on her braids and took Freeman's hand to show him the wheel wells of the huge tires. Then she and Freeman circled each other in the side yard for a while, Freeman following her every move.

"I got plum wine," Red Man said to everyone. "Go on and try some."

"How plum wine gon be orange?" said Roscoe, and Marietta looked at the mayonnaise jar in her hand doubtfully.

"Cause he was so impatient he use them green ones in the summer, them things wasn't ripe for nothin," Mary said.

"The body and soul of impatience," Roscoe said, smiling at

Marietta. "You should be able to tell by now that the man doesn't wait for anything."

"I don't need none," Marietta said, handing the jar back to Mary.

"Them wasps don't want to give up," Roscoe said, looking at Marietta's bag.

"I only live here a month, and that the second time they been in he side yard," Marietta said.

"And I bet he told you nobody could get close to the Cadillac." Roscoe laughed.

"As if anybody even thinkin bout fixin that thing," Mary said.

"Plenty people think about it," Roscoe said. "That's all they do." He made a face at the wine. "This stuff tastes like ten-year-old Kool-Aid."

Red Man stretched, and his pale chest rose above the V in his T-shirt, much lighter than the dark-burned skin on his arms and neck. "Y'all leavin more for me then," he said. "That Chicago game on TV—you want to watch it over here?" he asked Marietta.

"I see what Carolanne fixing to do. She said she want try some weekend beauty routine she see in a magazine."

Everyone was quiet, waiting for the small pickup truck that blared music to pass the house. She had seen many of them, all driven by young men, the trucks low and flat as house slippers, the beds filled with speakers. Roscoe's son had one.

"What they good for?" she had asked him.

"Making noise," he had said. She watched the shiny black thing stop at the corner. Cain't haul no people nor fish in there. Bitty thing.

"When that baby due?" Mary asked.

"January. Super Bowl Baby," Marietta told her.

"We both too young to be grandpeople," Roscoe said. Marietta was embarrassed. He had told her her face was classic, whatever that meant.

"Young as you act," Mary said.

Marietta stood up.

"I need for get home and give this boy he dinner," she said. "Freeman!"

Roscoe said, "We going to the dump on Monday. I'll come by and move the rest of that junk."

She nodded and took Freeman's hand to pull him away from Hollie. "I preciate that."

He brought wood, though, when he came. "We cut down a pepper tree," he said. "You might need some wood later, and we got plenty. Wind knocked down a lot of eucalyptus and pepper trees this year, and we had more than we could use."

"I have to get me a ax," she said, looking at the thick stumps and trunks.

"Don't worry about that," Roscoe said. "But let me move this junk first."

Stacks of plywood that Calvin had torn from the windows were in the corner of the dirt yard, and scattered in a few piles were the vials, clothes, and trash that had been swept from the inside of the house. Marietta had pushed them all to the far edge, near the garage, so she wouldn't see them all the time.

"My son was hanging out here," Roscoe said, throwing the plywood onto the truckbed. "He got busted with the rest of em when the cops came. Rock house. But the other guys told the cops Louis wasn't selling it." He wiped his forehead. "I don't know what he was doing."

"Where he stay now?" Marietta asked.

Roscoe shook his head and got a rake from the hooks on the wooden gate of the truckbed. "You coming to Red Man's on Sunday for the game?"

"I guess I might," she said. "Freeman ain't much company for football yet. He only like for see he daddy two, three time, and then he bored."

"I look forward to seeing you," Roscoe said. "And don't touch that wood."

Inside, she looked at the shiny wood floor, remembering the thick dirt clotted with beer and urine, the glass vials, the cigarette butts. Damp clothes in the corners of the big front room, and the dank smell. Last time for somebody else dirt, she had thought when she first stood inside the boarded-up house. I run away for the last time. I make my own dirt now.

She had sat down with Nate and Calvin, just the three of them, and talked about the money. The accountant called a real-estate agent, who said the house was only $42,000. "The neighborhood isn't really that good," the agent said to her on the phone. "That's why the price is so reasonable. Location really means a lot. Are you thinking of renting it out after purchase?"

The boys decided on the money themselves, without her. They set up an account after the accountant drafted the check to buy the house, and like Tiny Momma, they gave her money every month. But she only let them put $1,200 in the account, saying, "That all I need for feed us and buy book and toy. Pay my utility. You save the rest."

Calvin said, "I'ma need to buy a new car, since you taken the Lincoln." He laughed. "I never liked no big car anyway. I want me a Z-car."

When she swept out the dirt and bottles, she saw that though the varnish was pitted and scarred the wood floor was solid. And three bedrooms—one for her, one for Freeman, and one for visitors. Calvin slept on the foldout couch.

She liked the words, calling Tiny Momma to say, "This my new phone number. I got me a house, with a big yard and plum tree. In Rio Seco. Only half hour from them two, and they gon visit. When you coming out?"

She asked Red Man about the floors, and he brought a thin young man with a drum sander, which sent fine dust everywhere and left sweet-smelling bare oak. He smeared golden stain onto the wood, then brushed over clear varnish, and even Carolanne said, "It came out nicer than I thought. But wood floors are so much trouble to keep clean, and it's gonna be cold in the winter."

"Sweep em out easier than fool with that huge vacuum you need for all you carpet. And me and Freeman wear socks, huh, baby? You gon stay with you gran while Mama have a new baby."

"Fireplaces are really dangerous," Carolanne said. "You need a screen." Marietta remembered all the brass-trimmed screens she had polished in Charleston.

"I let you pick me out a nice one," she said.

The floor man put new linoleum in the kitchen. He said the

house looked like it was built in 1920 or so, and then he brought a young white man, who painted the kitchen cupboards pale blue and the rest of the walls white. Marietta scrubbed the sink, gleaming white enamel with ridged drainboards on each side; she loved to wash dishes or clean greens and see the rivulets of water run in tracks down to the double sink.

Nate and Calvin had come three times, during the week, to hose off the outside after she had moved in. Then she asked them to paint the windowsills dark blue. Blue for keep spirit away, window and door all.

Carolanne didn't like it, that they were working on the house when they should have been resting, but Marietta painted, too, listened to their voices, and watched the way they moved slower in the yard. She went to the window now and looked out at the wood. Nate don't need for throw chair at no wall, he chop wood. No—he ain't want for do that. Wood for winter.

Roscoe had been finding reasons to come by. Red Man teased him about being a poet, about the way he shifted his languages, too. He reminded her of Baby Poppa sometimes when he talked, but he was different. He stood close and talked low sometimes. Red Man and Mary watched, she saw, but she didn't mind. And when he was out of the yard, they told her how he had taken his son's daughter, how he had protected his son from the cops during the summer when there was trouble in the neighborhood. She washed the breakfast dishes, cut up a chicken, and thought about the outline of his lips.

He came early in the morning to tell her that he and Red Man were cutting down a carob tree today, and the thick branches would make even better firewood than the pepper trees.

"What you cookin?" he said, bending over the stove.

"Grits."

He laughed. "Rich woman like you gon eat grits for breakfast? That's poor folks' food!"

She had to laugh, too, because he was so obvious about wanting to stay in the kitchen. "I beena have grits without groceries many time."

Then he said, "You want to see what poor California folks eat, if they come from the desert like me? See, I ain't from Georgia or South Carolina like the rest of you. I couldn't go out and get fish like you're always talking about. I'm part Mexican, part Indian, desert people. Let me make you my specialty."

He left abruptly and came back by the time she had finished making coffee. Freeman looked up from the kitchen floor, where he was racing trucks. Roscoe dropped a brown bag on the table and said, "I'ma make you the Mexican equivalent of ground-up cornmeal. Each culture dresses up cornmeal as best they can. I've written poems for tortillas."

He stood at the spattering cast-iron frying pan and slid something onto the plate: crispy-fried envelopes filled with melted cheese and a vein of hot sauce inside. "Quesadillas," he said, and then, "Sun circles of yellow corn, keep us alive with their heat." A poem—she heard it in the rhythm.

While she ate slowly, he leafed through the *Sports Illustrated* she had left on the table, the one with her picture. She said nothing, but he told her, "I've already seen it, everybody has. Red Man's son Darnell bought four of em. I just want to look at you again."

"All in the Family" was the title of the photo essay: first there was a crinkle-eyed white woman with curly hair and her two sons who played hockey. "Twin Sticks," it said below them. Then two teenaged girls, with braces and freckles, and their father: "Double the Racket." A Mexican woman with a gold eyetooth and shy smile, and her two sons, who played soccer in college. Sidekicks. And then the stark photo of Nate and Calvin's bare chests, plates of bone hard-edged in the light, and her face and shoulders rising above them. "Blood Sport," the title said. Below was a line reading, "Marietta Cook, who now lives in California, and her sons, Calvin and Nate, rookie teammates on the Los Angeles Rams."

"My wife died when Louis was six," Roscoe said abruptly. "She was in a car accident."

Marietta nodded.

"Your husband?"

Marietta almost said it. He dead, too. It fit perfectly. But she waited, and he stood up to turn another tortilla in the pan.

"The boys' daddy—he here and gone people."

Roscoe nodded, finished the quesadilla. She watched the hot sauce drip from the corner, remembered Pinkie and Laha always wanting "vinecka-peppa sauce" at lunch in the fields. Then Roscoe said suddenly, "I like that, the way it sounds. Here and gone people." He sat down across from her. "But is he gone?"

She smiled into his eyes. "Been gone—longer than twenty year."

"Okay," he said. "I like the way that sounds, too."

He finished his quesadilla and washed his hands. "Let me take Hollie for the day," she said. "You bring me all that wood."

"Who you plan to invite for a fire, with all this wood?" he said. She looked away.

"I ain't decide yet. Go on and get Hollie for me. She play good with Freeman."

Hollie loved to boss Freeman around, telling him, "Go put that dirt in the bucket," and he loved to follow her orders. Marietta sat in the beach chair she'd bought at K Mart, watching the lake. The fishing here was hard to get used to, different from the lapping edges of the waterway and the sliding creeks.

The Vietnamese men crouched near her, gathering those tiny clams that breathed in the black mud around the edges of the lake. "I don't know why they want to fool with them things," Red Man had said. "Whole lotta work for a toothful a meat." Marietta watched her line floating, the fat larvae from the wasp eggs shifting below the water, and listened to the Vietnamese men's low, quick syllables. Their voices thudded in their throats almost as fast and hard as Aint Sister's old-time talk. Their feet were much smaller than hers in their rubber thongs.

She could stand the pole up the way the others did here, maybe work on a basket. She turned the circle around and around, wishing again that she knew how to make a bassinet like Aint Sister had made for her, a long round-cornered cradle with pine-needle squares in the sweetgrass. She had finished a low round for Carolanne, to hold baby powder and lotion and all the things she needed on the changing table. The grass and reeds she and Freeman collected near the swampy pipe didn't smell sweet, but they bent under her fingertips.

After an hour, she only had three bluegill thumping against the sides of the water bucket, and she thought she'd better take the kids home soon. Hollie wanted to try to make a basket, but Freeman snatched her grass away, shouting, "My Dig Ma! My Ma!"

She had wanted to catch a few catfish to fry for tomorrow, bring them to Red Man's house, since she was going to watch the game there and she knew he would serve her something. But this lake fishing wasn't the samc. She would have to practice.

"You want fish?" Roscoe said when he came to get Hollie. "I'll take you to the fish market tomorrow before we go to Red Man's and you can buy anything you want—red snapper, oysters, catfish. I don't eat much fish, but Mary loves it."

They drove in his truck, in the morning, with the kids between them in the long cab. It was a tiny storefront with bars on the windows and SEAFOOD SPECIALTIES painted on the white stucco over the door. When they walked inside, the two small tables with red-vinyled chairs, the warm-oiled air, made her blood turn to foam. A plump woman stood behind the counter, where the fish lay on ice, and said, "How you doing? What can I get for you?"

Waiting for the catfish and snapper to fry, she had to sit down and breathe, the smell coursing through her. Freeman and Hollie pressed their noses to the glass case, and Roscoe sat across from her. "You okay?" he asked.

"Fine," she said.

He was quiet during the game, while Red Man and Lanier and Red Man's sons yelled and drank beer and ate. Marietta sat with Mary at the table, eating a plate of fish and greens, but when she was finished, she moved to sit on a chair near Roscoe. "Thanks for take me to the market," she said. "You don't even like no fish. You ain't ate nothing."

He watched Nate on the screen, and Marietta waited until Nate had fallen inside the pack of players near the line. "Nice to see your sons play," Roscoe said strangely. "They big time. Make you feel good."

"Yeah," she said. "But make you feel nervous, too."

"Nervous better than nothing," he said, and he got up to go outside, where Red Man's daughters, who were in grade school, shouted with Freeman and Hollie.

Red Man watched Roscoe go, and he came to sit in the empty chair. "He don't like to watch sports," Red Man said. "His son used to play basketball, Roscoe was pushin him to play in college, and now the boy don't do nothin. Run wild with them dope dealers. Roscoe don't even like to watch the Lakers."

Marietta stayed in the chair, counting Nate's tackles and seeing Calvin play a few downs, listening to the men, but Roscoe didn't come back until the game was nearly over. The Rams won, 14–3, and Marietta felt Roscoe circle the room until he worked his way back to her.

"You want some a that wood done?" he said.

It was late afternoon, and the kids smoothed racetracks in the dirt near the plum tree. Marietta brought the chopped wood to the porch, stacked it, and watched him swing the mallet onto the wedge in the huge stumps. Sliding around the handle, the wood smooth in his hands—she remembered, the motion, the rhythm, the palms hot. The sun hung low in the sky, and he stopped chopping suddenly to point at the sky. "There go the crows," he said.

Flock after flock of big crows, fighting and croaking, went over the yard, and he stood mesmerized. "They're going to the riverbottom—that's where they sleep," he said. "They go home at this time every night."

The kids looked up, too, and the birds washed across the sky, darting at each other, flapping gracefully. "They got gold inside their wings," Roscoe said to her. She looked hard: at just the right moment, the sun reflected gold in patches on the undersides of their wings, close to their breasts. "My son loves birds," Roscoe said. "He used to."

"Mine just love fish," Marietta said, but he didn't even hear her.

"You can find gold in a lotta places, if you look the right way," he said, his head still thrown back, his skin tight.

"You have for look hard, huh?" Marietta said softly.

"No, I didn't mean hard. Just *right.*"

She thought about Roscoe's face, about what he'd said his son had lost. Every day she read the newspaper articles about the Rams' game, the analysis and features on the players. Carolanne said Nate was being good, that she thought he was off the steroids, but that he still stomped around before games. He told Marietta, "Take me two days to get up, get mad and pumped, and take me two days to come down after the game. With the game day, I only got two days for rest."

Calvin just got more and more quiet before games, and lost in his own face afterward. That was how he'd always been, running plays back and forth in his mind, correcting everything, he said.

This was the bye weekend, and they were all coming to spend two nights. She had planned carefully about what she would say, how she could keep them coming out to see her, how she could do her job from Rio Seco. She had asked Roscoe to bring her the things for Nate and Calvin, because she didn't know where to go for them, and she had bought Carolanne's birthday present and something for Freeman. Maybe this wouldn't work at all; maybe it would be as disastrous as the red-and-white dinner she had served. But she still wanted to keep an eye.

When Nate's BMW pulled up, she was waiting on the porch. They stood in the yard and Nate pulled off the strange things he had attached to the windshield wipers, some expensive thing everyone wanted now. Carolanne ran for Freeman, who shouted, "Mama! Mama here!"

"Rock said bring them things from the wipers in the house if we gonna park the car on your street," Carolanne said to Marietta, pressing her cheek against Freeman's. "He still can't believe you bought this old house."

"I can," Calvin said. "Old cheap Mama."

"You better hush all that. I don't need you tell me nothing, just come on back here cause you got work to do," Marietta said. She thought she might as well just get it over with.

"Great—more painting and moving furniture," Carolanne said, arranging Freeman's legs over her bigger belly. "Just what we need—strain on Nate's sore knee and paint fumes for me and the baby."

"No, not paint," Marietta said. "Nate's knee bad?"

"Naw, just had for put some ice on it last night," Nate said. "It ain't no big thing."

"I see you been eating," Marietta said to Carolanne when they walked around the house. "I'm happy you get some rest and fat." She pointed to the yard when the boys came. They saw the carob logs, the ash trunk Red Man had brought, and the new ax blades glinting where they leaned against the wood.

"Oh, man, Mama, you crazy," Calvin said.

"You see that thing, man?" Nate said, pointing to the Rototiller Roscoe had chosen. "She more than crazy. Don't crack you teeth at me, Mama. What Laha's Mr. Jerry always say—'I see that much work, I take my foot in hand for head on down-road.' *You* tell we that."

"Sound crazy to me, too," Marietta said. "But my neighbor say it really do get cold enough for fire here. And they say planting season in California come fall. Strangest thing I ever hear."

"Your coach is gonna love this, Nate. Don't you even think about it until the season's over," Carolanne said.

But he and Calvin were already examining the Rototiller. "Remember Baby Poppa use to tell us about some mule he had, said he had to cuss and fuss for get straight line in the field. Check out this blade. Mama, how big we gotta make this plot? You don't know how for grow no vegetable in California. Gon be too hot."

They started on the wood, though, the sledgehammer singing against the wedge in the log when Nate went for the biggest stump first. "Man, coach gon be hot he find out we chopping wood," Calvin said, holding the ax.

"He don know," Nate said.

"What if you bang up you knee?"

"Man, Muhammad Ali use to chop wood, get ready for fight."

"Yeah, but he was by heself, he mess up, it was on he back. We got the whole team lookin to you," Calvin said.

"Scary nigger," Nate said. "I ain't doin this by myself. Go on."

Freeman covered his ears when the metal rang against metal, and the ax thudded into the wood. "Owie," he said, watching them. Marietta had given him an old paintbrush and a pail of water, and he got busy wetting the plum-tree trunk, the side of the garage, the faded boards of the back fence. Carolanne stood uncomfortably, refusing to sit in the beach chair Marietta had brought outside for her. Marietta raked splinters and branches from the dirt. She'd been watering it, but nothing grew yet.

"Look at Freeman getting filthy," Carolanne said. "Y'all look just like a bunch a country niggers."

"We are," Marietta said. She took Carolanne's arm and led her back into the house. "Don't be mad," she said. "Nate tell you if you ax he—he like for see what he do, and this work gon calm he mind. He still got too much time on he hand, you beena tell me youself. Let he sweat some." Before Carolanne could answer, she said, "I ain't lecture. And if they don't want for work out there, they come back in. They grown. I didn't pay hardly nothing for them thing. But I get something for you, too, for you birthday next week." She handed Carolanne a small basket, with a box inside.

"This is beautiful," Carolanne said. "Did you buy this one where you got the ones you gave me, when we just moved into the condo?" She ran her fingers over the sides of the grass. It was darker than sweetgrass, too, but Marietta had tried to make the pattern clear.

"I make it. Them other one made by someone back home in South Carolina."

Carolanne tilted her head and looked at Marietta. "Are you serious? You *made* this? This is great, it looks so African, like something I see in books. You know, you could probably sell these for a lot of money, to a boutique or something. Maybe even a museum."

Marietta smiled. "That thing no good at all. My mama laugh at it. But it good enough for hold baby stuff, like you call it. Open the other one."

Carolanne pulled the ring from the tiny box. Marietta was ready for a fake smile and "Oh, how pretty." The stone was an emerald, big and green as a June bug, and Marietta thought Carolanne would think it was tacky, as she always said. But she hadn't been able to resist it at the store, and even though it had cost a lot of her saved money, it reminded her so much of Carolanne's eyes. She said quickly, "I seen in one a you magazine they wearing big jewelry now, call f-a-u-x, but this one real. It look like you when I see it."

The ring was huge on the thin gold finger, but Carolanne just laughed. "If I wear it, Tina Brigham and them want one, too. But I ain't wearing it to Soul Gardens, okay? I'd like to keep all my fingers attached to my hand."

Freeman came back from the bathroom with the toilet paper trailing behind him, and they both jumped up.

Marietta saw Carolanne stop at the counter where the *Sports*

Illustrated was still open to the picture of her. She hadn't been as angry as they'd all thought she'd be. She said now, "I'm glad they didn't use me. My face is all puffy from being pregnant, and I look a lot better in color, anyway. I hate black-and-white photography." She studied the picture closely again and said to Marietta, "You do have a great collarbone."

"I rather have eyebrows," Marietta said, surprising herself.

"Eyebrows?"

In the bathroom, Carolanne was tender and commanding, showing her how to stroke on black powder Marietta had bought, embarrassed, at the drugstore. Carolanne even said, "Here, you can have this eyebrow pencil, too, I'll get another one. Just be careful to blend—so it looks natural." She brushed with her fingertips, and Marietta saw the brows arch a little. She touched them herself, the ends soft and pointed.

Carolanne frowned and said, "You know, you could always get a curl," and Marietta had to laugh.

The boys were carrying the wood to stack on the side porch, and Marietta sat with Carolanne on the steps, watching Freeman raise dust with the dry hose, when Roscoe drove past slowly. He looked at Marietta, at the boys, and kept driving. He didn't smile or wave.

"What that dude lookin at?" Nate said, brushing splinters from his palms.

"He the one give me the wood," Marietta said. She stared after the truck—Roscoe's eyes had been blank, casual.

"Uh, oh," Calvin said. "Some dude try to sweetmouth Mama? Bring she wood, next gon give she vegetable seed!"

Carolanne said, "He doesn't look bad, for an old man. I like his eyes."

"You all best hush," Marietta said, going inside to make dinner. "He ain't that old."

While she fried the fish, she couldn't figure out why he wouldn't stop and say something. Why had he looked at the boys that way? She thought about his son, but still—he'd been happy to meet the boys that first day. She turned the four little bluegill she and Freeman had caught the day before, and Carolanne came into the kitchen, herself again.

"You got those at that city lake, huh? You don't know what's in those fish—they probably live on poison and toxic waste. Freeman might as well eat old tires."

Marietta let her talk. Super Bowl Baby. She knew what she wanted to ask Carolanne, watching her round belly touch the counter, and she knew she wouldn't. Marietta had thought about when Freeman came, when this one would, and she knew Carolanne had gotten pregnant whenever Nate did something big, something that would make him famous. Maybe make him restless. Carolanne had conceived Freeman just before the Rose Bowl, and this baby the month of the NFL draft. Marietta remembered Calvin telling her, whenever she prodded him about a girlfriend, "Mama, I gotta be too careful. These women *want* a baby, like it's a job. Like have a baby for Patrick Ewing or Tony Dorsett, you gon get two grand a month for a long *time.* Depend on how much the dude make. I don't know—I'm just looking."

But Carolanne had seen something else in Nate, she knew. Something in her voice when she told Marietta about Nate carrying her. Marietta put the fish, greens, and rice on the table. Slices of ham for Carolanne, who said that was what the baby craved. That and peanut-butter cookies. They ate at the table in the dining room, and Freeman looked at Carolanne when he dropped bits of fish and ham on the floor. "So?" Marietta said to him. "You go clean it up. You know where the broom stay."

"I still can't believe you bought this house, all the way out here, and all you say is you like the trees," Carolanne said.

"Yeah, Mama. You had a peach tree one time, huh?"

"She said Nate use to get sick off them peaches," Calvin said. "No sense back then, no sense now. He ate five banana in a row yesterday, look like a fool."

"I had leg cramps, man. Shut up. I needed some potassium. So why you like these tree, Mama?" Nate said.

She chewed, not knowing how to explain. She motioned that her mouth was full. Them little toothbrush tree by the condominium, all so scrawny you pull em up in a second for lightwood. She said, "I got a plum back there, got a fig, apricot. I like for have shade cause it so hot around here. Don't worry why I like a tree."

They complained that there was nothing to do, so they made her come to the movies. She sat in the dark theater, holding Freeman, who fell asleep, listening to the huge sounds of car crashes and shooting surrounding them, hearing Nate whisper to Carolanne and Calvin. But she closed her eyes to the giant flashing screen and saw Roscoe, his eyes half-lidded. What he do now, tonight? He drive someplace else, laugh and talk like he do for somebody young. He don't like for look straight in my eye.

She watched the late-night sports roundup with the boys. Carolanne and Freeman slept, and she was glad to be alone with Nate and Calvin, talking about who won the Atlanta game, and who had the most sacks for the league so far. They seemed more comfortable now, watching other players and highlights. Nate talked about the team, what they had to do for the season, and not just himself. Calvin said, "Letey better than that dude, man, look how many interception he get."

"That just what Rock like," Nate said. Marietta nodded. I know wood don't make all that big difference, she thought. But I try. I hope Carolanne don't laugh at she ring. I want them see me when I not there. I try.

All day Sunday, football games marched back and forth on the TV, and no one went outside. Marietta let them eat in the living room so they wouldn't miss any of the plays or scores, and then suddenly the windows were dark and the boys said they had to get home. Carolanne had been quiet, napping on the couch, and she said, "These guys got two road games—you know that, Mama. I gon take Freeman home for now, since I'll be by myself. I miss him. But I'll bring him back after Houston, in two weeks."

"Yeah, we turn up the dirt with that machine next time," Nate said. "I hope you water it some, cause it like cement now and you ain't gon get no rain." He put the strange things that looked like eyelashes back on the windshield wipers.

"Give Big Ma kiss," she whispered to Freeman's cheek close to hers. She breathed in his smell, holding him hard. "You get fishing pole when you come back. Give me sugar, one more time."

After they'd gone, she swept out the porch, and inside she looked at the empty fireplace. It was blackened and clean. You gon have for tell he, not no sit and wait. Maybe you do something wrong. Maybe he have somebody else all this time, just talk like Sinbad. Just for hear he voice.

She waited until early evening the next day. Monday Night Football would start at six, and it was still grayish light when she walked down Picasso Street. Her brows tingled from the pencil's tip. She knew people would be at Red Man's—maybe Roscoe would, too. I thank Red Man for the wood, anyhow. Pepper wood. That some big tree. People were sitting under the drifty-thin branches of the pepper tree in Red Man's yard, near the gnarled trunk.

"Hey," Red Man called. He and Mary, the older woman named Miss Ralphine from across the street, and Lanier and his wife, Mozelle. They had barbecued yesterday, Red Man said, and they had plenty left over.

"You watch all the games with your boys?" Red Man asked her.

"You know they had to see what everybody do," Marietta said. She hesitated. She thought she wanted to give him the tickets—Carolanne had told her yesterday that she and Freeman wouldn't be going to games. "It's too boring for him," she had said, "and I'm not fitting in them little seats."

Red Man and Roscoe and she could go, Marietta thought. She

wanted to sit next to Roscoe, but she liked the idea of sitting by Red Man just as well so she could hear him hoop and holler after each play. He knew almost as much as Baby Poppa.

Before she could say anything, Mary said, "Come on inside, get you a plate. I think it's gon rain, and Lord know we need it. I'm not gon complain."

They sat in the dim living room, with plates on their laps, and their voices wove around her. "These is some good greens, Mary."

"Lord, I hate to wash greens."

"Me, too. All that grit, and you gotta check em over two time. Take so much greens to make a good pot," Miss Ralphine said.

"And my daddy use to set up there and say, 'Don't complain—them greens keep you alive.'" Mozelle laughed. "Me and my sister be done sat at the table two hours cleanin em. Men love a pot a greens cause you don't never see no man having to wash em."

Red Man came in and said, "Hey, the game gettin ready to start."

Marietta listened. She heard Pinkie and Laha and Rosie, Big Johnny and all the others, but she wasn't wild Marietta, that girl say hi to tree fore she say boo to you. So tall she ain't got no sense. And she wasn't Big Ma; she knew she could be quiet and no one would mind. But every time the door opened and a kid or neighbor came in, her heart jumped like she was sixteen again.

And when Roscoe did finally walk inside, he was with a bearded younger man. "This is Lobo, remember, the one want to be a poet back when he was teaching school with Nacho and them?" Roscoe said. "Call himself Brother Lobo back then, when he thought he was a militant."

He introduced Marietta last, after the others had all said, "Boy, I ain't seen you, ain't you the one. . .": "This is Marietta Cook, mother of the famed Rams twins," Roscoe said, and the younger man nodded.

"I've seen you a few times," he said. "I notice you always wear a scarf."

Marietta looked away from Roscoe and said without thinking, "We keep we head cover where I from." She didn't know why she had said it like Aint Sister.

The younger man got excited, saying to Roscoe, "Her head covering, her face, her speech. See, it's the African way of putting the community first, the collective. I told you about my theory. . ."

"Don't pay him no mind," Red Man interrupted, touching Marietta's arm. "He look for Africa in everything."

"He find Africa in the way Red Man wrap baling wire around a starter," Lanier grumbled. "I find lazy."

"You can find your way out, nigger. If you don't like my ways you don't like my food," Red Man hollered, and everyone laughed.

Lobo went into the kitchen with Mary to get a plate of food, and Red Man moved into the big leather chair by the fireplace, where he always sat to watch television. Roscoe said, "You have a nice visit with the celebrities?" He stayed standing.

Marietta thought, He make me tell he. I see that. He scare as me. "Mmm-hmm," she said. She took a breath. "But I have enough football," she said. "We watch too much yesterday."

He squatted beside her chair. "Does that mean you plan to leave, or are you staying here with the experts?"

"It turn cold," she said softly, hoping no one would hear but him. "I fixing to build fire."

"That's my wood, you know." He smiled.

"You need for watch it burn, too?" she said. "Where Hollie?"

"I went to get her at Mrs. Rollins' and Rachelle wanted her to spend the night over her house. Rachelle is Mrs. Collins' daughter, and she loves Hollie to death. Hollie loves Rachelle's nail polish and makeup collection." He shook his head.

"Freeman gone with he mama," Marietta said. "He can't stay up for fire anyway." Her face was hot, but Red Man and Lanier were shouting at the screen already, and when she stood up to take her plate into the kitchen, Mozelle and Miss Ralphine didn't laugh.

The wind blew outside, and Roscoe said, "You walked down here?"

"I too old for walk that far?" she said, remembering his face passing the yard.

"What?" He stopped, said, "Well, I brought Lobo from his place downtown, so I got the truck. You want some fish?"

"From the market? Well, she cook it too hard for me," Marietta said.

Roscoe said, "We can buy it and you can cook it." In the truck, he said, "You know, she probably has to cook it hard so people can't get food poisoning. I guess she has to guard against that possibility, right?"

Marietta looked out the window. He heard everything she said, all the time: he thought it over, considered it, remembered it. He listen for me talk, look at my eye. She was scared.

While she was buying the fish, he went next door to a Mexican bakery and brought back a paper bag. Then he stopped at his dark house for something else, and when they were in her kitchen, he showed her the package of bacon.

"This is from Lanier's pigs," he said. "He and Red Man and me, we split a pig. He feeds those animals religiously, and it's rare that he kills one. But I've got some ham and bacon here. Real bacon."

They ate bacon, fish, rice, and the Mexican sweetbread, which was heavy and vanilla-flavored, sprinkled with sugar. She started to lay the fire while he brought in the wood, and he went to make coffee. "I can't sit down without coffee," he said, and the smell of new smoke and coffee filled the house.

When the fire had crackled down to a steady burn, and they sat on the couch, Marietta was so afraid that she couldn't hold the cup. She watched it sway on the table until the black stilled, and then she couldn't look at him, so she concentrated on the embers instead. She stopped her fingers from touching her eyebrow. Maybe I say something bout the ticket, she thought, but Roscoe said, "I'm too old to make flowery, hey-baby speeches."

She thought. "I too old for listen." Each word was important for him. She had to be careful.

"You used to here and gone men?"

"What?"

He looked at the fire, too. "Some women are—that's the only kind they really like, no matter what they say. They want exciting. They want trouble."

"I ain't custom to nothing right now," she said slowly. "What you custom to?"

"I'm accustomed to disappointment. How poetic." He smiled.

She didn't know what to say. He had his words already chosen, the right ones. "Why you didn't stop when you pass?"

"Because I don't want to intrude on you and your sons." He bit his lips. "And they make me nervous—they make me think about things I don't want to sometimes. But I guess what I did can't be undone." He leaned closer. "I still don't have an answer—about what you want."

When she didn't answer again, he said, "I like to cook—I want you to try my chili beans, and my enchiladas. I like to read, and that's boring. Ain't nobody like to read what I do, and I don't bore people with poetry, so don't worry. But I'm not dangerous—not exciting enough for some women."

"Nate and Calvin dangerous enough for me watch," she said.

"I'm not gon lie," he said, and he was beside her cheek. "I like other things. I want to see your hair, and your shoulders. Like in the magazine. I bought one, too." He pulled her face softly. "I hope you show me," he whispered. "But I'll take the parts I can see right now. If you let me get custom to that."

She put her mouth on his lips, imagining with her eyes closed that she could feel their outline pressing, and even then she was afraid of his hands, that they would clutch at her back and pull too hard. But all she felt was his thumbs just behind her ears, in the tender skin, holding her still.

They talked about rain for days, Red Man and Roscoe and Mary, but it wasn't until the next week that the sun didn't wake her. She looked, wondering, out the bedroom window, and clouds hung in the branches of the plum tree. The first wet sky she had seen since she came to California. Everyone said this had been a drought year, unusually sunny, but she had told Roscoe the sky here couldn't hold water, she didn't believe it; the sky couldn't be anything but blank, hard blue from day-clean to out-the-light. He teased her about the old-time talk, always wanted to hear something translated to the way Aint Sister would have said it, and he shook his head, laughing. "Your family just spouted poetry all day long, huh?" he said. "And nobody thought twice about it."

She dressed and drank a cup of cinnamon tea. Maybe the fish would be happy today—or maybe California fish didn't like gray sky any better, the way other fish did. She remembered the tickets then, that she had forgotten to ask Red Man and Roscoe if they wanted to go to the home games with her. The boys played New Orleans on Saturday.

She walked quickly down the street, thinking that she wouldn't go fishing, but she'd work in the yard in case it did rain. She could loosen the dirt where she wanted the vegetable garden, so the water wouldn't just run off. It would sparkle itself into the roots.

Only Mary was at home, sleepy-eyed from her night shift. Marietta said, "I just come to see if you husband want Carolanne's season ticket for the home game? He and Roscoe like to come with me, you think?"

Mary said, "Well, I know James Sr. would." That was Red Man's real name. "But I better tell you, I don't think Roscoe would go." She put her hands across her chest to hold her shoulders, as if she were embarrassed. "I know you gettin to know him, but he don't do too well with sports, cause of his boy, you know. Louis and him had that falling out over basketball. Roscoe don't even go to the junior college games when James Sr. and Lanier and them go."

Marietta thought quickly, remembering the hot sun, the beer, the knees, and she said, "You think your boys like to go sometime? I don't go to all the game, sometime I like for watch on TV. Maybe Darnell and James Jr. can go with they daddy this weekend."

"They would faint if you told em they could sit in your seats," Mary said. "You sure you want to give that up?"

Marietta smiled and said, "I seen plenty football. Let em tell everybody they Nate and Calvin's cousins." When she heard the first drops of rain on the roof, she looked up.

"I didn't really believe it gon rain," Mary said. "Roscoe and James Sr. went to San Bernardino to check on some big tree-trimming job—I wonder if it rainin over there? They inside anyway, suppose to empty out a building, too."

"I better run," Marietta said. "I bring them ticket tomorrow." She went out hurriedly and started back down the street, feeling the drops only a mist on her face now. She wanted to sit on the porch in the dripping.

I rather watch on TV, she thought. By myself, don't have to listen for nobody ax me question, don't have for feel nobody stare. Red Man and them go this time, maybe I go with him next. Roscoe ain't need for be bother with none of it. She went inside to close all the windows, just in case this gentle dripping turned to real rain, and while she was in the bedroom, someone knocked. She went to the door cautiously—I know California people don't go out in no rain. Roscoe working. Opening the door a crack, she looked down, expecting one of Red Man's daughters, but she saw a thin stomach and a belt. Raising her eyes taller than herself, she saw the angular gold face and the boys' thick eyebrows.

"Lord God," she said. "Sinbad."

"That's my basket name."

He came inside and she stood awkwardly away from him. He stopped by the door. "How you know where I live?" she said.

"Your picture. This dude at work was talking about these two football players all the time, and I never paid any attention. He's a big 49er fan, and he hates the Rams. So then he brought this magazine to work and showed me your face. And the twins." He said it strangely, of course. They not boy to he, not no men—he don't know what for call em.

"Where you work?" she asked.

"At a hotel. San Francisco, I guess you can tell. I'm in the kitchen, but it's a big kitchen and they pay big money." Water glittered on his hair, but he didn't move.

"You wife know you here?"

"I ain't married. Divorced."

"The boys don't live here."

"I know. My friend called the Rams, said he was your uncle or something like that to get their number." He stopped. "I didn't come to see them, or to bother you."

She looked out the front window at the rain. "You drive all this far from San Francisco?"

"You remember—I love to drive."

"What you got now?" she said, squinting at the car. "A new Ford what?"

"Hey, you didn't use to know anything about cars," he said.

"I know enough now. I got a Lincoln, from Nate and Calvin."

"What are their basket names?"

She had to laugh. "They ain't got basket name. But I do."

"Yeah?"

"When we live in Charleston, I was Big Ma."

He rubbed his fingers nervously when she said the names. "You don't look like a Big Ma."

"To you. But what I ever look like to you, huh?" She stood very still. The dirt outside was so hard she could hear each drop of water from the roof.

He moved his shoulders a little, stretching. "When I saw that picture, you looked exactly the same as you always did. Like somebody I was sort of scared to see."

"I scare everybody," she said, hard. "Blueblood. They afraid black rub off on em."

"No," he said, and she saw just a flash of his narrow, gap-toothed smile. "Nuh-uh. Scary because you knew too much. Looked right through me every day, didn't listen to my rap."

"I musta listen," she said. "I had two baby."

He smiled big then. "You know better."

"How many lady you keep now?"

"I have somebody off and on. Not serious."

"Yeah," she said. "I have somebody, live close by. Maybe serious." She was silent again, thinking of his breath, the feel of his back. "You ain't gon sit?"

"I don't know—you standing there like you don't know if you really want me in the house. What you want me to do?"

"Stand." She went close to him, holding her breath, and his hands on her back still made her shake a little, made her eyes hot. She felt his lips there, just below her hair, and then she stepped back and took his arm. "Come out here and sit," she said, opening the door and leading him out to the porch.

"It's cold out here," he protested, but he sat. "I ain't good enough to sit inside, huh?"

"No," she said. "But I don't know when it ever rain again here, and I like for see it come off the tree." She watched him put his long feet up on the porch rail. "So where you read about?" she said. "Tell me all the place you been."

After he'd gone, his car hissing down the street, she sat sheltered under the eaves, and the silver-gray water rushed from the pepper trees by the street and the plum tree in the side yard. The sky was very dark now, like the woods at home. Home—you gon still call that home? Still plan for run? Near forty—you best not run. You best stay. She thought she'd make some of the bacon Roscoe had brought. Real bacon—streak a fat, streak a lean, she thought. Not that yellow-tan flimsy stuff, like Carolanne call bacon, thin as ribbon and curl at the edge. Nothing but a crunch and then a dust a grease on you teeth.

The water already made puddles in the baked dirt. Close to the street, a long, wide wallow was filled with rain, and Roscoe had told her that every year a wide swath of sunflowers grew wild there, huge flowers nearly as tall as little trees.

© Felisha Carrasco

SUSAN STRAIGHT has published eight novels and a memoir, *In the Country of Women.* She has been a finalist for the National Book Award and received the Robert Kirsch Award for lifetime achievement from the Los Angeles Times Book Prize, the O. Henry Prize, the Lannan Literary Award for Fiction, and a Guggenheim Fellowship. She was born in Riverside, California, where she lives with her family.

Printed in the United States
By Bookmasters